Wilde in Love

Wilde in Love

The Wildes of Lindow Castle

Eloisa James

HARPER LUXE

An Imprint of HarperCollinsPublishers

This is a work of fiction. Names, characters, places, and incidents are products of the author's imagination or are used fictitiously and are not to be construed as real. Any resemblance to actual events, locales, organizations, or persons, living or dead, is entirely coincidental.

HarperCollins books may be purchased for educational, business, or sales promotional use. For information please e-mail the Special Markets Department at SPsales@harpercollins.com.

FIRST HARPERLUXE EDITION

ISBN: 978-0-06-268822-4

HarperLuxe™ is a trademark of HarperCollins Publishers.

17 18 19 20 21 ID/LSC 10 9 8 7 6 5 4 3 2 1

This book is dedicated to my dear friends
Cecile and Rachel,
who read this book in several forms,
texted endless encouragement,
and proved brilliant plotters,
helping me plot, and re-plot, and re-plot yet again.
Thank you, Sweethearts!

Acknowledgments

My books are like small children; they take a whole village to get them to a literate state. I want to offer my deep gratitude to my village: my editor, Carrie Feron; my agent, Kim Witherspoon; my Web site designers, Wax Creative; and my personal team: Kim Castillo, Anne Connell, Franzeca Drouin, and Sharlene Moore.

People in many departments of Harper Collins, from Art to Marketing to PR, have done a wonderful job of getting this book into readers' hands: my heartfelt thanks goes to each of you.

Finally, a group of dear friends (and one teenage daughter) have read parts of this book, improving it immeasurably: my fervent thanks to Rachel Crafts, Lisa Kleypas, Linda Francis Lee, Cecile Rousseau, Jill Shalvis, Meg Tilly, and Anna Vettori.

Chapter One

June 25, 1778
London

There wasn't a person in all England who'd have believed the boy who grew up to be Lord Alaric Wilde would become famous.

Infamous? That was a possibility.

His own father had given him that label after Alaric was sent down from Eton at the age of eleven for regaling his classmates with stories of pirates.

Piracy wasn't the problem—the problem was the uncanny way young Alaric had depicted his small-minded Etonian instructors in the guise of drunken sailors. These days he avoided portraying self-righteous Englishmen, but the impulse to observe had never left him. He watched and summarized, whether he was in China or an African jungle.

He had always written down what he saw. His Lord Wilde books were a consequence of that impulse to record his observations, a drive that appeared as soon as he learned to write his first sentences.

Like everyone else, it had never occurred to him that those books could make him famous. And he didn't think any differently when he rolled out of his berth on the *Royal George*. All he knew in that moment was that he was finally ready to see his family, all eight siblings, not to mention the duke and duchess.

He'd stayed away for years, as if not seeing his eldest brother Horatius's grave would make his death not true.

But it was time to go home.

He wanted a cup of tea. A steaming hot bath in a real bathtub. A lungful of smoky London air.

Hell, he even missed the peaty smell that hung over Lindow Moss, the bog that stretched for miles to the east of his father's castle.

He was drawing back the curtain over the porthole when the ship's boy knocked and entered. "There's a mighty fog, milord, but we're well up the Thames, and the captain reckons we'll be at Billingsgate Wharf any minute." His eyes shone with excitement.

Up on deck, Alaric found Captain Barsley standing in the prow of the *Royal George*, hands on his hips. Alaric started toward him and stopped, astonished. Through the fog, the dock glimmered like a child's toy: a blurry mass of pink, purple, and bright blue that separated into parts as the ship neared the pier.

Women.

The dock was crowded with women—or, more precisely, ladies, considering all the high plumes and parasols waving in the air. A grin tugged at the corners of Alaric's mouth as he joined the captain.

"What in the devil is going on?"

"I expect they're waiting for a prince or some such foolishness. Those passenger lists they print in the *Morning Chronicle* are utter rubbish. They're going to be bloody disappointed when they realize the *Royal George* hasn't a drop of royal blood aboard," the captain grumbled.

Alaric, who was related to the crown through his grandfather, gave a shout of laughter. "You have a noble nose, Barsley. Perhaps they've discovered a relation you never heard of."

Barsley just grunted. They were close enough now to discern that ladies were crowded as far back as the fish market. They appeared to be bobbing up and down like colored buoys, as they strained to see through the fog. Faint screams suggested excitement, if not hysteria.

"This is Bedlam," Barsley said with disgust. "How are we supposed to disembark in the midst of that?"

"Since we've come from Moscow, perhaps they think the Russian ambassador is onboard," Alaric said, watching a rowboat set out toward them, manned by a dockworker.

"Why in the devil's name would a flock of women come looking for a Russian?"

"Kochubey is a good-looking fellow," Alaric said, as the boat struck the side of the ship with a thump. "He complained of English ladies besieging him, calling him Adonis, and sneaking into his bedchamber at night."

But the captain wasn't listening. "What the devil are those women doing on the wharf?" Captain Barsley roared, as the dockworker clambered over the side from the rowboat. "Make way for my gangplank, or I won't be responsible for the fish having a fine meal!"

The man dropped to the deck, eyes round. "It's true! You're here!" he blurted out.

"Of course I'm here," the captain snarled.

But the man wasn't looking at Barsley.

He was looking at Alaric.

Cavendish Square
London

Miss Wilhelmina Everett Ffynche was engaged in her favorite activity: reading. She was curled up in an armchair, tearing through Pliny's eyewitness account of the eruption of Mount Vesuvius.

It was just the kind of narrative she most loved: honest and measured, allowing the reader to use her own imagination, rather than ladling on sensational detail. His description of seeing a cloud of smoke shaped like an umbrella spreading ever higher and wider was fascinating.

The door burst open. "Madame Legrand delivered my new bonnet!" her friend Lavinia cried. "What do you think?"

Willa plucked off her spectacles and looked up as Lavinia spun in a circle. "Absolutely perfect. The black plume was a stroke of genius."

"I fancy it adds *gravitas*," Lavinia said happily. "Making me look dignified, if not philosophical. Like you in your spectacles!"

"I only wish my spectacles were as charming as your plume," Willa said, laughing.

"What are you reading about now?" Lavinia asked, dropping onto the arm of Willa's chair.

"Pliny's account of the eruption that buried Pompeii. Just imagine: his uncle headed directly into the smoke, determined to rescue survivors. And he wanted Pliny to go with him."

"Lord Wilde would have gone straight to the disaster as well," Lavinia said with a look of dreamy infatuation.

Willa rolled her eyes. "Then he would have perished, just as Pliny's uncle did. I must say, Wilde sounds like just the type to run straight at danger."

"But he'd be running toward danger in order to *save* people," Lavinia pointed out. "You can't criticize that." She was used to Willa's scoffing at the explorer whom she claimed to love above all else.

Except new hats.

And Willa.

"I am so happy my bonnet came in time for the house party at Lindow Castle," she said, "which reminds me that the trunks are stowed and Mother would like to leave after luncheon."

"Of course!" Willa jumped to her feet and tucked her spectacles and book into a small traveling bag.

"I am looking forward to seeing Lord Wilde's childhood home," Lavinia said, with a happy sigh. "I mean to sneak up to the nursery as soon as I can."

"Why?" Willa inquired. "Are you planning to take a keepsake? A toy he once played with, perhaps?"

"The gardeners can't keep the flowerbeds at the castle intact," Lavinia said with a giggle. "People want to press flowers between the pages of his books."

Willa could scarcely imagine the chaos if Lord Wilde himself made an appearance, but the man hadn't been seen in England for years. If you believed the popular prints, he was too busy wrestling giant squid and fighting pirates.

Sometimes Willa felt as if a fever had swept the kingdom—or at least the female half of it—leaving her unscathed.

During the Season that just ended, young ladies had talked very little about the men whom they might well marry and spend a lifetime with, and a great deal about the author of books such as *Wilde Sargasso Sea.*

Wilde *Sargasso Sea*? Wilde *Latitudes*?

The only rational response was a snort.

Willa was fairly certain that in person, Lord Wilde would resemble every other man: likely to belch, smell of whiskey, and ogle a woman's bosom on occasion.

She tucked her hand under Lavinia's arm and brought her to her feet. "Let's go, then. Off to Lindow Castle to burgle the nursery!"

Chapter Two

Lindow Castle, Cheshire
Country seat of the Duke of Lindow
June 28, 1778
Late afternoon

Alaric walked down one of the long corridors of his childhood home, a deep feeling of satisfaction in his belly. His older brother, Lord Roland Northbridge Wilde—or North, as he preferred to be called—was at his side.

The heir and the spare. The courtier and the explorer. The duke's best beloved and the disgrace.

The infamous disgrace, it seemed.

He and North were of equal height, with similar

features and cut of jaw. But the resemblances stopped there. Had they consciously tried, they couldn't have been more different in personality.

"I did not bed the empress," Alaric said once they had reached the bottom of the stairs. He stopped at the gilt-encrusted mirror hanging in the castle entry to slap a battered, powdered wig on his head and then grimaced at his reflection. "Maybe I should change my mind and return to the Russian court. At least I wouldn't have to wear this monstrosity."

"Seriously, there's no truth to the rumor?" North persisted, coming up at Alaric's shoulder. "Joseph Johnson is selling a print entitled *England Takes Russia by Storm*. It's set in Empress Catherine's bedchamber, and the fellow looks remarkably like you."

Their eyes met in the glass, and North visibly recoiled. "Good God, is that your only wig?" He frowned at the lumpy mound on Alaric's head. "Father won't like to see that at dinner. Hell, I don't like it."

That wasn't surprising. North was wearing a snowy towering creation that turned him into a cross between a parrot dipped in plaster dust and a fancy chicken. Alaric hadn't seen his brother in five years, and he'd scarcely recognized the man.

"I came straight from the dock, but I sent my valet into London. Quarles should arrive in a few days, new wig in hand, although his acquisition won't come close to the elegance of yours."

North adjusted his cuffs. *Pink* silk cuffs. "Obviously not, since this wig is Parisian, enhanced by Sharp's best Cyprus hair powder."

Just then the family butler, Prism, came into the entrance hall. He was the sort of butler who firmly believed that the aristocracy could do no wrong. Butlering for the Wildes offered constant assaults to this conviction, but he was wondrously able to dismiss evidence to the contrary.

"Good afternoon, Lord Roland, Lord Alaric," he said. "May I be of service?"

"Afternoon, Prism," Alaric said. "My brother is determined to disrupt the duchess's tea by introducing me to his fiancée."

"The ladies will be shocked and delighted," Prism said with a cough that managed to convey his dismay at Alaric's unexpected fame.

"I'm as baffled as you are," Alaric told him. He had escaped the crowd on the wharf by throwing on Captain Barsley's hat. None of the women shrieking his name recognized him as he made his way through the crowd, which made the experience all the stranger.

"Give me a minute," North said, adjusting his elaborately tied cravat in the glass. "Brace yourself, Alaric. I suspect every woman in that room has at least one print depicting your adventures."

"The duke says that in the years since I left England they've littered the entire country. Actually, I think the word he used was 'defiled.'"

"The way people gossip about you, not to mention collecting portraits, does not please our father. He thinks your celebrity is ill-becoming to our rank. Do you remember Lady Helena Biddle? Supposedly she's papered her house in prints of you, so she might faint when you walk in."

Alaric bit back an oath. Helena Biddle had already been in pursuit of him five years ago.

"She's widowed now," his brother added, starting to tweak the curls that hung over his ears.

At this rate, they'd be here for an hour. "I'm looking forward to meeting your fiancée," Alaric prompted.

North had the trick of looking severe no matter his mood, but now his mouth eased. "Just look for the most beautiful, elegant woman in the room."

Who cared if North had transformed into a peacock in the years Alaric had been away? His older brother had clearly fallen in love.

Alaric gave North a rough, one-armed hug that

risked the perfection of his brother's neckcloth. "I'm happy for you. Now stop fiddling with your wig, and introduce me to this lovely creature."

Prism threw open the great doors leading to the green salon, where the female half of the duke's house party had gathered for tea. The room before them was crowded with things that Alaric loathed: silks, wigs, diamonds—and insipid faces.

He loved women, but aristocratic ladies, bred to giggle and talk of nothing but fashion?

No.

There were twenty assorted gentlewomen in the room, including his stepmother, the duchess, but North's gaze went directly to a lady whose overskirt was bunched into no fewer than three large puffs. Other women's arses were adorned with puffs, but this woman's puffs were larger than anyone else's.

It seemed the bigger your bum, the more fashionable you were.

"That is she," North said in a low voice. He sounded as if he had caught a glimpse of some royal being.

If sheer volume of attire were indicative of rank, Miss Belgrave would certainly be fit for a throne. Her petticoat had more bows, her open gown more ruffles. And she wore an entire basket of fruit on top of her head.

Alaric's brows drew together. Could his brother really intend to marry a woman like that?

"Lord Roland . . . and Lord Alaric," Prism announced.

The ladies registered his presence with an audible gasp. Alaric's jaw clenched. He turned to his brother. "Billiards after?"

North winked. "I'm always happy to take your money."

With no help for it, Alaric entered the room.

Thankfully, Willa happened to be facing the door when the great explorer was announced, which meant she didn't shame herself by spilling her tea as she swung about—as did almost every other woman in the room.

Willa could hardly blame them. Lord Wilde's image smoldered from bedchamber walls all over the country, and yet no one ever expected to meet him. Confronted by the real man, the lady to her right clapped her hand to her bosom and looked as if she might faint.

It was positively tragic that Lavinia was late for tea; she'd be furious with herself for dawdling once she heard the news.

The man who strode into their midst, looking neither left nor right, was wearing sturdy boots rather than the slippers commonly worn by gentlemen indoors.

He had no rings, no curls to his wig, and no polish.

Willa snapped open her fan, the better to examine this paragon of masculinity, as *The Morning Post* had called him. He certainly wasn't a paragon of fashion.

He looked as if he would have been at home in another century—the Middle Ages perhaps, when gentlemen fought with broadswords. Instead he was stuck in a time when gentlemen's toes were often rendered invisible by the floppy roses attached to their slippers.

At that moment, the silence that had gripped the room broke and there was a swell of chatter and more than one squeal.

"I see his scar!" someone behind her yelped.

Only then did Willa notice the thin white line snaking down one sun-browned cheek in a manner that should be objectionable but somehow wasn't.

There were many stories about how he'd acquired that scar, but Willa's guess had always been that Lord Alaric fell in a privy and knocked his head against a corner.

Lavinia's distant cousin, Diana Belgrave—Lord Alaric's future sister-in-law—had been moodily staring out the window at the gardens. Now she scurried over, positioning herself with her back to the room. "Do you think Lord Roland caught sight of me?" she hissed.

The two brothers kissed their stepmother's hand, and . . .

Turned directly toward them.

Willa almost sighed, except she'd made a rule years ago that Wilhelmina Everett Ffynche never sighed. But if there ever was a situation that called for a sigh, it was when a young lady—Diana, for example—was so dismayed by her future husband that she would do anything to avoid his company.

"Yes, he has," she stated. "Turning your back is no disguise when your wig is taller than anyone else's. They're headed this way like homing pigeons to a roost."

Watching them approach, Willa suddenly understood for the first time why prints of Lord Wilde adorned so many bedchamber walls. There was something shocking about him.

He was so big and—and vital in a primitive way.

Which would be an uncomfortable quality to live with, she reminded herself. She possessed only an engraving of Socrates: a thoughtful, intelligent man whose thighs were doubtless as slim as her own.

"Willa, I *beg* you to do the talking," Diana whispered. "I already endured an exchange with Lord Roland at the breakfast table."

Her fiancé reached them before Willa could answer.

"Miss Belgrave, may I present my brother, Lord Alaric, who has just returned from Russia?" he asked Diana.

While Diana demonstrated her remarkable ability to curtsy while balancing half a greengrocer's stall on her head, Willa discovered that Lord Alaric had sculpted cheekbones, lips that wouldn't shame an Italian courtesan, blue eyes . . .

Oh, and a straight nose.

Those portraits of him that could be found in every printshop?

They didn't do him justice.

He bowed before Diana with surprising finesse, given the breadth of his chest. His coat strained over the shoulders. One might think that a body so defined by muscle would find it hard to bend.

One might also think that a duke's son would employ a better tailor.

"It is a pleasure to meet you, Miss Belgrave," he said, kissing Diana's hand. "I am honored to welcome you to our family."

Diana managed a wan smile.

Willa almost stepped backward as Lord Roland turned to her. Lord Alaric was so large that she had the absurd feeling that he might be swallowing up the air around them.

At least that would explain her slight feeling of breathlessness.

Lord Roland was eager to converse with his future spouse, and promptly drew her aside for a tête-à-tête, which left Willa alone with the explorer. "Lord Alaric, it is a pleasure," she said, holding out her hand to be kissed.

The elite seminary she had attended had excelled at teaching the protocol of awkward social situations. In this case, it meant that Willa pretended that the circle of ladies behind her, breathlessly awaiting the same experience, did not exist.

Interestingly, Lord Alaric appeared to be paying no attention to them either. As he brought her hand to his lips, the smile in his eyes seemed to be for her alone. "I'd say the pleasure is all mine," he murmured.

His voice was deep and husky, as unusual as his costume. It wasn't the voice of a courtier. Or of a boy, as were many of her suitors. It was the voice of a grown man.

Instead of kissing the back of her hand, he raised her curled fingers to his mouth, and their eyes met as his lips touched them.

She wasn't wearing gloves, but that didn't explain the way her skin prickled to life. Willa felt her lips curling into a smile entirely unlike the calm expression with which she usually greeted a stranger.

"I understand that you have just returned to England," she said, hastily withdrawing her hand. "What do you miss when you are traveling abroad?"

Lord Alaric's eyes, fringed by thick eyelashes, were the blue color of the sky at twilight.

Beauty was an accident of birth. But eyes? That was different. Beautiful eyes had feeling in them.

"I miss my family," he said. "After that, mattresses without lice, brandy, welcoming servants, an excellent plate of ham and eggs in the morning. Oh, and the company of ladies."

"It must be intoxicating to be so adored," Willa said, nettled by the way he ranked ladies below a plate of ham.

Lord Alaric's mouth quirked into a wry smile. "Adoration is a bit strong. I think myself lucky that my readers find something to enjoy in my work."

She let a trace of scorn shine from her eyes because . . . false modesty? Ugh. "I enjoyed reading Montaigne's essay on cannibals, but that didn't spur me to hang his image in my room."

He looked faintly surprised. Did no one ever disagree with him? Or was he not aware that his image was enshrined in so many bedchambers?

"Where do you plan to travel next?" she asked, changing the subject.

"I haven't decided. Do you have a suggestion?"

"I am not certain where you've already been," Willa admitted. "I'm afraid that I'm one of the few people in the kingdom ignorant on the subject of Lord Wilde's peregrinations."

His heavy-lidded eyes opened slightly, the tilt of his mouth hitching up a bit more. "A large word for an inconsequential subject. I assure you that you aren't alone in avoiding my books."

Willa would really have liked to shrug, but shrugging was like sighing: an inelegant way to indicate an emotion better kept to oneself. "There's little evidence for that," she pointed out. "You have been away for some time, but you'll find that your work is read widely."

"Do you prefer novels?" he asked.

"No, I'm afraid I'm not attracted to invented stories of any kind," Willa said. His eyes were so intent on her face that she was beginning to feel slightly dizzy.

Annoying man.

"I do not invent the events I describe," Lord Alaric said, a thread of laughter in his voice.

"Certainly not," she said hastily. Then, unable to resist, "Although, from what my friend Lavinia has told me, wouldn't you agree that your adventures tend to be, shall we say, larger than life?"

"No," he replied, seemingly even more amused. "What are you reading at the moment?"

"Pliny's letters to Tacitus, but I'll put it to the side and read one of your accounts. Where would you recommend that I start? With the cannibals, perhaps?"

One of his brows shot upward. "Cannibals?"

"Oh, that's right," Willa exclaimed. "Lavinia told me that cannibals appear only in the play."

Like a dot on the end of a sentence, that put an end to his amusement. His brows drew together. "Play?"

"*Wilde in Love*," Willa answered, astonished that Lord Alaric knew nothing of the hugely successful play depicting his life.

"I presume the spelling of that title includes an 'E'." He did not look happy. "Exactly what happens in *Wilde in Love*?"

"As you might have guessed, you meet a lady," Willa said, rather enjoying watching his pained expression deepen.

Lord Roland startled her by clearing his throat. It seemed Diana had fled, leaving Lord Alaric's brother to rejoin them. "I forgot to tell you," he said, giving his brother a mischievous grin. "A group of us made a special trip to London to see your play, Alaric. Aunt

Knowe bought up every single locket they had for sale outside the theater."

Lord Alaric frowned.

"Reproductions of the locket you gave your fiancée," Willa explained.

"I not only fall in love, but become *betrothed*?"

"She was your one true love," Lord Roland said, his smile growing ever wider. "You wrote and recited a great deal of love poetry—that took up most of the first act—and finally handed over a locket as a sign of your devotion. You're sure to see ladies wearing them; yesterday Aunt Knowe was handing them out like gingerbread men."

"What utter hogwash. I've never had a fiancée nor written a scrap of poetry. What else happens in this farce?"

"I'm sorry to say that it's not a farce but a tragedy, since cannibals eventually make a meal of your beloved," Willa said, unable to stop herself from smiling along with Lord Roland.

"I can't say that I feel very sad on hearing of the death of the fiancée I never met," Lord Alaric observed.

"If you don't mind the advice," his brother said irrepressibly, "you should have skipped breakfast and overcome your fear of water in time to save the missionary's daughter from the cannibals."

Lord Alaric's body stilled. "Just what do you mean by 'missionary's daughter'?"

Willa reflexively moved back a step. All of a sudden he reminded her of a predator on the verge of pouncing. Not that anyone else seemed to notice.

The moment Willa broke their little circle, the gathering of impatient ladies at her back surged forward, elbowing her to the side.

She ought to leave without a backward look, and began to do just that, but halfway across the room, she turned, only to find, embarrassingly, that Lord Alaric was watching her.

Presumably he was accustomed to ladies throwing longing glances over their shoulders, because one side of his mouth curled up as their eyes met.

Was he *mocking* her for retreating?

Willa snapped her head about. He couldn't have made it clearer that he paid no attention to the rules of civility that dictated well-bred behavior.

The man was a menace to polite society.

An appealing menace, but a menace all the same.

Chapter Three

The billiards room
Early evening

I don't remember ever seeing you in silk, let alone pink silk," Alaric said. He was leaning against the billiards table, watching his brother pocket the red ball over and over with careless mastery. "If you're not careful, you'll turn dukish. Remember Horatius?"

When he was alive, their older brother Horatius had relished the nonsense of being heir to a dukedom. He had already been pompous in short pants. Hell, probably even in nappies.

"'Dukish' isn't a word, and this is what an English

nobleman wears," North said flatly. "Now you're back in England, you'll have to dress to your station."

"I shaved," Alaric observed.

North slammed his white cue ball into the red ball, which dropped into a pocket yet again. "It could be that the air around a future duke is poisoned. I'll admit that I astonish myself sometimes."

"Isn't it my turn yet?" Alaric took a healthy slug of French brandy.

"No."

"I've decided that your wig makes you look like an African parrot crossed with a fancy chicken."

North flipped his cue, using the slender end to carom his cue ball off one rail, then another, and finally into the chosen red ball—which surprisingly failed to pocket. "Horatius died. I had to grow up."

Alaric pushed away a familiar pang of sadness. "You have three curls over each ear," he pointed out. "Add them to the pretty ruffles at your wrists and the coat tarted up with gold embroidery, and the result cannot be explained by maturity alone."

"You can't imagine how uninteresting I find your sartorial commentary," North said. "Since you are preoccupied by my wardrobe, shall I take the next round?"

"Go ahead," Alaric said, taking another swallow. "It

isn't just your wardrobe. When I left five years ago, you were wig-free, with a plump dancer in one pocket and a sulky Italian singer in the other. And now you're getting married."

North leaned to position his cue. "People change."

"You're wearing heels," Alaric said, catching sight of his brother's feet. "Damn it, they aren't even black, are they?" He bent down and said, with some revulsion, "North, your stockings are striped, and your heels are yellow. *Yellow.*"

"This is the newest style. You left in 1773, and it's 1778. Fashions change." He sank the red ball.

"You've turned into a damn fop. I wouldn't be surprised if you start wearing great silver buckles on your shoes."

His brother straightened. "Alaric." His voice was dangerously quiet, a tone that in their childhood days would be followed by an attempt to pound his brothers into the floor.

But Alaric had never been able to stop himself from poking the beast—in this case, the man who scarcely resembled the brother he remembered. "Should I steel myself to watch you mince down the aisle in scarlet heels? Wearing rouge, no doubt, and patches?"

North narrowed the dark blue eyes that were uncannily similar to Alaric's own. "Should I assume that you will look like a blacksmith in the church? Because you do at the moment."

"Quarles would be very wounded to hear that," Alaric said. His valet did his best, inasmuch as his master refused to wear silk, heels, ruffles, or rouge.

Their family was large by any standard—their father's third wife was on the verge of giving birth to yet another little Wilde—but Horatius, he, and North had been the first three in the nursery.

He would have said that they knew each other inside out: Horatius had been arrogant, but true; Alaric was adventuresome, verging on foolhardy; North was rakish and half-mad.

Rakish and mad were nowhere in evidence now. In their place: Prissy. Fashionable. Flowery. *Soon to be married.*

It was hard to believe.

Impossible.

"What is Miss Belgrave's given name?" Alaric asked. He'd scarcely managed to speak to his future sister-in-law. For one thing, he'd been distracted by that fiery little termagant who hadn't read his books.

Damn, she was lovely, though. Delicate features paired with plump lips that curved in a way that made a man instinctively think about bedding her—even though her mouth had been crooked in a sardonic little smile, because she had obviously decided that he was a storyteller at best, and a fribble at worst.

A deceitful fribble, at that: one who created the events in Lord Wilde's books from thin air.

Never mind her smirk: when he was looking at her, he understood the whole wig business.

A wig kept a woman's hair to herself—and her lover. Made it a private delight.

Then, just when he'd learned about that absurd play, he'd been mowed down by ladies who had seen *Wilde in Love* and seemed to believe that his life actually bore some resemblance to that rubbishing play.

"My fiancée's name is Diana," North replied, smiling. It was an involuntary smile that lit up his eyes.

"*Diana?* Hell, she's practically already part of the family," Alaric said, shaking off thoughts of *Wilde in Love.*

Their father had named all his children after warriors; Alaric and Roland used to stage battles between Alaric, king of the Visigoths, and Roland, chief paladin to King Charlemagne. Horatius had been too lofty for such childish games; as he liked to remind them, *his* namesake had fought an entire army on his own.

"I told the duchess that she couldn't have the name for the new baby," North said.

"They'll run out of appropriate names soon." Alaric counted off the names. "There's you and I and Horatius from Mother. Leonidas, Boadicea, Alexander, and Joan from the second duchess. The third has given us Spartacus, Erik, and whoever the next one will be."

"Don't forget Viola," North said. Viola was the current duchess's daughter from her first marriage. Their father had met his third wife a few years after she was widowed.

"Viola doesn't have a warrior's name because our father wasn't around to name her. My point is that Diana will fit right in. Tell me about her."

"You saw how beautiful she is," North said, his face softening. "She's one of the most fashionable ladies in London. She's bringing a substantial dowry to the estate."

"We don't need it," Alaric said. "Unless things have changed?"

"They haven't, but money is always useful."

"True. What are her interests?"

His brother looked blank.

"Besides fashion," Alaric prompted. "Is she interesting?"

"I don't need, or want, an *interesting* wife," North

said, plucking the red ball out of the pocket. "In fact, I think an interesting wife is anathema to a man like me."

"'A man like you,'" Alaric repeated. "Exactly what kind of man have you become, North?"

His brother's mouth tightened into a thin line. "*You* may be able to racket around the world, calling yourself Lord Wilde, chasing pygmy tribes and wild elephants, but I cannot. The estate takes a great deal of work: our father has just acquired a sixth property, in Wales."

"I didn't know you needed me," Alaric said, feeling as if he'd taken a blow to the stomach.

"I don't," North said immediately. "I don't give a damn whether you've been roasting in Africa or freezing in Saint Petersburg."

But clearly he had. He did.

Damn it.

Alaric put down his glass. "I apologize for staying away so long, and for leaving you with the care of my estate on top of the rest."

"On that front, I meant to tell you that I hired a few men to guard your house, but people keep sneaking up and prying out bricks."

"What the hell for?"

"Keepsakes," North said with a shrug. "Mementos of their love. Damned if I know."

Alaric swallowed back a curse. A tall hedge would

keep them out. Maybe a hedge and a few wolfhounds for good measure.

"There's quite a trade in Wilde memorabilia," his brother continued, "so I suppose some of the bricks make their way to London."

"That bloody play," Alaric said with disgust. "I have to get it shut down." Yet he couldn't leave for London immediately, given his long absence. His father had asked him to remain at Lindow Castle for a few weeks, at least until the birth of his new sibling.

"I don't think it's against the law to write a play about someone's life. *Wilde in Love* is everything you'd expect: melodramatic, ridiculous, a lot of fun. Tickets have been sold ahead for months."

"It's one thing if a play's about Julius Caesar," Alaric pointed out. "I'm alive. How would you like a bunch of nonsense up on the stage about you?"

"You're the one who wrote books about yourself," North retorted.

"I wrote *books*. I didn't write a play. The books are accurate, whereas I have had nothing to do with cannibals." Alaric threw the last of his brandy down his throat, welcoming the burn.

The missionary's daughter had to be a lucky guess. He could imagine a playwright deciding to make a penny by dramatizing spurious adventures under the insipid title *Wilde in Love*. But how in the hell did that hack know to include a missionary's daughter?

It was actually thanks to the only missionary's daughter he'd ever met, Miss Prudence Larkin—who had loved him, though the feeling was not returned—that he stayed far away from virtuous young ladies. In fact, he vaguely put ladies and cannibals in the same category: ravenous beings with a taste for Englishmen.

But neither the play nor his thieving readers were as important as North's earlier revelation. "I am sorry that I left you with the care of my estate." His jaw tightened. "It was easier to board another ship than to come home and imagine Horatius losing his life in the bog." He dipped his head in the direction of Lindow Moss, the huge stretch of wetlands east of the castle.

"Did you think that you were alone in that feeling? We all miss Horatius. But we missed you as well." North's cue ball thumped into the table's cushion, spun, and narrowly missed a pocket. "I actually read your last book, not because I'm one of your throngs of admirers, but so that I had some idea what my brother was doing and where he'd been."

"I apologize," Alaric said. He raked his hand through his hair again. "Hell and damnation. I'm truly sorry."

"Horatius would have loved your latest book. He would have been bloody proud of you. Probably dragged us to that play every night of the week." North slammed his ball so hard that it skipped the rail and rolled across the floor.

"Your turn," he said, looking up.

In more ways than one, it seemed.

Chapter Four

Later that evening

When Lord Alaric entered the drawing room, Lavinia's eyes got round. "He's even prettier than his prints," she breathed.

"Pretty?" Willa took a look at the man, who was immediately surrounded by a circle of ladies. To her, he looked like a tiger someone was trying to fence in with rosebushes. It wasn't going to confine the beast.

"No, not pretty," Lavinia agreed, ogling Lord Alaric without shame. "He's too large to be pretty. His chin is too strong."

"Strong" was one word for it. Willa thought his chin looked stubborn. That was a quality she'd made up her mind to avoid in a husband. Stubbornness led to uncomfortable marriages.

Lord Alaric was enthralling in much the same way that tigers in the Royal Menagerie were. She liked to observe them, but wouldn't dream of taking one home.

She leaned over and said in Lavinia's ear, "Personally, I think the imminent demise of his pantaloons is more striking than his chin." Lord Alaric's thigh muscles were straining the silk in a manner that was remarkably eye-catching.

Indecorous, but eye-catching.

"Wil-*la*!" Lavinia said, choking with laughter. All the same, she flipped open her fan, and from behind its shelter, her eyes dropped below his waist. "If that's the fashion in Russia, I approve," she whispered back.

"I never before gave much thought to thighs," Willa observed, "except perhaps those frog legs your mother served at her last dinner."

"Frogs?" Lavinia yelped. "He's no frog. Frogs are green and slimy."

"With large thigh muscles," Willa pointed out, laughing.

"I simply can't believe Lord Alaric is under the same roof as I am," Lavinia said breathlessly. "Just last week, *The Morning Post* reported that he was lost in the Russian Steppes. I knew it wasn't true. He's far too experienced a traveler to succumb to bad weather."

"I remember the print you have of him caught in an Arctic ice storm," Willa said.

"I left that at home," Lavinia said. "I only brought one with me, showing him at the wheel of a ship, pursued by another flying the Jolly Roger. It's a representation of *Wilde Latitudes*."

Willa wrinkled her nose. "That title is a good example of why I haven't read his books. What does that mean? He's a latitude, all to himself?"

"No, just that his ship roamed the islands where pirates make their home."

Willa laughed. "We should take out the print and make a close comparison. Perhaps we could ask Lord Alaric to stand in profile, holding a wheel, to make certain that your money hasn't gone to waste."

"We'd have to beat off his admirers."

"And that's far too much work." Willa linked her arm with Lavinia's and drew her in the opposite direction from Lord Alaric and his thorny tangle of admirers.

She disliked the hungry expression that had swept the room like a contagion when he walked in. Many ladies had clearly dressed for a hunt: Bodices couldn't go any lower without a display of bellies better kept private. Patches had been applied to women's faces with such abandon it was as if the skies had showered scraps of black silk.

Rather surprisingly, Lord Alaric didn't seem to be basking in all that adoration. In fact, if she had to guess, she'd think he hated it.

She refused to be part of the frenzy—or allow him to think of Lavinia in that light either. What if Lavinia made up her mind to marry him? Not that Willa thought it was a good idea, given Lavinia's infatuation. In her opinion, no woman should adore her husband; it led to flagrant abuses of power.

"Good evening, Mr. Fumble," she said, smiling at the young man who stepped into their path.

He bowed. "Good evening, Miss Ffynche." And, with a yearning look, "Miss Gray. I hope you are quite well." When they'd met the day before, he'd promptly succumbed to Lavinia's charms.

Lavinia, meanwhile, was making a half-hearted pretense at being overheated, so she could stare at Lord Alaric from behind her fluttering fan.

"Did you chance to read the *Morning Chronicle* at breakfast?" Willa inquired. "It was dated several days ago, but there were copies at the table this morning."

Mr. Fumble blinked at her uncertainly. "His Grace invited us to a hunt this morning, but I read the first page. Most of it. Some of it."

Willa brought up the proposed Act for the Prevention of Vexatious Proceedings touching the Order of Knighthood, but it was clear that Mr. Fumble had no interest. He was, however, fascinated by the habits of red foxes. He was still lecturing them about fox tunnels when Lavinia interrupted.

"Lady Knowe is behind you, Willa," she cried. "She has Lord Alaric with her, and I believe they are coming to speak to us!"

"I beg your pardon," Willa said to Mr. Fumble, turning about. Lady Knowe, the duke's sister, was a large-boned woman with a wry wit and an infectious laugh; since the duchess was expecting a child in the not-too-distant future, Lady Knowe was acting as her brother's hostess. She had the family's slashing eyebrows and height.

She was using that height to cut through a froth of ladies trying to cling to Lord Alaric. She looked like a mother duck striking out for land with a cluster of ducklings in tow.

When they all reached Willa's side, Lady Knowe gave Miss Kennet and Lady Ailesbury such a hard-eyed glance that they actually fell back a step. Lady Helena Biddle seemed to be of tougher stuff, because she clung obstinately to Alaric's other arm.

"Lady Biddle," Lady Knowe said in an awful voice, "I trust that you will unhand my nephew. I am *waiting*."

"We are reuniting," she replied, with a touch of desperation. "I haven't seen Lord Wilde for such a long time!"

"Lord Wilde is a fictional character," Lady Knowe retorted. "As such, you may reunite in your imagination, which doubtless is the wellspring of many such enthralling encounters. I wish to introduce my nephew, Lord *Alaric*, to these young ladies."

Lady Knowe was the closest thing there was to a queen at this distance from London, so Lady Biddle acknowledged herself beaten and fell back a few steps.

"Miss Willa Ffynche and Miss Lavinia Gray," Lady Knowe said. "May I introduce Lord Alaric Wilde? Alaric, these are two of my favorite young ladies, other than our family members."

"Good evening, Lord Alaric," Willa said and, to his aunt, "I was fortunate enough to meet your nephew over tea, Lady Knowe."

"It is a true pleasure to meet you, Lord Alaric," Lavinia said. "I find your work most enthralling."

Somewhat surprisingly, Lord Alaric didn't assume

the glazed look of admiration most men got when Lavinia brought her most dazzling smile into play, but
perhaps he was a slow starter.

It would help to give him the full force of Lavinia's
charm and beauty.

"Mr. Fumble was just giving us an account of this
morning's hunt," Willa said to Lady Knowe, turning
her shoulder and leaving Lavinia to dazzle the explorer.

"We were all very sorry," Lady Knowe said to Mr.
Fumble. "I blame it entirely on your mount. The duke
should clear his stables of horses that are so difficult to
handle."

It seemed Mr. Fumble had taken a tumble. Willa
managed to keep that poetic sentence to herself. For
some reason, she was wrestling with a rebellious streak
as regards ladylike conversation. Likely it was just a
response to the Season.

She and Lavinia had presented a resolutely ladylike
front for months, saving all commentary, ribald and
otherwise, for home. Or, if it couldn't wait, for whispered conversations in the ladies' retiring room.

Now she felt like sighing, shrugging, disagreeing,
and disobeying all the self-imposed rules that had
turned their first Season into such a success. But to give
in to that impulse would be disastrous. The "real" Willa

would be an unwelcome shock to most of her suitors, who wouldn't have imagined that she wore spectacles while reading—or that she loved bawdy jokes.

"I agree," Mr. Fumble said stiffly. "My mount was deaf to all persuasion and refused to take a hedge that any decent pony could have managed."

"I trust you weren't injured?" Willa asked, putting on a sympathetic expression.

"He went arse over teakettle into a stream," Lady Knowe answered. "Which broke his fall, no doubt."

This proved such a terrific insult that the gentleman gave her a huffy scowl and stomped off.

Glancing at Lavinia, Willa saw that things were not going as well as they might. Her friend was gazing at Lord Alaric precisely as one might imagine Pygmalion gazed at his statue before it came alive.

Silently.

The statue likely didn't notice, but Lord Alaric was looking restless.

Lady Knowe obviously came to the same conclusion. "Your older brother tells me that you claim to have never met a single cannibal, Alaric," she said. "I meant to tell you that *Wilde in Love* is riveting. I enjoyed every moment of it."

Lord Alaric's eyes darkened. "While I am sorry to

disappoint you, Aunt, I am unacquainted with cannibals."

"Oh, come, come," Lady Knowe cried. "You could
find a cannibal if you tried hard enough. I would chase
one down, were I you. *Wilde in Love* has led your readers to expect just such an account. Explorers mustn't
be cowardly."

Looking at the brutal contour of Lord Alaric's jaw,
Willa thought it most unlikely that cowardice played a
part in his decisions, or for that matter, that a cannibal
would be able to catch him unawares.

Lavinia was staring dreamily at his profile, ignoring
the conversation.

Willa gave her a surreptitious pinch. The man was
only a man, no matter how many books he had written.

No matter how beautiful and powerful and rich
he was.

Or dazzling.

He was only a man.

"Lavinia and I had a diverting conversation about
that subject this very afternoon," she said. "We were
wondering whether cannibals from different tribes
would be allowed to marry if one had previously enjoyed a feast that included a relative of the other."

"How grisly," Lady Knowe exclaimed. "I can say

categorically that I would never marry someone who had ingested a relative."

"If we believe Hamlet," Lavinia said, coming to life as if *she* were Pygmalion's statue, "the dust of our ancestors is everywhere. We're likely drinking it in these glasses of sherry."

"That's most unlikely, considering that our ancestors were not Spanish," Willa pointed out. "I'm pretty sure this is Amontillado wine."

"I have a Spanish great-aunt," Lady Knowe said, grinning. She raised her glass. "I'll have to change my mind about eating relatives. To Aunt Margarida!"

"But what if your relatives were more corporeal than dusty?" Willa asked.

Lord Alaric's eyes glittered under their heavy lids but he said nothing. Willa hadn't the faintest idea what he was thinking.

"Lord Alaric," she asked—*again*—"what do you think about the possibility of a union between members of warring cannibal tribes?"

"The likelihood would change from tribe to tribe," he answered. "The respective reasons for the practice of cannibalism would be important. For example, some cultures view dog meat as a delicacy, while others view eating it as unthinkable."

"Are you saying that for some tribes, cannibalism

might be just an efficient way to dispatch of an enemy while putting supper on the table?" Lavinia asked. "That wasn't my understanding."

"You are *both* morbid!" Lady Knowe exclaimed. "What has happened to young ladies? In my day they understood a great deal about needlework and hardly anything else."

"In some cultures, sacred animals are never eaten because they are believed to be incarnations of gods," Lord Alaric put in. "In another, the same animal might be eaten daily."

Willa was in the grip of an overwhelming urge to prove him wrong—somehow, anyhow. Unfortunately she knew nothing about sacred animals.

"My father viewed his hunting dogs as sacred," Lavinia said, "but my mother could not abide the way they would cluster around his chair at supper. Talking of sacred objects, Lord Alaric, I gather this locket is *not* symbolic of a lost love? Lady Knowe was kind enough to give me one." She held up her locket.

"I'm afraid no meaning can be attached to that object, other than my aunt's reckless inclination to part with money."

Lady Knowe gave an exaggerated sigh. "Your lockets are beautifully designed, decorated on both sides, and so pretty, Alaric darling. Everyone adores them."

"Do you have a locket as well?" he asked Willa, his voice forbidding.

She had the idea that people usually quaked in fear at the mere hint of his disapproval. If so, she was just the person to acquaint him with a new emotion.

"I didn't qualify," she answered, giving him a sunny smile.

He frowned. "What were the qualifications?"

"Devotion," Willa said. "When Lady Knowe disclosed her purchases, there was very nearly a squabble."

"Like bulldogs fighting for territory," Lavinia put in, her eyes gleaming with laughter. "I assure you, Lord Alaric, that my possession of this locket was hard won."

"I had to establish rules," Lady Knowe explained. "Every locket went to a true devotee. Though some people had already bought their own." She coughed delicately. "Helena Biddle owns a replica made from true gold."

"What were the rules?" Lord Alaric was definitely grinding his teeth.

Almost . . . *almost* Willa felt sorry for him. But if he disliked his own fame that much, he shouldn't have written books about himself.

"Lady Knowe held a contest," Lavinia explained. "The questions were all drawn from your work. Oh, and the play, of course."

"You surprise me, Aunt," he said. "I didn't have the idea that you read my books so carefully."

"Oh, I didn't come up with the questions," Lady Knowe said blithely. "I went to the nursery for that. The children are forever acting out your adventures. They know the books by heart."

He looked even more taken aback. "The children are reading my work? I visited the nursery this morning, but no one said a word."

"Your father commanded that they not pester you on your first day home. Believe me, they have memorized every sentence. Their poor long-suffering governess has read the books over and over at bedtime. In fact, that might be one of the reasons why she left. We haven't found a new one yet."

Willa swallowed another grin. Lord Alaric had the look of a man contemplating a flight to the nearest port, perhaps to set sail for cannibal country.

"The children haven't seen the play, but Leonidas gave them a thorough account on his last trip home from Oxford," Lady Knowe continued. "Betsy does a fine, if somewhat histrionic, rendition of the missionary's daughter declaring her love just before she is captured by the cannibals."

Lord Alaric subtly shifted his weight. Willa guessed that he was irritated to the bone by the whole discussion, by the news about his siblings, by the lockets, and most of all, by the play itself. Every mention of it put a deep furrow on his forehead.

But he was too polite to explode before his aunt. It was rather adorable, actually.

"Are you more nettled by *Wilde in Love*, or by the missionary's daughter's untimely death?" she asked.

"They are one and the same," he answered. "Both of them sprang up like a weed while I was abroad."

"That makes the play sound like a black eye," she commented, enjoying the way a muscle was jumping in his jaw. "As if it happened when you weren't noticing. Explained by running into a door in the dark, that sort of thing."

"It did happen while I wasn't noticing—or rather, not even in the country. My brother tells me that the wretched playwright hasn't even had the courage to acknowledge the piece. No one knows who he is."

"Are you planning to shut down the production?" Lavinia asked. "I would appreciate advance notice, because my mother hasn't allowed us to see it yet."

He looked to Willa inquiringly.

"Lady Gray disapproves of the fact that your enthusiasm for your beloved is expressed in heated terms," she told him.

It was clear Lord Alaric had no trouble interpreting

what she meant because he scowled. "It's reprehensible to stage a play about a living person, especially one that's no more than a mess of inaccuracies and apparently lewd ones at that."

Lavinia turned to Willa. "We must insist on attending it as soon as we return to London."

"You'll pay upwards of ten guineas for each ticket," Lady Knowe warned.

"We could just visit the nursery," Willa pointed out. "Request a command performance from actors with true knowledge of the hero."

"It's not fair to call the play entirely inaccurate," Lady Knowe said to her nephew. "Act One begins with two boys playing at sword fighting. You and North, pretending to be a king and a warrior. I remember those bouts quite well."

"I see."

A quiet voice, Willa was discovering, did not necessarily mean that the man who possessed that voice was less dangerous than a man who bellowed.

She had thought that Lord Alaric was irritated by the play, but now—on hearing that true details of his life were playing out on the stage—his expression became truly forbidding.

"How cross you look! You oughtn't to be," Lady Knowe said. "*Wilde in the Andes* sold every single copy on the first day, and everyone says that part of its success must be put up to the triumph of *Wilde in Love.*"

Ouch.

"I suppose it is taxing to have so many admirers," Willa said, changing the subject.

At that moment she made the unsettling discovery that not only was Lord Alaric outrageously handsome, but his eyes were nearly . . . irresistible.

The very idea made her feel a little ill.

The man was notorious.

Notorious. Whereas she was an adamantly private person.

Yet here she was, smiling at him with practically the same fervor that had driven Lavinia to spend her pin money buying those prints.

"I expect Lady Gray is looking for us," she said.

Lord Alaric didn't glance around the room, but his expression suggested that Lavinia's mother would have appeared at their side if she wished to interrupt the conversation.

Likely he was unaccustomed to women cutting a conversation short.

"Are you disappointed?" Willa asked Lavinia, when they were out of earshot of Lord Alaric and his aunt. "So often an idol turns out to be unsatisfactory in person. You remember what a shock Mr. Chasuble, the Oxford philosopher, was."

"You were put off by the luxurious black hair growing from his ears," Lavinia agreed. "But did you see a single objectionable physical detail about Lord Alaric? Because I did not."

"No," Willa admitted. In fact, she still felt the shock of his raw earthy charm in her whole body.

It wasn't something she would have anticipated, but—she reminded herself—it simply meant she was a member of the female sex.

And if she told herself that a few more times, she might actually believe it.

"Alas, I think he's too masculine for me," Lavinia said thoughtfully. "Too perfect."

"He's not perfect," Willa objected. "He has a scar on his forehead as well as the one on his cheek; did you see it?"

"I don't mean physically. He's intelligent and yet there's something almost brutal about him. I've lost the desire to love him madly." She looked disappointed.

"Isn't it more comfortable this way?" Willa inquired. "It's not as if you'd want to become an explorer's wife, Lavinia. Remember how seasick you became from rowing on the Thames."

"True!" Lavinia said, her natural optimism asserting itself. "I'll have to find someone to take my collection of prints. I don't want them, now that I've met him." She wrinkled her nose. "It would be odd to have him on my bedchamber wall."

Willa had never, ever thought of buying a print of Lord Wilde. Or rather, Lord Alaric.

Of course she didn't want Lavinia's prints. "Right," she said, "they should be easy enough to give away. Let's find your mother."

"He knew that that was an excuse," Lavinia said. "I know you don't think much of his books, but I promise you that Lord Wilde's accounts are more captivating than you have assumed."

"I am sure you are correct," Willa said. Leaving it at that.

A footman presented a tray with glasses of sickly sweet ratafia. "I wish that young ladies were allowed to drink more than a single glass of sherry," Lavinia said with a sigh.

"The Season is over," Willa pointed out. "We can allow ourselves some leeway." She sent the footman off for sherry instead.

"It's a good thing Mother didn't overhear you," Lavinia said, very entertained.

"You're not alone in your aversion to ratafia. I feel

the same way about the drink as Diana does about Lord Roland."

"Just look at Diana now," Lavinia said. "She is in *anguish*."

Willa's imagination was a pale, stunted twig in comparison to Lavinia's bountiful creativity, and as such she tended to discount Lavinia's more fanciful opinions. But she obediently turned to look across the drawing room at Diana, trying to decipher signs of anguish.

They had spent a good deal of time together during the Season, since Diana and Lavinia were distant cousins, but somehow Willa never felt she got to know Diana. At the moment, she looked pale, but then Diana had a porcelain complexion. After Lord Roland fell in love at first sight, general opinion declared that her complexion must have played a signal role.

"She may have slept badly," Willa suggested.

Lavinia shook her head. "It's monstrously unfair that she caught Lord Roland when she obviously doesn't want him. I wish a future duke would fall in love with my complexion. It's such a *pure* emotion. I suspect most of the men who offered for me have far more indelicate inclinations."

Willa agreed. Lavinia's suitors had trouble keeping their eyes off her chest, and for good reason. "I watched Lord Roland talking to Diana at breakfast, and his motives are definitely not pure. His eyes were quite desirous."

"Thank you!" Lavinia said to the footman, who had returned with sherry. "We can't rule out the possibility that he was experiencing lust for her wig rather than her person," she told Willa, with a wrinkle of her nose. "I don't think I could bear to be with a man who took his attire so seriously."

Lord Roland was certainly a peacock, from his golden heels to his tall wig. This evening he was wearing a coat of silver silk with cherry twill. The combination would have made most men look effeminate, but the violent black slashes of his eyebrows saved him. In fact, in an odd way that bouffant wig just made him more masculine.

"I have the impression that he wears lip rouge," Lavinia added.

His lordship had a deep ruby lip, but it might be natural. "He has the courage to do so," Willa acknowledged. "I've never seen a man in a wig that high."

"He must have acquired it in Paris," Lavinia said. "Mother doesn't approve—although if he'd fallen in love with my complexion she would have changed her mind—but I must say that he carries it off."

Lord Roland was a beautiful animal, and any woman

in his vicinity would find her eyes resting on him pleasurably.

His brother was just as beautiful. But Lord Alaric was rougher. Untamed. Their features were equally pleasing, she supposed. But somehow the same jaw on Lord Alaric looked harsher, more stubborn.

More troublesome for anyone in his life, such as his wife. It was just as well that she hadn't the faintest wish to audition for the role.

"We can't join my mother until we finish the sherry, so we ought to talk to Diana," Lavinia said. "Since she's over there by herself. Again."

Sure enough, Diana was standing with her shoulder turned to the room, staring out the darkened window with passionate interest. Enough to make it clear that she did not care for company.

"I'll join you after a visit to the ladies' retiring room," Willa said. "Just imagine what a fuss there will be if she changes her mind about the marriage, given that this entire house party is in honor of her betrothal."

"You may be a natural philosopher, Willa—and I'm still not certain what that entails—but I can read faces," Lavinia said. "I could make a fortune if I set up a stall at the fair. My cousin is in despair."

Diana's expression was indeed curiously tragic, as if she'd prefer wearing sackcloth and ashes to a Parisian gown covered with ruffles and bows . . . to say nothing of all the fruit pinned to the top of her wig.

"Her eyes resemble a basset hound's," Willa said thoughtfully. "A basset looks glum even if given a bone all to itself."

"Lord Roland undoubtedly has a very fine bone," Lavinia said, deadpan.

Willa choked with laughter. "You have no knowledge on that subject. He might have a twig, for all you know."

"I'm telling you now, Willa, that if Diana breaks her engagement, I mean to see what that man has to offer. Under his wig, I mean, of course."

"A shaved head," Willa said blandly. "As bald as a nut. To go with his bone, *of course*."

"Wil-*la!*"

Chapter Five

W hat do you think of the young ladies I introduced
you to?" Lady Knowe whispered, throwing
Alaric a smirk. "They were the undisputed toast of the
Season; the only question was which of them received
the most proposals."

He had no time to answer before he was surrounded
by admirers. His aunt began tossing out introductions
as if she were announcing the field of horses at the
Royal Ascot.

The interruption was just as well, since he wasn't at
all sure how to answer her question.

He felt as if he'd taken a sharp blow to the gut.

For some reason, Willa Ffynche inspired intense
interest, a fierce impulse to know everything about
her. What she thought, and why she thought it. Willa

looked as if she kept her thoughts to herself—and he wanted them. All of them. He wanted to learn her private language.

He couldn't remember ever meeting an English-woman who managed to be so courteous while being transparently skeptical. Not just about his books, but about *him*. She didn't like him. Even looking at him made her turned-up little nose wrinkle.

Frankly, she might as well have waved a red cloth in front of a bull. The uncivilized male inside him, the one who hated wearing a wig, had got wind of a hunt.

Willa Ffynche didn't look flirtatiously from under her lashes. She didn't want a signed book, a proposal, or a baby.

She had absolutely no interest in becoming Lady Alaric Wilde.

She wanted nothing from him.

In fact, he had the impression that she considered him akin to a circus barker trying to charm visitors out of ha'pennies by boasting of a two-headed giant hidden in his wagon.

At one point, she had flicked him a glance that implied she believed his travel accounts to be blatantly dishonest.

Another thing: she didn't seem to giggle. He was

WILDE IN LOVE · 57

surrounded by giggling women at this very moment, so he appreciated her restraint.

Add to those qualities her beauty. It wasn't just the clean way her cheek swept to her jaw. Or the wide eyes that had undoubtedly been serenaded by a hundred dubious poets.

The sum of her was so much greater than the parts. Lashes, pale skin, arched brows—

Long legs and a surprisingly deep bosom. Nothing like her friend Lavinia's, who had breasts about which men wrote real poems, as opposed to doggerel about pretty eyes.

Lavinia's bosom wouldn't suit him, though. Willa's breasts were creamy mounds that would just fit his hands.

They were perfect.

He smiled mechanically in response to a fawning comment, even as his body tightened at the thought of those breasts.

Willa held herself apart, and it undoubtedly drove men mad. Put together with that face and figure, the poor sods who frequented polite society hadn't a chance of maintaining their equilibrium.

Even as he kissed hands and accepted yet more compliments, most of which had nothing to do with his books but everything to do with his stage portrayal as a lovelorn fool, he kept sorting through the difference between Willa and, say, a pirate. "Fascination" wasn't quite the right word.

He'd never wanted to kiss a pirate, for one thing.

He wanted to kiss Willa Ffynche's impudent mouth into silence, and then coax her to talk again.

The thought gave him a feeling of vertigo, followed by a wash of nausea. What in the bloody hell was he thinking?

"Lord *Wilde*," a lady insisted, and he realized that he had lost track of the conversation.

"I do apologize," he said. "You were telling me of your ancestor in the East India Company."

She nodded. "I have his diary, and my husband and I think you are just the person to turn it into a book. He was dreadfully brave, you know. Frightfully so. It's a family trait; my son takes after him."

Alaric thought about explaining that he didn't write for hire, but discarded the notion. "Is your son also a member of the Company?"

She bristled. "I hardly think I can be taken for the mother of a grown man!"

"Margaret, your son is only six years old," Lady Knowe said, intervening. "I don't think he's been on the earth long enough to demonstrate familial courage."

Alaric stopped paying close attention after that. He had the feeling that Willa didn't give a damn about her beauty, or how old people thought she was. In fact, it was more the other direction.

She would be put off by praise. All those poor dogs who courted her during the Season likely wrote poems to her eyes. She would give a poet a sweet smile, count him a fool, and disregard whatever he said thereafter.

His aunt poked him in the ribs. "Miss Haverlock asked a question, Alaric."

"What punishment did you mete upon the cannibals? The play unaccountably neglected to finish the story," Miss Haverlock chirped, clearly hoping to be told that he had laid waste to an entire tribe of men he'd never met.

His smile thinned to a grimace. "I've never encountered any cannibals, Miss Haverlock. The play is a fantasy written by someone who has never met me."

The lady seemed unconvinced but she moved on. "Then what *really* happened in Chapter Six of *Wilde Latitudes?*"

"It was precisely as I described," Alaric said. "I don't have much of an imagination. I merely write down what occurs."

"Impossible!" she said, smiling at him roguishly. "You must give me more credit, Lord Wilde. I am not one who shies away from the truth. I know perfectly well that natives wear little more than strategically placed coconut shells."

He managed to stop himself from growling at her.

"You invented clothing in order to spare the gentle sensibilities of your readers," Miss Haverlock persisted. "But my uncle voyaged to the Antipodes and he told me that the natives are practically naked."

"There are many islands in the Pacific," Alaric replied, "and peoples with many different styles of dress on them."

He wasn't going to turn away and follow Willa Ffynche to the other side of the room.

That would be absurd—a conclusion he came to at the precise moment he caught sight of her slipping out the door.

Willa remained in the ladies' retiring room just long enough to give herself a lecture. She hadn't rejected fourteen proposals of marriage—one of them from a future marquess—only to follow in the footsteps of Lady Biddle.

Mooning after Lord Alaric, in other words.

The problem was that he appealed to the worst side of her. One of the reasons that she and Lavinia had come up with an ironclad set of rules governing their debut into society was that they were well aware that correct behavior didn't come naturally to either of them.

As Willa saw it, Lavinia's infatuation with the Wilde books had had less to do with their author than with the freedom depicted in the books. Lord Wilde could and did go anywhere he pleased. He could talk to anyone.

Not so for a young lady.

Willa had resisted the books, but the man himself, walking through the drawing room as if the straitlaced world of high society was irrelevant? She felt the pull of his presence as if it were the tide going out.

With a start, she discovered that she was staring blindly into the glass and had bitten her lower lip until it was ruby red. Enough!

She opened the door to the corridor.

Walked through—and froze.

Lord Alaric was leaning against the opposite wall, as casually as if he were waiting to enter the ladies' retiring room.

He looked up, and all that raw masculinity he wielded like a weapon focused on her. It took everything she had for Willa to say casually, "Good evening once again, Lord Alaric."

He straightened and gave her a slow smile. "Miss Ffynche."

"Is there something I can help you with?" Willa

managed, proud of keeping her voice from rising to a squeak. Willa Ffynche never squeaked. Or sighed. Or . . .

The comforting list of rules slipped from her head because the door swung closed at her back, which left them alone in the shadowy corridor.

"I'm not sure," he said, looking down at her, his eyes curious.

Willa could feel a flush rising in her cheeks. She never blushed. She never squeaked. She never sighed—

"I think I'm having an odd reaction to returning to England," he said, almost to himself.

"I can certainly understand how you might wish to flee a drawing room full of ladies," she answered. "*People*," she corrected herself hastily. "Drawing rooms full of people, because—because I suppose there is a great deal of solitude onboard a pirate ship."

She groaned inside. A pirate ship? She sounded like such a ninny.

"Would it surprise you to know that I've never been aboard a pirate ship?"

"Indeed not," she said, flustered. "I know that pirates board English vessels, rather than the other way around."

The smile in his eyes deepened. "I confess to piratical tendencies."

Was he implying that he viewed her as an English vessel eager to be boarded? *Boarded?* Willa felt her cheeks flame, and be damned with that rule about flushing. What on earth made him think she would welcome a blatant proposition of that nature? She was no Helena Biddle.

She flashed him a look and made a move to go, but he caught her arm before she could leave. "I succumbed to a pun, which was outrageously ill-bred of me. I've been too long outside of England."

Willa agreed, so she kept her silence.

"I had no intention of casting aspersions on your chastity." His voice was peppery and deep. "I'm not used to watching my tongue, and I've an idiotic weakness for puns. All plays on words, in truth."

In that case, he didn't belong in polite society, because if there was one thing English gentlepeople did, it was watch their tongues.

Perhaps that was why he had spent years wandering the world—so he needn't be constantly thinking about the implications of every utterance. The realization gave her a strange sensation under her ribs: a mixture of envy, censure, and wariness, all jumbled together.

"I expect attention to language is essential for a writer," she murmured, tacitly accepting Lord Alaric's apology.

His fingers slid from her arm, leaving a sensation of heat in their wake.

"I enjoy the discipline of shaping my experiences on the page, but I never imagined gaining all these admirers," he said flatly.

"Your readers?"

"For the most part, the ladies I've met in the drawing room are not readers. They seem infatuated with a character in a play, who has nothing to do with my books." His eyes were rueful, but sincere. "Not something I welcome, I assure you."

She was trying not to think about how close to her he was standing in the dim passage. He smelled like mint.

"I've been away from England long enough to forget many rules, but I remember the important ones. This one, for instance." He picked up her hand and brought her fingers to his lips again. "I like this one. What a marvelous way to greet a woman, say goodbye to her, or apologize to her."

His lips touched her hand and she felt the shock of it down her whole body. Followed by a withering sense of shame. She was *not* going to succumb to the allure of such a public figure, whether he welcomed his admirers or no.

She withdrew her hand and nodded coolly. "If you'll

forgive me, Lord Alaric." She strolled past him to the comfort of the drawing room and her boyish suitors—any one of whom could call to mind upwards of a hundred social rules without prompting, and likely thrice that if given time.

She knew he was watching her go, and she did not turn around.

Chapter Six

Diana and Lavinia were standing together, staring out the window. Willa forced herself to walk calmly toward them, pretending that her heart wasn't racing and her cheeks weren't flushed.

"What are you looking at?" she asked a moment later, peering out at the lawn. Diana made a noise that sounded like a sob. Abruptly, Willa saw that Diana's shoulders were shaking, and Lavinia was standing in such a way as to shield her from the room.

She hastily reached into her knotting bag and produced a handkerchief. "Is something wrong?"

"Oh, no," Diana said unconvincingly, dabbing her eyes with the handkerchief. "I'm merely overtired. I traveled through the night yesterday. Mother didn't want to insult His Grace with a belated arrival but she was occupied in London. She sent me ahead with my maid, knowing Lady Gray would act as my chaperone, and it was a tiring journey."

That betrayed a profound lack of understanding of the nature of house parties. One didn't worry about arriving late; people sometimes appeared a fortnight after the party began.

But while Diana's late father had been a distant relation of Lavinia's, her grandfather on her mother's side had been a Lord Mayor of London—a fact everyone tactfully pretended to overlook while talking about it constantly.

Love at first sight is more romantic when it has a touch of *mésalliance* about it, and Diana's grandfather—a rich grocer—was rarely forgotten when Lord Roland's proposal was mentioned.

"Lady Gray is generally late to every occasion," Willa said comfortingly.

"We told my mother that the house party began three full days early," Lavinia said, rubbing small circles on Diana's right shoulder blade. "Otherwise, we might have arrived a week from now, and you'd have had no chaperone at all."

Diana gave them a wobbly smile. "My mother felt I had to be here on the first day of the party. She is terrified that it will dawn on my fiancé that we don't belong in the highest circles. She keeps trying to disguise me." She gestured toward her wig.

"Your wig is a disguise?" Lavinia asked. "How so? I would think it makes you more obvious, if anything."

"I know," Diana said miserably. "I feel as if I'm an entry at the fair for the largest marrow grown in the shire. I couldn't sit down in that infernal dress I wore this afternoon because it felt as if I had a washing tub strapped to my hips. I just stood in one place and ate so many muffins I felt ill."

"I suppose all clothing is a disguise of one sort or another," Willa said, thinking about it. "Just look at Lavinia."

Diana glanced at her blue gown.

"My bodice is extremely small," Lavinia said helpfully.

"Which disguises her face," Willa followed up. "When Lavinia wears it, gentlemen are incapable of looking anywhere else."

"I could cut one of the bundles off the back of my Polonaise gown and it would contain more cloth than your entire bodice," Diana observed, looking slightly more cheerful.

"Mother wasn't entirely pleased when I ordered this gown," Lavinia said—something of an understatement in light of the ensuing hysterics—"but she changed her mind after seeing its effect on gentlemen."

"I wish my mother would allow me to select my own gowns," Diana said.

"Soon enough you'll be a married lady and you can wear whatever you wish," Willa pointed out. "Will you live in London, or here at Lindow?"

"I haven't the faintest idea," Diana said, in a voice that welcomed no further questions on that subject. "You were speaking to Lord Wilde, or rather, Lord Alaric, earlier, weren't you? I have the feeling that he doesn't like me very much."

"He has a brusque manner," Willa said. "Could you be mistaken? He frowns easily, but I don't think he dislikes me."

In fact, she had the unnerving conviction that Lord Alaric liked her quite a lot.

"My fiancé says that his brother is frightfully cross about that play," Diana said. "It seems that *Wilde in Love* is akin to his books; to wit, entirely fictional."

"The plot may have been elaborated upon by the playwright," Lavinia said defensively. "I am willing to accept that the missionary's daughter was added for the sake of melodrama. But Lord Alaric's adventures, as described in his books, are not exaggerated. I am certain of it."

Across the room Lord Alaric had his head bent as he listened to Helena Biddle, who was cuddled so close to him that her bosom was practically in his armpit.

"Do you suppose she'll be able to lure him into her bed?" Diana asked. Then she clapped a hand to her mouth. "I am so sorry. I'm not used—"

"That's all right," Lavinia assured her. "We both plan to remain faithful to our husbands if at all possible, but one can't pretend that more creative arrangements don't exist." She studied the couple, and added, "Even though she's a widow, Lady Biddle is remarkably assertive."

The lady was clinging to Lord Alaric's arm, one of her hands pressed to her heart, her eyes round.

"Perhaps he's telling her about his adventures," Willa said, feeling a visceral flare of dislike for the lady.

"Or the location of his bedchamber," Diana put in.

Lavinia tossed her head. "If his taste is that wretched, I shall definitely stop adoring him."

Diana laughed, but it was a small, stunted sound. "Do you believe that is within your control?"

"Yes," Lavinia stated.

"I have the impression that Lord Roland would like to stop adoring me," Diana said.

Willa was surprised into silence by her frankness.

Lavinia, naturally, was not. "For your sake, I would hope not. I have every intention of ensuring that my husband adores me. It will prevent any number of problems."

"It's awkward to marry someone who doesn't share one's feelings. We are both uncomfortable."

They all three instinctively looked toward her fiancé. From this distance, he resembled an advertisement for a French tailor.

"Likely you will come to love him in time," Lavinia said. "Lord Roland is quite handsome. If nothing else, he will present a pleasing vision at the breakfast table."

"And the bedchamber," Willa said.

"Wil-*la*," Lavinia hissed, under her breath.

Diana gave the two of them a quizzical look.

"Lavinia is reminding me to avoid improper subjects in public," Willa explained. "But just think how pretty your children will be."

"Mama mourned my father for well over a year," Lavinia said. "Yet she absolutely detested him during the first year of marriage. *Detested.*"

"Why?" Diana asked.

Lavinia laughed. "She says he smelled like a horse, because he spent all his time in the stables. She taught him to bathe regularly, and then he taught her how to ride a horse, and after that, they began loving each other."

"I don't think it will be so simple," Diana said.

"Are you in love with someone else?" Lavinia asked.

"No!" Diana said. And then: "Will you both stay at Lindow Castle for the entire six weeks of the house party?" There was just the faintest shake in her voice.

"We plan to travel to Manchester for a few days next week," Willa said, "and you should definitely join us, unless your mother has arrived by then. Lady Gray has some friends whom she wishes to visit."

"Look at that," Diana whispered. Lord Alaric was headed across the room toward his brother at a pace scarcely short of a jog. "He's escaping!"

They watched as the two men met in the center of the room. Lord Alaric's face lit with laughter as he slung an arm around his brother's shoulder.

"There's something remarkably attractive about all those muscles," Lavinia said. "Your future husband has them, Diana, and he doesn't even climb mountains. You are very lucky."

"I'll try to keep it in mind," Diana replied. "Lord Alaric's life sounds so uncomfortable, doesn't it? Arctic ice, mountains, pirates, cannibals, and likely no afternoon tea, either."

"I know," Lavinia admitted, with a sudden flash of common sense. "I adore his books, but I certainly wouldn't want to *be* him. Or marry him. What will you do if he falls in love with you, Willa? Everyone else did."

She and Willa had come to the duke's country house party straight from their first Season, during which they had been fêted and proposed to with remarkable fervor.

Willa's heart skipped a beat at the idea of Lord Alaric at her feet. "None of those men truly love me. Nor you either, Lavinia, to be blunt, even though you were as popular as I. They don't know us at all."

"He would make an excellent spouse," Diana said, adding in a lowered voice, "I heard that Lord Alaric's estate is easily the size of his father's, with one of the biggest apple orchards in the county."

Lindow Castle could be seen for miles about, which suggested that the Wilde books were far more profitable than Willa would have guessed. "Lavinia must own at least one of those apple trees, given all the prints of his face that she's bought," she pointed out.

As she was laughingly backing away from Lavinia, who was threatening her with a fan, the duke hoisted his pregnant duchess out of her chair, which served as a signal that everyone should make their way to the great hall on the upper floor, where supper would be served.

"Will you sit with us?" Lavinia asked Diana. "We shall be near the bottom of the room, because Willa has asked the butler to place her at a smaller table with a scholar who's transcribing Egyptian hieroglyphs."

"I know that sounds dire, but it's an interesting subject," Willa promised.

"You're not seated at a table with Lady Gray?" Diana said doubtfully. "My mother wouldn't approve."

Just then her fiancé turned and headed in their direction.

"I'm sure the scholar will be enlightening," Diana said, setting out for the door at a brisk pace.

They had almost escaped when Lord Roland cut them off. "May my brother and I have the honor of escorting the three of you upstairs to dine?"

That rumble in his voice betrayed far more about his emotions than a man of his caliber would ordinarily care to reveal. Diana certainly didn't like it; her whole body had gone rigid.

"Not tonight," Lavinia said, giving them both a cheerful smile. "We have plans to educate ourselves."

Lord Alaric was looking at Willa, which made her feel pleased and uneasy at the same time. "I am always in need of education," he said. "Who is dispensing instruction this evening?"

"We have made plans to dine with Mr. Roberts, a young Oxford don who has been working in the duke's library," Willa explained.

"Roberts, the Egyptologist?" Lord Alaric inquired.

She nodded. "I want to ask about his work on hieroglyphs and the Egyptian alphabet."

"What are hieroglyphs?" Diana asked, edging around to Willa's other side, away from her fiancé.

"It's a way of writing with little pictures," Willa said. "Lavinia and I saw an exhibition of ancient Egyptian scrolls covered with them."

"I've always been interested in hieroglyphs," Lord Alaric said. "And so has North."

He elbowed Lord Roland, who was gazing at Diana. "Absolutely," his brother said. "Fascinated."

"If I'm not mistaken," Lord Alaric added, "Roberts is working on the barrel of papyri I sent home. I'd forgotten all about that. It's just like our father to have someone in to translate them."

"You cannot translate hieroglyphs," Willa said, before she could stop herself. "The alphabet isn't understood at this point."

"She's got you there," Lord Roland said, snapping out of his study of Diana's downcast eyes to elbow his brother back.

"I'm more interested in the present than the past," Lord Alaric said. "But I shall be interested to see what the fellow thinks of the papyri. I had them off an old man who swore they were found in one of the pyramids."

"Perhaps we should continue to the dining hall," Willa said. Lady Biddle was bearing down fast behind Lord Alaric, the way a thundercloud bundles up on the horizon, and then manifests as a black cloud just over your head.

To judge by her scowl, she had decided that Willa was *persona non grata*.

Willa aimed a smile over Lord Alaric's shoulder.

The thundercloud darkened.

Lord Alaric's eyes narrowed, but he did not turn.

"Ladies, I shall speak to Prism and arrange to join you at the meal," Lord Roland said, bowing.

"Excellent idea; I'll join you," Lord Alaric said heartily, turning on his heel without further farewell.

Lady Biddle arrived just too late, drawing up short in the aggravated way a horse does when a carriage nips out from a side alley and blocks the road.

Diana, Lavinia, and Willa all curtsied.

"You three act as if you're so different from the rest of us," the lady said, in an astonishing display of poor manners. "As if you didn't want him. The truth is that he's a handsome beast, and we all want him."

"I *beg* your pardon," Diana said frigidly, doing an excellent imitation of a woman who would someday become a duchess.

"As a matter of fact, I've changed my mind," Lavinia

said with her usual ready friendliness, even though Lady Biddle was glowering. "He seems like a real person now, if that makes sense."

"Lord Alaric is not a beast," Willa stated, wondering why she was bothering to defend the man.

Lady Biddle laughed. "He's a primitive. That's the thrill of it." Her mouth twisted. "Oh, why am I trying to explain to you? Green girls are so tiresome. Don't think he isn't bored by the three of you, because he is."

"I have no doubt," Willa said, keeping her tone even. "If you'll please excuse us, Lady Gray will be looking for us."

"That woman is extraordinarily ill-bred," Diana said, as they climbed the stairs to the great hall. "When I am married, I shall give her the cut direct."

"I was fascinated to see Willa throw her hat into the ring," Lavinia said, twinkling at Willa. "You practically challenged Lady Biddle to a duel, or a version of it."

"I most certainly did not," Willa exclaimed.

"You raised an eyebrow," Lavinia crowed. "I saw you! That was a challenge. Your expression implied that Lord Alaric was at your feet and you were contemplating whether to accept his hand. And then you defended him!"

"Really?" Willa said, trying to decide whether defense could be construed as a challenge.

"Absolutely," Lavinia confirmed. "If you were a man, you would have slapped her cheek with a scented glove and challenged her to meet you on the heath, and there in the early dawn, you'd have to defend your—"

"Don't say 'love,'" Willa advised.

"I wasn't going to. You'd have to defend your desirability over Lady Biddle's. Obviously, you would win."

"That's not high praise," Willa said, thinking about Helena Biddle's eyes. They were beady. And greedy.

"Don't you want the famous Lord Wilde at your feet?" Diana asked, peering past Lavinia. "You would be my sister-in-law."

"I'm sorry, but no, even under those circumstances," Willa replied.

She couldn't imagine Lord Wilde at her feet. He was the explorer, the man who leaned close to Lady Biddle, who spoke knowledgeably about Egyptian pyramids, and seemed to await praise of his books. If not his profile.

But Lord *Alaric*?

That was a different story. The very idea of *him* at her feet, or in her bedchamber, made her feel hot all over.

Lord Alaric was livid at the idea of his personal life playing out on the stage. He didn't want all his admirers. He made terrible puns and looked as if he'd like to pounce on her.

Carry her from the room and into his bedchamber.

"Think of how many ladies are mad for Lord Wilde. It would be such a triumph," Diana insisted.

Willa shrugged, breaking her own rule. "I'm not interested."

"Willa!" Lavinia hissed.

Lord Alaric was looking down at them from the top of the stairs, certainly within earshot. Willa stopped short, hand frozen on the balustrade.

He opened his mouth and almost said something, but instead took himself off down the hallway.

"Well, that was awkward," Lavinia murmured.

Willa bit her lip. She hadn't intended for him to overhear her. All the same, she'd meant what she said. She would hate it if women pursued her husband, sniffing at his feet as dogs do after a fox's tail has been dragged over a path.

She would never marry a fox's tail.

That didn't quite make sense. She didn't want to marry a man whom everyone wanted, as Helena Biddle put it. The lady was wrong to call him a primitive, but she was right about his desirability.

No one lusted after Socrates, she reminded herself again.

Her engraving of the philosopher pointed directly to the type of man with whom she could be happy.

Chapter Seven

Lavinia's mother, Lady Gray, had the easy confidence of someone whose great-great-grandfathers rubbed shoulders with kings. "Of course, you may eat wherever you wish. But why would you wish to do such a peculiar thing?" she sighed, before waving the girls away.

The moment Lady Gray was out of earshot, Diana murmured something about a headache and fled to her bedchamber, so Prism escorted Lavinia and Willa to a small table at the very bottom of the hall, managing—as butlers do so well—to mask his disapproval of their voluntary displacement with an impassive face, while somehow still making his feelings known.

At their approach, the young scholar, Mr. Roberts, sprang to his feet. He was thin as a billiard cue and was wearing an old-fashioned wig with a queue. Twists of sandy hair escaped around the edges of his wig, making him look like a dandelion gone to seed.

Willa was surprised to see his eyes widen in something like awe, as he'd been perfectly composed when the duke had introduced her earlier in the day. Then she realized that Roberts was reacting not to her, but to Lord Alaric, who was looming just behind her.

"Good evening, ladies," his lordship said, bowing. "I'm afraid we'll have to dine without my brother. Once made aware that Miss Belgrave had retired for the evening, North decided he wasn't as interested in hieroglyphs as he thought."

"Lord Alaric, may I present Mr. Roberts?" Willa said.

The scholar's eyes were as round as saucers. Evidently, Lord Wilde's books had been well received in the university. "I am . . . I am honored," he stammered.

Interesting.

Willa would have thought that an academic would disdain authors of popular travel narratives. But not this author: Roberts proceeded to reveal that he had read every one of the books.

Willa watched Lord Alaric respond to Roberts's lavish praise politely, but with no life in his voice. In fact, it was as if an impassive veneer had settled over his expression.

He wrote the books; why would he be so disinclined to tell Mr. Roberts what the "true story" was behind some incident that had taken place in the Americas? Instead, Lord Alaric insisted, in a voice courteous but remote, that there was no "true story" other than what he had put on the page.

Mr. Roberts seated himself to Willa's right, his expression frankly disbelieving. Just as she had decided that Lord Alaric's scar was the result of an accident in the privy, Mr. Roberts had apparently come to his own conclusions about that incident.

And no matter what Lord Alaric said about it, Mr. Roberts was not inclined to change his mind.

Much to her own surprise, Willa discovered that she trusted the author. The quiet, even way he affirmed the events he had described in his book made her believe him.

Annoying though Lord Alaric was, it seemed he told the truth. No literary flourishes, no extra characters added for the sake of drama.

No cannibals. Which meant no missionary's daughter. There was no logic to the relief she felt at that idea.

When all four of them were seated, Lord Alaric looked across the table and said, "I'm very pleased that you invited me to join you, Miss Ffynche."

It was a blatant provocation, as she had *not* invited

him. And so was the naughty smile he was giving her. Willa had been taught not to speak across the table, so she merely nodded, and turned to Mr. Roberts.

"I was most interested by the article you published in *The Gentleman's Magazine* about Egyptian papyrus rolls. I wonder if you've made progress deciphering the hieroglyphs."

Mr. Roberts cast her a wary look. "You read my article in *The Gentleman's Magazine*?"

"Yes," Willa said, keeping it simple because it appeared that even notable scholars had trouble understanding the English language. "Have you been able to make progress on the scrolls?"

He frowned. "Matters of ancient philology cannot possibly interest ladies of gentle birth. I thought you wished to discuss my travels in Egypt." He turned to Lord Alaric. "Don't you agree, your lordship?"

"I'd think you'd welcome intelligent conversation with anyone even slightly familiar with your work." Lord Alaric glanced at Willa, a gleam of laughter in his eyes. "I'm sure I find it easier than talking to people who boast of never having read a page of my books."

Willa swallowed back a grin.

After that blunt appraisal, the scholar got over his reluctance to discuss hieroglyphs with ladies, and admitted that he thought he had made some valuable discoveries.

"The most contentious question is whether each individual hieroglyph represents an idea or a sound."

"Which do you believe?" Willa asked.

He puffed out his chest like a bantam rooster, and spoke over her head to Lord Alaric. "I have come to the conclusion that each hieroglyph represents an idea."

"Could you give us an example of a hieroglyph?" Lavinia asked. "I must admit that I didn't pay close attention to the exhibition of papyrus."

"Regrettably, I haven't a way to draw one," Mr. Roberts replied. His expression suggested he thought ladies were incapable of deciphering such mysteries in any case.

"That is no matter," Lord Alaric said, picking up his bowl of spring pea soup. He poured a thick green glop on the white plate underneath the bowl. "Draw your hieroglyph here."

Mr. Roberts picked up his knife and scratched a shape.

"I know what it is," Lavinia cried. "It's a golden idol, the sort they used to worship. A baby. Yes, it is certainly a baby. With a crown!"

That was characteristic of Lavinia's imagination. Willa didn't see a baby. Or a crown.

Lord Alaric was frowning, perhaps because he was viewing the image from the side. "Is it a swan?"

"Very close," Mr. Roberts said. He turned to Willa.

"It's a duck," she said. "I must say that while I applaud your drawing skills—and those of the ancient Egyptians—I find it hard to imagine what concept a duck might represent."

"I am working on the hypothesis that because a duck loves its children, this image means 'son.'"

There was a moment's silence. "Miss Ffynche," Lord Alaric said at length, "what do you think of Mr. Roberts's proposition?"

"Mr. Roberts's reasoning isn't immediately clear to me," Willa replied, discarding the rules of dining etiquette in order to respond directly, "but perhaps that is because I don't know as much about the species as he."

"I don't think closer study of ducks would help," Lord Alaric drawled. "Even if one discounted animals unknown to ancient Egyptians, any number of animal hieroglyphs could indicate parental affection."

Mr. Roberts started rapidly blinking his eyes. "The duck was particularly known in antiquity for its care of its offspring."

"I noticed many cats in the scrolls on display in the British Museum," Willa intervened. "What do you think they represent, sir?"

"I vote for 'daughter,'" Lord Alaric said, before Mr. Roberts could gather his thoughts.

"We have a tomcat in the stables who must have fathered hundreds of kittens, but he dislikes them all," Lavinia said. "Even mother cats care for their young only until they are able to kill their own mice, which contradicts your suggestion, Lord Alaric."

Mr. Roberts appeared rattled by the turn the conversation had taken. "The ancient Greek word for 'duck'—"

Lord Alaric cut him off. "Ladies, are you aware that a duck will feign an injury in order to draw a fox away from her nest? The bird runs the risk of being eaten, putting her life before her offspring's."

He had switched sides, Willa thought with some indignation. The discussion was merely a game to him.

"I have read about that behavior," she said. "However, Mr. Roberts did not indicate that the image of the duck connoted the idea of sacrifice. He specified 'son,' thus I believe he has further reasons for his argument."

Mr. Roberts's pained expression suggested he was not enjoying the conversation, no matter how respectful her phrasing. Willa was used to that; it sometimes took gentlemen a good half hour to get over their conviction that the additional body parts men possessed indicated their brains were extra large.

It was one of the reasons that she and Lavinia had

decided to question but not counter their beaux during the Season: men were so tiresomely afraid of being proven wrong.

She gave Mr. Roberts yet another encouraging smile. "I do hope we are not making you uncomfortable by engaging with your intriguing idea."

"Willa is forever discomfiting knowledgeable gentlemen," Lavinia remarked, "and nothing our headmistress said could dissuade her from it."

"Please explain the reasoning behind your association of 'duck' and 'son,'" Willa said, ignoring Lavinia.

Lord Alaric was sitting back in his chair and was watching her with a faint smile that was absurdly unsettling. In fact, it gave Willa a warm feeling in her chest and belly that—

That was unacceptable. She was not affected by a man.

Mr. Roberts, for his part, was seemingly still trying to adjust to the fact that his conclusion was being called into question by two women.

"I believe you were about to say something about the Greek word for 'duck'?" Willa prompted. "Am I right in thinking that it is 'Penelope'?"

Lord Alaric gave a bark of laughter. "What was your headmistress like?"

"Are you asking whether Willa and I belong to the

Bluestocking Society?" Lavinia inquired. "They'd never have us. We're entirely too fond of dancing, and I, for one, am remarkably frivolous."

Willa was wrestling with the uncharitable instinct either to kick Lord Alaric under the table, or lead him to believe that she knew Greek.

Which she did not.

"I do not read Greek," she admitted. "But in Greek mythology, Icarius was angered by the sex of his eldest child, Penelope, and threw his infant daughter into the water to drown, whereupon she was saved by a family of ducks. My understanding is that Penelope's name means 'duck.'"

"It's a lovely story," Lavinia said. "I can imagine a family of ducks anxiously keeping the baby afloat with a great deal of diving and quacking."

"Lavinia is likely the only person I know capable of writing that play you disparage so much," Willa said to Lord Alaric. "She has a remarkable imagination."

Lord Alaric grinned. "Miss Gray, did you author a disgraceful farce entitled *Wilde in Love*?"

"I wish I had," Lavinia said. "Because then my mother would have been forced to allow us to see the production, don't you think?"

Mr. Roberts was gaping from one to the other.

"I assume that Lady Gray would feel confident that

your girlish innocence could not be tarnished by listening to heady poetry that you yourself wrote," Lord Alaric agreed.

He was addressing Lavinia, but looking at Willa.

She broke his gaze—which was harder to do than it should have been—and turned back to the scholar. "If you don't mind my asking again, Mr. Roberts, how did Penelope's experience with ducks influence your thinking about the Egyptian hieroglyph?"

Chapter Eight

Alaric was experiencing that disagreeable emotion again. It was an emotion that brought an unpleasant physical response with it, like seasickness.

Or the consequence of too much brandy.

Perhaps the sudden onset of a fever.

He sat back, thinking it over, while the young fool from Oxford painstakingly tried to explain to Willa the links between a mythological girl named Penelope and the figure of a duck drawn in pea soup.

Roberts's efforts weren't helped when the lady, with exquisite tact, noted that she was confused by how the Greek civilization, which had begun thousands of years after the Egyptians invented hieroglyphs, could have influenced the earlier system of writing.

Alas, Roberts was unable to respond with anything resembling clarity.

If he had anything logical to say, which Alaric doubted.

"I believe I understand," Miss Gray put in after Roberts had repeated himself three or four times in the forlorn hope his thesis would sound better in different words. "You think that the myth of Penelope is much older than scholars believe."

She was nearly as smart as her friend, and equally pretty.

What in the devil had happened to English ladies in the years he'd been traveling?

Helena Biddle was as lustful and foolish as he remembered, but Miss Gray and Miss Ffynche seemed as akin to her as . . . as an ancient Egyptian to an ancient Greek.

When Willa Ffynche was intrigued by something, her blue eyes darkened to indigo.

Roberts had at last figured out that the two women were as intelligent as he, if not more so. He leaned forward in order to reply to Lavinia, causing his sleeve to brush Willa's bare arm.

Primitive instincts had kept Alaric alive on more than one occasion. The instinct to run was a powerful one. Very useful.

The emotion he was feeling right now?

Just as powerful, but not as useful.

He stared at Roberts until the man uneasily glanced at him . . . and sprang back into his seat, removing his person from the vicinity of Willa's arm, as if Alaric had put a torch under his nose.

Perhaps not a useful emotion, but an effective one.

Alaric was accustomed to evaluating new situations and extricating himself without undue haste if danger presented itself. There were occasions—the Empress Catherine's invitation came readily to mind—when prudence had forced him to refuse what might have proved a memorable experience.

In another example, no matter what *Wilde in Love* depicted, while traveling in Africa he had deliberately avoided incursions into cannibal territory; they didn't sound like fellows who would welcome him in their village.

He had, however, made the acquaintance of friendly chaps whose heads barely came to his waist. In the last half decade, he'd seen an enormous white whale, the Great Wall of China, and the aurora borealis.

And now he'd seen Miss Willa Ffynche.

She had a tip-tilted nose, absurdly big eyes, and mounds of hair. Tonight she wasn't wearing a wig, but he still wasn't certain of its natural color, because it was concealed under a blanket of snowy-white powder.

Her eyebrows provided a clue. Presumably dark hair would swirl around her shoulders when she was unclothed.

He even liked her dress, although it was green. He'd never liked green, but on her . . . he liked green.

Right now, she was taking apart Roberts in the sweetest, most reasonable voice in the world. A sympathetic voice. Asking him whether there was any chance that the hieroglyph of a duck might stand for a D sound.

Roberts began babbling about the Arabic, Coptic, and Greek alphabets while Willa kept those unnerving eyes fixed on his face as if she had forgotten that Alaric was sitting opposite her.

Alaric did not consider himself vain, but he was well aware that if he wanted to, he could bed any number of women at this house party, married and unmarried.

Willa Ffynche wasn't one of them, since she was obviously a proper young lady. A virgin.

The word lit a slow burn in his groin. She was a virgin, untouched by another man. Unkissed, most likely. She had that look.

Naturally, he wouldn't sleep with her, because he

wasn't interested in marriage, and she had marriage written all over her.

But he saw no reason why he shouldn't be the first to kiss her.

Just now she was leaning toward the Oxford man as they discussed whether hieroglyphs might actually be magic spells or attempts at magic spells. Willa did not believe in magic, which didn't surprise Alaric at all.

If she was trying to spark his jealousy, she was succeeding. Even more so, because she was still pretending to forget he was there, though he was staring at her with all the boldness of a beggar—

No, not a beggar. He was no beggar, and never would be.

Surely Roberts's lecture had gone on long enough.

Abruptly, footmen swirled around them like water around a rock, whisking away everything from their table, including the plate adorned with a lopsided Egyptian duck.

Willa, Lavinia, and Roberts didn't stop talking for a moment. The two ladies weren't bluestockings, per se. They showed no burning desire to learn Greek or deliver a lecture on the Stoic philosophers.

To Alaric's mind, they were more appealing. They were people who went through life driven by curiosity and intelligence. The realization made him feel as if he were walking close to quicksand, so he remained silent, broodingly watching the conversation.

Any man would concur that Willa Ffynche was exquisite, from her slender eyebrows to the curve of her cheek. But it was the self-contained part of her nature that made him feel like a schoolboy.

It made him want to poke her, tug her braid, offer her an apple. A wash of disgust broke over him, and he wrenched his eyes away—and met those of Helena Biddle.

She must have come into the room at his heels, because she'd positioned herself at the very next table. *Her* smile had nothing contained about it at all. Across the table from her, another woman offered a glowing smile.

Perhaps he should just sleep with Helena. Hell, it was better than being ignored by a young lady with a sardonic smile.

He stood and broke into the conversation. "Miss Ffynche, Miss Gray, Mr. Roberts, I must ask you to excuse me. I have no stomach for sweets tonight."

Willa looked up, confused. Then she gave him a charming smile, inclined her head in a nod, and turned directly back to Roberts.

She really had forgotten his presence altogether.

In fact, she didn't give a damn whether he stayed at

the table or not. Considering the speed with which she returned to the skirmish with Roberts, she would have shown considerably more dismay if the scholar had tried to escape the conversation.

His brother came up behind him just as Alaric took a step away from the table, toward Helena Biddle. He needed . . .

He needed to exorcise this aggravating sense that he should pick up Willa Ffynche, walk out of the room, and give her that first kiss.

Sleeping with Helena would force the irritating virgin out of his head before he made a fool of himself by . . . by courting her or some such nonsense.

North slung an arm around his shoulder. "Come along with me."

Helena saw that he'd been intercepted, launched herself out of her chair, and anchored herself to Alaric's arm. "I am longing for some fresh air," she said, in the husky, practiced tones of a woman confident of her ability to satisfy any man.

But North shook his head. "You must forgive me, Lady Biddle. Our younger brother Leonidas has just arrived and will want to see Alaric directly."

She seemed mollified by this intimate murmur. "I look forward to tomorrow," she said to Alaric, her eyes fairly eating him up. "I'll be staying in the castle for over a month; I do hope you are not fleeing to foreign parts immediately?"

Once they'd left the hall, Alaric said to North, "Where is Leonidas?"

"Billiards room," his brother said. "I imagine that's why he was sent down from Oxford again. Last year it was for winning twenty-five pounds off some young fool."

"Billiards? We played billiards all afternoon! Aren't you tired of them yet?"

"I never tire of billiards," North said. "Besides, you fool, I saved you before you did something you'd regret later."

"I rarely indulge in regrets," Alaric said.

North laughed. "I've been watching you from the long table. You would have regretted a tryst with Helena Biddle, probably for the rest of your life."

Chapter Nine

Late the following afternoon

D amn it, I apologize." Alaric put down his glass of brandy and followed his brother to the door. "Don't be an ass, North!"

"It runs in the family," his brother retorted. But he stopped before walking out of the billiards room, his back rigid.

"I'm the ass. I'm sure Miss Belgrave is deliriously in love with you. Whispering to her friends about your eyebrows at this moment. Likely she was just uncomfortable in my presence."

"What makes you think that?" his brother asked dryly, turning around. "Because the notorious Lord

Wilde intimidates ladies? Did she look intimidated at luncheon?"

No, she hadn't.

In fact, Diana Belgrave appeared as unimpressed by him as Willa Ffynche had when she told her friends that she had no interest in him.

"I am happy to say that your fiancée seems not to be an admirer," Alaric said, grimacing. "That would have been awkward."

His brother snorted. "Do you realize that if the king and queen knew that Lord Wilde was attending this house party, they might well have joined us? *Wilde in Love* played at the castle in the last Christmas season."

"I can't stand people fawning on me," Alaric said tightly. "Royal or no."

North smiled. "Diana won't fawn on you, any more than she fawned on me, though I'm heir to a dukedom."

Alaric already knew that. Whenever he spoke to his future sister-in-law, she looked vaguely as if someone had put an insect in her tea. She had dropped his hand after the slightest touch.

More problematically, she seemed to do the same for North.

"She is skeptical of your claims about Africa," his brother said now.

"She's not the first to think I'm a habitual liar,"

Alaric said. "Englishmen prefer to believe that everyone longs to walk around in a wig, even given much evidence to the contrary."

North grinned at him. "She once asked me if your next book would describe people carrying their heads in their arms. Or riding giant dragonflies. In short, she's not a true believer."

Sadly, that was the best thing that Alaric had heard about Diana Belgrave to this date. "How did you meet her?"

"I saw her in a ballroom, sitting at the side of the room."

That made sense. Miss Belgrave had the air of a wallflower, for all she was so fashionable.

"How did she respond when you were introduced?" he asked.

North turned his head, and their eyes met. "I'm heir to a duke," he said flatly. "Her grandfather was a mayor of London. Did she have a choice other than to be overjoyed?" He picked up the cue he had discarded and slammed the red ball into a pocket without appearing to position the shot.

Alaric shook his head. "No."

"She was laughing," North said.

To Alaric's mind, his future sister-in-law had a glower that made it hard to imagine her laughing.

"I saw her, and I wanted her to be mine," North stated.

Alaric opened his mouth and closed it again.

Damn.

Love was like an infection, apparently. Disease of the brain.

"I knew," North said, sounding like a man in a fever dream. "I knew that I had to have her."

If Alaric believed in love spells and the like, he would have thought his brother had been struck by one. Except that would imply Miss Belgrave had administered said charm, which would in turn imply she actually wanted to marry his brother.

"Have you ever felt that way?" North asked.

"Absolutely not," Alaric stated. "I doubt it's in me."

North flipped his cue, the gleaming wood catching the light. "I think it runs in the family. Look at our father."

Alaric shrugged. "What about him?" The duke's third wife, Ophelia, had bright red hair, a pointed chin, and a temper. Alaric liked her. She and their father seemed to have a passionate, if tempestuous, union.

"Years ago, the duke entered a room and saw our mother lying on a sofa being fanned by three suitors. He says that he knew at that very moment that he would marry her. He got rid of her suitors, tossed the fans, and kissed her."

Alaric laughed. A portrait of their mother, the first duchess, hung downstairs; with few memories of his own, he'd formed the opinion that their mother was a beautiful minx who had led their father on a pretty chase.

"I don't see the point of emulating Father's methods of courtship," he said. "Remember, his second duchess ran off, leaving four of her children behind, never mind the three of us."

"After Mother died, Father made the pragmatic decision to provide his three orphaned sons with a mother." North paused, and then added blandly, "His choice of mother for those orphans was, perhaps, unfortunate."

Alaric's bark of laughter echoed his brother's. The second duchess hadn't had a maternal instinct in her body. She had dropped babies in the nursery as if they were abandoned kittens; none of them—including her own children—had further contact with her.

After her fourth baby arrived, six years into the marriage, she'd run off with a Prussian count, and Parliament passed a Private Act granting their father a divorce without discussion.

"I realize it casts some doubt on the duke's judgment," North said. "But he maintains that he felt the same certainty about Ophelia as he did for our mother, and both his first and third marriages are successful."

"God willing, I'll never be struck by a 'certainty' of that nature," Alaric said. "If this is what love does to a man"—he waved his hand at North's costume—"I want nothing to do with it. I'm right, aren't I? She is the reason you turned yourself into a popinjay?"

For the first time Alaric saw a trace of discomfort on his brother's face. "Diana is fashionable. She cares for such things."

"You put on yellow heels in order to win the lady's heart."

"She had no choice in whom to marry, so I wanted to—to make it a more appealing proposition, that's all."

"Diana Belgrave is a lucky woman," Alaric said. "Damn lucky."

Even if she doesn't recognize it.

But he kept that thought to himself.

"It's your turn, by the way," North said, flipping his cue again.

"I don't suppose you'd like to box a round instead?" Alaric asked. "I went for a ride earlier, but I'd welcome more exercise."

"Absolutely not." North eyed him. "I'm sure you

strip to advantage; I suppose you kept yourself fit on board ship by taking on the sailors."

"Under all that silk, you've still got a muscle or two. Where's Parth, by the way? Unless he's changed as much as you have, he was always game for fisticuffs."

Parth Sterling, a former ward of the duke, had grown up with them from the age of five. The four of them—Horatius, North, Alaric, and Parth—had racketed about the estate for years, leading a pack of boys whose fathers ranged from the estate blacksmith to the village butcher. Parth was like a brother, an irritable bear of a brother, a Wilde in everything but name.

"He was supposed to arrive today. Perhaps tomorrow." North pocketed a ball. "He'll spar with you."

"Should I expect an egg-shaped wig?" Alaric asked warily.

North laughed. "He's too busy building his empire to bother with fashion. Are you still one of his main shareholders?"

"Certainly. I paid for my estate with returns from my initial investment. What's his focus at the moment?" Parth had started by trading in China, but he had an eagle eye for anything that would return a huge profit. Letters from his solicitor trailed Alaric around the world, each noting how much money Parth had recently made for him.

"A power loom. Oh, and he's talking of starting a bank."

"A power loom," Alaric said, his interest caught. "Have you seen it?"

North nodded. "He bought an estate west of here, not far from yours, and housed the loom in a barn, along with the men who are working on it. The old manor had burned, so he's building a house with cast-iron balconies made to his own design."

Alaric detected a tinge of envy. "You don't mind living in the castle, do you?" He glanced around. Even now, at the height of summer, the stone walls were a little damp, and the place smelled like old books and dogs. Like home.

"No more than anyone does who had planned to build his own house," North said wryly. As a boy, he had spent hours sketching buildings he planned to construct someday.

"Being the heir doesn't mean you can't design a house. I brought you back a pattern book by a fellow named Palladio."

"Andrea Palladio, I assume," North said. "Thank you. I haven't time to design a house, though the dairy went over in a storm, and I designed a new one." The savage undertone to his voice surprised Alaric.

He stayed silent, watching his brother play billiards

as if it were a game of war, on a battlefield with only one army. A man's dreams can be flattened by responsibilities.

He himself had spent years exploring the globe.

Perhaps it was time to come back home.

To take over responsibilities and allow North to spend the next decade doing as he wished. Perhaps he would build a mansion with ceilings high enough to accommodate his wife's wigs.

"I'm back now," he said, keeping it simple. "I could take over the estates, including working with Father. You can do whatever you like. Though your future wife might have objections if you set out to travel around the world."

North's eyes met his. "I appreciate your offer, but it's my responsibility. I'll be the duke someday. Father can't do it all, even with three estate managers. These days he is spending more and more time in Parliament. And you love to travel."

"Neither of us was born to be duke," Alaric retorted. "Horatius was. He would have relished it, but I won't leave you to do it by yourself any longer. We'll share it. I took the first bout of freedom; you take the second. I'll travel again later."

"No," his brother said. "I appreciate it, but it's my lot, and I won't impose it on anyone else."

North turned, slotting his fancy billiard cue into the holder to the side of the door. Alaric watched his broad shoulders, dismay pricking his spine. There was something brittle about his older brother, something near damaged.

He felt a surge of dislike for his fashionable, sulky future sister-in-law, but he shook it off. Diana Belgrave was likely more a symptom than a cause.

English gentlemen didn't hug each other. It wasn't a rule that had to be voiced, in the nursery or elsewhere. It was intrinsic to the heartbeat of high society, to the stiff upper lip that shaped male relationships.

But as Alaric had discovered, it was a rule that many parts of the world considered absurd. He strode after his brother and wrapped his arms roughly around him.

North stood stiffly for a moment, then his arms reluctantly encircled Alaric. "You intend to bring foreign customs home?" he murmured in a wry voice.

"We would both hug Horatius if we could," Alaric said.

The truth of that hummed between them. North's arms tightened, before they both stepped back.

Chapter Ten

The following day
The Peacock Terrace

Willa had made up her mind that she would treat Lord Alaric with exactly the same courteous attention she paid all the other men at the party. No more, no less.

That would be the same attention she paid to men who were entirely ineligible for marriage.

Like married men. Or toothless ones, if any such had made their intentions clear.

Lord Alaric was married to his fame and his readers and his explorations. That was a good way to think of him. Off limits.

Regretfully, she seemed to have a susceptibility to warm blue eyes. He merely looked at her and she felt it all over her body, like a promise of breathless pleasure and wild, unsteady feelings.

No sensible person married for those reasons.

Lavinia had danced with him twice the previous night and reported that he turned the wrong direction once and entertained her with tales of dancing around bonfires. The three times he'd approached Willa, she had managed to claim either a previous engagement or an impromptu trip to the ladies' retiring chamber.

Whenever they were in the same room, she felt his presence like the rumble of a carriage that came too close to the walkway, bringing with it a stiff breeze and a sense of danger.

But she couldn't spend the whole month running away from the man like a frightened rabbit. It wasn't ladylike. It wasn't *Willa*-like.

Lavinia popped her head in at her bedchamber door. "I can scarcely believe I'm saying this, but for once you are late and I am not! It's time for tea. The gentlemen will be rioting, wondering where you are."

"Pish," Willa said. "Far more likely, they're pining for you. After all, *The Ladies' Own Memorandum-Book* declared that blonde hair is the most desirable."

Lavinia giggled. "*Your* dark eyebrows emphasize

your eyes, which are—allow me to remind you—the cornflower blue of Venus's own."

"No one knows the eye color of a mythological goddess," Willa said, slipping past Lavinia into the corridor. "More to the point, why would Lord Noorland think that a poem would warm me to his suit? He doesn't know me at all. Didn't he call your eyes 'pansies'?"

"He should have given you a blue-eyed kitten, instead of a poem about your blue eyes. Remember how much you longed for a cat when you first came to live with us?"

Willa's smile faded. The memory of the year when she'd come to live with Lavinia, after her beloved parents died, was not a happy one.

"I always thought that Mother should have let you have a cat," Lavinia said, as they made their way down the stairs.

"No need. I couldn't have taken it to school." After the death of Willa's parents, the girls had been dispatched to a select seminary in Queen Square. Lady Gray's generosity toward her ward did not extend to having children or felines underfoot.

"I know Mother doesn't care for animals in the house, but she should have made an exception for you," Lavinia said, pursuing her own train of thought. "But you never asked again. Why not?"

There was a very practical answer to that question: a nine-year-old orphan needs a substitute mother more than a pet. Willa had made a rapid study of Lady Gray and turned herself into the perfect daughter.

Somewhat ironically, the same attributes that had pleased Lady Gray led to Willa's success on the marriage market ten years later. It was astonishing how quickly a man expressed devotion if a lady was happy to speak of his interests, whether the intricacies of heraldry, or the nesting habits of herons.

"I'll have a dog or cat someday," Willa said. "More to the point, I feel the same way about my suitors as your mother does about cats."

"*All* your suitors?" Lavinia said with a twinkle, as they entered the library. "Including Lord Alaric?"

"Is he hurting your feelings?" Willa asked, catching her hand to bring her to a halt. "I can order him to stay away from me. I certainly have no interest in marrying a man of such notoriety."

"It's terribly unfair," Lavinia said cheerfully. "Just think of the years when I adored Lord Wilde, while you scoffed at him. I used to imagine him walking into the room and falling straight into love with me. Instead, I was late to tea, and he saw you instead."

Willa bit her lip. "I'm sorry."

"Don't be silly," her friend said, breaking into laughter. "If I had been on time, he still wouldn't have given me a second glance. More importantly, I don't feel the slightest bit faint-headed around him, whereas I used to feel swoony just by glancing at his image on my wall."

"You loved him with great devotion," Willa said.

"Yes, but my devotion evaporated with alarming rapidity. I'm a little worried that I'll end up a hard-headed old maid, living in a cottage with four cats and no husband."

Willa grinned. "I have the same fears. Might we share a summer cottage on the Isle of Wight as well?"

"I have the distinct impression you won't be with me," Lavinia said.

She drew Willa through the tall doors leading from the library to the Peacock Terrace, a wide expanse of flagstones abutting the castle's south face and stretching out across the lawn. It was one of those days when the sky was clear and blue, with just a few ragged clouds.

"They look like swans floating across a lake," Lavinia said, pointing.

Willa looked up, but to her the clouds resembled crabs or spies scuttling for cover—which was such a ridiculous thought that she didn't voice it. She didn't believe in flights of the imagination.

"Forget the swans," Lavinia added, "where are the peacocks?"

Indeed, there wasn't a peahen to be seen on the wide lawn. They were joining perhaps a dozen ladies and as many gentlemen, standing or seated at small garden tables scattered around the terrace. The ladies' gowns gleamed with rich colors, spangles, and embroidery, and their wigs were tinted with colored powder and adorned with plumes. Willa's imagination stubbornly presented her with another comparison to the animal world.

"There's no need for peacocks," she said softly to Lavinia. "Just look at all the parrots gathered for tea."

Lord Alaric was nowhere to be seen. All the better, Willa told herself.

Lady Knowe presided over an enormous silver teapot, from which two liveried footmen ferried teacups to the guests.

She looked up as they arrived. "Darling girls! I've been wondering where you were. Willa, that is a lovely gown."

Over breakfast that morning, Lady Knowe had declared that "miss" was one of the most objectionable words in the English language, and that she meant to address Diana, Willa, and Lavinia by their given names.

Willa gave her a wide smile. "Thank you! I am particularly happy to hear that, because Lavinia thought I should add blonde lace to the bodice, and I disagreed."

"Your taste is exquisite, dear Lavinia, but in this instance you were mistaken," Lady Knowe pronounced. "Blonde lace reminds me of morose wives of penurious pedants."

Like many of Lady Knowe's pronouncements, this had no obvious logic, and was left unchallenged.

"I wish to introduce you to Mr. Parth Sterling, who is as dear to me as one of my own nephews," Lady Knowe said, rising. "Parth!"

"Aunt Knowe." A deep voice answered the call.

Mr. Sterling's jaw was strong; his nose was aristocratic; his hair was thoroughly powdered. He was attired like a perfect gentleman.

And yet he had the look of a pirate. Or a smuggler.

It was his skin, Willa thought, as Lady Knowe made an introduction. His cheeks had a sun-warmed hue that she associated with seamen or field laborers. It was remarkably . . .

The thought trailed off because the gentleman was bowing before her with the graceful elegance expected of an aristocrat.

Not a pirate, then.

"It's a pleasure to meet you," she said. Beside her, Lavinia dropped into a curtsy that was just slightly deeper than Willa's, because they'd realized long ago that gentlemen were slavishly grateful for a glimpse of Lavinia's bosom.

Mr. Sterling kept his eyes on Lavinia's chin.

"Parth, do escort these young ladies over to those chairs at the edge where they can see Fitzy," Lady Knowe ordered. "We have only one peacock," she explained to Willa and Lavinia. "It's better for Fitzy, since he fancies himself as the cock of the walk."

Lord Peters lunged from his chair to escort Lavinia, so Mr. Sterling offered Willa his arm.

"I don't believe we met during the Season," Willa said as they strolled the short distance to the other end of the terrace. Behind them, Lavinia was asking Lord Peters whether he had tame peafowl at his country house.

"I attend no such events. I do not count myself a gentleman or, at least, not one who belongs in polite society," Mr. Sterling said. "I grew up as a ward of the duke; my father was governor of Madras and sent me back to England as an infant."

Willa was conscious of a deep feeling of surprise. She was extremely good at identifying a stranger's pedigree. Mr. Sterling's attire alone would have placed him in the gentry, if not the nobility.

It wasn't a matter of silk breeches; it was the way he wore them.

"Do your parents live in India still?" she asked, curling her fingers around his arm. It was strong and muscled.

Easily as muscled as Lord Alaric's, she thought with a touch of rebellion. This absurd . . . *affinity* that she felt for the adventurer had to be stamped out. Ruthlessly eradicated.

"No," Mr. Sterling said. "They both died of a fever when I was a boy. I have no memory of either of them."

"I am very sorry. I, too, was orphaned. My parents died when I was nine," Willa said sympathetically.

"I sometimes think it's not the tragedy it might seem to others, to grow up without parents," Mr. Sterling said. "It left me free to construct my own ideas about life. Although you knew your parents, which changes the situation entirely."

"I do miss them," she admitted. "Still, it forced me to be far more observant than I might have been. To fashion my own ideas, as you said."

They reached the small table Lady Knowe had pointed out. Lord Peters assisted Lavinia, and Mr. Sterling pulled out a chair for Willa. "Having been given no further instructions, I shall claim the seat beside you, Miss Ffynche, unless you wish to reserve it for someone."

There was an odd inflection to his voice, as if the implied question had more consequence than a cup of tea on a summer afternoon. "I would be very happy for you to join me," she replied, smiling up at him. And then, when he was seated: "Since you are not in society, Mr. Sterling, may I assume that you are occupied with more than morning calls?"

A footman placed a tea tray before them, with silver spoons shaped like peacock feathers and a bowl of sugar.

"I have a number of interests," he replied. "The tea before you traveled from China in one of my ships."

Lavinia promptly leaned over the nearest cup and sniffed. "Pekoe!" she exclaimed, straightening and smiling.

Mr. Sterling appeared unmoved by her dimples. "You are correct, Miss Gray."

"Do you import silks as well as tea?" Willa asked. "Porcelain? You must have excellent relations with the Hong merchants."

A corner of Mr. Sterling's mouth curled up.

"Don't ruin things by being patronizing," Willa exclaimed. The Hongs were the only Chinese merchants licensed to trade with foreigners; it was hardly a state secret. "The newspapers talk of the Hongs whenever China is mentioned."

"I do beg your pardon. I didn't mean to seem patronizing."

"Men rarely do," she said, a bit crossly. "They simply can't help it, if a woman shows the slightest knowledge of something other than fans and slippers."

"In that case, I apologize for my sex," Mr. Sterling said. "We're an absurd lot of fools, and as you likely know, Miss Ffynche, we become even more inarticulate in the presence of a beautiful young lady."

It was a deft compliment, so she smiled at him. "Have you made the trip to China yourself?"

Mr. Sterling laughed as he glanced over her head. "I seem to be seated beside one of the few English ladies who knows nothing of your books, Alaric."

Willa turned and saw, somewhat to her dismay, that Lord Alaric had joined their group and was taking the seat on her other side. Even worse, he edged his chair so close to hers that she could smell a spicy male scent, a wildly expensive eau de cologne.

No, Lord Alaric would never wear scent.

The scent was just *him*. Or him and soap.

"I haven't yet read Lord Alaric's books, but I fully intend to," she said, as the footman put a cup of tea before him. She took a sip of hers, hoping for a clear head. It was unusual to feel out of her depth . . . but she felt it.

She and Lavinia had ruled the ton during the Season by acting precisely as they had discerned gentlemen wished them to: as young ladies with spirit but docility, spice yet innocence.

They had shaped this plan around the desires of boys. Lord Alaric and Mr. Sterling were *men*.

She looked past Mr. Sterling and saw the same awareness in Lavinia's eyes. But whereas Willa felt like retreating upstairs and making up some new rules, Lavinia waggled her eyebrows with madcap bravado.

"Our voyage was the subject of Alaric's first book," Mr. Sterling was saying now.

"I understand it takes a year to reach China," Lord Peters said, with languid disapproval. "Seems like a rotten loss of time, if you'll forgive the impertinence. Though I suppose some might feel the profit was worth it."

Lavinia gave him a narrow-eyed look that turned his cheeks faintly pink. She had strong feelings about impoliteness.

"It did take nearly a year to reach China," Mr. Sterling said indifferently. He couldn't have made it more clear that he considered Lord Peters an impudent puppy.

"Oh, hello!" Miss Eliza Kennet, who had debuted with them, dashed up to their table and began bobbing curtsies. "I'm so happy to see you, Lord Alaric! And

Lavinia and Willa!" Her hair was so thickly powdered that white dust lay on her shoulders like snow on two fence posts.

"Good afternoon, Miss Kennet," Lord Alaric said. "May I introduce Mr. Sterling?"

The girl's eyes paused on Mr. Sterling's face, just long enough to register that she didn't know him, and went straight back to Lord Alaric. "I've seen *Wilde in Love* twice! You are my favorite author," Eliza gushed. "You and Shakespeare. You are both geniuses! But you are more intriguing."

Lord Alaric gave her a brief smile. "I didn't write the play in question, so Shakespeare has nothing to worry about from my side."

"Given the choice of a dead author or a live one," Lavinia said, her husky voice taking on a laughing undertone, "I must say that I agree with Miss Kennet."

"My dear," Lady Knowe said, appearing behind Miss Kennet, "you mustn't rearrange my tea party; I shall be quite cross if you do." Without further ado, she took her elbow and towed the young lady away.

Willa turned to Mr. Sterling. "Did you dock in Canton?"

At his startled look, Lavinia burst into laughter. "You remind me of one of the teachers at our seminary, when Willa would confound him by knowing more about cotton plants or coal mines than he did."

"I merely read the newspaper," Willa said firmly. "There is nothing extraordinary in that."

"Yes, but you *remember* what you read," Lavinia retorted.

Willa could feel Lord Alaric's gaze on her. It gave her a thrill, one that she didn't trust. There was something heady about his attention, and not only because so many ladies longed for it.

He wasn't a sedate man, she told herself. Furthermore, he didn't have a widow's peak, which had been one of her girlhood requirements for a husband.

Now that seemed like a remarkably frivolous consideration.

"Do tell us what happened when you reached Canton, Mr. Sterling," she said hastily.

"We showed ourselves to be the two young fools we were," he answered.

"I'm sure you weren't fools," Lavinia protested.

"We were cork-brained, but in our defense, we were not yet nineteen," Mr. Sterling said.

"We fully expected to be invited to meet the emperor," Lord Alaric said, sitting back in his chair as a footman offered a plate of cucumber sandwiches.

"Imagine our surprise when it was made clear to us that, from the point of view of His Imperial Majesty, the son of an English duke is no better and no worse than a dock boy."

"We finally bribed a local governor to invite us to his house," Mr. Sterling put in. "We were given a cup of tea and told to go back home."

"That tea," Lord Alaric said meditatively, "was pekoe." He raised his teacup to Willa. "Precisely what you have in front of you, Miss Ffynche."

"We made up our mind to travel to the mountains where pekoe was cultivated, but because we stood a head taller than the local men," Mr. Sterling said, picking up the tale, "we couldn't disguise ourselves."

Lavinia laughed. "I remember this part of the book."

"The only thing to do was to become people whom everyone avoided."

"Beggars afflicted by leprosy?" Willa suggested.

"Good guess. No, night-soil men," Mr. Sterling said. "Worst job in the world, but perfect for interlopers like ourselves."

"You become foul-smelling Trojan horses," Willa said, laughing.

Mr. Sterling's face was naturally stern in repose, which made his smile unexpectedly endearing.

"Trolling around with a wagon so people could

throw excrement out their windows meant that no one gave us a second glance," Lord Alaric said, giving his friend a sharp glance. "All the work is done at night. And we had an excellent excuse to keep scarves wound around our faces."

Willa smiled again at that image—and then realized that Lord Alaric's eyes had moved to her mouth. She abruptly straightened her lips.

He made a sound deep in his throat, so low that only she could hear it. Willa drew in an unsteady breath. She felt as if he had caressed her, given her a lingering kiss—and all he'd done was gaze at her lips.

That sizzling heat she felt low in her belly? It was merely because he was unreasonably handsome, she told herself. Any woman would feel it.

"We wandered around China for three or four months," Mr. Sterling was saying, "making our way from village to village at night, reeking to high heaven."

"We managed to find the tea groves," Lord Alaric interjected. "Pekoe is a form of Bohea tea, which is mixed with small white flowers until their perfume infuses the leaves. In comparison to our scent at the time," he added with a rueful twist of his lips, "the tea was delightful."

"I can imagine," Lavinia said, gurgling with laughter.

"When we returned to Canton, we filled the hold of

our ship with pekoe and cloud tea, which I will brew for you one day," he said, looking directly at Willa. She had the sense that he was leaning forward, though he hadn't moved a muscle.

"I doubt we shall have time for that," she said, picking up a cucumber sandwich.

Just then the resident peacock crossed the lawn toward them. He was the most magnificent bird Willa had ever seen, even with his long train furled. His throat was bright cobalt blue and his feathery crown was equally dazzling.

"How beautiful he is!" Lavinia exclaimed. "Is there any way to entice him to fan out his tail?"

"Peacocks show their tails to attract a mate," Mr. Sterling drawled, glancing at Lavinia as if to suggest that she had something in common with a peacock.

Willa swallowed a grin. One could say Lavinia's bosom was akin to a peacock's tail, but with the sexes reversed. She wasn't wearing the blue dress, but her bodice was quite revealing.

"I've offended you again," came the voice of a beguiling devil in her ear. "I didn't mean to do so. I'm making a hash of what can and cannot be said in polite society. Do you mind if I call you Willa, by the way?"

"Yes," she said flatly.

"You could call me Alaric."

"No, thank you."

"I find formality tedious."

"*I* find boredom indicates a lack of application," Willa replied, keeping her voice steady, though she felt as if she were trembling all over. "Life is always interesting, if you pay attention."

"I am not at all bored at the moment," he said.

His gaze burned right down Willa's spine and she felt color rising in her cheeks. "That is beside the point," she managed.

"You didn't mean to imply that men and women should carry out flirtations in order to avoid boredom?"

Lavinia clearly found Mr. Sterling irritating; she'd hopped up from her chair and accepted some grain from a footman. Now she was bent over the balustrade, trying to bribe Fitzy into spreading his tail.

"No, I do not," Willa said. "Society is interesting, because *people* are interesting. There is always more to learn. Conclusions to be drawn, rightly or wrongly."

They watched as Lord Peters joined Lavinia. "I'm not sure there's anything very riveting about Peters," Lord Alaric said in a low voice. "Is that an example of Miss Gray's spread plumage, by the way?"

Willa frowned. "That is not only improper, but downright rude," she whispered. "I have no idea what you are talking about."

"*That*," Alaric responded, unconcerned by her rebuke. He nudged her with his elbow.

Lavinia was leaning toward Fitzy, who was regarding her with a beady eye, but showed no inclination to spread his tail.

Willa looked back at Alaric, mystified.

"Look at Parth," he said.

Mr. Parth Sterling had showed no sign of being charmed by Lavinia—rather the opposite. But now he was staring at her as she leaned over the rail. The small side panniers she wore under her gown merely enhanced her already generous curves.

As they watched, Lord Peters laughingly put his hands around her waist, presumably to keep her from toppling over the parapet.

Mr. Sterling made a rough sound, snatched up a cucumber sandwich, and got to his feet.

"Is a cucumber sandwich a more effective bribe than grain?" Willa asked Lord Alaric, unable to stop amusement from sounding in her voice.

"Fitzy loves cucumbers. But more to the point, the peacock responds to other males, even the human variety."

Sure enough, as soon as Mr. Sterling moved to the edge of the terrace and barked, "Fitzy!" the peacock made a burring sound, shook himself, and fanned out his tail in a spectacular display of purple and green feathers.

Then he stalked to and fro, obviously daring Mr. Sterling to show some plumage of his own.

Instead Mr. Sterling tossed the sandwich toward the bird, said something to Lavinia, and returned to his seat.

"Thank you!" Willa said. "His tail is quite remarkable."

Mr. Sterling shrugged. "Fitzy is decorative, for all he's an irascible fellow." He gave her that quick, rare smile of his. "May I be so bold as to guess that you and Miss Gray are very high society, indeed? She just gave me a look that would have done a queen proud."

"Mr. Sterling," Willa said, "do you think that you might be romanticizing your position? You were raised by a duke, and remain best of friends with his sons. I would guess that you have a formidable estate. Could it be you are simply avoiding the reality that you would be perfectly welcome at society events?"

"I was raised to believe that rank is contingent on blood."

"That certainly used to be the case," Willa said, "but from what I have observed, it is less and less so each day. A fortune, together with excellent breeding and powerful friends, is a great leveler."

"Huh," Mr. Sterling said.

"This house party celebrates the betrothal of a future duke to a woman whose grandfather was a grocer," Willa said, proving her point.

She glanced at Lord Alaric for support in her argument only to see faint irritation on his face. Evidently, he didn't like it when she spoke to other men, even his childhood friend.

"I will take your idea into consideration," Mr. Sterling said.

"Take what into consideration?" Lord Alaric asked.

"I merely told Mr. Sterling that I think he would be welcome in high society," Willa said.

At that moment a hush fell over the party; the duke and duchess had arrived. As they stepped onto the terrace, a cluster of footmen moved among the guests, offering glasses of champagne. A chair was quickly brought, and the duchess carefully lowered herself onto it.

"The last of our guests arrived this morning, and thus we are complete," His Grace announced. "I would like to officially open this party in honor of my son's betrothal to Miss Diana Belgrave by offering a toast to the happiness of the betrothed couple."

He turned to Lord Roland, who was standing beside Diana at the far end of the terrace. "In centuries past, we would have gathered to make certain that Miss Belgrave had not been kidnapped by my son. I wouldn't have been surprised to find that North had been forced to kidnap such a beautiful, intelligent woman."

Everyone laughed, but Lavinia's eyes met Willa's. In view of Diana's lack of enthusiasm for the match, that was a tactless remark.

"My father has an odd sense of humor," Alaric said in Willa's ear.

His Grace raised his glass. "I offer this toast to my future daughter-in-law, whom I have discovered to be a gentle, thoughtful warrior, with an impeccable flair for dress and an even more impressive skill at chess."

"She beat him," Alaric supplied in a low voice.

"Welcome to the family," the duke concluded. Everyone drank.

"I should like to add my voice to His Grace's," Alaric said, rising.

The heads on the terrace swiveled in his direction, like poppies toward the sun.

He kept his eyes on his brother's face. "I am very fond of a fourteenth-century Persian poet named Hafez. I'll ask your forgiveness in advance for butchering this translation, but he says that we are all holding hands and climbing. Not loving, Hafez says, is letting go."

Lord Roland nodded.

"So don't let go," Alaric said, his deep voice holding everyone captive, "because the terrain around here is far too dangerous for that." He raised his glass. "To my future sister-in-law, whom we are honored to welcome into the family."

"I will never let go," his brother said into the silence, as everyone drank to the betrothed couple. Diana turned visibly pink.

Willa thought it sounded like a vow. "Are your books as eloquent as that?" she asked Lord Alaric, when he was once more seated.

The question seemed to startle him. "As the poet, Hafez? Not at all. I wouldn't describe myself as eloquent."

"'The terrain around here is far too dangerous for that,'" Willa quoted. "I'm hopeless at understanding poetry, but he wasn't talking about Persia's mountain ranges, was he?"

He smiled at her, a smile so intimate that Willa drew in a breath. A girlish part of her soul that she hadn't even known existed cheered.

"No," he said. "No, the terrain he was referring to is quite different. I haven't been there myself."

"Ah."

"But I hope to in the very near future."

"Girlish" was not a strong enough word for what

Willa was feeling. "Giddy" came closer. Something about that made her suddenly cold, despite the warm sunshine.

Even if Lord Alaric's intentions were honorable—which now struck her as possible, if unlikely—she had absolutely no desire to be married to a man whose printed image was concealed in young ladies' Bibles.

"I wish you the best of luck in your exploration of new terrains," she said coolly. "I have no interest in journeying around the world myself, but I understand it must be quite intoxicating."

"Yes, it seems to be," he said, grinning. "Surprisingly so."

The man could make anything sound suggestive.

Willa had decided long ago exactly what she wanted in a husband. She wanted a decent man who didn't drink to excess. It would be nice if he had a fortune, but since she had inherited her father's estate, it wasn't necessary.

He had to be steady; to have all his teeth; and she would like him to have his own hair. She even knew what his voice would be like: quiet, and private.

Very private.

If possible, she would prefer him to look clever and pale. Not gaunt, but lean and unlikely to run to fat later in life.

Lord Alaric was not only not a private man, but everything that happened to him—and several things that hadn't—was displayed for public consumption.

The engravings were a prime example of the problem. Whoever married him would find her likeness in the windows of printshops. A lifetime of seeing one's face depicted in bookstalls.

Or—how ghastly!—on the stage.

With that thought in mind, Willa turned back to Mr. Sterling. Now *he* was a man whom she ought to consider seriously. He may think he wasn't suited for high society owing to his parentage, but to Willa's mind, that was an advantage. Whomever she married would be accepted everywhere; she had no worries about that.

He was extremely good looking, and seemed unencumbered by a Helena Biddle. But she had to clarify something first.

"Mr. Sterling," she said, "am I right to think you might have some connection with Sterling Lace?"

"I am honored to think that you know of my lace," he said, taking her hand and pressing a kiss on the back of it.

A growl sounded near Willa's ear, but when she turned to look incredulously at Lord Alaric, he smiled at her as placidly as if he were a vicar.

"Stop that," she ordered.

"Stop what?" he asked innocently.

"That," Willa said, less than articulately.

He snatched the hand that Mr. Sterling had just kissed. "I think you just soiled your hand." Before she could stop him, he brought it to his lips and kissed the same spot.

"Better?" he inquired.

Willa frowned at him. "Lord Alaric, please stop." She could feel pink rising up her neck. She glanced over his shoulder and realized that a good many of the guests was watching them. Naturally, they were watching.

They would always be watching whatever he did.

In that instant she understood exactly what was happening. The man was unused to women who didn't collapse at his feet. A woman who remained upright?

An undiscovered country. *Terra incognita.*

Lord Alaric was flirting with her because he was a man who had to win. He didn't understand that she was not—and never would be—a prize. She meant to choose her spouse after a thoughtful review, and no part of that review included being "won."

"I am not someone who cares to be a spectacle." She said it quietly but firmly as she drew her hand away.

His lordship turned his head to survey the terrace. Eyes fell, and a murmur of sound rose again from the tables. He scowled.

"Notoriety is a great facilitator of book sales, my lord. Of that I have no doubt."

He opened his mouth but she lifted her hand to stop him.

"I am not a territory to be conquered for the mere sake of it. I would be grateful if you would direct your attentions elsewhere."

His jaw flexed, but Willa held his gaze. It was essential she make this clear, because he was used to intoxicating women, and his successes had made him confident. Or arrogant. Whatever one wanted to call it.

She was as susceptible to him as any woman. But she had no intention of being conquered.

"I do not see you in that light," Lord Alaric stated. If Willa hadn't observed the darkening of his eyes and the way his shoulders stiffened, she might actually have believed that he was merely issuing a polite correction.

"In some sense, we are all foreign countries," she said, not giving in. "In my analogy, your shores are frequented by ambassadors like Lady Biddle."

His jaw tightened again.

"When I become a citizen of a foreign land, it will be one without pomp and circumstance," she said, rising. "Without ambassadors."

She smiled at Mr. Bouchette, sitting at the next table, and he sprang to his feet. As he eagerly asked her to accompany him on a promenade in the rose garden, she overheard Lord Alaric speaking behind her.

"She's angling for dinks too tiny to keep," he said to Mr. Sterling, the rest of his remark unintelligible.

She had the vague idea that a dink was a fish. Was he saying that Mr. Bouchette was too small to keep? A minnow, in fact?

Lavinia gave Willa a look that reminded her, in the nick of time, that ladies did not empty teacups over a lord's head.

"Might you escort both of us?" Lavinia asked Mr. Bouchette, who beamed with pride.

A lady could not spill tea, but she could walk away, exaggerating the sway of her hips.

So Willa did.

Chapter Eleven

The following day

Willa successfully avoided Lord Alaric all that evening, and over the next day's luncheon, even though he seemed to be always within earshot. For example, the moment that Lavinia expressed interest in walking to the nearby village of Mobberley, he appeared out of nowhere and declared he would accompany them.

The truth was that his lordship had paid no attention whatsoever to her command that he not woo her. Every time she looked, he seemed to be watching her, even while surrounded by his admirers.

She had to remain resolute. That, and cling to her

suitors, who were as assiduous as his. They made Lord Alaric curl his lip, but why should she care? They might be boys compared to him, but they were safe, biddable young men who would never make her infamous by association.

Mobberley was a half hour's walk from the castle, down a long lane lined with elder bushes just beginning to fruit, and ditches full of cowslips, with a sprinkling of poppies. It was a perfect day for a stroll, and a party of twelve set out not long after luncheon.

She and Lavinia each had two suitors in tow to Lord Alaric's three, among whom Helena Biddle seemed to be leading the pack. The mathematics of the situation was amusing. Willa left the suitors to Lavinia, dropping back to walk with Lady Knowe while ignoring Lord Alaric, who was shepherding his flock in the rear. Mr. Sterling had Lady Biddle on his arm, and while he wasn't scowling, he seemed less than happy.

"The villagers call cowslips 'paigles,'" Lady Knowe told Willa, nodding at the wildflowers. "They make an excellent wine around here that will have you dizzy as a goose after a glass or two. By the way, I meant to ask whether Prism has lectured you about Lindow Moss yet."

Willa nodded. "He warned us to stay out of it, and I

believe he also talked to our maids and grooms. Do you find it difficult to live on the edge of such a dangerous wilderness?"

"'Dangerous wilderness' is an exaggeration," Lady Knowe said. "It's merely a bog, and quite beautiful in the right weather."

Willa hesitated, thinking of Prism's revelation that the eldest of Lady Knowe's nephews had perished in Lindow Moss. To her, that fact alone qualified it for the label "dangerous wilderness."

Before she could formulate a sentence, Mobberley came into view on the far side of an ancient bridge. The village consisted of a small cluster of houses lining a single street. Their gables seemed to lean toward each other, as if the buildings on either side were having a cozy chat.

Lady Knowe gave a whoop. "Bless me, Mr. Calico is here!"

"Who?"

"The peddler!" her ladyship crowed. "Mr. Calico is the most reliable source of pleasure in this area. I'm on subscription lists for novels, so they arrive by the post. Traveling theater troupes come through the village. But Mr. Calico? He's a magician."

"I'm surprised that he's still traveling," Lord Alaric said, catching up with them. "I considered him already ancient when I was a child. Good afternoon, Aunt Knowe." His voice lowered. "Willa."

"I address Miss Ffynche by her Christian name, Nephew, but what's sauce for the goose is definitely not sauce for the gander," Lady Knowe declared, casting him an admonishing look.

"I agree!" Willa exclaimed. "Lord Alaric has misspoken."

To which he just laughed.

His deep voice licked at the back of her neck and she almost squirmed. But she didn't. She was determined to be a perfect lady today. She'd achieved it without a problem all Season, and there was no reason why the arrival of one arrogant explorer should cause her to behave differently.

Lady Knowe and her nephew began trading stories about Mr. Calico's wagon as they drew nearer. To hear them tell it, he often had the one thing that you most desired, even if you didn't know you wanted it.

"I gathered from your discussion of Egyptian hieroglyphs that you have no faith in magic," Lord Alaric said to Willa.

"I believe!" Lavinia skipped forward. "I can't wait to see what I find in the wagon."

"What would you like from Mr. Calico?" Lady Knowe asked Willa.

"Actually, nothing," she said, feeling somewhat apologetic, as if she were letting down the peddler. "I have all the ribbons I need."

"Ribbons are the least of it," Lady Knowe replied, grinning widely.

The peddler's wagon was painted a lively green. Its lathwork sides were flipped out and up, so they rested against the yellow roof. The shelves exposed by the hinged sides were decked out in yellow, as were the gaily painted wheels.

Mr. Calico was a thin, white-haired fellow with a luxuriant mustache, wearing a weathered coat that glittered in the summer sun. He hopped down through the red door of the wagon as the group spread around its sides. "If it isn't my favorite lady in all the north," he cried, bowing. "The best of afternoons to you, Lady Knowe!"

In return, she dropped a deep curtsy, as if he were a courtier. "Please tell me that you've brought something wonderful from London!"

"Many things," he said jovially. "I meant to make my way up to the castle later this afternoon, but here you are, come to find me. You have the pick of my goods, at least those which the good people of Mobberley have not already purchased for themselves."

"Miss Ffynche and Miss Gray," Alaric said, as seriously as if he were presenting the king himself, "may I introduce you to Mr. Calico, the proprietor of this fine wagon? As children, we would have been bereft without his visits."

"I think Mr. Calico has a fair claim to have made you into the traveler you are," Mr. Sterling said, joining them. "After all, Mr. Calico, you brought Alaric any number of things from foreign countries over the years, and now look at him, addicted to visiting strange places."

"I was around eight when Mr. Calico offered me a curiosity box full of exotic objects," Alaric acknowledged.

"Where did you find it?" Willa asked Mr. Calico.

"I travel about," he said, with a smile that made his mustache seem bushier and more jolly. "People sell things to me in one place, and I sell them in another. As I recall, the curiosity box came from the attic at Rumpole House, in Sussex. I didn't buy it; I traded it for . . ." His brow wrinkled. "I traded it for a pair of beautiful slippers that happened to be just the young lady's size."

"The curiosity box may have been a push toward your chosen occupation," Mr. Sterling said to Alaric, "but the tiny, dried-up head was the key."

"No!" Lavinia gasped, with a shiver.

"It was in reality a withered apple," Lord Alaric said ruefully. "By the time Mr. Calico came back around this way and told me the truth, I'd made up any number of stories about an Amazonian chief who shrank the head of his greatest enemy."

"The genesis of Lord Wilde," Mr. Sterling said. "He terrified Horatius, North, and me out of our wits every night."

"Mr. Calico," Willa said, stepping forward. "Would you mind if I asked you a question about your shiny coat?"

"Pins, my dear. Pins of all shapes and sizes, with pearl heads, and diamond heads, and these new clever ones, all shiny, that come from Portugal. Pins made for all occasions: hair pins, hat pins, pins for a rip, or a tear, or a drooping chemise."

Lavinia clapped her hands. "I should like a pin!" She circled him. "May I buy one of those sparkly blue ones?"

"These pins come to me, not the other way around," Mr. Calico said, shaking his head. "These aren't for sale. I have some lovely pins in the wagon, if you'd like to buy one."

After Lavinia set off to find the basket of pins, Mr. Calico bent to greet the butcher's fat cat, who was busy sniffing his boots. "You're Peters, aren't you? I know what you're smelling."

Willa crouched down and rubbed the cat's head. Mr. Calico undoubtedly had nice things for sale, ranging from pretty inlaid combs to shiny pins, but she didn't need anything. Or want anything.

Behind them, Lavinia was squealing over a book she'd found hidden under a stack of fashion plates.

"That's my American sable you're smelling," Mr. Calico told the cat. "You'll not have met her like, as her relatives live far from here, over an ocean and even further."

Willa straightened. "What is a sable? I read a book about the American continent's animals, but a sable wasn't mentioned. Unless I've forgotten."

"Somehow I doubt it," Mr. Calico said, beaming at her.

"Perhaps not," Willa allowed. She forgot very few things she read.

A hand touched her shoulder, and a shiver went down her spine. She went rigid with embarrassment, but Alaric seemed not to notice. His ungloved fingers spread on her shoulder blade in something perilously close to a caress.

When had she started thinking of him simply as

Alaric, rather than Lord Alaric? She jerked her attention back to the conversation.

"'American sable'!" he scoffed. "That'll be a skunk, plain and simple, Mr. Calico. You know it as well as I do."

The peddler shrugged, eyes twinkling, utterly unrepentant. "I bought it as an American sable, my lord, and that's what it will remain." His gaze moved to Willa. "Until I can find a good home for it."

"I'm afraid I am unable to care for an animal," Willa said politely. "I reside with Miss Gray's mother, who doesn't care for domestic animals, let alone exotic ones."

"My sable's no more than a baby," Mr. Calico said. "Once she's grown, she'll make a fine tippet. Better than a fox, really. More exotic. Everyone will ask you where you found it."

Willa flinched. She didn't wear fur of any kind, and the idea of raising an animal solely to make it into a neck scarf was abhorrent to her.

"Mr. Calico, you haven't changed a bit," Alaric said. "Do you remember how you talked me into buying that withered apple?"

The peddler tilted his head to the side with a frown. His coat flashed in the sunlight. "No," he admitted.

"You told me it wasn't for sale because your next stop was the rectory, where the minister would bury it in the churchyard."

"He would have," Mr. Calico said promptly. "A nice apple tree would have grown in its place."

Alaric grinned. "In short, Miss Ffynche is now as curious to meet the American sable as I was to own that dried-up apple."

"No, I am not," Willa stated. The very mention of a baby animal whose future was being a neck ornament made her feel slightly ill.

Alaric put a hand on her back again, as if he didn't notice what he was doing. Nor how improper his touch was. "Better luck elsewhere," he said to Mr. Calico.

"Everything finds its place in time," the peddler said, clearly unperturbed. "No doubt I'll stop by a house where the lady of the manor fancies the idea of a tippet the exact length of her neck."

As he turned away, Willa focused on the absent-minded caress of Alaric's fingers on her back. "Stop that!" she whispered fiercely.

"What?"

He appeared honestly surprised. She cleared her throat and moved away. "You are touching me," she said, walking over to the wagon. The shelf before her held two peacock feathers, a linen cloth embroidered with a prayer, an oddly shaped rock, and a silver bowl full of thimbles.

Alaric followed and touched her back with one finger. He looked down at her with a lazily innocent expression. "Like this? I was merely guiding you to the wagon."

Willa noticed from the corner of her eye that Mr. Calico was opening the back door and helping Lavinia up the narrow wooden stairs.

Before she could come up with a response to Alaric, she saw Lavinia reel back, handkerchief clapped to her face, and throw herself off the wagon with a little shriek.

She might have landed on her own feet, but Mr. Sterling lunged forward with remarkable speed and caught her in his arms.

"Mr. Calico, I fear for your health!" Lavinia cried. "Your wagon is not a salubrious place."

"My chambermate is rather fragrant," Mr. Calico agreed. "I'll admit to taking a room in an inn this evening. I was told that her scent glands had been removed, but I begin to suspect that was a falsehood."

Willa found herself scowling, and never mind that a lady was supposed to be placid at all times. "Her scent glands were removed? So the poor creature is unable to smell anything?"

"The other way about," Mr. Calico said. "She is now able to make *us* smell, although she would do so only if she felt threatened."

"May I?" Alaric stepped forward, gesturing at the stairs.

"Please do, my lord! My house is your house," Mr. Calico said.

With a bound Alaric disappeared into the wagon.

"Have you found anything you wish to buy, Lavinia?" Willa asked.

Mr. Sterling said mockingly, "She's a young lady, isn't she? Naturally she has."

"I'm certain you didn't mean that remark to be as impolite as it sounded," Lavinia said, showing laudable restraint, to Willa's mind.

He shrugged. "In my experience, women are insatiable when it comes to fripperies, and if you'll forgive me, Miss Gray, you almost ripped a pin from Mr. Calico's coat."

Lavinia narrowed her eyes. "I wonder if it's better to be insatiable about money or pins," she hurled back. "Is it better to ask for a pin, or ask for a mansion and when refused, burn it down?"

Willa blinked. Lavinia obviously knew something about Mr. Sterling that she hadn't told her about.

With that, Lavinia turned her nose in the air and twirled, skirt flying around her ankles. She marched to the other side of the wagon where she joined Lady Biddle.

Mr. Sterling's face was indifferent. "It seems my reputation precedes me."

"Did you indeed burn down a building?"

"I unsuccessfully attempted to buy an estate near here. Two years later, after the mansion burned to the ground, I was offered the land. But I had nothing to do with that fire."

"Then how did the rumor start?"

"North and I were up to no good as boys," Mr. Sterling said, his eyes glinting with amusement. "It was the work of a moment for the locals to decide that I must have been at fault."

"Lord Alaric was not a member of your naughty tribe?" Willa said, incredulity leaking into her voice.

"We were far more reckless than he ever was." He hesitated. "I'm surprised that Miss Gray brought up that rumor. It wasn't a strictly ladylike comment, was it?"

"Ladylike is a matter of tone of voice," Willa told him. "If you had offended me, I might have mentioned a fact that I remember reading in the *Times*: Sterling Lace employs children, but I would say it in a pleasant tone of voice." She met his gaze without allowing a shade of condemnation to enter her voice. "If you were to make an unkind comment about ladies' fondness for pins, I mean."

"Damn it, that's—" He cut the words off. "Very kind of you to forewarn me."

"Hopefully, we shall have no opportunity to discuss it," Willa said. She gave him a cordial—entirely ladylike—smile and moved to Lavinia's side.

"Thank you," Lavinia murmured, leaning forward. "Look at these adorable baby dolls, Willa! Perhaps we should buy some. Sometimes I miss being five years old."

A stifled noise, like a snort of laughter, came from behind them.

Just then Alaric appeared in the wagon door.

"You are right," he said to Mr. Calico.

"Taking her, are you? I've grown fond of her, but it *will* be a pleasure to have the wagon to myself again."

"I imagine it will be," Alaric replied, jumping down. His hands were empty.

"By 'her,' do you mean Mr. Calico's fragrant companion?" Willa inquired.

Lavinia shuddered. "The entire castle isn't large enough to contain that stench."

"A harsh judgment," Alaric said. "I think she merely needs a bath and a larger box."

He reached into his pocket and brought out a tiny creature, only half the size of his hand. It had a white fluffy tail and a black head with a stripe between its eyes.

It poked up its head and looked straight at Willa with shiny black eyes that looked like little currants.

"Yes, I'll take her," Alaric said to Mr. Calico. "I can't allow her to be made into a tippet, as you bloody well knew, you old reprobate."

"I don't know why not," Lady Biddle said, coming closer. "That tail would frame a lady's face quite nicely if it grew long enough. How long will it become?"

"You might buy her as a gift," Mr. Calico suggested to Alaric, completely ignoring Lady Biddle.

Willa tore her eyes away from the baby. "I cannot own a pet . . . but may I hold her?"

Alaric placed the animal into Willa's outstretched hands, where she promptly curled her little claws around Willa's forefinger, using it to balance herself.

"Ugh," Lavinia said. "She reeks, Willa."

Lady Biddle pressed a handkerchief to her mouth and backed away, suggesting that she might faint. Willa rather hoped she would, but wishes like that never seemed to come true.

She raised her cupped hands closer to her face and the animal looked back at her fearlessly. After a second, the baby stretched forward and brought her nose close to Willa's.

"You are a darling," Willa breathed.

"As a gift," Alaric was saying, behind her back.

Willa and the baby looked at each other. Then, with a graceful twirl, the little animal turned and curled into a ball. Her fluffy white tail draped over Willa's wrist and her head rested against Willa's finger.

Her eyes closed.

"My mother is going to have spasms," Lavinia groaned.

"I have never asked for anything," Willa said, meeting her friend's eyes. "Never. If Lady Gray won't allow my American sable, I'll set up my own establishment."

"No, you won't!" Lavinia retorted. She reached out one finger and drew it down the baby animal's back. "Perhaps Lord Alaric is right and a bath will help. She is very soft."

"What do I do now?" Willa asked. She didn't dare move her hands.

Willa hadn't noticed Mr. Calico retreat into his cart, but now he stepped down, carrying a basket. "This is her bed," Mr. Calico said, "along with her favorite blanket, a list of food she likes to eat and, importantly, her soap, Miss Ffynche. Bathe her once a week and she will smell as fresh as a daisy. If you wish, you may give her a bath in chamomile in between."

"Do you know how old she is?"

"Something over four weeks," Mr. Calico said.

"I shall call her Sweetpea," Willa decided.

Sweetpea opened one eye and looked at her. Then she made a chuffing noise, closed her eye, and lapsed back into slumber.

"She's nocturnal, by rights," Mr. Calico said. And then, to Alaric, "If you would be so kind as to inform Mr. Prism that I shall arrive at Lindow Castle in the late afternoon, I would be most grateful."

Lavinia was holding an armful of things she wished to purchase: some French fashion plates, two books, a few lengths of sprigged muslin, and a baby doll. Her two suitors were bickering over which of them would pay her bill.

"Bloody hell," Mr. Sterling said, handing Mr. Calico a note. "That should cover it. Can you deliver the lady's trinkets to the castle, along with those prints?"

Mr. Calico bowed, just as Lavinia realized what had happened. "I shall pay you back," she said to Mr. Sterling.

"As you wish," he said, making it absolutely clear that he didn't give a damn.

Lavinia huffed and swept past them, a suitor on each arm, toward the lane that led back to the castle.

Alaric took Sweetpea from Willa and put her into her basket, his hands so gentle that the baby animal scarcely stirred. "If you'll allow me, I'll carry Sweetpea, but first I must pry my aunt away from Mr. Calico's enticing wares."

Sure enough, Lady Knowe was adding a couple of books to a stack on the steps of the carriage.

He slung Sweetpea's basket over his arm—and against all the laws of nature, he just looked more manly. Willa couldn't stop herself from looking at him from head to foot, cataloguing his tousled, unpowdered hair—no wig and no hat—broad shoulders, a body made to *do* things.

Not just to dance.

Mr. Sterling fell in beside Willa and they wound their way up the hill in silence. Ordinarily Willa had no difficulty making small talk, but now she was at a loss. The notorious Sterling Lace Factory employed children. One child had been found dead in his factory, but likely there had been others.

So she remained silent until he said, out of the blue, "The report wasn't true."

Willa had been wondering whether it would be bad for Sweetpea's fur to give her a daily chamomile bath.

Chamomile was so delicate that it wouldn't sting her eyes.

"Ah," she said, pulling her attention back to her companion. "You are referring to the report in the *Times*?"

"The newspaper claimed I employed children, one of whom died on my premises. I didn't, and I don't. I ended the practice immediately when I bought the lace factory, and all of those children are safely housed in the country."

Parth Sterling had the look of a soldier: dangerous, a bit wolfish around the eyes. Not a man who would bother with lies.

"All right," she said.

Silence.

"You're not asking me for details? For proof?"

She shook her head. "I believe you. Lavinia might be harder to convince."

Mr. Sterling glanced ahead at the figure of her best friend. "I have no interest in convincing her."

Right.

Alaric was wild in the way animals were wild. You could see a need in him for open windows and wide expanses. In contrast, Mr. Sterling was dangerous, like a trapped animal, a large predator.

One had to wonder what led to that hard chin and

hard eyes to match. The way he carried silence with him like a weapon.

Perhaps he was interested in power, although that *Times* article had described the owner of Sterling Lace as one of the most powerful commoners in Britain.

Or perhaps he wanted more money, although it sounded as if he had more than one man could use.

"I hope you find it," she said, turning her head and smiling at him.

"What?"

"That thing you're looking for," Willa said. "Since you have searched in the manure wagons of China, and the lace factories of England."

He stared at her.

"I hope you find it," she repeated.

Chapter Twelve

After Aunt Knowe decided to join the vicar for tea, Alaric set out on the path leading to the castle, walking at a brisk pace. Smelly Sweetpea was as good as a suit of armor—his admirers decided they would prefer to walk back to the castle in the company of Willa's suitors.

A few minutes later, he caught up to Parth, walking behind Lavinia and Willa, who had their heads bent together, talking.

"That's a skunk," Parth observed, gesturing toward the basket. "American sable, my ass! That's a skunk."

Alaric nodded absently, watching Willa lean close to Lavinia.

Willa didn't know it, but she'd sealed her fate when she kissed that little skunk on the nose. She was curious, adventuresome, and not put off by stinky creatures. Damned beautiful as well, but did that really matter? Catherine of Russia was beautiful, and she was—well, sexual curiosity was something, but not what a man wanted to spend his life with.

Spend his life with?

The phrase dropped into his head with no warning. And now there was no way of unthinking it. He wanted her.

He wanted to spend his life with her: a sharp-tongued, self-contained, prim miss who—according to his aunt—ruled London high society. He hated society.

This meant marriage, children, death in England, not abroad. Buried in the family chapel alongside all the other Wildes, most likely. With God's luck, he'd breathe his last as an old man, surrounded by those he loved.

Not lost to the snow in the Steppes, or eaten by the cannibals he'd never met.

"I can't believe you gave Miss Ffynche a skunk," Parth was saying. "You're out of your mind, and so is she."

"Scent glands removed," Alaric reminded him. "Perhaps."

"You're supposed to give ladies flowers. Gloves. Lace.

Pretty things for pretty people." His voice conveyed disgust.

"Willa smells like orange blossoms," Alaric observed.

Parth grunted. "She likely has a bar of soap that cost a guinea."

"If she bought it from you, then you made money, so stop griping," Alaric said. "My point is that Willa is also smelly. In a good way, but smelly."

"You're an odd man."

"A smelly pet for a smelly woman."

Lavinia turned about and looked at them. Alaric waved.

"You're taking the only acceptable one," Parth said grudgingly. "I assume that you're taking her?"

"Yes." The word hit the bottom of his soul with a satisfying clunk. A good feeling, a grounding feeling.

"Good luck," his friend said. "She's an odd woman."

"Willa is beautiful. Intelligent. Not too frilly. Not as frilly as North's fiancée, Diana, for instance."

"More beautiful than Catherine of Russia?"

Alaric glanced sideways and found his friend had a wicked smile.

"I bought a very interesting print that suggests you know the empress. Intimately, shall we say. *England Takes Russia by Storm.*"

"North told me about that particular print. It's untrue."

Parth shook his head. "I don't believe it. The notorious Lord Wilde didn't bed the empress?"

"All I'll say is the opportunity was there," Alaric said dryly. "She issued a public invitation, in the interests of raising Russian morale."

Parth gave a shout of laughter. "The burden of improving national morale would put some pressure on a man's performance, I'm guessing."

"I declined the challenge and took the first ship out of Saint Petersburg."

"Fearless when faced with a herd of elephants, yet he flees a lascivious empress," Parth mocked. "A sad reflection on England's greatest adventurer since Sir Walter Raleigh."

"I avoid man-eating tigers as well," Alaric said.

"A touch of Casanova in your writing wouldn't go amiss," Parth said. "Enough with the hardship, woe, and duels with two-headed men. On to randy royalty. If I were you, I would have bedded the empress and called it research."

"As soon as you take to the roads and head for Russia, I'll make an introduction. I'm sure you'd love to bed a woman who addresses you as a badger of delight," Alaric retorted.

Parth let out a crack of laughter. "Badger? Are you sure she didn't mean stallion? Imagine the book sales for *Wilde Stallion of Delight.* To say nothing of the prints."

Just then a ragged woman with unkempt hair stepped from behind a hedge and onto the path. It was Mrs. Ferrus. Years ago, when they were boys, her husband had been arrested and hanged on a charge of treason.

After that, she went mad, and now some called her a hedge-witch, and worse.

"Mrs. Ferrus," Alaric said, stopping, "how are you?"

She looked at him from strangely lightless eyes. "I'm as limp as a piece of seaweed." She turned to Parth and scowled. "You!" she said. "I remember you."

Parth's body went utterly still, a knack Alaric remembered from innumerable boxing matches as children.

Mrs. Ferrus spat words at him. "The angels will come at dusk, their wings ragged as crows—"

"That may well be," Alaric said, cutting her off. Then, more kindly, "May I offer you something for your supper, Mrs. Ferrus?" He held out a couple of shillings.

Her eyes moved from Parth's face to his own, and she took the money.

The young ladies turned around, and before Alaric could catch Willa's eye to warn her, she returned, bringing Lavinia with her.

Mrs. Ferrus looked like an aged stork. Her hair stood in nests around her head, one knot over her right ear and another toward the back. Her dress looked as filthy as her skin.

Neither Lavinia nor Willa flinched. Instead, they smiled, as if they were encountering a duchess.

"Won't you introduce us, Lord Alaric?" Lavinia asked.

"This is Mrs. Ferrus," Alaric said. "She lives in the village. Mrs. Ferrus, these are friends of ours, Miss Ffynche and Miss Gray."

"Do you have children, Mrs. Ferrus?" Willa asked, nodding to her.

It was hard to say whether Sweetpea or Mrs. Ferrus were the more pungent, but Alaric thought Mrs. Ferrus had the better odds. Her glassy eyes slowly focused on Willa.

"Two boys," she answered.

She did? Alaric had no idea. Those sons must have grown up by now.

"Do they resemble their father?" Lavinia asked.

"Me mother's eyes," Mrs. Ferrus said. "And their father's chin. They like potatoes and mash. Aye, and

I'd better be cooking for them. I don't always . . ." Her voice trailed off.

"Do you live close by?" Willa asked.

"On the other side of the church." She jerked her head and looked down at her skirts for the first time, as if realizing how she was dressed. "I'd better go," she said. "I haven't made any bread."

"Permit me to walk you to your cottage," Alaric said. He handed Sweetpea's basket to Parth.

Willa watched Alaric escort the madwoman away. It was her impression that Mrs. Ferrus had been raving when they first walked toward the men, but she was quiet now, looking up at Alaric and shaking her head to whatever he had asked her.

"When did she become mad?" Lavinia asked, as they set off on the path again. "Are her boys still living at home? Is her husband alive?"

"Do you ever ask one question and wait for an answer before the next?" Mr. Sterling met her questions with his own.

Lavinia considered it. "Not usually. I have five or six questions at any moment, so I try to marshal the two most compelling."

"When we were boys of around ten, Mr. Ferrus attempted to blow up the king, his court, and all of Lindow Castle," Mr. Sterling said.

"The king!" Willa exclaimed. "How awful for everyone involved."

"He was hanged, deservedly so," he said.

"Everyone says that about a man who tries to blow up the king," Lavinia said to him, her voice irritated. "They ignore what his deed did to his family. Willa and I have noticed it time and again."

"He should have stayed away from gunpowder," Mr. Sterling stated.

Lavinia shrugged. "That's the easy response, isn't it? He should have stayed away from gunpowder. But he didn't, for whatever reason. And the people who were hurt most, since he was caught before he could do damage, were his family. Those boys grew up the sons of a notorious, albeit failed, assassin."

"As well as a mother maddened by grief," Willa added.

"I suppose you'd put that at Mr. Ferrus's feet as well?"

"Wouldn't you?" Lavinia retorted.

"It's hard to say," Mr. Sterling replied.

Willa walked between them, feeling as if she were a wall between two warring nations.

Chapter Thirteen

In the drawing room that evening, the marvel that was Mr. Calico's wagon was the principal topic of conversation. He had driven up in great style and proceeded to sell most of his inventory to those house-party guests who hadn't walked to Mobberley.

"Tell me about your American sable," Lady Knowe said to Willa. "I didn't get more than a glimpse of her."

Sweetpea was upstairs, having been bathed in Mr. Calico's soap, then given a second bath in chamomile-scented water. She had showed herself a curious little animal who loved to rise up on her back legs and grab a treat from Willa's fingers.

"Lord Alaric insists that 'American sable' is a misnomer," Willa said. "'Skunk' is less grand-sounding, but more accurate."

"How are you managing her necessaries?" Lady Knowe asked.

"We put a box filled with earth on the balcony," Willa explained. "Once Sweetpea understood what it was for, she appeared happy to use it. She's the most intelligent animal I've ever seen."

Lady Knowe put a hand to Willa's cheek. "You are a darling girl," she said. "I'm so happy that my nephew gave you Sweetpea." Her hand was large and rough, presumably from riding. But her smile was beautiful.

"Thank you," Willa said. "What did Mr. Calico bring you, Lady Knowe?"

"A hat with a wig attached," Lady Knowe said. "Or perhaps one could call it a wig with a hat attached? It's for riding, because hats and wigs aren't designed to stay together in the midst of a stiff breeze."

"How clever!" Willa exclaimed.

"Are you talking about Lady Knowe's cunning new hat?" Lavinia asked, joining them. "I mean to buy one for myself, as soon as we return to London. It's absolutely darling, Willa. The hat is set at a rakish angle."

"I mean to have a habit designed to match," Lady Knowe said.

"Did Mr. Calico sell you the fabric?"

Lady Knowe grinned. "Certainly. I can't think why the man hasn't retired his wagon on the basis of the hundreds of pounds that I have given him over the years."

Lavinia had a mischievous look. "I can tell you who spent the greatest sum of money this afternoon."

"Who?" Lady Knowe asked. "I happily bought a stack of books, so I retired to my bedchamber and paid no attention to everyone else's purchases."

"Mr. Sterling bought every Lord Wilde print in the wagon!" Lavinia said. "He said they were for darts practice, which does not surprise me. A more disagreeable man I never met."

"You wound me," said a sardonic voice. Mr. Sterling stood just behind her.

"You truly mean to throw darts at Lord Wilde's image?" Willa asked him.

"If he does, I'll use his arse for archery practice," Alaric growled, joining them.

His big, warm body crowded behind Willa's, though the drawing room was large enough that no one need touch.

Her heart hammered in her chest, but she steadied her voice. "What would you prefer Mr. Sterling do with the prints he bought?" she asked, stepping to the side.

"Burn the confounded things," Alaric said without

hesitation. "If I'd known Mr. Calico had them on the wagon, I would have bought them myself."

"He's sold hundreds in the last few years," Mr. Sterling said, laughter running through his words.

"So there is something that makes you smile," Lavinia said to him. "I am astonished."

What about these particular men was making both Willa and Lavinia forget the exquisite manners that had carried them through the Season? The sweet smiles and thoughtful replies?

"That, and foolish women," Mr. Sterling retorted.

Alaric groaned.

"I deposited the prints in the nursery," Mr. Sterling continued. "My favorite depicts you on a boat with an enormous tentacle curled around the stern. How did you escape that particular predicament, Alaric?"

"I haven't got that one!" Lavinia exclaimed.

"You're part of the puling parade?" Mr. Sterling said, deep disgust in his voice.

"'Puling parade'?" Lavinia repeated, narrowing her eyes.

"Ladies, weeping every time the newspapers announce that Lord Wilde is lost at sea, which means every three weeks or so, or more often when Parliament isn't in session and there's nothing else to report."

"Who wouldn't admire him?" Lavinia demanded. "Lord Wilde is such a gentleman, if you'll forgive me, Lord Alaric, for referring to you by your alias. Wherever he goes, he rescues people. He's so *chivalrous*."

The full force of her admiring smile was directed at Mr. Sterling.

Whose face darkened as a muscle ticked in his jaw. "Perhaps I should clarify—" he ground out.

"Lord Wilde is a credit to the English people," Lavinia said, cutting him off. "He neither hoards money nor tramples those—including children—who get in his way."

"God almighty," Alaric breathed into Willa's ear. "I don't remember anyone taking on Parth since we were in the schoolroom together."

"And I do?" Mr. Sterling inquired.

Lavinia smiled at him, the smile a tiger gives a rabbit. "Is that not an apt summary of your philosophy of life?"

At that, Mr. Sterling and she launched into a ferocious argument, Lavinia all the sweeter for being utterly furious.

"I'm a little afraid of Lavinia," Alaric said, displaying a useful instinct for self-preservation.

"She doesn't usually lose her temper," Willa observed.

A large hand curled around her waist. "We should leave them alone." He tugged her backward. "It's like watching a husband and wife fight: intriguing but awkward. Would you like some sherry?"

She nodded, grateful for his ignorance of the societal rules that dictated she drink ratafia. He moved his hand to her back and guided her toward the butler and his tray of crystal glasses.

Willa decided that she absolutely must make Alaric stop touching her, because it was befuddling. All the same, she allowed herself to be drawn away.

"Did you notice that I called Miss Gray by her first name?"

"Yes, I did."

"That means you should call me Alaric."

After all, he *had* given her Sweetpea. She yielded. "Very well." He looked at her steadily, so she added, "Only in private. Alaric."

"I have a private question. Do you have a temper like Lavinia's, which you are keeping leashed?"

"No," Willa said. "I'm a very tidy, boring person."

"You are not boring," he said. "Whatever you are, you're not boring."

The compliment sank into Willa's bones, but she refused, absolutely refused, to allow pleasure to show on her face. The man was entirely too confident as it was.

"Have you seen any of the prints they're talking about?" he asked.

"Lavinia had a few on the wall of her bedchamber when we were in school," Willa admitted. The shudder that went through him was small but visible. "She kept her favorite in her Bible," she added, enjoying the look in Alaric's eyes.

He handed her a glass of sherry, and took a healthy swallow from his own. "I could never have imagined all this nonsense when I left England."

"The way prints are bought and traded is new," she explained. "The mania began around three years ago, I believe, but of course the play brought you into even greater prominence."

His mouth twisted with disgust. "Surely they'll forget about me soon."

Willa felt an unnerving wish to soothe him, although she had the distinct impression that even if he wrote no more books, a significant number of people would adore him for the rest of their lives.

"Have you ever seen salmon flop their way upstream in a spring frenzy? Or geese migrating as winter approaches?"

"That bad?"

"Think about migrating geese. The foremost goose

flies at the top of the V, but they're all intent on the same goal."

He gave her a reluctant grin.

"You are the promised land," Willa said. "And, Alaric, don't forget all the clamor they make as they pass overhead."

"Oh, bloody hell." But his eyes had cleared. "It's almost worth it to hear you call me Alaric."

She shook her head at him. "That means nothing."

"So, Lavinia is one of my geese?"

Willa opened her mouth, and shut it again.

"Let me guess," Alaric said, his voice full of mock resignation. "After meeting me, her adoration has waned."

"I'd hate to put it that way," Willa said, but she couldn't keep back a smile. "She *might* be less inclined to think your nose is a perfect specimen."

He rubbed that nose thoughtfully, keeping his eyes on her. As Willa was discovering, Alaric's attention was like brandy: burning hot, enticing . . . habit-forming. He didn't give a damn what women thought of his nose, or any other part of him.

"I should rescue Lavinia," she said.

"Your friend doesn't need rescuing; if anything, mine does."

As they watched, Lavinia delivered a final retort and turned on her heel, the tip of her nose pointed straight at the ceiling.

Mr. Sterling strode toward them, unabashed and furious.

"That woman is a plague and a—" He bit off the word, his eyes cutting to Willa.

"Congratulations," she said, smiling at him. "You are the first gentleman on the marriage market this year to see the true Lavinia."

"Who would want to?" he snarled. "I pity the man who marries that termagant. He'll find out on the wedding night, no doubt. Poor sod."

Eliza Kennet had entered the room and was trotting toward them, her face alight with excitement. Having no wish to see her gush over Alaric, Willa decided to surrender the field. "Please excuse me, gentlemen," she said. "I'll follow my favorite termagant."

"I don't want to discuss him," Lavinia snapped, as Willa joined her. "The man is outrageous . . . offensive. I can't imagine why anyone thinks it appropriate to have him in the house. He's not domesticated."

"Worse than Sweetpea?"

"Far worse. Sweetpea is learning. That man is a cur, one who's been given his own way far too many times."

"It's probably that air of command he has," Willa said. "Like an admiral."

"Like a spoiled boy who has been coddled," Lavinia retorted.

"Somehow I don't think Mr. Sterling has been coddled," Willa said. "But let's join Diana, shall we? I want to know what she bought from Mr. Calico this afternoon."

The answer was unexpected.

Diana drew them down on a sofa to sit on either side of her. "I saw nothing I wanted for myself, but I bought presents for both of you. I'm so grateful to you for coming to my betrothal party."

Opening her knotting bag, Diana gave them each a gold locket, oval in shape and embellished with seed pearls and scrolled designs.

"This is exquisite," Willa said, opening it and inspecting the compartment, which could handily carry a needle and thread.

"You shouldn't have," Lavinia cried, "but I absolutely love it, Diana. Thank you!"

"My mother prefers French jewelry," she answered uncertainly.

"Your mother has excellent taste," Lavinia said.

Diana nodded. "I *would* have chosen them for you,

because I like you so, so much. But . . ." In truth, the pieces were too costly for a gift between friends, and Diana knew it.

She stopped helplessly.

"I adore this locket," Willa said. "It's useful as well as beautiful, and in my estimation, that's high praise for a person or a locket."

"I shall pass my Wilde locket to another admirer, and wear this instead!" Lavinia cried.

"Everyone is talking about you and Lord Alaric," Diana said to Willa, lowering her voice. "He's never shown such marked attention to a lady." She turned to Lavinia. "They're also talking about you and Mr. Sterling."

Lavinia snorted. "I would ignore him, but it's like ignoring an enormous, surly dog that snarls at you from the corner."

"Is Lord Alaric a snarling dog as well?" Diana inquired.

"No," Willa said. "He's decided I'm a challenge."

"Why does it matter if he thinks of you as a challenge?" Lavinia asked.

"He's a man who would climb a mountain simply because it's there," Willa explained. "He doesn't see me as a person."

"He's monstrously wealthy, well-born, and handsome," Diana said, dismissing the question of identity.

"His face is stuck on bedchamber walls all over England," Willa said flatly.

"That is a drawback," Lavinia conceded. "I spent an entire year kissing the print in which he's wrestling a polar bear every time I left for French class. And I had French five days a week."

Diana's brows drew together.

"For good luck," Lavinia explained.

"I don't want to be 'conquered' by someone who thinks of me as a polar bear he's wrestling to the ground," Willa said. "Nor do I want my husband to be a good-luck token for schoolgirls."

"Kissing a print is not the same as kissing the actual man," Diana pointed out. But she sounded uncertain.

"I'm curious about what will happen to the prints Mr. Sterling bought," Lavinia said. "If he wasn't so rude, I'd give him mine to add to the pile."

The duke and duchess were slowly making their way toward the drawing room door, which signaled it was time to go upstairs to dine.

Willa didn't have to glance around to know that North was headed toward Diana, and Alaric toward her. She stood up, overwhelmed all of a sudden. "I believe I will take dinner in my chamber. I have a headache."

"Are you ill?" a deep voice asked, as a hand settled on the middle of her back.

Lavinia and Diana rose. "Good evening, Lord Alaric," Diana said.

Lavinia echoed the greeting, adding, "Did you learn to walk so silently in the jungle?"

"Please don't tell me you own the print depicting me swinging from a vine?" Alaric groaned.

"I do indeed!" Lavinia said, grinning.

Having outgrown her infatuation, Lavinia seemed to have decided that she liked Alaric. That wasn't her polite smile; it was the one she reserved for friends.

"Please excuse me," Willa murmured, feeling an even stronger desire to get out of Alaric's presence. He was pursuing her with every weapon in his arsenal. But to what end? He was an adventurer, a man who would wander away. Right now, she was the challenge—the mountain that simply happened to be there—but if she gave in, he might turn his attention elsewhere.

At that idea she felt a surge of emotion stronger than she'd felt in years. It made her lightheaded.

Without another word, she bobbed a curtsy and headed for the door.

Chapter Fourteen

Alaric watched Willa leave with a rising sense of disbelief.

She didn't have a headache. She was avoiding him.

He poked at the idea the way one's tongue pokes at a sore tooth. He was surrounded by women longing to spend time with him, so it shouldn't matter that one young lady didn't feel the same.

Willa was extraordinarily beautiful, but the world was full of lovely women.

His brooding was interrupted a second later as Eliza Kennet attached herself to his arm. Trying politely to shake her free, he realized again that his retinue—as it were—was a genuine problem. He could hardly carry Sweetpea around in a basket to ward them off.

The only thing he wanted to do was follow Willa. Scoop up that tantalizingly curved bottom and throw it over his shoulder.

Go to bed.

Go to bed and never climb out. Not for at least a week, until he had memorized the contours of her body. And the colors. He was fascinated by the dark- ness of her eyebrows against her pearly skin. Thick, dark-tipped eyelashes. Not a freckle to be seen.

Perhaps she had hair like a raven's wing, hair that would swirl over a man's chest when she sat on top of him, taking her pleasure, riding to her heart's content.

Or perhaps it was a deep mahogany, the color of tree trunks at twilight.

Bloody hell.

He really was losing his mind.

There was no sign of Willa the following morning at breakfast. Nor did she appear at luncheon.

Aunt Knowe caught him after the second meal and informed him that his presence was required at archery, to even the numbers. Teams of two would advance to the archery range and take their turns with bows and arrows.

"It's Diana's favorite sport," she explained. "North has had a set of arrows with brass filigree made for her."

They silently acknowledged between them that lavish gifts would not win North his fiancée's heart. In fact, it crossed Alaric's mind that Diana might accidentally shoot his brother, but he pushed it away.

There were better ways to avoid marriage than manslaughter.

Willa's arms were slim but taut. Perhaps she was an archeress as well. She couldn't hide in her room forever. "I'd be happy to," he told his aunt.

She snorted, shrewd eyes on his face, but said nothing, for which he was grateful.

The duke had erected a tent on the lawn, where guests could take refreshment and seek shelter from both wayward arrows and the midsummer sun. The moment he appeared, Lady Biddle curled her fingers around his arm and claimed him as her partner. Willa was still to be seen, so he followed Helena from the tent to the archery field.

She took the first turn, squealing as her arrow missed the target. After the third such failed attempt, she demanded he stand behind her and show her how to hold the bow. When he complied, she promptly nestled her arse against him.

"What's that I feel?" she giggled, rubbing against him like a cat in heat.

"Nothing," he stated, which was the truth. He

glanced at the tent, where everyone was enjoying lemonade. Some were watching, but they were out of earshot.

He turned her around and caught her eyes. "I'm going to be very blunt, Helena. I am not interested in having an *affaire* with you."

Her face reddened. "It's that girl, isn't it? Willa Ffynche. You think to marry her. The marriage won't succeed."

"Oh?" He picked up his bow, took careful aim, and released the string. The arrow whipped forward with the sound of slashed wind, and slammed into the center of the target. He lowered his bow. "I cede this match."

"You'll have to cede your hope of that particular marriage," Lady Biddle said, her voice sharp. "May I point out that your image is spread all over England—precisely so that ladies can drool over it in the privacy of their bedchambers?"

The words lacerated his gut.

"Willa Ffynche is a lady. She will go nowhere near a life that's played out in the open marketplace. You think there wouldn't be prints sold of your wedding? Of your first child?"

The thought had never occurred to him.

"You couldn't have chosen worse," she swept on, her words fueling a bottomless pit of dark emotion.

"Willa Ffynche is a private woman. Very private. In fact, she—"

Alaric turned on his heel and left her in mid-sentence. If that provoked gossip, it couldn't be helped.

Damn . . . *Damn.*

Willa *was* private. That was part of her allure. She was all hidden depths and secret thoughts. She didn't display herself for everyone to see.

For a man who loved the idea of an undiscovered country, she was the ultimate temptation. At the mere thought of her, his body fired with heat.

North's words came back to him: "I saw Diana, and I had to have her." Alaric didn't want a betrothal—or, God forbid, a wedding—like his brother's, characterized by longing on one side and reluctance, if not dislike, on the other.

He had braved pirate waters in *Wilde Latitudes.* Sailed into sheltered coves in a boat so small that it could hold only one person. He'd won over pirates with games of chance, with spicy tales, with a true lack of desire to steal their treasure.

He had to win her as a friend. That's where North had gone wrong, in his opinion. His brother had courted Diana, had gone so far as to don a towering wig to please her. But last night, Alaric had overheard North's lecture on how a duchess should behave when greeting the queen. Diana had been listening without expression.

North was only trying to ease his future wife into the role of duchess-to-be. But it wasn't a good idea, to Alaric's mind. They should discuss anything other than the responsibilities of a duchess.

To this day North didn't know what his fiancée's favorite ballad was, or which book she most disliked.

Alaric dropped the arrows he held, and stretched. Helena Biddle strode past him, her shoulders rigid, furious.

North strolled over to him. He looked more splendid than Fitzy, a befringed and beruffled jewel in the midst of the green lawn.

"Frankly," Alaric said, unable to resist, "if I had to dress like that in order to win Willa's hand, I'd probably be heading for Africa right now."

"An unlucky destination," his brother pointed out. "You do know that in the play, your beloved—the innocent, dewy missionary's daughter, the lovely Angelica—ends up in the stew pot?"

"*Angelica*?" It was less a question than a groan.

The one good thing about that detail was that its sheer preposterousness confirmed lack of information about Prudence, the real missionary's daughter. Angelica's background must have been a lucky guess on the part of the playwright.

"It's a heart-rending scene, particularly enjoyed by the apprentices in the pit. They pelt the stew pot with apple cores, but the playwright cannily had the pot appear and disappear without showing actual cannibals, saving his actors from assault." His brother threw an arm around his shoulders. "We'll have to stock up on apples to defend your future wife."

"I would never take my wife to Africa. Perhaps Paris."

"Not to defend her from cannibals," North said, just as several women turned about and smiled lavishly. "From English ladies."

Alaric groaned.

Chapter Fifteen

Willa spent a lovely afternoon playing with Sweet-pea. Like a small child, the little skunk seemed to require a daily bath. Luckily she loved water, and paddled around in a large basin, joyfully diving for dried peas.

At one point, Willa caught a glimpse of Alaric out on the lawn, playing at bows and arrows with Lady Biddle. She told herself that she didn't care.

Late in the day, after the archers had disappeared, she decided it was a good time to introduce Sweetpea to her leash. Lavinia had fashioned a little harness out of a gold ribbon sewn with spangles, so it glittered against Sweetpea's dark fur.

"There," Lavinia said, once they managed to fasten

it comfortably around the baby's round stomach. "She looks like a princess, ready to survey her realm."

Sweetpea swung up her tail, tipped, and fell on her nose.

"Oh, no!" Lavinia cried, dropping to her knees.

"She does that without the leash as well," Willa said with a gurgle of laughter. "I don't think she's learned how to balance her tail."

"It is longer than she is," Lavinia said, measuring it with her hands.

"Every time she flips it up, over she goes." Willa picked up Sweetpea and tucked her into her basket. "Would you like to join us? I thought we'd go to the rose garden."

"No, thank you," Lavinia said, yawning. "It's time for a nap. Archery was exhausting; as many feelings as arrows whizzed through the air."

"Diana's?"

"No, far more diverting! Alaric said something to Lady Biddle that made her despise him. She marched away from the archery field in high dudgeon, and by all reports she's ordered her trunks packed."

Willa drew in a silent breath.

"Isn't that fascinating?" Lavinia demanded. "She's given up the idea of bedding him, and spent the last hour telling anyone who will listen that men only set out for foreign lands if they are incapable of satisfying women at home."

"Characteristically vulgar," Willa said, leaving it there.

The rose garden was set in the shade of a high stone wall, so that the flowers received morning sun, but were sheltered from the worst of the storms that raged across Lindow Moss, the bog that stretched into the distance on the other side of the wall. An intriguing smoky odor in the air competed with the roses, presumably coming from peat.

Willa sniffed the air. She was deeply curious about what uncut peat looked like, but that would require disobeying the edict keeping all guests out of the bog. It was just her confounded curiosity that made her wish she could see over the wall.

She set Sweetpea on the path, but the baby skunk headed straight into a flowerbed. She meandered here and there, winding around rosebushes, waiting politely while Willa disentangled her skirts when they caught on thorns.

"You are allowing that animal to drag you around as if she were a puppy. Or a young child of two or three."

Willa spun about.

"I saw you from the tower." Alaric jerked his head backward. "My bedchamber is up there."

"Ah."

"But that's a secret," he added.

Willa wouldn't dream of inquiring into people's sleeping arrangements, so she merely nodded. She could guess the unsavory reason his bedchamber's location had to remain undisclosed.

"I assure you that your secret is safe with me," she said, trying and not quite succeeding in keeping distaste out of her voice.

"I did not choose to be the object of people's . . ."

He couldn't seem to find the word, so she supplied one. "Adoration?"

"That's not quite it." Sweetpea batted at his boot, her claws leaving tiny scratches. "'Adoration' implies devotion, even worship. Playgoers and readers of my books seem to feel something like ownership of me, which is far from devotion."

"How unpleasant for you," Willa said, meaning it. She could imagine few things worse than a stranger believing that he—or she—had a claim on her time or person. She decided to change the subject. "Sweetpea has eaten an earthworm, three leaves, and a small mushroom. She tried to eat a fly, but it flew away. She also contemplated a bee, but I picked her up in time."

"In short, she'll eat anything," Alaric said.

"Yes. This morning she enjoyed a bit of egg, and last night she ate fourteen berries."

"No wonder she's so plump." He squatted down and caressed the skunk's ears. Sweetpea swung up her tail, lost her balance, and went nose down into the dirt.

Alaric scooped her up. She looked even smaller in his large hand. "You are not a good walker." His deep voice was coaxing and affectionate.

Sweetpea touched her nose to his.

"She's kissing you," Willa said, smiling.

"Let's try again," Alaric said, setting Sweetpea back on the path. Willa's throat grew tight at the sight of the huge man, a warrior if there ever was one, bending over her pet.

Once again, Alaric hadn't bothered to put on a wig or powder his hair. Dark locks fell over his forehead and around his neck as he gently traced the pretty white stripe that began at Sweetpea's nose and ended in her plumy tail. "She's a beauty," he said, straightening.

"More importantly, she is remarkably polite, as well as curious," Willa said. "This morning she dragged my slippers from under the bed and brought them to me."

"A man of the Meskwaki tribe once told me that skunks are wiser than cats and more loyal than dogs."

"Does an American sable even exist?"

"No. Sweetpea is a skunk. No one there would make a skunk into a fur stole, since they are famous for their odor. Thus the fancy name."

"Sweetpea doesn't smell," Willa protested. Then she laughed along with Alaric. "Or not very much. After a bath, she smells woodsy, like an autumn forest. I haven't had a chance to say thank you," she said, feeling a surge of gratitude. "I adore her. I always wanted a cat, but I agree with your wise man. Sweetpea is better than a cat."

"Cats are fairly uninterested in their owners," Alaric agreed. His eyes crinkled as he smiled.

"I left my knotting bag hanging from a chair overnight," Willa said, the words tumbling out. "She pulled it down, and took everything out. She didn't break anything, although my locket suffered."

"How so?"

"Gold is easily marked by sharp teeth."

Something twisted in the area of Willa's heart every time Alaric laughed. It endangered the shell she had constructed around the inner her. The shell she'd built after her parents died, and she'd turned into Lady Gray's perfect daughter.

"What is it like to travel?" she asked impulsively.

"There are long days when nothing happens," Alaric said. "Weeks spent on a ship without an island in sight, and nothing but a trunk of books and some grumpy sailors for company."

"You read all day?" It sounded like heaven.

He nodded. "You read, fish, listen to salty tales. Watch for whales and bad weather. At length, a shore appears. Contrary to those engravings, I have no interest in danger, but I am fascinated by the different ways people live."

Sweetpea clambered into her basket and curled against the silk lining.

"Do you like roses?" Alaric asked.

"Yes, certainly," Willa said. "The white ones are so beautiful."

To her surprise, he took a knife out of his boot and began gathering a bouquet. His face was all the more beautiful for the austerity of his black coat. He was confident but not arrogant, likely the distinction that allowed him to walk into the midst of a tribe like the Meskwaki. Listen to their stories, eat with them, walk away undisturbed.

"The Meskwaki?" Willa repeated. "What a curious name. You don't make up any of the stories in your books, do you?"

He turned to her, his arms full of white roses. "The world is a strange place. I've never had to embroider the truth. I'll send a footman back for these so that I can carry Sweetpea's basket." He put them to the side of the path.

Willa suddenly realized that she would forever associate the perfume of those roses with Alaric. White roses would bring to mind smiling blue eyes, shoulders too broad for their coat, honey skin marked by a scar.

The scar gave him a wickedly rakish quality.

She could feel pink creeping up her neck. "Lord Alaric—"

"Not 'Lord Alaric,'" he said firmly. "We have already agreed on that. I am Alaric and you are Willa. Actually, I learned from Aunt Knowe that you are Wilhelmina Everett Ffynche. I like Everett. Is that your mother's name?"

"Yes."

Most improperly, Alaric reached out and ran a hand over her hair. "I was curious to know what color it was and here it is: dark as midnight without a moon."

"I prefer not to powder," Willa confessed. "It's so tiresome to wash out."

"Obviously, I feel the same." He had a half-smile now, direct and yet subtle. "My brother says I resemble a blacksmith."

"It doesn't appear to chase away your admirers," Willa said, before she thought.

"Does it chase away detractors like yourself?"

"I'm not a detractor," she said primly. "I now accept that the stories you recount are true."

Alaric bit back a smile.

Willa Everett pretended to primness, but he saw through her now. She was adventuresome, but not reckless. Intelligent and logical. *Funny.* Behind that placid demeanor, she was funny.

"Thank you for the roses," she said. "I've never had so many at once."

"It's mating fervor," he said thoughtfully.

Her brows drew together. "'*Mating* fervor'?"

Too late, he remembered that a gentleman shouldn't discuss mating with a gently bred young lady. He shrugged mentally. "Haven't you noticed that when spring comes, all the male animals begin flinging themselves around, trying to impress the female of their choice?"

"Like your peacock Fitzy?"

"And my brother North," he said wryly.

Before she could hide it, he saw that she agreed.

"I need a friend more than a mate. One who isn't impressed by Lord Wilde," he added.

"Lavinia would be an excellent choice," Willa suggested, her bright gaze making him want to laugh again. "She would do an excellent job of keeping your bravado in check."

He shook his head. "Lavinia's collection of prints makes her ineligible for friendship."

"What if I read your books, and succumb to the appeal of Lord Wilde?" Her expression made it clear that was most unlikely.

"I wouldn't discourage you." He couldn't stop grinning at the thought.

"It won't happen."

Willa was so sure of herself that the urge to prove her wrong ripped through every pretense of civilization that clung to him, childhood training, everything.

"Will you accompany me back to the house?" she asked, seeming not to notice his hungry gaze. Like a gazelle frolicking in sight of a tiger, he thought.

"Are we friends?"

No gazelle had such a direct gaze, unwavering and solemn, as Wilhelmina Everett Ffynche. "We shall be friends," she said, nodding, "but only if you don't try any nonsense."

"Meaning what?"

She waved her hand. "You know what I mean. Gallantry."

"I'm not known for gallantry."

"The way you bend your head to listen to Lady Biddle," she said. "And there's that look. The look you have right now!"

"The one where I'm suppressing a smile because I can make neither head nor tail of the conversation? Helena Biddle has left for London, by the way. I have also informed Miss Kennet of my penchant for dark-haired women."

"You do realize that ladies often dye their hair?" she asked, with that contained smile that made him half-mad. "Poor Eliza will probably appear at breakfast tomorrow with hair the color of Sweetpea's fur."

"How old were you when your parents died?" he asked, picking up the basket and turning back toward the castle.

"Nine years old."

"A difficult age for a girl."

"How on earth would you know?"

"My sisters. When Boadicea was nine, she was a terror."

"I haven't met your younger siblings. Did you say 'Boadicea'?"

Alaric nodded. "We are all named after warriors. Boadicea prefers Betsy, and Spartacus insists on being called Wilder, after spending his nursery years as Sparky."

"Wilder?"

"I believe it is something of a jest; I am accused by my siblings of having ruined our last name with my books," Alaric admitted.

"They do have intriguing titles," Willa said in a tone of reserved congratulation.

But he was coming to know her. She was most polite when she was most disapproving. "You don't like *Wilde Sargasso Sea*?" he asked, glancing at her. "That's my favorite title."

"I prefer *Wilde Latitudes*, if only for the boldness of renaming a significant part of the world after oneself."

"Ouch," Alaric said, with a grin. "In case you're wondering, I believe that my writing days are over."

"Over?" Her voice squeaked, waking up Sweetpea, who looked around groggily.

Alaric carefully rocked the basket back and forth; Sweetpea tucked her nose under her tail again and lapsed into sleep. "I fancy new challenges. I own an estate near here that my brother has been managing for me."

He looked up to find her blue eyes assessing him. *That's right,* he thought to himself—not letting anything but friendship show on his face—*I am an agreeable man. I will stay in England and spend my days peacefully tending to my estate. I am an excellent prospect for marriage.*

"I see," she said. "As opposed to fighting off pirates, now you're going to spend your time paying morning calls?"

"Would you believe me if I said yes?"

"No."

"Paying a call on a pirate is not so different from a visit to a duke," Alaric observed.

Willa was enormously relieved to discover they had reached the castle walls. They were carrying on two conversations at once, and she wasn't certain that she understood the second.

Alaric's face was harsh in its angles: the way his eyebrows flared above his eyes, the line of his jaw, the shape of his nose. It was the face of a man who strolled into a den of pirates and made friends.

He probably looked at the pirates the way he looked at her: with that piercing interest backed by raw, masculine strength. She wanted him to look at her again. To listen to her. To ask her questions.

To put his arms around her.

Willa's heart was beating a syncopated rhythm that she'd never experienced before. Part of her—the logical part—was thinking, *Flee. Flee.*

Flee before he strolls in, sits by your fire, takes your stories and possibly your heart, and walks away just as casually.

And yet . . . he was big and strong. He would take the world and make it into a smaller, protected place.

"Thank you for the walk," she said, marshaling years of careful civility.

He put the basket down and took a step toward her. Her back touched the castle's stone wall.

"What's the matter?" Alaric asked.

"Nothing," she said, giving him a little push in the chest.

"Willa."

The way he looked down at her surprised the truth out of her. "I do not believe that you are back in England for good."

"Why not?"

"You're an explorer—" Her voice died out because he was tracing the plane of her cheek with one finger.

"I'm getting old." He was so close that the minty smell of his breath washed over her face.

"You are not old." The look in his eyes suggested that she was about to be kissed.

She'd been kissed before. She and Lavinia had decided a great deal could be learned about a man by allowing a small intimacy. Both of them had been kissed by a reasonable number of men—eight in the case of Lavinia and two in hers.

Alaric's mouth came close to hers, hovered, and waited. That was part of his allure. He didn't take, from the pirates or anyone else.

He waited for an invitation. The nearness of him was like kindling, making pinpricks of fire spark throughout her limbs.

Willa felt the weight of her eyelashes sweeping down as her eyes closed. It was acceptance. Joyful acceptance. His hand slid under her hair, curled around her neck, pulling her closer. Finally his lips brushed hers, asking a silent question.

Willa welcomed him, opening her lips. His tongue took her mouth with an assured, slow masterfulness that made her ache with need, though his touch was still light. His hand clung to her neck but his body didn't touch hers.

Enough, she thought. Yet reining in her desire felt like reining in the dusk. Or the rain. Something real, natural, uncontrollable.

That thought was absurd enough to make her eyes snap open. Alaric was looking directly at her, his blue eyes slumberous.

She gave him another push, her hand flat on his chest. He wasn't wearing a waistcoat; under the fine cambric of his shirt his chest was hard with muscle.

"You surprise me, Willa." His gravelly voice skittered along her skin and made her shiver with the sudden wish to demand another kiss.

He tilted up her chin and licked her lips, teasing her

mouth open, then stroking inside. Their mouths clung together as Willa's heart beat faster. He tasted potent, like brandy heated over an open flame.

"Willa," he said. And then, again, heavily, "Willa." He shook his head. "The name doesn't suit you."

"Wh-what?" she managed.

"*Willa* is cool and dispassionate. *Willa* kisses a man to know whether she could bear to meet him over the breakfast table."

It was somewhat shocking to hear him summarize her justification for kissing suitors so accurately.

"I would like to call you by a name that's known only to the two of us," he told her, brushing her mouth with his again.

She pulled away. "There's no need for that."

In her basket, Sweetpea stretched and yawned, little teeth flashing briefly in the sun.

"It's time to return," Willa said, wondering what on earth had got into her. She bent over and picked up the basket, holding it against her chest.

"Everett," he said, looking at her.

It was her mother's name, and the very sound of it made her smile. "That is not a proper name to call any-one," she said. "It was my mother's maiden name."

"Ah, but it suits you. In another world, you'd be a man."

She narrowed her eyes.

"But thank God, you're a woman," he added, eyes alight with amusement. And desire. "Everett," he said again. Then: "Evie!"

Willa shook her head and circled him so she could return inside. She was finished with this dalliance. She had another kiss to add to her tally, which was good.

Experience was always valuable. Before she chose the man she would marry, that is. Her brain felt oddly woozy, but at the same time, her senses were keenly alive.

Alaric walked just behind her, at her shoulder. She could feel the warmth of his body, and a hint of spearmint.

"Why do you taste and smell like mint?" she asked abruptly.

He wrapped his arms around her from behind and breathed into her ear. "Do you like the way I taste, Evie? Because I *love* the way you taste." He kissed her neck.

Willa shook him off. "This is not the way friends behave." She hesitated, then turned and told him the truth. "I don't wish to marry someone like you."

His face stilled.

"My father was rash and impulsive. My mother as well. They died after he accepted a bet to drive a coach and four from Brighton to Croydon in under two hours."

"An impossible goal," he observed.

"I would never be comfortable or happy with someone with such an adventurous nature. *Please* do not importune me."

He was silent as they headed back toward the front door of the castle. Once in the entry, he paused to tell Prism about the roses.

"Your maid is waiting for you in your chamber, Miss Ffynche," the butler said.

"What's this?" Alaric asked, staring at a print stuck to the wall behind Prism.

Willa hadn't seen that particular one, but the subject was clear: his jaw and eyebrows were all too familiar.

"It's entitled *Something Wilde*," she said, smiling as she took a closer look. "My goodness, just look at that bull you're riding. What a rakish hat."

"Why is it on the wall, Prism?" Alaric asked, his voice even.

"They're hung all over the house, my lord," the butler said, hastily taking it down. "As soon as I discover them, your brothers put up more."

"My brothers?"

"Master Leonidas returned home with a great many prints in his luggage," Prism said. "As you know, Mr.

Sterling bought Mr. Calico's entire collection yesterday; Master Spartacus claimed them, I believe. The nursery is papered in prints of Lord Wilde and they are multiplying about the castle like mice."

Willa had been in danger of forgetting the reasons why Alaric was the wrong man to kiss, but the world intervened with a reminder just when she needed it.

"My lord," she said, curtsying. She turned without further ado to climb the stairs.

A hand caught her elbow. "Evie," Alaric said in a low voice.

She steeled her heart against those blue eyes. "Good afternoon, my lord."

Chapter Sixteen

Wherever Alaric looked, he found the hellish prints. The escutcheon on the dining room side table boasted two, the candelabra in the drawing room was doing duty as a picture hanger, and the fireplace in the morning room was adorned with three versions of himself with Empress Catherine.

He tore them all down as he went. When he reached the breakfast room—hearing giggles floating from just outside the door—and found two more images of himself (entitled *Wilde Revealed*), he gave up.

It wasn't the prints making emotions rampage around his chest. It was the look in Willa's eyes.

For a moment she had looked stricken, and then her eyes had gone utterly blank. Courteous, but blank. The empty face that she presented to the world: that of the governed, perfect lady.

His kiss had only momentarily shattered her façade.

But he was coming to realize that he had shattered more than *her* reserve. Something inside himself had changed, too. He felt a sudden, desperate need to turn back the clock. Push her, force her, into acknowledging Alaric, rather than Lord Wilde.

She disliked Lord Wilde. No, stubble it: Willa didn't *dislike* anyone. She observed them, with the same friendly curiosity with which he observed people in other countries.

She was curious about her fellow Englishmen.

But . . . and this was a huge *but* . . . he thought she showed only her friend Lavinia her dizzy sense of humor. Remembering the way she looked at the little skunk—a stinky animal bred to be a fur scarf—made his chest tighten with crushing weight.

Willa deserved a peaceful life with a man who would keep her safe from vulgar eyes and gossiping tongues. A man whose face was plastered across half of England was ineligible. His notoriety meant that whoever married him would always be in the public eye.

Most of the guests were upstairs in their chambers, engaged in the elaborate process of dressing for dinner, the same process that would spit forth his brother as varnished and polished as a seashell. If he encountered one of those guests right now, especially a lady, the odds were that he would be greeted with a mixture of vulgar curiosity and awe.

Looking down at the prints in his hand, he went in search of his younger siblings. They'd been giggling outside the door only moments before, but now they'd vanished.

He found his sister Betsy alone in the nursery, where she seemed to be working on a large drawing.

"Where are they?" he demanded, tossing the prints to the side.

"The boys? I have no idea." She bit her bottom lip as she concentrated.

Alaric felt a wave of affection. Betsy had been a mere girl when he'd left England, and now, at sixteen, she was nearly grown.

"What are you drawing?" he asked, coming closer.

She scowled at him and covered it with her arm. "Don't!"

"No wonder there are so many of these things around the house," he groaned, catching sight of her subject. "You're creating them."

Betsy grinned with all the evil mischief that his siblings had in force. "It's only fair!" she cried. "Do you have any idea how much teasing I've endured because of you?"

Alaric frowned. "You have been teased?"

"You do know that I've been attending a seminary, don't you?"

He shook his head. "When I left, you were here, with a governess." He looked around. "Tall, gaunt woman?"

"Mr. Calico kept bringing her letters from a gentleman whom she knew in Kent," Betsy said. "One day she climbed on the back of his wagon and left, without a word of warning. Papa was most displeased."

"I imagine so."

"But it turned out for the best, because Joan, Viola, and I were sent to school, which we *love*, except that all the girls have prints of you on their bedchamber walls." She wrinkled her nose.

"I apologize," Alaric said.

"So you should!" she cried, eyes sparkling. "I can't tell you how many girls befriended me merely because they thought I would invite them home to meet you. Or introduce you later, once we debut."

"That is unpleasant."

"I agree," Betsy said, turning back to her drawing. She moved her arm, enabling Alaric to get a good look.

It wasn't the nose he saw in the glass every morning, but the likeness wasn't bad.

"What am I doing with that sword over my head?" he asked.

"You're fighting a polar bear," she said. "I shall put him in this blank space once I find a picture to copy, because I can't remember what they look like. Right now I'm just trying to get your nose right. It keeps going overly long, if you see what I mean."

"I do," Alaric said, nodding. "If I actually resembled your portrait, I would lose the greater part of my female admirers, which would be a blessing."

Betsy sighed. "I tried telling the girls scurrilous things about you, but it had no effect."

"What scurrilous things?" Alaric inquired.

"Oh, that your lover had been cooked for a cannibal breakfast, and things like that."

"Don't tell me you were allowed to attend that blasted play?"

"Not yet, but I've heard all about it. Papa says that I will be able to see it, the next time we go to London. You might as well stop taking them down," she said, almost kindly, as she gestured at the crumpled prints he'd brought with him. "Leonidas has lots more. He bought every copy he could find. He's adding some embellishments and then he means to put his up to-morrow."

"Embellishments," Alaric said hollowly. "Such as?"

"Oh, whiskers and so on," Betsy said. "Demon horns. He has some red ink so he can make a pretty devil's tail . . ."

This was all going to be marvelously helpful when it came to courting Miss Wilhelmina Everett Ffynche.

"Do you suppose there's anything I might do to dissuade him?"

"I do not," Betsy stated. She was sketching rapidly now. The Alaric on the page held his sword above his head in such a position that he wouldn't be able to fight off a sparrow, let alone a bear.

"The flat of the sword does nothing in a fight," he observed.

She glanced up at him. "Do you think I care?"

"I suppose not," Alaric said. Truth was relative; he knew it as well as his sister did. But he had the strange feeling that Willa saw things in a less ambiguous fashion.

For her, the stream of tawdry portraits that multiplied by the day would be evidence of his ineligibility, no matter his dislike of his own fame.

He left the nursery, trying to think how to rein in the maelstrom of public attention so it was acceptable to a reserved virgin with a dislike of celebrity. Nothing came to mind.

In fact, he would say that he was the antithesis of everything Willa wanted in a spouse.

A reluctant grin curled his mouth. One thing could be said for him—for all the Wildes, it seemed.

When they went down, they really went down.

Chapter Seventeen

The following evening

Lavinia burst into Willa's room, eyes glowing. "Let's go! We're playing piquet this evening." Lavinia adored card games; Willa, less so, because she disliked the element of surprise involved.

People behaved irrationally when playing card games. They bid high when they had a weak hand. They became fearful when a simple mental tally of the cards already played would tell them that they had a good chance of winning.

"We have to be the first to arrive," Lavinia commanded, holding the door open. "Yesterday Mr. Silly

Sterling dared to inform me that ladies are never on time. You look lovely, by the way."

Willa's deep amber gown was designed to emphasize her slender shape by parting to reveal a saffron petticoat that frothed around her feet.

It also left most of her bosom exposed. She didn't have Lavinia's generous shape, but everything she had was presented for admiration. She took a last look at the glass, slipped on the striped silk shoes made to match the gown, and followed Lavinia down the stairs.

Lavinia's eagerness to prove Mr. Sterling wrong resulted in their being the first to arrive in the green salon, where several tables seating four or six persons had been set out, just enough to facilitate a lively game of piquet. No sooner had they entered the empty room than Alaric appeared, Parth Sterling in tow.

"Could that man look any more wretchedly ill-tempered?" Lavinia whispered as they approached. All the same, she greeted both of them with a wide smile. She had a tendency to become even more charming in the face of bad humor.

Willa thought it was a habit she'd developed as a child because her mother, Lady Gray, was so plagued by nerves.

"Good evening, Lord Alaric, Mr. Sterling," Lavinia

said, ignoring Mr. Sterling's cantankerous look. She tucked her arm under his, uninvited. "Do walk me around the room," she cooed. "You are a trifle early, though not as early as Willa and I were."

Willa shook her head. For some reason, Lavinia was bent on tormenting the poor man.

Alaric moved forward as Lavinia towed his friend toward the other side of the salon. "Your friend is a menace."

"And yours is absurdly bad-tempered," she countered.

"He likes to keep to himself, but Lavinia deliberately provokes him."

"That's true," Willa acknowledged.

"It's because the two of you are used to having every man in the vicinity at your feet," Alaric said.

She shook her head. "Nothing parallel to your admirers, Lord *Wilde*. Any moment now, an adoring horde will surge through those doors."

He looked down at her, eyes sober. "If I'd had the faintest idea that someone would write a farce about me, leading to this lunatic situation, I would never have written my first book."

Willa put a hand on his arm, enjoying the corded strength under her fingers. "I'm sorry," she said, meaning it. "It's unfair. I never paid much attention to the reason for your fame, but I do see that it is unfair."

His eyes lightened. "Do you know what is truly unfair?"

Willa's heart thumped. When he had that expression . . . "What?"

"All these ladies are making pilgrimages to my home, and adoring me from afar, yet I can't get the one woman I want to pay me any true attention."

"I do pay you attention! We're friends, remember?" The look in his eyes made her prickle with warmth all over her body.

He bent close. "I want *close* attention, Evie. Very, very close attention."

Willa swallowed. "There are plenty of women who would give you whatever you wish."

"Lady Biddle and her ilk are no competition for you." Alaric's voice was quiet. His eyes caught hers, and then he bent his head and his lips touched hers. Willa gasped, and his tongue darted between her lips, sending a lick of flame straight down her legs.

She should push him away; guests were sure to flood the salon any moment. Instead, she glanced over her shoulder. Lavinia and Parth Sterling were standing at the far end of the room, and from the looks of it, they were engaged in yet another pitched battle.

Alaric's grin was pure, wicked *fun.* "No one is here to see us. Did I tell you that I haven't given my attentions to a lady in a very long time? I might be out of practice."

Willa's mouth crooked up on one side despite herself. "Am I expected to offer advice?"

He bent his head to hers again. Broad, capable fingers cupped her face, tilting it just so. His were callused hands that knew how to unfurl a sail, how to climb a tree, how to scale a mountain.

Willa's toes curled. She didn't move, just looked into those beautiful eyes until Alaric's mouth came down, eyes still locked with hers, and he plundered her mouth.

For a moment she luxuriated, arms wreathing around his neck, and then she began to plunder back, her tongue fencing with his. Every touch made her body tighten, like a clock being over-wound. A whimper rose in her throat, answered by a growl in his.

As if the sound brought Alaric back to himself, he moved back just enough to kiss her nose. "You're mine," he growled, low and sure.

"No," she said. But she wasn't as certain as she'd been the afternoon before. "I don't . . ."

"I want you enough for both of us," he said in her ear. The door to the drawing room opened, admitting a cluster of guests, and he stepped back. "And with all due respect to your father, Evie, I would never be reckless when it came to your safety, and I don't make bets I can't win. In fact, I don't make bets at all."

Willa snapped open her fan, hoping that her cheeks weren't as rosy as they felt.

The duke and his sister walked in, heading directly toward the two of them. "Alaric, what do I hear about your entourage?" Lady Knowe said with a twinkle. "The duke just informed me that Lady Biddle has departed."

"She has another party to attend," Alaric said, his tone bland.

"Should we expect your other admirers to flee?" his aunt asked. "Goodness, we would be left with a nearly empty house."

"After the initial flurry of excitement, perhaps our guests are recognizing that Alaric's fame is all out of proportion," His Grace said.

"Not if my siblings have anything to do with it," Alaric said. "Those wretched prints are posted all over the house, and being hourly supplemented by the artistic efforts from the nursery."

"They're making new images?" Willa asked, intrigued.

"Paintings and sketches." The duke gestured toward the fireplace, which was adorned with a sheet of foolscap which bore no resemblance to the room's otherwise elegant furnishings.

His Grace went over to the mantelpiece, plucked the picture from it, and returned. He was holding a depiction of a stick figure surrounded by blobs that vaguely resembled animals, seeing as they had four legs and a great many sharp teeth.

"I was surprised to find such artistic talent in the family," the duke said, the mischievous look in his eyes making him look much younger than his fifty-some years. "Here my son Erik represents Alaric—or rather, Lord Wilde—in the jungle. I might add that Erik is six years old."

"Enthusiastic, but unpracticed," Alaric said, looking it over.

"I like the way he portrays your teeth extending below your chin," Willa said appreciatively. "When he's a bit older, Erik will be able to draw your profile and sell it for five shillings."

"By then, the market for those particular images will be gone." Alaric sounded very sure of that.

"Someone has to depict your next decade's adventures," Lady Knowe said. "Why not a family member? I could set up my own stall in front of the theater. Lockets would be redundant, but original portraits are sure to sell."

Alaric dropped a kiss on her cheek. "You surprise me, dear aunt. Who would have thought you proficient with watercolors? I have never seen you sewing a fine seam. Perhaps I'll ask Mr. Calico to bring you an embroidery hoop."

Prism entered the drawing room. "Lord Alaric, forgive me for interrupting, but a young woman is insistently requesting to see you. I have shown her to the library."

Willa discovered, to her dismay, that she did not care for the fact that a lady was calling at this hour of the evening. That didn't happen in the normal course of events. Ladies paid morning calls, with chaperones and family in tow.

"Not another one," Lady Knowe groaned.

Alaric frowned. "What on earth do you mean by that?"

"Pilgrimages," his father explained with a sigh. "They want to see the place where you were born. They invariably request to be taken to the nursery so they can gaze at your hobbyhorse."

Willa's tension eased, but Alaric stiffened.

"That's bloody nonsense."

"Not in front of ladies," his aunt scolded, ignoring the fact that she often cursed herself. "Your father and I have developed an excellent routine for dispatching such unwanted visitors. If you make an appearance it might overcome her sensibilities. I suppose I had better send Prism for spirit of hartshorn. Or *sal volatile*."

"In case she swoons?" Willa asked, reluctantly fascinated.

"Lord Wilde's admirers do occasionally feel faint on meeting members of his family," the duke said dryly. "Lord knows what will happen if Lord Wilde himself makes an appearance."

"I apologize," Alaric said, his voice colorless.

"Do you mind if I inquire about your routine?" Willa asked, wishing she could put a hand on Alaric's arm just . . . because.

"We terrify them," Lady Knowe said, with all-too-obvious glee. "It comes naturally to my brother, but I have discovered a gift for it as well." She drew herself up—which brought her almost to the duke's height—and regarded them imperiously down the length of her nose.

"My goodness," Willa exclaimed, impressed.

"Do they turn tail and run?" Alaric asked.

"Pilgrims have the courage of their convictions," Lady Knowe said. "Some of them have even read your books. But after seeing *Wilde in Love* twelve times—"

"*Twelve?*" The word exploded out of Alaric's mouth.

"Or twenty," his father confirmed.

"Poor Lord Wilde. Plagued by too much love," Willa said, wanting to lighten Alaric's expression.

He shot her a look that reminded her of their kiss, with no need for words. Heat washed into her face and she hastily brought up her fan.

The duke chuckled. "If you wish to join us in greeting the young lady, Alaric, you are more than welcome."

He and Lady Knowe strolled away.

"This is remarkably distasteful." Alaric's jaw tightened.

Willa gave in to her impulse and put a hand on his arm, her fingers curling around his strength. "I think your father and aunt are enjoying themselves."

"Will you—" He paused.

"Will I what?"

"Will you wait a few minutes and then come to the library on some pretext?" His eyes searched hers and Willa thought there was more than one question buried in his words.

How could she say no? He had kissed her, but even more than that, he had somehow become a *friend*.

A strange word for a man. She and Lavinia had many suitors, whom they flattered and bandied words with. But Alaric had somehow crashed through all that.

"Evie?" The word was a rasp.

"Yes, I will." She frowned at him. "I am only agreeing to rescue you from your uninvited admirer. Nothing more."

That smile?

The one he gave her now?

That was the arrogant smile depicted in the engravings. It was the smile of a man who had conquered mountains.

"Thank you." He bowed and kissed her hand. His lips pressed against her fingers and his tongue—

She snatched her hand away. "Alaric!"

Chapter Eighteen

Alaric made his way to the library, feeling generous toward the lady who had made a pilgrimage all the way to Cheshire. Whoever she was.

When the butler mentioned that he had a visitor, he'd seen a flash of something in Willa's eyes that he chose to think was jealousy. It was cheering to see that trace of possessiveness.

He opened the library door, expecting to find his father on his high horse, every inch the duke. In fact, he thought His Grace and Lady Knowe would be towering over the visitor.

Instead they were all seated. He approached them, his shoes making no noise on the thick Aubusson carpet covering the library floor. Their visitor was talking in a soft voice, her back to the door.

Soft brown ringlets, unpowdered and unadorned, fell to her shoulders. She was wearing a gray dress, cut high around her neck and made of cloth that had no interest in the shape of a human body, but formed a box that hung from the shoulders.

That dress advertised itself and its wearer. It was a dress that might be worn by a missionary's daughter.

The thought, and a second look, sent a sickening jolt through him.

Unless he missed his guess, the woman sitting in his father's library was Miss Prudence Larkin, who had neither been given a locket, nor—obviously—been eaten by cannibals.

He'd last seen her years before, when she was fourteen, and although the skin that had been spotty then was now milky white, her snub nose and slightly protruding teeth were unchanged.

Prudence turned her head. "Alaric, my dearest," she cried, springing to her feet, her eyes shining. She dropped into a low curtsy, head bent as if she were greeting royalty.

Why in the hell was she addressing him with such familiarity? "Good evening, Miss Larkin," he said, bowing. "I see that you have met my father and aunt."

They had risen as well; she turned to them with a

smile. "I was just telling your family everything that passed between us in Africa."

"You were?" Alaric's mind reeled. In his opinion, a woman would be humiliated by the memory of their last, profoundly awkward encounter—when she had stolen into his bed and had to be unceremoniously ejected. Yet here she was, beaming at the duke.

"At times the heart can mend itself only in silence."

The duke frowned. If there was a man in the world unimpressed by vague metaphysical statements, it was His Grace. "I beg your pardon?"

"I was dead, you see." She took a step toward Alaric. "Verily, I know that you must be shocked to the very core. But I lived . . . I *lived*!"

After a moment's silence while everyone digested the fact that, indeed, the lady seemed to be living, the duke said, "Alaric." It wasn't a question.

"Miss Larkin is the daughter of Charles Pearson Larkin, a missionary with whom I stayed in Africa some years ago. I believe she was fourteen years old at that time. I know nothing about her death nor, indeed, her return from it."

Prudence gave him a beatific smile. "Alaric and I shared a special . . ." Her voice dropped. "A special bond."

Bloody hell.

"No, we did not," Alaric stated.

She gave him a sympathetic look. "I understood that you would have tried to raze me from the tablets of your heart after discovering that I had passed from this earth."

There was silence again as everyone wrestled with her idiosyncratic language.

"When I left Africa, you were perfectly healthy," Alaric observed.

The duke said, "May I say that for someone who claims to have died, and lived again, you are looking remarkably well."

"It was a miracle," Prudence said. Alaric was starting to find her glowing smile unnerving. "I came here, among the tents of the wicked, with sobriety and humbleness, not taking pride in my love for Lord Wilde, but certain of it."

"A Puritan, I gather," his aunt said.

Prudence turned her head and her eyes narrowed as she looked closely at Lady Knowe. Then she said, with a little gasp, "Let not your eyes be drawn aside with vanity, Prudence, nor your ear with wicked noises."

"I beg your pardon, but did you just address yourself?" His aunt seemed to be working out how best to handle this eccentric stranger.

While Lady Knowe appeared undisturbed by Prudence's rudeness, Alaric was appalled. What in the devil was Prudence doing, insulting his aunt and raving about a "special bond"?

He had clear memories of her as a spotty young girl who prayed more loudly and fervently than did her parents. All the same, she'd had an unhealthy anger about her, as if she was always on the verge of loud sobs.

Then the night came when he'd discovered her tucked under his sheet—belying her claims to godliness. He had pried her from the bed, escorted her to the door, pushed her out of his bedchamber, and left the next morning.

"Why are you here, Miss Larkin?" he asked.

"I came for you, dear one."

"I am not your dear one, and there is nothing between us."

"It is a sin of obstinacy, great obstinacy, high and horrible obstinacy, to deny the truth."

"There is no truth in what you are saying." He'd heard enough. Prudence was more than eccentric; she was deranged.

"What I wish to know," his father said, intervening, "is whether there is a connection between you, Miss Larkin, and the play depicting a missionary's daughter that is currently on the stage in London."

Prudence turned to Alaric with a gentle smile. If it was a mask, it was a complete one, one which the woman herself believed in. "Indeed, there is," she said. Her smile widened. "I wrote *Wilde in Love.*"

"*You* wrote that play?" The words grated from Alaric's chest.

Her eyes fell. "You are right to admonish me, husband."

"*Husband?*"

"I think of you as my husband, though I know the word is an ensign of pride, a banner of pride," she said, stumbling over her words for the first time. She squared her shoulders and that eerie sweetness stole over her face again.

To Alaric, she looked like a woman smiling at a baby, rather than at a small circle of hostile aristocrats.

"My father calls the theater the smoke of vanity, made by Satan himself to draw us to fleshly errors, things of the world, of the devil, and the flesh."

"Does he indeed? And I would call your play a tissue of lies," Alaric said. He crossed his arms over his chest. "I feel myself justified in calling the sheriff."

"Do not be angry with me," Prudence pleaded. "Everything I have done, I did for the pure love of you."

This was an unmitigated disaster.

"Where is your father?"

"After you left, I fell into such a fit of longing that I was deemed not likely to survive." Tears glimmered in her eyes. "I died, verily, I died. When I awoke, I knew that I had to follow you, though you went to an impure place, yea, even into the fires of hell itself."

"She's deranged," Lady Knowe said, bluntly but not unkindly. "Daft as a brush, and that's the truth of it. I always said those Puritans prayed too much. Fasting isn't good for a body either."

"*You* should not address me," Prudence said, her chin firming. "You have the marks of the devil about thee. You partake of pitch. You—"

"Do not speak to Lady Knowe in that tone," His Grace said.

He did not raise his voice, but something about the duke made Prudence instantly fall silent.

"Where is your father?" Alaric repeated.

"I ran away. I came here, not to partake of sin, but to cleanse you of it." A silence, and then she added practically, "You weren't in the country when I arrived."

"So you wrote the play?"

A hint of pride crept into her face. "I composed it on the voyage. The men aboard the ship were quite unkind and forced me to keep to my room."

"You had no right to make a play out of my nephew's life," Lady Knowe said.

"I had every right," Prudence retorted. "I am his *wife*."

"I have no wife." Alaric didn't allow himself to move a finger.

"Yes, you have," Prudence insisted. "We may not have exchanged words in the presence of a minister, but we were moved in the Spirit together, and God rewarded our zeal and glory."

Alaric shook his head. "I have no idea what you are talking about. After you crept into my bed, I put you out directly. I did not tell your father about your actions, though I see now that was a mistake."

"You took my heart with you when you left . . . I died. But I live, and die, every night in the play that I wrote for you. All that remains is for us to say the words in our heart under a sacred roof."

"You can't possibly think that Alaric would actually marry you," his aunt said, visibly surprised.

"He will marry me because he loves me."

Silence.

What in the hell could he say that would convince

her? What did one say to a woman who seemed to think that she'd been brought back from the dead? "I will never marry you."

"I will wait for you," Prudence cried, her voice trembling. "I will wait until you change your mind. I will wait my entire life."

The duke moved forward. "Miss Larkin—"

"Thou canst not rule my tongue," she said desperately. "My tongue is my own, and so is my pen, and with it I will keep loving you no matter how often you slay me, reject me, hate me."

"This is turning Shakespearean," Lady Knowe observed. "I think she's threatening to write more plays about you, Alaric."

"I rejoice in my afflictions," Prudence said. Then she scowled at Alaric's aunt. "*Thou*, thou art all abomination!"

The duke sighed. "Miss Larkin, I'm afraid you must go your way now. You've said enough."

"I'll pay for your passage back to your father," Alaric said. "I would guess that he's worried about you."

"No, he isn't," Prudence said, her voice trembling. "He knows we are to be married, because of our love. Because I came to you, and spent the night with you, and married you in my heart."

"We did not spend the night together." Behind Miss

Larkin, his father shook his head, and Alaric realized the duke was right. There was no point in attempting to reason with her.

"I shall find you a ship headed for Africa," he said, schooling his voice to what he hoped was a persuasive key.

"I was terrified in my inner heart that you would have found someone else, but now I see that my prayers are answered. You are mine, and though you may not—"

"No," he said, "I am not yours. I *have* found someone else."

Her eyes narrowed for a second and then, like a veil, the sweetness fell back over her expression. "You are teasing me, dear one. It isn't kind. Not after the privations I've suffered for your sake."

"A rest cure might help," Lady Knowe suggested, sounding unconvinced.

Behind them the door opened and Willa entered. Alaric's heart bounded at the sight of her. She was so frank and honest in comparison to this frighteningly strange madwoman.

"Please forgive my interruption," she said, once she reached the group. "I came to fetch a book that Miss Gray left here earlier in the day."

Alaric held out his hand. "Miss Ffynche, please join

us." Then he held his breath. Willa had theretofore refused his courtship in no uncertain terms. But there
was something between them . . . an invisible bond as
strong as steel.

He needed her help.

Chapter Nineteen

It seemed to Willa as if she'd entered a theater after missing the first two acts of a melodrama.

Before her stood the brave heroine, amidst a circle of uncaring aristocrats. This would be the scene in which the hapless, seduced maid denounces the evil squire for taking her virginity and getting her with child.

That speech was typically capped by the squire's rejection, leading in Act Five to the heroine's tragic plunge from a high tower, cliff, or church steeple.

But in this scene the evil squire was Alaric, and he was holding out his hand. He needed her. Her heart was pounding in her chest, even though there was no logical reason she should be so thrilled by the expression in his eyes.

"Lady Knowe, Your Grace," she said, dropping a curtsy. Then she came a few steps closer and murmured, "Lord Alaric." He promptly reached down, caught up her hand, and held it to his lips.

Willa felt herself turning pink. The duke was looking at them, his eyes speculative, but unsurprised. Lady Knowe outright winked at her.

"I cannot and will not marry you, Miss Larkin," Alaric stated. "I did not seduce you, or even spend time with you. I do not know you, and you are clearly disturbed."

Marriage? Willa's guess at melodrama seemed correct; the state of affairs was not as simple as an enthusiastic pilgrimage to Lord Wilde's birthplace.

Alaric would never act in a shabby way toward a woman. For a fleeting moment, Willa thought about how much her opinion of him had changed since they'd met. He was no longer Lord Wilde, the famous explorer.

He was *Alaric*. Alaric of the honorable eyes and hungry kisses.

"Even as you say that, I just love you more," Prudence breathed, moving a step toward Alaric. Her voice dropped. "Think of me as your spaniel."

Goodness.

Hadn't Miss Larkin noticed the object of her devotion was pressing kiss after kiss on another woman's fingers?

It seemed not. Willa withdrew her hand; it was awkward to stand there and be theatrically kissed when the designated audience was paying no attention.

"The more you beat me, the more I will fawn on you," Miss Larkin said in a panting voice.

Ugh.

Willa instinctively moved closer to Alaric, her arm brushing his. She caught Miss Larkin's eye and gave her a direct stare that she hoped would clarify that there was to be no "beating" in Willa's presence.

Nor fawning either, to be frank.

"Lord Alaric, won't you introduce me?" she asked.

"Please forgive me," Alaric said. "Willa, *my love*, this is Miss Prudence Larkin, whom I knew exceedingly briefly when she was a young girl in Africa and her father, a missionary, showed me hospitality. We have just learned that she traveled to London some time ago, and is the author of that wretched play."

All signs of fawning love fell from the playwright's face. "My play is not wretched!" she snapped. "It has been widely proclaimed as brilliant!"

Alaric's adjective had certainly been less than tactful, though most people would agree that he had reason to be annoyed. "I must congratulate you on your extraordinary success, Miss Larkin," Willa said. "I have not been lucky enough to see the production myself, but it is certainly popular."

Miss Larkin glanced at her. "Yes, well, the tickets have been sold ahead for months. I suppose I could find you a ticket or two if you happen to be in London."

That was so extraordinarily rude that Willa bit back a smile and Lady Knowe actually guffawed.

Ignoring them, the playwright took a step toward Alaric, her hands clasped before her. "Spurn me, strike me, neglect me, lose me," she said in a low, broken voice. "Only give me leave, unworthy as I am, to follow you."

Oh, for goodness' sake.

"That sounds awfully familiar," Lady Knowe muttered.

"Because the speech was written by Shakespeare," Willa pointed out. "It first appeared in *A Midsummer Night's Dream*, as did most of her lines since I entered the room."

"What worser place can I beg in your life than to be used as you use your dog?" Miss Larkin cried, her voice rising feverishly. She swayed and Willa had a horrible sense that she was about to fall to her knees. "I am sick when I—"

"I am betrothed to Miss Wilhelmina Everett Ffynche," Alaric said, cutting her off.

Willa let out an involuntary gasp. Lady Knowe broke into another bellow of laughter, and even the duke smiled.

"Miss Larkin, this is not a stage, nor are you in a Shakespeare play," Alaric continued. "I'm afraid I must ask you to leave."

The lady's eyes grew round. She slapped her hands to her cheeks, falling back a step.

Overacting, Willa thought unsympathetically. What could you expect from someone who adopted Shakespeare's wilder lines for her own? If Willa remembered correctly, this particular character, Helena, was drugged with a love potion when she said those foolish things.

Shakespeare was a good example of why Willa disliked fiction. Helena ran around on stage abasing herself. There was enough of that in real life.

"I expect this is a shock," she said.

A large tear rolled down Miss Larkin's cheek. "Verily, it breaks me. I think I will die again."

She was a terrible actress. Perhaps she was a brilliant playwright, but Willa was beginning to have suspicions about that too. The cannibal stew pot had sounded dubious, and it could be that *Wilde in Love* was utter rubbish.

Perhaps even plagiarized rubbish.

"Dying is not allowed in Lindow Castle," Lady Knowe said. She wasn't laughing anymore; instead she looked sympathetic.

Alaric's aunt was eccentric, brusque, and funny, but Willa was also starting to think that she was one of the kindest people she'd ever met.

"You proposed marriage to this woman before you knew that I still lived," Miss Larkin gulped. "You will change your mind because you loved me first, and I know you still love me. I saw how many times you glanced at me across the table in Africa. I've read every one of your books!"

"What does that have to do with anything?" Lady Knowe asked.

Alaric had the feeling that he was caught in a nightmare. Willa was the only stable fulcrum of his world.

"Alaric left clues for me in his books," Prudence cried. Eerily, that sweet smile broke over her face again. "As I read his lines over and over, I came to see that he spoke to me through the pages."

"Why would I be speaking to you if I believed you dead?" Alaric asked.

"Love is eternal," Prudence explained. "You were talking to my soul, little knowing that I had survived the tempest."

"Alaric and I are betrothed," Willa said, putting a hint of outrage in her voice. "It is presumptuous, not to mention inaccurate, to suggest that my fiancé might fall out of love with me and marry you. Lord Alaric is *mine*," she concluded, nudging him with her elbow.

"And she is mine," Alaric said, taking her cue. "Miss Ffynche is mine."

Prudence's large eyes moved from one to the other. "My heart is a wasteland," she rasped, as tears began to flow down her cheeks.

"Oh, for goodness' sake," Lady Knowe said, moving forward. She towered over Prudence like a pine tree. "Come along, my dear."

"Where are you taking her?" the duke asked.

"We can't simply throw her out of the castle," his sister said.

"We could send her to the village and drop her at the parsonage," the duke suggested. "Perhaps the vicar can remind her of the prevailing moral principles governing relations between men and women. Those followed by Puritans and all people of good taste."

Prudence broke into louder sobs.

"Prism will find her a bedchamber, and she can

remain here while she decides what to do next," Lady Knowe said.

Alaric was about to disagree—there was something about Prudence Larkin that he truly disliked—but it struck him that as long as Prudence was in the castle . . .

He and Willa would have to pretend to be engaged.

"I don't mind," he said.

"Two days," His Grace said, meeting Alaric's eyes. His father had a way of smiling without moving his face. He was smiling now, even as he regarded Alaric with perfect sobriety. "Miss Larkin may remain here for two days, during which time you must decide what to do with her."

"Keep me!" Prudence wailed. "Keep me because I am yours!"

Lady Knowe pushed a handkerchief into her hand. "If you haven't anything sensible to say, keep silent," she told her, not unkindly.

"I l-l-love—"

"As do I," Willa said, cutting her off. "I love Alaric, and he is mine, Miss Larkin. I will not give him to anyone. You must come to terms with that fact."

For the first time Prudence seemed to be struck dumb. She stared at Willa as if she were a burning bush.

Willa gazed calmly back.

To Alaric, Willa was a study in clear lines: patrician nose, high cheekbones, a Cupid's bow of a mouth. In contrast, Prudence had a round cheek, soft jaw, her blurred features underscored by the tears dripping from her cheeks and creating dark splashes on her gray dress.

"Why her?" Prudence whispered. "Why *her*, why not me?"

"I don't even know you," Alaric said, allowing astonishment to leak into his tone. "You were a tiresome fourteen-year-old when I first met you, Prudence, and you will have to accept that there was, and is, absolutely nothing between us."

Prudence started weeping again.

"She is bedazzled," Willa observed.

"I had nothing to do with that bedazzling," Alaric said. "Her father was living in a house that wasn't much bigger than a hut; it was hot as blazes; we couldn't bathe in the river thanks to crocodiles. There was nothing dazzling about me."

"However it happened, it has," Lady Knowe said, and led Prudence away, the young woman's shoulders shaking with sobs.

Alaric did not feel a shred of guilt. Prudence had written the idiotic play that was endangering his chance to marry Willa. She was at least partly responsible for the hordes of women who were stripping his flower-beds and stealing his bricks.

"There seems to be a great deal of drama surrounding Miss Larkin," Willa said, as the door closed behind Lady Knowe. "She certainly knows her Shakespeare."

"Will you pretend to be my betrothed for a few more days, just until we work out what to do with Miss Larkin?" Alaric asked.

The duke bowed before Willa could respond. "If you'll forgive me, I should inform Her Grace that we will be entertaining another guest."

"Prudence Larkin can scarcely join us at the table, given her delusions," Alaric said.

"In fact, I believe she ought to do just that," His Grace said. "Rumors are far more pernicious than discovering the lachrymose daughter of a missionary at the table. What's more, given enough contact with you, she might well drop her infatuation."

Alaric grinned at his father. "Questioning my desirableness, are you?"

"Miss Larkin's command of logic is debatable," his father said dryly, "but propinquity will inevitably have an effect."

When he'd gone, Alaric stepped forward and wrapped his arms around Willa.

"I will pretend to be engaged to you," Willa said,

not pushing him away. "But that doesn't mean that I agree to marry you. Once Miss Larkin leaves, or comes to her senses, we are no longer betrothed."

Alaric nodded. He'd accept that for the time being.

It was a step better than friends, because betrothed people could kiss. *Did* kiss. "We should practice intimacy so as to be convincing," he suggested.

Willa pushed him away, her mouth curving up. "I think we shall have no problem with that."

Chapter Twenty

That evening Willa settled down with a book in her hand. Lady Knowe had lent her a tale of great derring-do, with knights dashing hither and yon, wasting a great deal of energy.

The novelist had not depicted a realistic world. Yet Willa kept reading. The castle had fallen silent by the time a large piece of fictional armor fell from the fictional sky and crushed one of the fictional characters.

At that, she sighed and closed the book. She simply didn't see the purpose of fiction. Events like these made her too curious about things for which there was no answer.

Why armor, for example? Why not a chicken? A chicken as big as a house, perhaps?

Lindow Castle was full of fascinating people. She

saw no reason to read about invented events when life was complex enough as it was.

Her bedchamber was bright with moonlight that flooded in the windows of the castle along with the scent of honeysuckle. Sweetpea kept running through the pool of light, a black-and-white streak. She was busily taking everything out of Willa's knotting bag and stowing each piece under the dressing table.

Willa squinted at the moon; when she was wearing her spectacles she couldn't see much beyond the printed page. Still, she could tell that the moon was flattened on one side and round on the other, like an overstuffed pigeon.

Right there was the reason why she could never be a novelist. The moon was supposed to be a silver disc, or the goddess Diana's face . . . not a fat bird.

The quiet rap on her door was a welcome interruption; she'd been longing to tell Lavinia about the mad missionary's daughter, but the encounter with Prudence made her feel oddly unbalanced, and she had retired to her chamber rather than return to the salon to play cards.

When she opened the door, cautiously so that Sweetpea couldn't dash past her, Alaric—not Lavinia—was in the corridor.

There was absolutely no occasion on which a gentleman may acceptably pay a visit to a lady's chamber—unless that lady had issued an invitation to an *affaire*. To dally, in plain English. Evidently, Alaric thought she was a lightskirt.

Willa stared at him for a second, feeling a crushing sense of disappointment. It was one thing to kiss her. Or contrive a pretend betrothal. It was quite another to conclude that either fact could be construed as an invitation to further intimacies.

"Lord Alaric," she said coldly. "You have so many doors to knock on at night. I assure you this one is not a possibility."

"I didn't think any of the ladies behind those doors would be interested in this." He uncurled his hand, which he'd held in a fist. Willa took off her spectacles and looked down to find two roly-polies and an earthworm on his palm. It wriggled.

Willa raised her eyes to his, dumbfounded.

"I brought them for Sweetpea," he said. "I noticed this afternoon that while she ate insects of several varieties, she is particularly fond of roly-polies."

"How on earth did you determine that?"

"She pranced," Alaric said, eyes innocent. Too innocent, to Willa's mind. "Did you not notice her celebratory response?"

"I did not," Willa said. "She already had a piece of

chicken for dinner." She was unenthusiastic about the idea of touching vermin of any kind.

"Would you like me to give them to her?" Alaric asked. "I promise I won't be overcome by lust if you allow me in your bedchamber. As you say, there are many doors that would open should I be that desperate to bed a woman."

"You're making fun of me," Willa said.

"Only a trifle. Because you're jealous."

"I beg to differ."

He grinned. "In that case, you might as well let me in. Unless you'd like to keep the roly-polies for a morning snack? I could find a small box so that they don't crawl around your room."

Sweetpea would probably love a snack, and Willa was far more covered in this nightdress and dressing gown than she'd been in her evening gown. Alaric was honorable, and she was being silly.

She opened the door and stood back. As soon as he entered, Sweetpea made a happy chattering noise and scampered to him. He crouched down and held out both hands, curled into fists.

"Don't squish that worm," Willa said urgently.

Sweetpea was sniffing his hands.

"I'm not," Alaric said. "Look, she's figured it out."

Willa put her spectacles on her bedside table and got

down on her knees, making certain that her dressing gown covered every inch of her ankles.

Sweetpea had put a small clawed hand on one of Alaric's fists and was trying to pry back a finger.

"She's so clever," Willa said with delight.

Alaric uncurled the finger and Sweetpea eagerly poked her nose into the gap. When she couldn't reach her treat, she tapped his hand with her claws. Her chuffing noise took on a commanding tone.

"You know who's in charge, don't you?" Alaric murmured.

Willa stopped watching as Sweetpea ate her snack— she was not fond of her pet's enthusiasm for earth-worms, let alone roly-polies—and watched Alaric instead.

He wore no coat, and his white shirt was open at the neck.

His brother, North, would never present himself to a lady in such a state of undress. But she had the strong feeling that the state of his attire hadn't occurred to Alaric.

"She definitely likes the roly-polies best," he said now, his voice deep in the quiet night.

Willa took a hasty look down and discovered that Sweetpea had gobbled the roly-polies and was circling the worm. She sprang into the air, as if the poor creature had offered some defense. Her tail flew up . . . down went Sweetpea on her nose.

They both laughed. "She'll grow into her tail," Alaric said. He wasn't looking at Sweetpea, though.

Willa could feel color creeping up her neck. This was precisely why gentlemen and ladies weren't allowed to be together unchaperoned. She felt as tipsy as those nights when she and Lavinia had smuggled bottles of wine up to their room and made plans to conquer polite society.

Talking about boys half the night. Or rather, men.

Talking about men.

When Lavinia wasn't chattering about Lord Wilde.

Alaric's eyes narrowed. "What are you thinking?"

Willa turned away, leaving the poor worm to its fate. She washed her hands at the basin. Then she said, over her shoulder, "How many evenings I've spent with Lavinia discussing her adoration for Lord Wilde."

He gave a half-stifled groan and joined her, washing his hands as he glanced at her under his lashes. "You were never tempted to read one book?"

"No. I don't mean to insult you," Willa said.

He turned, leaning his hip against her dressing table, so close that his breath stirred the tendrils of hair that had sprung free of her nighttime braid. "I am not insulted. Will you be insulted if I tell you how adorable you look in spectacles?"

Of course she wouldn't be.

That look in his eyes?

It made her want to betray the self she had painstakingly constructed. The self who never sighed, never kissed adventurers . . .

He moved forward, cupped her face in his hand, and said in a dark rumbling voice, "Evie, may I kiss you?"

"Is that Lord Wilde or Lord Alaric speaking?"

"What do you mean?"

"Lord Wilde is reckless and impetuous," Willa said, spelling out the obvious. "Lord Alaric is far more restrained and thoughtful. I am currently in a sham engagement with Lord Wilde."

"Interesting." There was a moment's silence.

Then: "Neither one. Not a lord. Just a man who would very much like to kiss you, Evie. Not Willa, who is perfect in every way, but Evie, who is captivating. I think Evie wears spectacles, by the way. Willa has perfect vision."

She met his eyes and had to freeze to avoid throwing herself into his arms. Damn it, the man was like a fine liqueur. He bent his head and brushed his lips across hers, making her shiver.

"Open your lips," he said, his voice ragged. "Pretty Evie, open your mouth for me."

His voice was a caress in itself. It made her feel wanton. She leaned forward and put her lips on his, her breath catching as his tongue traced the seam of her lips and then licked its way inside.

She dimly registered that he tasted of wintergreen. But it didn't matter because her senses were bombarded and her skin tingled all the way down her back and belly, down her legs. Between her legs.

As Alaric's tongue curled around hers and his arms closed around her, Willa melted against him. Her fingers curled into the hard muscles of his shoulders and then moved to wind into his hair.

Alaric kissed as if he could imagine nothing else he'd rather do. He didn't move a hand to her breast, or pull her more closely against him.

Willa's mind raced, taking note of his steely arms (good), his minty breath (good), his height (good), the silky feel of his hair (good) . . .

No other man's kiss had ever pleased in so many ways.

A few kisses later, her brain was beginning to feel dull and foggy. He wasn't pulling her closer; it was she who was pressing against him, her heart racing.

The taste and feel of him swept all intelligent thought

aside, until she was moaning in the back of her throat and running her tongue over his white teeth. Clinging to him.

Lust, she thought dimly. Lust was flushing her skin and making her heart pound in her throat.

"Evie," Alaric said, and the name slipped out from his lips like a pagan, carnal prayer.

The wonderful thing was that if he addressed her as Evie, she didn't have to think about Willa's rules. It made her feel like a young girl again, certain that the world was full of fascinating information merely waiting to be discovered. That little girl had no thought of rules, because her mama and papa loved her just as she was.

She pushed the thought away, her lips drifting along the hard line of his jaw.

Alaric turned his head and took her mouth again in a languorous kiss, one that sent aching sensation down her legs and through her body until she felt as if honeyed wine was running in her veins.

Everything about Alaric, from the low rasp of his breathing to the rock-hard muscles in his shoulders, enticed her.

"Evie," he said again, some time later, his voice hoarse.

"Hmmm," Willa responded happily. She wasn't

thinking at all. Every bit of her being was enjoying this moment.

"We must stop."

"I could kiss you all night," she said with a gasp. She threaded her hands through his hair and looked at him from under her lashes.

He groaned and caught her against him, his mouth coming hard down on hers as a rumble came from his chest. The sound made her head fall back so he could devour her mouth, his tongue curling around hers, his hands spread to hold her hard against him.

"No," he said a time later. A minute or an hour. A kiss, or five kisses, or five hundred. Willa was pressing against him, trying to tempt him to run one of his hands down her back. Or, daringly, up her front. Or even through her hair.

He could loosen her braid and free her hair with his fingers. He could clasp her bottom with those strong fingers and jerk her against him.

She'd never imagined that thoughts like these would go through her mind. Dimly she remembered the bawdy freedom she felt when she and Lavinia laughed about that erotic book they found.

This was another side of that same person. A bold, lustful person. Possessive, too.

She jerked her head back, narrowing her eyes.

Alaric had a dark flush, and his eyes were gleaming with desire.

Was she merely the last of many women to see him like this?

The thought was a dash of icy water.

"Have you kissed any other women at this house party?" she asked.

An expression she couldn't interpret crossed his eyes. If it was amusement, she'd have to slay him.

"No," he said.

"Are you certain?"

It was amusement, damn it. "There was a lady a few years ago," he said musingly.

She gave him a little shove. "I didn't think you were a saint. That's not what I was asking."

He snatched her up again, kissing her until she was breathless, her mind hazy again.

"Evie."

"Hmmm?"

He laughed. "You are the most formidable, articulate woman I know, and at the same time . . ."

She traced the line of his deep bottom lip with her fingers, her eyelids growing heavy because the only thoughts in her mind were wild.

Imagining those lips caressing her body all over. Imagining moans coming from his throat as he . . .

"You're dazed."

"Hmmm."

He was laughing and she didn't care. He wasn't laughing *at* her, anyway. He was laughing with her.

"We mustn't do this," he said regretfully.

She looked at him from under her lashes and sighed. Sighed!

She never sighed.

But faced with a man like that, his eyes desirous, even sinful. His body beautiful . . .

How was she different from Helena Biddle?

She jumped back at the thought. All those women staring at Lord Wilde with lust in their eyes . . . wasn't that precisely what she was doing?

"Willa is back," he said, with something that sounded perilously like a *male* version of a sigh.

"I temporarily lost my mind," Willa acknowledged, her voice husky. She stepped back, tightening the tie on her dressing gown. He hadn't even loosened it, which distinguished him from the boys she'd kissed previously. They always sneaked a hand toward her bodice.

"As did I," he said.

They looked at each other for a moment in silence. Then he shook his head. "Saucy Evie . . . where does she go?"

There was no point in lying. He was no fool, and she'd exposed her true self in the last hour.

"She is private. You must leave."

"If you insist." He went to the door before turning.

Willa kept her chin up, absolutely certain that not a trace of emotion was revealed in her eyes. Those dark blue eyes focused on her, and something tightened and twisted deep in her belly.

"You are fearless, unafraid of me," Alaric stated.

"I see nothing to fear. You would never hurt me. Or any other woman."

He ignored her. "You respect my father, but you don't want to be a duchess. You respect Parth, but you aren't interested in him, despite the fact he's the richest man in England."

Willa shrugged. Everything he said was true.

He wasn't finished. "Your mouth damn near kills me every time I see it because I want to kiss it until it's dark red, the color it is now. It's a mouth I want to kiss me, wrap around me, bark at me . . . love me."

Willa couldn't find any words.

She thought he was going to kiss her again, but he slipped through the door, closed it behind him, and was gone.

For a moment she stood motionless, hand pressed to her lips. Then she walked to the large glass on the wall.

She was still *Willa*, wasn't she? Willa, who was extraordinarily competent, organized, curious?

Her hair had fallen from its braid in a way that suggested it had been rumpled by a lover.

And her mouth?

He was right. It was ruby red. Swollen by kisses.

He hadn't touched her, but her body felt like the map of a foreign country, an undiscovered country that he had explored without touching.

Willa didn't have absurd thoughts like that.

Evie did.

Chapter Twenty-one

Willa was rudely awakened by the force of a body landing on the bed beside her. "What?" she mumbled. She knew who it was. The scent of Lavinia's pear soap announced her presence wherever she went.

"You must wake up," Lavinia replied. "You've missed breakfast. Everyone is riding to a ruined abbey in an hour or so. Lady Knowe says that King Arthur is buried there, but I don't believe her."

"What time is it?"

"After ten o'clock. You've missed breakfast."

Snippets of thick paper were falling over Willa's face and hair. "What on earth are you doing?" she asked foggily, blowing a scrap from her lips. She sat up, sending a shower of scraps across the coverlet, and saw that Lavinia was wielding a pair of scissors, busy attacking prints. The same prints that she had until recently collected with the zeal of a true devotee.

"I have three of the new Lord Wilde prints, and I'm sacrificing the one I brought with me as well," Lavinia explained, cutting busily.

"Why are you destroying them?" Willa swung her legs over the side of the bed. "Where's Sweetpea?"

"Alaric took her for a walk."

Willa spun around. "He came to my *room*?" She did that indignant tone fairly well, considering that she had never been any good at lying.

More bits of paper flew over the bed. "You were soundly sleeping, so your maid gave him Sweetpea."

"Why are you cutting up prints?" Willa asked again, ringing the bell for tea.

"I'm turning them into decoration."

"That's Alaric's head!" Willa exclaimed, picking up one of the cuttings. "And his feet. Is that the cannibal pot?" At Lavinia's nod: "I can't believe you're cutting up your favorite print."

Lavinia's hands stilled, and she looked directly at Willa. "My mother has a terrible toothache and stayed abed herself, so no one remarked on your layabout ways—except Lord Alaric, who knew you would be tired this morning, and told me at breakfast that he would walk Sweetpea."

Willa bit her lip. "We kissed."

"Most of the night?" Lavinia demanded.

At Willa's silence, Lavinia went on. "In other exciting news, it seems my best friend has accepted an offer of marriage and *forgot to tell me!*" She slid off the bed and waved her scissors in the air. "Wilhelmina Everett, unless you have an excellent excuse—such as you kept kissing until dawn—you have some explaining to do!"

"He *told* you?" Willa gasped.

"He told everyone," Lavinia said. "Willa, did you let that man spend the night in your chamber?"

"Absolutely not! It's not a real betrothal," Willa admitted. "You know that I would have woken you up and told you myself if I had accepted a proposal, no matter what the time of night."

"Not a real betrothal?" Lavinia said, gaping at her. "What other sort of betrothal is there? Lord Alaric informed the entire breakfast table of your not-so-real future together. Although he neglected to mention that he had asked you for your hand at extremely close quarters—in this very room!"

"That is not what happened," Willa protested. "We are not engaged to marry."

Lavinia sank back on the bed. "Why not? I no longer want him for myself—thus my demolishment of his image—but I quite *like* him, which is far better than worshiping him."

"We are pretending a betrothal in order to dissuade a deranged woman. Your newfound affection for Alaric is not a sufficient reason for me to marry him!"

"As your closest friend, I naturally—" Lavinia stopped short, her mouth forming a perfect O. "Prudence Larkin! I met her at breakfast, where she shared her feelings far and wide. I have to say that it made me ashamed of my former adoration."

"Did she tell you that she wrote the play?"

Lavinia nodded. "You're truly not betrothed?"

Willa shook her head.

"I'm disappointed," Lavinia said, picking up her scissors and assaulting another print. "I do like him. Much more than I did when I adored him," she added with a faint look of surprise. Then she turned back to trimming the scrap of paper. More snippets fell onto the coverlet. "Because there isn't enough thrilling gossip to go around, Diana told me this morning that she is pretty certain she's going to jilt Lord Roland."

"Oh no," Willa groaned.

"Her precise words were, 'I can't bear my life, and I hate my fiancé.'"

"Mrs. Belgrave will be furious," Willa said, picturing the lady's gasping face. "It's lucky for Diana that her mother stayed in London. She has her heart set on the match."

"Diana does not. Oh, I almost forgot," Lavinia said, putting down her scissors and reaching into her pocket. She dropped a gaudy locket into Willa's hand. "You are engaged to Lord Wilde—at least outwardly—so obviously, this should be yours."

It was large, with an ornate W enclosed by a heart engraved on the front.

Willa flicked the catch. Inside was Alaric's face, cut from an engraving. "You need to practice your scissor work," she said. "You didn't make it a proper oval and he almost lost an ear."

"Would you prefer one in which he's wearing an admiral's hat? I have one of those, never mind Lord Alaric has had nothing to do with His Majesty's Navy."

"This will do," Willa said. She clicked the locket closed.

"You must wear it outside your gown today, so Prudence Larkin can see it," Lavinia said. "She told everyone at breakfast that she wrote the play because she was fated by God to be Lord Alaric's wife. Diana inquired if she was referring to a Greek or some other heathen deity—because the Anglican God isn't usually seen as a matchmaker—and Miss Larkin was not amused."

Willa groaned.

"But she wasn't truly overset until Lady Knowe pointed out that Prudence was acting as if Alaric were the god of her idolatry. At that point the lady became entirely incoherent. I thought she was going to fling her toast across the table."

"I shall never wear that locket," Willa said. She hated the play, and everything it had done to Alaric without his permission. She hated the locket, too, though she might put Alaric's picture in the exquisite locket that Diana had given her.

"The party is entertained by the news of your betrothal, except the ladies who had hoped to talk him into their beds," Lavinia said, picking up the last print and cutting a circle around Alaric's face. "I doubt Eliza Kennet will ever speak to you again, although that's not much of a loss, seeing as her conversation is limited to discussion of your fiancé."

General knowledge of the sham betrothal was such a terrifying notion that Willa felt unable to respond. Last night, she had stepped in to help without a second thought. But now . . .

"What are you doing with those cuttings?" she asked, pushing panic away.

"I'm going to paste the heads onto a sheet and paint gold halos on them, so that Alaric will never forget the heyday of his popularity."

Willa groaned. "He'll hate that."

"I know!" Lavinia grinned. "I might give you my artwork. For when you marry that dusty, boring scholar, the one with skinny thighs and a perfectly kempt wig."

"I never said I wanted to marry a scholar." But Willa had imagined just that. Scholars were so precise with their language. Comfortingly knowledgeable.

Lavinia patted her leg and went on snipping.

Willa opened the locket again and looked at Alaric's face.

"You'd better ring for a bath because Lady Knowe might come fetch you herself." Lavinia scrambled off the bed, leaving scraps of paper strewn over the counterpane. "She is determined to impress Prudence with your closeness to Alaric."

Willa was still thinking about Prudence an hour later, after her bath, as she put on her favorite riding habit. The skirt was crimson, worn with a white waistcoat under a tight crimson riding coat that opened in a dramatic fashion over her bosom. The matching straw hat was worn at an angle, and adorned with black plumes.

It was masculine, almost military, at the same time emphasizing her every curve. A neckcloth edged in white lace provided a feminine finishing touch.

A missionary's daughter would never wear anything so provocative.

Looking in the glass as she put on riding gloves, Willa felt better. It wasn't going to be easy to look Alaric straight in the eyes. Not after last night.

After those kisses.

But the riding habit helped. She felt braver in it. More in control. Not a woman joining a horde of admirers.

For some reason, it felt essential that he recognize that. She was edging toward a decision. Did she want to be Willa for the rest of her life? Or was she brave enough to marry a man who saw her as Evie?

Yet what if Alaric grew tired of England and English society? Or Willa? Or Evie?

Chapter Twenty-two

Willa arrived in the entry of the castle to discover that the party had already set out for the stables.

"It's a walk of a few minutes only," Prism told her. "Roberts will escort you."

"No, thank you," Willa said, straightening her hat to make certain that the sun would not touch her face. "I shall enjoy the walk."

"You cannot miss the stables if you keep to the path," Prism said, looking very disapproving at the idea that a young lady would venture to walk in the open air without escort.

She strolled out the great front doors of the castle, and followed a footpath that wound down a sweep of emerald-green lawn toward a riot of violet, burgundy, and pale pink rhododendrons at the bottom. The path curved alongside the flowering bushes, first skirting a beech wood and then ducking into it.

The woods were pleasantly cool, and Willa walked slowly as a heady smell of horse and straw began to eclipse the honey-nutmeg scent of the rhododendrons. The path turned again and opened on the stables.

If Prism had a sense of humor—which Willa thought unlikely—she would have judged his comment that she couldn't miss the stables a dry jest. The duke's stables were larger than most mansions, composed of a sprawling series of low barns surrounded by paddocks, any number of gallops, and training yards. One lush field held five foals madly racing each other about, and beyond that were snug cottages, presumably for the grooms and their families.

The largest paddock was crowded with people and horses, dotted with the duke's grooms wearing their dark ruby livery with almond-colored trim. Willa caught sight of Lavinia's guinea-bright hair amidst a crowd of gentlemen, her riding hat bedecked with a green feather.

She walked through the gate into the yard, and was looking about, wondering if there was a horse for her, when a large, warm nose nudged her neck, bringing with it the smell of fresh straw and clean horse.

"Your mount," said a deep voice.

Her heart leapt to her throat.

Alaric held the reins of a raw-boned black steed and a sweet-faced mare with a patch over her right eye. "I wasn't certain of your prowess in the saddle," he said. "This is Buttercup. She's not as young as she was, but she has a lovely seat."

He transferred the reins to a groom and put his hands on Willa's waist. She felt a surge of gratitude for her French corset.

"Do you have a whip?" Alaric asked, not yet lifting her onto her horse. He was standing entirely too close. And smiling down at her.

"Yes," she said with a little gasp. "I mean, no, I don't use a whip."

"Right." He effortlessly swung her into the air, placing her on the saddle. He turned away to help another lady onto her mount.

As Willa adjusted her leg over the pommel, Lavinia pranced over, riding a lovely sorrel mare.

"Thank goodness you're here!" she called. She gestured behind her. "These gentlemen simply won't accept that I have no need for an escort. They can escort the both of us."

Willa greeted two young lords and a future earl with a smile, and the five of them joined the rest as they all moved onto the road at an easy amble.

It was a perfectly splendid early-July day, and at least twenty-five gentlemen and ladies, laughing and talking, made up the riding party. Alaric was somewhere behind Willa's and Lavinia's small group. They set out at a walk, on a road bounded by hedges entangled with wild roses. The ditches were starred with great wheels of cow parsley.

After a few minutes, Mr. Sterling caught up, and his horse paced alongside Willa's. Lavinia kept flitting past and making inane remarks to him that made a pulse beat in his jaw.

"You must stop that," Willa said later, when their two horses were walking side by side. "You're teasing Mr. Sterling unnecessarily."

Lavinia bestowed a smile on her nearest swain. "What on earth do you mean?"

"You know he hates empty-headed society chitchat, and you're willfully inundating him with it."

Lavinia laughed. The merry peal made all the men around them turn to look at her—except Mr. Sterling, whose eyes remained fixed straight ahead.

"Like that," Willa said. "I don't know why you bother."

"He's such an ass," Lavinia said, *sotto voce.* "By the way, Prudence doesn't know how to ride, so she's in one of those carriages that went ahead. Oh, and look! Fiendish Sterling is getting in another argument."

Sure enough, Mr. Sterling—who did seem to be a trifle irritable—had started trading insults with Lord Roland.

"Where is Diana?"

Lavinia wrinkled her nose. "At the last minute, she told my mother that she was indisposed."

They were silent. There was no need to voice their shared opinion that Diana was doing herself no favors by fibbing.

"We're stopping for luncheon at that inn," Lavinia said, nodding toward a large building a short distance ahead. Men in the Duke of Lindow's livery were spilling out, waiting to take their mounts.

Behind the inn, a grassy bank shaded by huge willow trees led down to a river that ran flat and wide before winding out of sight. Snowy cloths and soft pillows had been set on the ground, and a picnic lunch was being laid out.

"I'm positively famished," Lavinia said. "Do you know what Despicable Sterling said to me at breakfast?"

"If you would stop taunting him, he'd probably let you be," Willa said.

"He said I was double-chinned!"

"I doubt that," Willa said. "For one thing, he wouldn't insult you, and for another, you aren't."

"In as many words," Lavinia retorted. "He said I ate like a horse and that I'd have a double chin by next week."

"What did you say to him to provoke it?"

Lavinia turned her mare at the gate of the inn. "I merely noted that if he ate all the bacon he had on his plate he'd end up looking like a poke pudding. I said 'if.' Whereas he as much as called me a lumpish hag."

Before Willa could answer, Alaric drew up beside her. In one smooth movement, he dismounted, tossed his reins to a waiting groom, and raised his arms to help her down.

He had removed his coat at some point and slung it over his saddle's pommel. Gentlemen never did that . . . but here he was, his white shirt tight against the planes of his chest.

"If you think I'm going to allow one of those fribbles to put his hands on you, you're wrong," he said, in a conversational tone. The three men didn't even try to compete; they turned to cluster about Lavinia instead.

Willa felt her cheeks growing hot. "You're making a show of me."

"The better to thwart Prudence," he said, grinning

as he scratched Buttercup's nose. "How did you do with this darling?"

"She's lovely," Willa said. And then she leaned forward into his hands because what else could she do?

A moment later her feet were on the ground, except he was standing entirely too close for propriety, crowding her against Buttercup's broad, warm side.

Willa wasn't used to feeling lightheaded and happy. Giddy, almost.

"You don't have Sweetpea stowed in a pocket, do you?" he asked. His hands slid down her back.

"Certainly not," Willa managed. "What if I dropped her? Or if I fell from the horse?"

"Are you likely to fall?"

Willa had the sudden conviction that if she said yes, he would forbid her to ride home. She could see it in his eyes. "No," she admitted. And then she smiled, because it was just so . . . *heady* to see that ferociously protective look in Alaric Wilde's eyes. She hadn't fallen off a horse since . . .

Actually, she'd never fallen off a horse.

"Willa!" Lavinia called.

Alaric stepped back, and she took a deep breath. He smelled of mint, and leather, and horsehair.

"Are you going to put your coat back on?" she inquired.

He reached out and grabbed it from the pommel just before a groom led his mount away. "If you wish me to."

"It's proper."

"You are not a proper young lady, Evie," he said in a low voice. "We both know that."

Had she thought his eyes protective? Now they were greedy. Willa wanted to take a gulp of air, but that would be too revealing. She tried to ignore her trembling knees.

"Are you hungry?" she asked.

His answer was tense, low. "Yes."

Willa made a face. "Stop that!"

"I can't." He stepped forward and brought his mouth to her ear. "I rode behind you all the way here. Your waist is enough to make me cry. But when Buttercup trotted and you bent forward, bottom in the air?"

He pulled back and met her eyes. His had turned smoky and dark. For a second, she had a sense of vertigo. Was this Lord Wilde—the man whom most of the female half of England adored—looking at her? Like that?

"You drive me mad," he said, his voice rasping.

Willa turned and marched toward the inn; it was either that, or yield, as she had last night, and kiss him.

"I stayed behind you on the road first, so that

I could enjoy the view, and second, so that no other man could," Alaric said at her back, keeping pace with her. They were ushered around the side of the building. "The meal isn't ready," he observed. Sure enough, serving people were still dashing in and out of the inn. "Are you hungry?"

She nodded. She'd risen so late that she hadn't had time for breakfast. "Wait for me," he said, striding forward.

Willa never obeyed men who gave orders; it set a bad precedent. But she stood as if her feet were rooted to the ground, watching as Alaric snatched up a loaf of bread and block of cheese. A bottle of wine and a couple of glasses.

Whatever he had in mind, it would not be proper. Willa was certain of it.

A voice inside was shrieking about her reputation. If Lady Gray even dreamed that Willa had allowed a man into her bedchamber last night, Lavinia's mother—her guardian—would quickly declare her ruined. *Ruined.*

Which translated to soon to be married.

Willa—docile perfect Willa—had been shoved to the side, and the girl who stood under the eaves of the inn, waiting for the absolutely wrong man to return to her . . .

Evie was waiting, not Willa.

Lavinia appeared at her side. "Do you know what that man just said to me?" she demanded.

"I said nothing importune," Parth Sterling snarled from behind her. His eyes were furious.

Lavinia wheeled around and pointed a finger, which was so impolite Willa could scarcely believe she was seeing it. "You said I was an ill-tempered harpy."

He folded his arms over his chest. Quite a broad chest, Willa couldn't help noticing. "If you don't want to be insulted, you shouldn't work so hard at making a nuisance of yourself."

Alaric was coming toward them, with Prudence— whose gown had a snowy-white collar that seemed to Willa ostentatiously Puritan—in hot pursuit. "Good morning, Lord Alaric," Prudence cried, reaching them and dropping a curtsy so deep that her knee nearly brushed the ground.

"Good morning, Miss Larkin," Alaric said. "You will remember my *fiancée*?"

Prudence's mouth tightened, and to Willa's surprise, an ugly look flashed through her eyes.

"Miss Larkin," Willa said, keeping it short. From what she'd seen during their ride, the announcement of her betrothal had had a dampening effect on his admirers, but of course Prudence had an ingrained tendency to ignore inconvenient facts.

"If you'll excuse us, Miss Larkin, we have made plans for a stroll," Alaric said.

Prudence stepped backward, waving her hand gracefully. "I would never deny you any pleasure, my lord."

Willa wanted to bare her teeth, but instead she took Alaric's arm. "Where shall we go?" she murmured.

"Out of sight," he replied grimly.

Lavinia bestowed a beatific smile on Mr. Sterling, just the kind they all knew he loathed. "Yes, I would love to go for a stroll with you," she trilled, tucking her hand through his arm. "Thank you for asking. I believe I'll address you as Parth, and you must call me Lavinia."

"That is more honor than I deserve," Mr. Sterling retorted.

"Nonsense! Alaric and I are on a first-name basis, obviously, since he is marrying my best friend. Just think how often we will find ourselves together in the coming years!"

She flashed a smile at Willa. "You must call him Parth as well, Willa," she said, blithely ignoring the fact that her escort's eyes were emitting sparks.

"I would be honored," Mr. Sterling—no, Parth— said to Willa, managing to sound genuinely pleased.

"I'd be happy if you addressed me as Willa."

Alaric tossed the bottle to Parth, who snatched it from the air. His hand now free, Alaric took Willa's arm and drew it close to his side.

The four of them followed the river until it wound away from the road between two fields. Cushions of violet-blue wildflowers and sweet-smelling lavender lined the water, which had turned from dark turquoise to pale and shimmering.

"Let's stop here," Lavinia said, walking over to sit beneath a willow, so tall and lush that it looked like a pale green fountain.

"Did anyone ever tell you just how much a man appreciates a riding habit such as the one you are wearing?" Alaric asked Willa, as she followed Lavinia.

"One assumes," she said.

"I don't often have the impulse to revere a piece of clothing," he said. "But your rear in those skirts, Evie . . ."

"Hush," she ordered, looking over her shoulder. She faltered at the look in his eyes and turned about. "Why are you flirting with me? You are an explorer. You'll board a ship and sail off . . . somewhere. I, on the other hand, have a domestic frame of mind."

That slashing eyebrow of his went up. "Domestic, are you? I'm glad to have the proper adjective. I had been trying some out in my mind."

She wouldn't ask, she wouldn't ask.

"'Domestic' wasn't one of them," he said, his eyes dancing.

If he imagined she would board a ship and explore the pirate latitudes with him, he was sadly mistaken. That was her father. No, her mother. She clearly remembered her mother's laughter, the morning her parents had taken off on that madcap race. They'd scarcely kissed her farewell.

"Willa!" Lavinia called. Sunbeams were breaking through the branches and creating a halo around her hair. She looked positively angelic. "Come join me."

"We'll have to share glasses," Alaric said when they reached the willow. He pulled a knife from his boot, flipped it open, and made quick work of the wine cork.

Lavinia took a sip of the wine he gave her, and passed the glass to Parth, fluttering her eyelashes as she did so.

He gave her a look of round dislike and took a deep draught.

"You're such a gentleman," she cooed, snatching the glass from him and drinking the rest. "Parth, would you mind terribly lending me your coat so I can lie down on this bank?"

Without a word, he wrenched off his coat and handed it to her.

"Thank you!" Lavinia cried, dropping it on the grass. Then she lay back, wiggling a bit until she was comfortable—and perhaps until the coat had acquired a grass stain or two. "Willa, do join me. Parth's girth is such that I'm sure we can both fit."

Willa unpinned her wide straw hat. Alaric's mouth brushed by her ear as he murmured, "You could have balanced a fruit platter on top of that thing."

She smiled. "I'll have you know, sir, that this is an exceedingly fashionable hat."

Lavinia lay against the emerald grass, buttery curls spread about her shoulders, eyes closed in an expression of pure contentment. Parth was staring out at the water, brow furrowed.

Alaric shook out his coat and spread it on the grass next to Parth's. Willa lay back, shoulder bumping Lavinia's, and squinted up at the sky through the willow spears. "You're going to get freckles on your nose, and your mother will be overset."

"Mmmm," Lavinia said sleepily. "I love it when the sun is warm on my face."

Alaric watched the two of them with amusement. Willa's closest friend was a diabolical woman, which said something about his future wife's personality.

"Think you can still skip a rock five times?" he asked Parth.

Parth instantly headed for the placid river. "You've kept your arm," he said, when they'd both hurled enough rocks to work up a heat.

Alaric took careful aim and skipped a rock seven times.

Behind them came a drowsy murmur of women's voices. He could pick out Willa's voice beneath Lavinia's lighter one. Lavinia always seemed to be on the verge of laughing, whereas Willa was an observer.

And a doer, he reminded himself.

He had the impression that Willa quietly managed the lives of a great many people around her. Lavinia's, for one. Lady Gray's, for another.

He drew back his arm thoughtfully. Life was an odd thing. He'd spent years floating around the world, only to come home and discover that he had an anchor waiting.

"I cannot bear that woman," Parth said quietly. "May I return to the inn now? Please?"

"You sound like an eight-year-old trying to shirk Latin class."

"I'd *do* a Latin tutorial to get away."

Alaric glanced back. The two prettiest girls in the world were lying side by side. Lavinia had an arm behind her head, a position that had a truly magnificent effect on her bosom.

Rather to his surprise, he wasn't interested. *He wasn't interested.* There was a distinct possibility that the man who wasn't interested in Lavinia Gray's breasts was dead.

Or something.

"If I leave, she'll think she's won."

Alaric shrugged, but before he came up with an answer, Parth muttered a curse, hauled off his boots, and headed into the water.

"What are you doing?" Alaric shouted. Behind him, Willa sat up. He couldn't see her, but he knew she sat up because . . .

Because he knew.

"There's something trapped in that tree," Parth shouted back. He was in up to his hips, plowing at a steady pace toward a tangle of tree limbs caught on a large rock in the middle of the water.

By the time Lavinia and Willa had come to their feet and joined Alaric at the water's edge, only Parth's head and shoulders remained above the surface.

"Excuse me, ladies," Alaric said, tossing his topboots well up onto the grass. "I believe I'll see whether Parth could use some help."

The water was warm, likely because the river was so shallow. When Alaric reached Parth, he had one arm buried to the shoulder in the tangle.

"Damn it," he bit out. "It scratched me."

"What is it?"

"Cat," he grunted. A furious howl came from inside the branches as he brought his arm back out, the drenched animal clutched in his hand.

Alaric burst out laughing. Parth had hold of the ugliest, scraggiest, and downright most hideous cat he'd ever seen. It was hissing and spitting like a teakettle on the boil, ears flat to its sodden head.

No, its single remaining ear was back.

"I don't believe he likes me," Parth said, straight-faced. The cat was twisting wildly in the air, scratching at him.

Alaric bellowed his laughter and headed back to shore. When the water was waist-high, he realized that his shirt clung to every ridge of the muscles that encircled his body.

He couldn't stop himself from grinning as he strode toward Willa. She was looking at him, a little dazed, her mouth slightly open. For her part, Lavinia was watching with pleasure as Parth wrestled the yowling tomcat.

The water was at Alaric's knees by the time Willa's eyes jerked above his waistband, her mouth snapping shut. "I'm afraid to say that I cannot ride on to King Arthur's grave," he said, splashing onto the bank. He spread his arms and sure enough, Willa's eyes drifted down his body again.

Parth strode by him, clutching the cat by the front and back legs, so it was rendered more or less immobile. "That's an ugly cat," Alaric said, impressed. It had lost fur on one haunch and there was an old scar across its nose.

Willa laughed. "He's almost as scarred as you are."

Alaric caught her hand, pulling her against his body. She gave a little shriek. "You're wet!"

His drenched shirt meant that he felt every bit of her bosom.

"You may not kiss me," she commanded in a low voice. But her eyes were shining.

"I want you," he said, low-voiced. "Damn it, Willa, these breeches are as protective as wet paper. My front is likely a crime in some part of the country."

"You must return to the castle," she said, stepping backward. Obviously she knew what he was talking about. She had *felt* it.

"That cat resembles you, Parth," Lavinia announced behind them.

Alaric wove his fingers through Willa's and turned. "Scrappy, lame, angry . . ."

The cat had stopped twisting and was hanging

from Parth's hands, making a good show of looking submissive.

Unless you caught the maddened look in its eye. It was merely biding its time.

Lavinia sauntered over. "I'll fetch your coat, Alaric," she cooed. "We wouldn't want you to take a chill."

Parth snatched up his coat and bundled the cat so only its furious head was visible. "You were so touched when Alaric bought that baby skunk for Willa," he said to Lavinia, a smile just touching the edges of his hard mouth. "Sweetpea's soft fur, dark eyes, and affectionate ways are a perfect match for her new owner."

Lavinia's smile cooled.

"I'll bring this creature back to the castle for you," Parth said cheerfully. "My present."

Chapter Twenty-three

Lavinia was rarely spitting angry, but she was now. "That man is arrogant, impossible, and just plain rude," she said, striding up and down Willa's bedchamber, too cross to sit.

Willa was curled in an armchair, snuggling Sweetpea. Parth Sterling had made good on his promise—or threat?—to make a present of the rescued cat; the beast had hurled himself through the door opening onto Willa's balcony, and had flattened against the stone balustrade outside. Occasionally he let out a low curse in cat language, meant to discourage anyone from encroaching on his territory.

"Are you laughing?" Lavinia demanded, swinging about.

"No!" Willa said. "That screeching noise is your cat."

"*My* cat! *My* cat! I don't want a bloody cat," Lavinia wailed. "I don't even like animals. You're the one who wants a cat. I'm giving him to you."

"I have Sweetpea," Willa said, alarmed. "I don't need a cat."

"Sterling is the most gratuitously rude man I have ever met. Ever." Out on the balcony, the tomcat continued to hiss, throwing in a little yowl now and then for variety. Lavinia continued to do the same, in English.

"Parth will be gone by the time you return from Manchester," Willa said consolingly, during a pause. "He's not a man of leisure."

Lavinia's face brightened. "Oh! I'd forgotten Mother and I leave for Manchester tomorrow! Are you certain you don't wish to join us, Willa?"

"I can't leave Sweetpea," Willa said, "and your mother would not enjoy her as a traveling companion. It's only a few days, and Lady Knowe will be an excellent chaperone."

"I shall miss you, but perhaps it's just as well; you should keep an eye on Prudence," Lavinia said. "I wouldn't put it past her to contrive a situation in which Alaric supposedly compromises her."

"Prism has already thought of that. The location of Alaric's bedchamber is a closely guarded secret." She wrinkled her nose. "I'm of the opinion that a frank conversation with her might solve the problem, but Alaric doesn't agree."

Alaric didn't believe that he needed anyone to champion him, but Willa disagreed. He never showed his feelings when women besieged him, but he hated it. Prudence represented the worst kind of devotee.

Lavinia shook her head. "She's not like one of his typical admirers. I'm afraid of her."

"That's absurd," Willa said, laughing. "She's merely another woman in love with Lord Wilde, albeit more zealous than most."

Willa had the distinct impression that Alaric was keeping Prudence in the castle because it allowed him to continue to claim her as his fiancée. It was a heady thought—a duke's son wanted her that much.

"Are you sure you won't come to Manchester?"

"I really can't."

"Perhaps I can convince Diana to join us. We have more than enough room in the carriage."

"If she were to agree, it would be to escape the company of Lord Roland," Willa said wryly.

"For now, I'm going to take a nap." Lavinia stretched her arms toward the ceiling. "Why, why do I allow that ill-tempered fellow to vex me so?" She poked her head onto the balcony, which provoked an ear-piercing yowl, and withdrew it quickly. "I was merely jesting about giving you the mongrel cat. I'll ask to have a groom take it to the stables."

Willa frowned. The poor animal was so terrified that she hated to think of him being manhandled immediately. "Leave him there for the time being," she said. "He used Sweetpea's box, which I thought was quite intelligent. And he devoured the chicken I gave him."

"Naturally he ate the chicken. I can see every one of his ribs. Don't grow fond of that ugly creature, because I forbid you to keep it. I don't want any memories of Appalling Parth."

"I won't," Willa promised. She stood up and put Sweetpea into her basket by the fireplace. "A nap sounds lovely; I believe I'll take one as well."

"Do you need me to help with your riding habit before I go?" Lavinia asked. "My maid took a half-holiday, as did yours."

Since the house party was supposedly exploring King Arthur's tomb, the butler had given the personal servants a holiday.

Willa shook her head. "Everything fastens in front, including my corset. You?"

"As well." Another pitiable screech came from the balcony. "I think I'll name that animal Parth," Lavinia said thoughtfully.

"Parth is an overly refined name for that particular cat," Willa said, joining her in the balcony doorway.

The tomcat had wedged himself into the corner of the marble balustrade. His fur had dried in mangy patches. "How about Hannibal?" Willa asked.

"Wasn't Hannibal a military commander?" Lavinia asked. "This cat looks nothing like a soldier."

"I don't agree; he's clearly a fighter!"

After the door closed behind Lavinia, Willa stripped to her chemise and collapsed on the cool linen sheets with a sigh. A peppery-sweet scent drifted into the bedroom from the balcony. Mignonette, perhaps, or roses.

She closed her eyes and thought about Alaric, emerging like Poseidon from the river, his thin shirt clinging to the sleek muscles of his abdomen. She'd never realized how much fun it would be to be *naughty*.

Sinful, even.

She stretched, thinking perhaps . . . but it was daytime. She didn't want to pull covers over herself, since the afternoon was hot and sultry.

Instead she curled up on her side, imagining that Alaric had followed her up the stairs. Imaginary Alaric entered her room and peeled off his shirt, tossing it to the side, a roguish smile on his face.

Would he say something? Quote poetry? Perhaps

poetry that talked of exploration—say, John Donne's "Oh, my America, my newfound land"?

No.

In Willa's estimation—she was a virgin, but she'd made a study of men—Alaric would give her a heavy-lidded look and not bother with speech.

Her imagination first placed his hands on her back; now it willed them to her front. Her breasts were smaller than Lavinia's, but they were nicely shaped, and in her imagination they fit neatly into his cupped hands. By the time her daydream became a little fuzzy, Alaric had lost his riding breeches. She wasn't entirely sure what he would look like unclothed, so she drifted off to sleep thinking it over.

She and Lavinia had studied the male anatomy, having found a couple of risqué books in Lord Gray's library. But they had decided the depictions of male anatomy contained therein had to be exaggerated.

But . . . in light of Alaric's wet breeches?

Perhaps not.

When his knock remained unanswered after several long moments, Alaric pushed open the door of Willa's bedchamber. It wasn't as if Sweetpea could answer, and a handkerchief full of roly-polies could scarcely be left in the hallway.

Willa was likely in the drawing room, or in the garden with Lavinia—

No.

She was curled on top of her bed, asleep. She'd unpinned her hair; dusky curls spread over the pillow. Dark eyelashes lay on her cheeks, a pink stain on her cheekbones, and her beautiful mouth was curved in a very slight smile. She was wearing a scrap of fabric that had drawn up tight around her thighs.

He froze, gaping at her with the handkerchief of roly-polies in one hand and the open door in the other. When his gentleman's training reasserted itself, he looked away, his eyes traveling slowly around her room as he weighed whether to quietly retreat or to give Sweetpea an afternoon snack. He'd gone to the trouble of finding the things, after all. It'd be a shame to deny Sweetpea.

The hell with it. He had never been very good at being a gentleman. He closed the door and stepped toward the little skunk's basket, not looking back at the bed—and uttered an involuntary curse.

The basket contained the blighted tomcat Parth had insisted on bringing back from the river. The cat fixed an eye on Alaric, and his single ear flattened against his head as he emitted a threatening rumble that sounded like a far-off thunderstorm.

Nestled in the center of a half-circle of matted orange fur was Sweetpea, her nose resting peacefully on one of the cat's paws. Alaric took a step closer and the tom's mangy tail rose in the air and thumped down once.

Right.

He emptied the contents of the handkerchief into the basket and stepped away.

Willa was his, though she didn't know it. And didn't believe it. Possibly didn't want him.

No, she did want him. She'd trembled all over when he kissed her. Her eyes had clung to his chest when he walked from the water. They had dipped below his waist, and stayed there when he emerged in skintight, wet breeches. Since he had a constant cockstand around her, she had had an eyeful.

Alaric went over to the bed and carefully lowered himself until he lay alongside her. Then he ran his hand down the riotous curls that fell over Willa's shoulders. He didn't let himself look below her neck.

Gaping at a woman while she slept was distasteful, but brushing his lips along the warm curve of her cheek?

Waking her up?

"Evie," he whispered, hoping his voice would drift into her dreams, rather than startle her.

"Mmmm," she sighed.

Mine, said the beats of his heart.

"May I kiss you?"

She didn't respond, so he slid his lips past the arch of her cheekbone to the silky gloss of her hair, and then to the delicate pink curve of her small ear. He was still kissing her ear when she made a happy sound and curled against him.

Alaric froze. His blood was pounding through his body and his cock was so stiff that it hurt.

"What did you say?" he whispered.

"You're talking," she said, sounding inebriated. "For . . ." Her voice drifted away and she turned onto her back.

"Evie," Alaric said, after a few seconds' thought informed him a gentleman would not ease her chemise farther up her leg.

He had to wake her. He propped himself up on one elbow, kissing her face in earnest, kissing her forehead, the small bridge of her nose, the rounded point of her chin.

She sighed, opening her lips. He was about to kiss her, really kiss her, when he realized that if he was kissing Willa Everett, he wanted her to be fully aware.

He nipped her bottom lip and whispered, "Wake up."

She sighed and one hand flattened against his chest. He watched in amusement as her fingers flexed . . .

Her eyes popped open.

Another woman might have yelped or even screamed.

But Willa looked at him and said sleepily, "Alaric, what are you doing in my bed?"

"Lying next to you." He met her eyes just long enough to make sure that she understood he wasn't a figment of her imagination—and that she had no intention of pushing him out of her bed.

Her blue eyes were no longer dreamy, but curious. Desirous. He bent over and kissed her hard and hungrily, his fingers sinking into her curls.

To his enormous satisfaction, Willa wound her arms around his neck as if he'd woken her like this a hundred times before. Which he had every intention of doing. A silent promise arrowed through him.

He would do whatever it took to convince her that he was the only man who would ever wake her with a kiss.

Chapter Twenty-four

Willa threw herself into Alaric's kiss the way a moth throws itself at a candle.

His kiss had a hint of the unknown, and at the same time, there was something familiar about it. He smelled a bit like the river, and a lot like lemon soap. He tasted a bit like Alaric and a lot like spearmint. He felt . . .

Bringing her hands down from his neck and resting them on his shoulders fogged her brain and she couldn't come up with a suitable comparison. Sleek muscles flexed under her hands and her pulse quickened.

"I . . ." she gasped.

Alaric pulled himself away with a mumbled word.

"What did you just say?" she asked.

"I can't repeat it in a lady's presence." That was a *wicked* smile. Sinful.

"You already said it, so you might as well repeat it."

"A man can take only so many liberties in one day," Alaric told her. His face was so close to hers that she could see that his eyelashes, a dark golden brown, turned to pure gold at the tips.

She brushed his right eyelash with a finger. "They are beautiful."

"What?"

"Your eyelashes. They're two colors."

He propped himself up on one elbow. "Yours are mink brown, and they curl up at the ends."

"Sometimes I color them black." Willa was trying hard to be casual under non-casual circumstances, but it was difficult. Her legs were trembling, for one thing, and she felt as if she were growing more rosy by the moment.

His eyes were ranging over her face, and although she didn't know what he was thinking, she knew he approved.

Willa cleared her throat, thinking it was time she suggest that he lever himself into a standing position and leave.

He must have seen it in her eyes, because he promptly kissed her again. She hadn't had much experience with this sort of kissing—the kind that seared her bones and her lungs with heat and made her feel breathless and hungry for more.

One kiss led to another, or perhaps it was all the same kiss. After a while, Alaric wound his fingers back into her hair. Willa decided he was ensuring that he didn't run his hands down her thighs, or over her breasts, or any of the places that were aching for his touch.

"Alaric," she murmured, the word sounding unnervingly like a plea.

His shoulders bunched under her fingers as the delicious weight of his chest lifted away. His eyes had turned the steely blue of the ocean where it's deep and cold.

But his eyes were not cold.

"Evie," he answered, giving her a small, secret smile.

"Do you mind if I ask you a question?" If they were to keep kissing, she had to—to understand him better.

"Anything."

"What kept you away from England for so long?"

He had been watching her, but as he thought about her question, he turned onto his back and stared at the stone ceiling far above them.

"Horatius died," he said, his voice flattening. "I couldn't imagine the castle without him. I loathed Lindow Moss because he lost his life there. I didn't come home because it allowed me to pretend he wasn't dead. That everyone I loved was still here."

"I'm sorry," Willa said, carefully. "I've heard of him, but we never met."

A large, warm hand caught hers and held it against his chest. "I don't think you would have liked him, at least, not until you came to know him very well."

"Certainly I would have," Willa said stoutly.

His eyes glinted at her, full of laughter. "Why do people always assume that the dead must have been delightful? Horatius was a royal ass. I loved him, but you wouldn't have."

"You don't know my preferences," Willa said.

"I know you do not like pretentious people. The color of your eyes changes when you think someone is being absurd. Horatius was often absurd."

Since she'd never seen her eyes in that circumstance, she could hardly counter his observation.

"He was as stuffed full of virtue as a pincushion is with pins," Alaric continued, his hand pressing hers tightly against his chest. "He was so intent on perfection that his halo gleamed. If there's a heaven, he's up there with a banner establishing that his is the topmost cloud. His harp is the largest."

"You wouldn't want him to be on a basement cloud," Willa pointed out. "May I ask how he died? I mean, I know he died in Lindow Moss, but what happened?"

Alaric turned his head again and met her eyes. "Foolishness. It's not impossible to cross the bog at night, but he was drunk."

Willa's fingers tightened on the warm muscles layering his chest. "I'm sorry," she whispered, leaning over and kissing his jaw.

"He was such a fool," Alaric said. "If you ever find yourself caught in the bog, don't move until you're rescued." His voice was sad, with a tinge of anger. "We couldn't even recover his body. He has a gravestone, but the coffin was empty."

"For years, I was furious at my parents for dying and leaving me," Willa offered.

"Raging at the dead is useless," Alaric said.

"I suppose it feels better to be distracted by foreign places."

Alaric rolled again and she found herself on her back.

"This is *so* improper," she gasped. "You must leave."

"I know," Alaric said, grinning at her. "But we're getting married, so it's all right."

"I haven't made up my mind," she countered.

"I've already begun providing for you. I brought Sweetpea roly-polies."

His eyes crinkled at the corners in a way that made Willa's heart skip a beat. It was intoxicating.

She sat up and pushed her chemise back down her legs. "You must leave, Alaric."

He sat up as well, winding his arms around her waist from behind. "Look at Sweetpea's basket."

Willa turned her head—and gasped. The baby skunk was splayed on her back, eyes happily closed, while Hannibal placidly washed her belly.

"Oh my," Willa breathed.

Alaric pushed her curls aside and kissed her neck. The brush of his lips made Willa feel raw and new. Vulnerable. She pulled free and got off the bed. "Please go."

A flash of disappointment crossed Alaric's eyes that made Willa's stomach roil.

"I would like to marry you," he stated, standing up.

She silently registered those words. He'd said them with about as much passion as one might mention a partiality for pears over apples. If there was one thing she was very good at, after her first Season, it was refusing offers of marriage.

"I am sorry to decline," she said, making up her mind. "I couldn't—I *cannot* marry someone whose life is shared by so many."

A nerve jerked in his jaw. "My life is not *shared*."

"Your many admirers would disagree."

"You have many admirers of your own. According to my aunt, half of London proposed marriage to you in the last few months."

She wrinkled her nose. "Those proposals reflect my penchant for following society's rules, along with the fortune my parents left me."

"In case you are wondering, I didn't know you have a fortune and I have no need of it. I'd note that your beauty is a factor as well."

She shrugged before she remembered that she never shrugged. "That too."

"Your personality."

"Lavinia and I present ourselves as ideal young ladies. Our personalities are unknown to our suitors."

Alaric crossed his arms over his chest. "I have no wish to marry the shiny version of you."

"I have no wish to marry you."

He narrowed his eyes. "If anyone knew we spent this time together, you'd be ruined."

"Are you threatening to tell anyone?" Willa smiled, because she knew to the core of her being that Alaric would never betray her. For any reason.

"I could." He shifted his weight, just the tiniest motion.

Her smile widened. "No, you couldn't. Now you must go. Did you give Sweetpea her roly-polies?"

He made a sound like a low growl. "Yes, I did. I'll go—for now." He walked over to the basket, and Hannibal hissed a warning. Alaric went down on his haunches beside the basket. Hannibal's front leg whipped out, as fast as the wind, and his claws dug into Alaric's sleeve.

"I'm not stealing your kitten," Alaric said, his voice deep and low.

Hannibal unhooked his claws, as if tacitly admitting the possibility of an error.

Alaric stood and crossed the room. When he reached the door, he turned around. "What if I were to write a poem and bring you more roses? All the roses in the garden? My father likes you; he would sanction their sacrifice."

"Are you in love with me, Alaric? Because in my experience, which, as you note, has been pleasingly full, such poems declare love."

His eyes narrowed. "Do you make fun of all your suitors this way?"

Willa grinned. "I do not."

"We get along uncommonly well," he tried.

"I'm sorry," Willa said, with genuine regret, because something about the way his voice had grown stiff was twisting her heart. "I want more from marriage."

"Did I tell you that I've made up my mind to stop writing?"

She opened the door. "Your readers love your work so much."

He left without another word. Her remark wasn't meant as an insult, but it seemed he had taken it as such. Willa closed the door behind him and sank into a chair.

Sweetpea tumbled from the basket onto her nose. Hannibal grumbled. He reminded Willa of a fussy nanny, the kind who has raised numerous children.

She'd done the right thing; she knew it.

In that instant the door was flung open with such force that it struck the wall. Willa jumped to her feet. Alaric strode over to her, wrapped his arms around her, and took her mouth.

He devoured her, forcing a moan from deep in her chest. Kissing, by definition, involved lips. But Alaric's kisses were a bodily experience. His tongue plundered her mouth; his hands went down her back, shaped her bottom and pulled her against his thighs.

Even had she been wearing four or five layers, instead of a thin chemise, she would have felt exactly what he had to offer.

"It's a good thing we're not on that damn bed any longer," he said, pulling away.

Willa gasped for air.

"Perhaps you could kiss *me* next time," he said.

With that, he was gone.

Chapter Twenty-five

The following afternoon

G iven the rain shower this morning," Lady
Knowe announced after luncheon, "I suggest a
few rounds of cards, which will allow the grass on the
archery field to dry."

To Alaric's disgust, a thicket of gentlemen surrounded Willa during the first game; every unmarried
man in the house party seemed to be hovering about her.
He stayed on the opposite side of the room, resenting
the ache he felt every time he saw her. He couldn't help
noticing as Willa lost the game, beaming at her circle of
admirers as she implied that she couldn't count cards.

She is lying, Alaric thought savagely. Probably she

could empty their pocketbooks if she wanted to, but she preferred to gaze at them with limpid blue eyes and collect betrothal rings instead.

She didn't accept the rings. But only so that she could keep looking for the perfect consort. The man with a private life.

To add insult to injury, Prudence persisted in fluttering around him like a demented moth, putting off discussion of her return to Africa by claiming exhaustion. Alaric was on the verge of tossing her forcefully into a carriage. Instead, he excused himself with the plea of work, and took himself off to the library.

His father's desk was piled high with ledgers. North had declined his offer to help with the estate, but Alaric thought he'd take a look at the ledgers, if only to get a sense of the scope of work North had inherited on Horatius's death.

An hour later, he had made considerable progress with the books when his Aunt Knowe burst into the room. "Prudence Larkin just told me that the two of you were matched in heaven by the Angel Gabriel himself," she said. "I asked her to describe him and she took offense."

"Thank you for rescuing me at breakfast. Again," he said wearily.

"I wouldn't have to rescue you so often if you would just stay where you belong."

"What do you mean?"

She scowled at him so ferociously that her slashing eyebrows touched in the middle. It was a Wildean feature, less unfortunate in the men of the family.

"I found this on the drawing room floor," she said, handing him a locket. It wasn't one of those cheap souvenirs engraved with a W; this one was gold, beautifully made, and opened easily.

A cutout of his own face looked back at him. One of his eyes was higher than the other. He closed it, turned the locket over, examined it more closely. The soft metal was dented by tiny teeth marks.

Sweetpea.

Willa owned this locket, and she was carrying his picture.

Lady Knowe's face was transformed by a broad smile. "It must be Willa's. If the castle has rats—which I doubt—they've never gnawed on my jewelry."

Alaric tore off a small strip from a sheet of foolscap. "Would you be so kind as to return Willa's locket?"

His aunt circled around behind him and watched over his shoulder as he wrote.

My dear Evie,

This note replaces a likeness of my face. Perhaps
I should stop by your chamber to reassure you that
my eyes are level with each other, unlike the image
you were carrying in this locket.

He pried his face from the locket, folded up the note, and tucked it inside. His aunt left, laughing under her breath.

Sometime later, as Alaric was steadily working his way through yet another of the ledgers associated with the castle's upkeep, a footman appeared bearing a silver tray. On it was the locket.

Alaric nodded. "Return in two minutes, if you please."

If I had a true betrothed, I would wish to reassure
myself about many aspects of his physique.

He stared at this for some minutes before a slow smile spread over his face. Willa was wickedly sensual underneath that placid exterior of hers. A wild woman hiding in plain sight.

How will you judge his worth, if you have nothing
with which to compare those "aspects"? You should

conduct a thorough examination. I offer myself as a standard for comparison.

He dispatched the footman and returned to the task at hand. The ledgers before him, bound in leather and made up of line after line of entries written in the crabbed, cramped hand of his father's chief steward, began to resemble Mr. Roberts's hieroglyphs.

He already had over two dozen questions to ask North. Why did they maintain the mew when no one had gone hawking since Horatius's death? Why did they send two deer to Lord Pewter, in the next county, every November? Who was drinking all this small beer? Why were twelve or more rolls of silk wall covering acquired every year?

Glancing around at the walls of the library, he thought he had the answer to that. Probably the dampness of the stone rotted silk within a few seasons. Wouldn't it be better to put a sturdier fabric on the walls?

He knew the answer to that too. The duke's consequence demanded silk. If her fussy, frilly style of dressing held true for decorating, his future sister-in-law Diana would cover every nook and cranny, including the ceilings, in silk spun from royal silkworms, if such a thing existed.

At length, the footman reappeared. This time, he

offered, along with the locket, the information that the ladies had removed to the archery field.

Alaric nodded, his hand clenched around the locket until the door closed behind the man. He instantly opened it, read Willa's missive once. Then over again.

Undoubtedly many ladies would be enchanted to learn of your generosity as a teacher. Others, like myself, envision themselves being schooled in these matters only once. By their husbands.

Schooled?

The slow burn in his blood burst into open flame. He had a sudden vision of Willa watching intently as a man, a faceless man, stripped off his shirt and peeled off his clothing.

No, not a faceless man. That was *his* body, *his* thighs. And she was watching with wide eyes.

He got up, strode over to the library door, and fastened the latch. Back in his chair he stretched out his legs and tore open his breeches. His cock sprang forward, stiff and swollen, into his hand.

He wrapped his right hand around himself and let his head fall backward with a sigh of relief. Damn it, he had a cockstand twenty-three hours out of twenty-four these days. Every time he caught sight of Willa's lips, or the curve of her waist, or the turn of her slender ankle.

Eyes closed, he drew his hand up tightly. Behind his closed lids, Willa's lips opened as she watched him kick his breeches to the side. He stood in front of her, letting her adjust to the size of him.

His Willa wasn't afraid, though. Her tongue ran over her lower lip, and a soundless groan escaped his lips. His hand tightened again, stroking himself as imaginary Willa reached toward him, her hand tentative.

"This is yours, Evie," he told her. "All for your pleasure."

Damn it, his imaginary voice sounded as rough and untutored as a lad of sixteen. He had the feeling that it would be like that with her. Completely different than it had ever been with other women.

He imagined her naked, pink, excited, on her back but propped up on her elbows, watching as he kissed his way up her inner thighs. His hand tightened to the point of pain as he imagined stroking her with his tongue.

A harsh groan broke from his lips as he envisioned her eyes squeezed shut, lips open, her hands gripping his hair so he didn't move. Making certain that he kept licking her.

An orgasm ripped through his body as his head fell

farther back. He thought he heard her panting, and his body spasmed again, his cock jerking in his hand, warm liquid splashing onto his belly.

No solitary pleasuring had ever felt as brutally all-encompassing as this.

He pulled out a handkerchief and cleaned himself up, but even his brisk touch made his tool harden again and strain forward, as if that first orgasm was just the beginning.

The idea of seducing Willa flashed through his head . . . yet the last thing he wanted was to take away her choice by compromising her. The moment North had made his courtship apparent, it was as if Diana had been compromised. She had no say in the matter. Diana's dislike was biting into North like acid.

They were trapped in a cage made from his future title of duke.

Alaric would rather live without Willa than marry her under those circumstances.

If only Horatius hadn't died in that damn peat bog. With that bleak thought, his tool went abruptly limp. He tucked himself back in place, buttoned his placket, and came to his feet, shoving his shirt into his breeches with the brisk movements of a man who rarely waits for a valet to dress him.

He went to the window and drew back the curtains.

Lindow Moss started on the other side of the wall at the east end of the rose garden and stretched into the distance like a rolling green ocean marked by brighter threads, reddish patches, brown moss, and ochre-colored mud. From here he couldn't see the heath butterflies or golden-ringed dragonflies, but he knew they were there.

Not for nothing was his family called the Wildes of Lindow Moss. His ancestor had tamed land no one else had wanted, and had erected Lindow Castle on the edge of the bog as a sign of his audacity.

Centuries ago, that early Wilde held off a siege by Oswald of Northumbria—who had successfully besieged Edinborough Castle. Lindow defeated Oswald. Only local men knew the bog's twists and turns, and food and supplies had flowed readily through Lindow Moss, while the bodies of Oswald's men sank without a trace.

Alaric stood at the window for long minutes, watching the rippling mounds of moss, grass, and peat. Horatius had truly loved the bog; he'd been proud of it and considered it their birthright.

Alaric had to make his peace with Horatius's death.

And with Lindow Moss.

He slowly returned to the desk, feeling older by a decade.

Chapter Twenty-six

Willa was shocked by her own disappointment when Alaric did not return her locket with another improper message. She should have been relieved that he had halted the game before other guests noticed the footman traveling back and forth.

Back in her room, she sank in a deep tub of warm water and afterwards gave Sweetpea her own bath. The little skunk paddled in a circle, nose scarcely above the water, waiting for Willa to drop peas so she could dive for them.

When Sweetpea tired of the game, Willa took her to the bed and toweled her until Sweetpea's tail waved like an ostrich feather. With a thump, Hannibal landed on the coverlet.

To this point, the tomcat had hissed every time she

came close to his corner of the room, or to the door leading to the balcony, if he was outside.

Now he glared at her, his eyes squinty.

"Oh for goodness' sakes," Willa told him. "I have no interest in hurting your baby; why would I?"

Hannibal put a paw forward. Willa didn't move. Still glaring at her, he bent his neck, grabbed Sweetpea by the scruff of her neck, leapt down off the bed, and padded over to the basket. Then he ostentatiously curled around Sweetpea and began licking her head, regarding Willa through slitted eyes.

She broke into laughter. She was surrounded by protective males. Absurd, protective males.

When dinner was announced that evening, Willa accepted Parth's arm into the dining room. She was tired of her suitors' simpering flattery. What's more, Alaric showed no reaction when she flirted with them—but he looked daggers whenever she talked to his old friend.

There was no need to feign interest in Parth's conversation; after he told her about his purchase of the infamous lace factory, their topics of conversation ranged from the ideas of Jean-Jacques Rousseau to exploration of the territory west of the Ohio River in America, to the war between Britain and the American colonies.

Surprisingly, North sat down with them and joined

the conversation about the war, revealing a nuanced and thoughtful interest in British skirmishes with American troops. The problem, to his mind, was that the British weren't fighting for their territory; instead, they'd filled the ranks with Hessians, German mercenaries.

The more they talked, the more Alaric glowered. Hemmed in by admirers who only wanted to talk of his books, he had no way of joining them.

She wasn't surprised when, late that night after the castle had quieted, a knock came at her door. Sweetpea, ever curious, headed directly toward it, as did Willa—without bothering to pull on her dressing gown.

Sure enough, Alaric stood in the dark corridor. "Roly-poly delivery. Plus one locket."

She pulled him inside, closing the door. He put the roly-polies on the floor in front of the delighted baby skunk and went to the basin to wash his hands. "What is it you like more about all those proposals you've received—the compliments or the kneeling?" he asked over his shoulder.

"The kneeling. It's so infrequent that men recognize how important women are to their lives."

Alaric turned, his eyebrow raised. "Just how important is that?"

"If you don't know, I shan't tell you," she said. "I

don't suppose you have spent a great deal of time with ladies in the last few years."

"None. And that includes Prudence, no matter what she thinks."

Prudence was no lady. "Do you intend to see her play?"

He flinched. "On the contrary. I intend to close it down."

"You're not curious?"

"No." Alaric prowled toward her with the effortless grace of a large cat. "I'm told Prudence characterized me as so terrified by water that I couldn't save the missionary's daughter from nearly drowning in a river."

His tone was so offended that Willa couldn't help laughing. "You showed no sign of hydrophobia when you helped rescue Hannibal," she observed.

"I prefer to maintain a respectful distance from crocodiles, but water in itself? No."

"I wish I could see it," Willa said. "From what I've heard, the play enacts not just one, but *two* scenes in which you fail to save the missionary's daughter."

"First the flood, and then the cannibals."

She nodded, watching his frown. He was a man who any woman would instinctively know would care for her. His strength and contained ferocity would be wielded to protect those he loved every time.

It made her think that Prudence had deliberately constructed the play to misrepresent him. But that implied that Prudence *hated*, not loved, him. "I begin to wonder whether Prudence wrote the play as revenge," she said, thinking it through as she spoke. "Perhaps she meant the portrayal to shame you, to make the audience believe that Lord Wilde was not a hero, but a coward. But instead—"

"It exploded in her face, and she turned me into England's most celebrated explorer!" He let out a bark of laughter. "I owe this damnable fame to a woman who tried to ruin me."

How like him to laugh on hearing something that would drive many men to a murderous fury. Of course, he didn't care whether strangers thought he was a coward. He knew himself and his strengths. That confidence made her feel weak in the knees.

Light from the candles on her dressing table flickered over his cheekbones and revealed a reddish tinge in his hair. Why did men ever wear wigs?

"If you look at me like that, Evie," he said softly, "I will take you to that bed, and be damned with the fact that I've made up my mind not to let you seduce me."

"Let *me* seduce *you?*" she cried. "I've no such intention!"

"It doesn't matter," he said, shaking his head. "You're

doing it without trying. May I kiss you goodnight?"
There was a raw note to his voice, a shocking, blatantly
erotic undertone.

Heat ripped through her, roaring up the back of her
neck and between her legs, and the tips of her breasts—
all parts of her that hungered for his caress. Somehow
it was even more erotic to know that he wouldn't approach her unless she gave permission. Not here, in her
bedchamber where she was vulnerable.

Modesty was called for, but she ignored it. Willa
didn't care that they weren't married, or even betrothed. Alaric looked as hungry as a man who hadn't
eaten in days, as if the only thing in the world that
would satisfy him was her. She'd never seen hunger like
that in any of the fourteen men who'd proposed to her.

He read the answer to his question in her face and
drew her into his embrace, bending his head until his
lips met hers, whisper-soft.

In that moment Willa understood that kisses were
like kindling for a fire yet to come. When her lips
opened, the spark caught flame. When Alaric invaded
her mouth, the blaze threatened to turn into a bonfire
and burn out of control.

She caught hold of his shoulders in order to steady
herself. Unfamiliar sensations crowded into her faster
than she could catalogue them: desire, hunger, tender-

ness. The hard length that pulsed against her, burning through her nightdress.

Many kisses later, she watched him, mute, new emotions crowding her throat so that she couldn't, didn't want to, speak. She wanted things that couldn't be said aloud.

She wanted to lick the severe line of his jaw. She wanted to make him groan. She wanted to eradicate every trace of Lord Wilde and make the man before her all Alaric, all hers, only hers.

None of that could be spoken aloud, and it all whirled in her head in a daze of possession and desire. He kissed his way down her neck, and she tipped her head to the side to let those lips go where they would, trembling as he pushed down the wide neck of her nightdress and kissed the line of her shoulder.

He made a sound, low and deep in his throat, when she tugged the nightdress farther down. Her breast was revealed, and they both stared at it as if surprised.

"Kiss me," Willa whispered.

Alaric's expression was somewhere between awe and yearning. "I don't dare," he said, his voice guttural. He eased her nightdress back up, wrapping her in a fierce embrace, his mouth ravaging hers in a possessive, dominating kiss that made Willa's mind tumble over and over itself, shattering into fragments of heat and light and desire.

"You are so beautiful," he said, his voice harsh in the quiet room as he eased away. She tried to see herself through his eyes, hair tumbling over her shoulders like a wanton, her skin gleaming in the candlelight. "You're demure during the day, but you are not demure in truth, are you?"

"I'm afraid not," she admitted. She ran a finger down the white line of his scar. "I believe I inherited a bawdy sense of humor from my father. I remember him roaring with laughter while my mother beat him around the head with her fan."

There was a question in his eyes, but he didn't voice it. He didn't need to; everything in her responded to his desire.

Without a word, she moved her shoulders just enough that the neckline of her unbuttoned nightgown slid down again. At the expression in his eyes, she allowed it to slide further, until the delicate cambric gathered in folds at her elbows and her waist.

Silence hung in the room for a long second. He looked at her breasts before meeting her eyes again. "You are certain?"

She took a breath, trembling with the pleasure of

the pure carnality of his gaze before she said steadily, "Yes. Alaric, yes." He reached toward her with a stifled groan, his palms clasping her breasts. Her groan followed his as his callused fingers rubbed her nipples and set her blood on fire.

Willa shook like a willow in a breeze as he slid one hand around the curve of her breast and lowered his mouth there, *there*, to skin that had never been touched by anyone other than Willa herself.

His lips were like a brand, hot and sensual, turning her inside out, making her mind slip away into some other place. Some other woman curled her fingers into Alaric's thick hair. Stared at the buttonholes of his waistcoat as he kissed her breast, her mind wordless for the first time in her life.

Delicious tremors ran up her legs and kept going through her, over and over, growing in strength as he suckled. Her hands stopped caressing his hair; they curled tight, keeping his head in place so that he would keep doing that mad, wild thing that made her want to surrender to him.

Her body, herself. Everything.

He felt it. She knew it, and he knew it. He raised his head and met her eyes. She couldn't find words. Perhaps there were no words for this intoxicating, glorious pleasure.

Alaric's gaze was heated, fierce . . . sane. "Is this a betrothal between us, a real betrothal?"

The look in his eyes lit an erotic fire in Willa's blood. Surely this was the definition of madness: when a woman throws away all propriety and all the rules that made her life what it was.

All the rules that defined her as a lady, as chaste, as sensible.

The word "betrothal" knocked about in her head as she tried to connect it to desire and possession, to the way Alaric looked at her, as if he could eat her up.

If she nodded, he would never give her up. She would be Lady Alaric Wilde to the end of her days, never just "Willa" again. She would be Evie. He would pull her into his sphere, with all the blazing attention and fame that entailed.

Alaric felt the change in Willa before she spoke. It wasn't as overt as a flinch, but her body changed: she withdrew without moving, cooled without notice.

She was afraid, though she would be angry if he were to say so.

Perhaps she was rightly afraid. He didn't know how to get rid of the admirers created by *Wilde in Love*. Willa wouldn't want to live in a house that was slowly losing its bricks and couldn't keep flowers in its beds.

He let his hand slip from her breast because Willa,

his Willa, deserved better than to be seduced. He wanted her to choose him free and clear.

Slipping her nightdress back over her shoulders, he kissed her with complete concentration, willing her to understand that a house missing a few bricks wouldn't matter if they were under the roof together. "I would have new white rosebushes planted every year," he whispered later.

"What?" Her voice was a gulp of air. She was trembling in his arms, a slim column of passion and flame.

"I will keep a bricklayer on the grounds," he promised. His hand rounded her arse and he pulled her against his aroused cock, consumed with hunger. "I will close down the play, and I will never write another book." Vows fell from his mouth, surprising him. And yet they felt right.

He had never written his books for the audience who bought lockets and thought of him as a romantic hero; after all, he had not even known they existed. His true readers enjoyed accounts of faraway countries and exotic customs. They were curious about the world, not about him.

"What did you say about a bricklayer?" Willa asked, her voice drowsy and drugged, her fingers trailing over his back.

It would not be seducing her to remove his waistcoat. Or his shirt. It would be . . . *chivalrous.* She was asking him without words. He stood back and wrenched off his waistcoat, tore off his shirt.

Even that took too long. He made his arms into a prison and kissed her, carnal, scorching kisses that did everything his body wanted to do: they explored her, caressed her, spoke to her.

Loved her.

He pushed the thought away.

"This is *very* improper," Willa gasped, sometime later.

"I love impropriety with you," he whispered.

She was still running her fingers over the muscles in his back. He was larger than most Englishmen, his shoulders widened from exertion. Climbing mountains, hacking his way through impenetrable jungles, sailing through a hurricane. Vigorous activity had changed his body.

"And Evie, you enjoy impropriety," he added.

Her hands moved to his chest, her eyelashes dark against her cheeks.

"Would this be the first time you've seen a naked man?" he asked.

Her long, curling eyelashes fluttered. In this light,

her eyes were darker than the bluebells they usually brought to mind. Perhaps it wasn't a consequence of candlelight; perhaps it was desire.

"Yes," she said. "I am sorry for myself that my first naked chest is such a defective one."

He laughed.

Her fingers gently traced a white scar that cut across his waist. "What caused this?"

"A whip," he said, shrugging. "I took a lash from an irate sailor before I managed to disarm him."

Willa had found another. "And this?"

The scar was so old that it had whitened and lay flat. He couldn't remember its origin, because his mind was engulfed by a wave of sharp desire.

"May I give you pleasure?" he whispered, drawing up her chin and pressing a kiss on her lips.

"You do give me pleasure." Now her eyes were lighter again, like a stormy sky in summer.

"I want to take you," he said, the words guttural.

She froze like a deer caught in the sudden light of a lantern.

"Not that way." He wanted her so much that his body longed to claim her in the most primitive of ways, to own her, to take her. "That is, I do want you that way, but I won't. Not until you agree to marry me."

The word "love" knocked through his mind again,

but he dismissed it. She hadn't understood what he'd meant by the bricklayers and the rosebushes. She had no idea that he would give all that up for her. Easily, for her.

He swept her into his arms and she gave a startled squeak. But when he laid her on the bed, she didn't protest.

Willa appeared delicate, but appearances were deceiving. She looked proper; she was not. She looked as if a strong gust might knock her over; he suspected she would live into her nineties if not longer.

His hands slid up her legs. Like her arms, her legs were slender, and the skin, always hidden from the sun, was tender.

She made a muffled sound and her thighs quivered under his touch. Swallowing a grin, he kissed her left knee.

Another on the right, to be fair.

A little farther up. She squeaked a phrase that didn't seem to be a protest so he kept going.

He reached the part of her inner thigh that began a shy curve inward.

Chapter Twenty-seven

A year or so earlier, Lavinia and Willa had bent their heads over a page in a book depicting a man lying between a woman's legs. The man's mouth was *there*, and one hand was on himself.

They had looked at each other and turned the page in unspoken agreement: either that was pleasant, or it wasn't.

It seemed Willa was about to find out.

Alaric looked up at her and the expression in his eyes made her legs fall open in a truly improper fashion. She did so instinctively—because he looked as if he were on fire to kiss her there.

Feeling welled up inside her . . . she laughed. No, she giggled. She never giggled.

But there it was. She giggled.

"You surprise me, Evie," Alaric drawled, his voice husky and suggestive. His thumbs were rubbing provocative little circles on her skin, leaving trails of flames and pure want.

Willa lost all inclination to giggle, and a startled gasp came from her lips instead. When a broad finger touched her, she melted backward, her head falling to the pillow, her lower back arching without conscious volition.

Gasp followed gasp as his tongue followed his fingers: one callused and strong, the other sleek and smooth. Both beguiling, both entrancing.

Hunger, this hunger, was like a fever, Willa discovered. It raged through her brain and took away conscious thought. It spread through her body as if her blood had been replaced by burning brandy.

It was a pleasure she could never have imagined. Touching herself was a pale thing compared to this assault on her senses and her body. She couldn't find words, but he did.

Hoarse, aching words spilled from Alaric's mouth. She felt unmoored, flung into a deep sea by the racking waves of desire sprung from his words and his mouth on her. She reached down and he laced one of his hands with hers.

Their fingers clung together and that fulcrum became her steady point in a world in which desire drove her higher and higher—

Until she broke, the feeling overflowing her body. Her fingers locked on his and a scream broke from her lips. He stayed with her, his tongue making the pleasure last, flowing from wave to wave, until she finally slumped, boneless.

He made a satisfied sound, and gave her a last caress. Willa pulled her fingers away from his and pushed hair back from her damp forehead, gasping for air. She was still panting when he crawled up beside her, his erection straining his breeches. "Alaric," she whispered.

He grinned at her, the triumphant grin of a bad man who knows his way around a woman's body. "You have a rosy splotch on each of your cheeks," he said cheerfully. The back of his hand felt cool against her heated skin.

Willa didn't know what to say. All the modesty and shyness she hadn't felt earlier came flooding in, making her skin tight with embarrassment. With a wiggle she restored her nightgown to something resembling decorum.

"The splotches are joining together and you're turning rosy pink all over." That twinkle in his eye should be outlawed in polite society.

She coughed. It was an expressive cough, the sort

one makes when a gentleman has overstayed his welcome: a morning call gone on too long; an unwelcome
request for another dance; a second marriage proposal
after the first was refused.

Predictably, Alaric paid no attention. Instead he
rolled onto his side and watched with interest as she
wriggled her nightdress all the way down to her toes.

He didn't seem to be taking the hint, so she finally
met his eyes again. He quirked up one side of his mouth
in a smile that made her feel unnervingly happy.

"That was quite lovely," she said candidly. "But I
think you should leave now."

"You are a hard-hearted woman," he offered, eyes
dancing with laughter.

"Why so?"

"You accepted my best ministrations with nary a
thank-you."

Color flooded up her neck again. "I apologize. I
wasn't . . . I'm not cognizant of the proper comport-
ment after ministrations of this nature."

He laughed so loudly at that, she felt obliged to clap
a hand over his mouth. When that didn't work, she
poked him in the side, and threatened to put a pillow
over his face to smother the noise.

"Hush, you utter beast," she said, giggling despite
herself.

"When a lady has been plundered and despoiled . . ." Alaric began. Caught sight of her face and gave another shout of laughter.

"Someone will hear you!" Willa squealed.

"If they heard anything, they heard *you*," he said, pushing himself up against the headboard, his eyes gleaming.

"Hush," Willa commanded. She was beginning to feel like herself again. Her heart had settled into a normal rhythm, and the pulsing heat between her legs had subsided. "I have been neither plundered nor despoiled," she said firmly.

Looking at the bare chest of the man lying in her bed made that throbbing sensation return, so she kept her eyes above his chin. "I am thankful for your . . . for you, Alaric. But you should return to your bedchamber."

He reached out and cupped his hand along the curve of her jaw, bent forward and pressed a kiss there. "Am I to take it that my skill has not changed your mind as regards making our sham betrothal into a true one?"

Willa's heart skipped a beat. Alaric was so . . . just so much himself. Beautiful in an untamed way, his rumpled hair, worn too long for fashion, if the truth be known. Most gentlemen were shaved these days. She and Lavinia had wondered what it would be like to kiss a man with a scalp as bare as a baby's bottom.

If she accepted Alaric's hand, she'd never kiss a bald man.

Or she might, if she refused him again. The arguments for and against tangled in her mind like a thorny hedge.

"If only you were an ordinary man," she said, hopelessly. "Even if you had nothing!"

"My ministrations must have truly pleased if you would accept me without a ha'penny to my name."

She reached over and gave his chest a little slap. It was warm and broad, and her fingers clung there. "Don't be silly. I mean *you*, Alaric. You. It's just Lord Wilde . . ." Her voice trailed away into helplessness.

"So you have said." He swung his legs over the side of the bed. Her fingers slipped from his chest. His expression wasn't cold in the least. Or angry, or anything unpleasant.

It was just . . . not there.

He was giving her his "Lord Wilde" face, Willa thought with incredulity.

She came to her feet as well. "Don't you dare bow to me."

"I beg your pardon?" His face, too startled for politeness, appeared through the neck of his shirt.

"You are Lord Wilde-ing me," she said, folding her arms over her breasts. Then she thought better of it and snatched up her dressing gown and put it on.

He looked bewildered, the way men do when they are being particularly idiotic. That was an unfair thought, but she couldn't make herself unthink it.

"You have a way of being Lord Wilde," she explained, tying her sash tightly around her waist, as if adding another layer would take away from the fact that her knees were still trembling. "It's all very well if you wish to behave that way with your legions of admirers, but not with me."

A smile softened his mouth. "You are not an admirer?"

"I am not," she said stubbornly.

His smile grew as he buttoned up his waistcoat. "Willa Everett, you are unlike anyone I have ever met."

"As you have already pointed out," she said. "And I will repeat that your circle of acquaintances must have been regrettably small, for all that you boast of having friends in many parts of the world."

"They are not friends," he said. "Merely acquaintances."

"Because they all met Lord Wilde," she said, nodding. "And not Lord Alaric."

A smile lit his eyes. "If you ban Lord Wilde, you will have a remarkably impolite spouse."

"I have not agreed to have you as a spouse," she reminded him.

"Yes, you have." His smile was wide, and warm, and sent a bolt of pleasure straight down her body. "You haven't quite accepted it yet, Evie, but you are mine. There's no rush, though. Take your time."

That was pure Alaric. That sinful, teasing look, the one that promised to come to her room night after night, roly-polies in hand, no doubt. It made her blood simmer with lust, weakened her knees again.

"Go," she commanded, ignoring her conviction that he would knock on her door on the morrow.

"As you wish," he said, amiably enough. He came over and kissed her with the brisk efficiency that she'd seen from husbands leaving their wives for the day.

"*Lord Wilde* is not who you want in a husband," Alaric said, with a grin. "He doesn't exist. *I* am precisely who you want, Evie. But I know it will take you some time to accept it, and I will wait for you."

He turned and was out of the room, the door closed quietly behind him, before Willa could open her mouth to reply.

Which was just as well.

She was afraid she would have agreed with him. Or disagreed, if only to say that she wouldn't need much time at all.

That she wanted Alaric Wilde now, here, forever.

Chapter Twenty-eight

The following day

Willa was captive to a lecture about partridge shooting all the way through luncheon. Neither Alaric nor Parth appeared at the meal. Lavinia wasn't due back from Manchester for another two days, and Diana was hiding in her room. Even Lady Knowe claimed to have a toothache.

By the end of two hours, Willa had learned everything there was to know about the magical hour before sunset, when partridges supposedly wandered about, waiting to be shot.

She was bored, horribly bored.

It drove her to consider that, while winning fourteen proposals of marriage had been a flattering and agreeable game, the idea of spending the rest of her life listening to a man lecture her was intolerable.

As they'd begun their Season, she and Lavinia had confidently assumed that suitors would appear who were compelling in their own right. Those men would fall into their beguiling trap but somehow be different. *Their* lectures would be engaging.

Only one man had seen through Willa's trap.

But . . . "Willa Wilde"? She wrinkled her nose.

An awful name. *Her* name?

She practiced saying it to herself, wishing Lavinia were there. How does one accept a proposal that has yet to be formally made? All the same, joy prickled down her back.

Her parents would have scorned a lecture about partridge shooting. They wouldn't have been bored by a conversation with Alaric.

Alaric had spent the morning in his father's library, so thoroughly buried in the account books that he didn't hear the gong announcing luncheon. He emerged at length with a firmer sense of the work to be done with the estate.

No wonder North was so morose. This work didn't come naturally to either of them, as it had to Horatius.

Their older brother would have relished the labor of managing the estate. He had been protective to the core, a worthy descendant of the medieval ancestor who had ridden out the siege. Horatius would have gathered his people and fought to the last stand before he gave up a blade of grass.

For the first time in years, Alaric smiled at the thought of his brother. This time, the pain of loss didn't constrict his heart as if it were in a vise.

As soon as he could get his father alone, he meant to suggest that the duke hire two more estate managers. North wouldn't inherit the estate for years; he couldn't see any reason why his brother shouldn't spend the next decade designing houses and building them. It would make him a happier duke in the end.

The archery range was across a long lawn. The smell of scythed grass and hedge roses drifted in the air. In the cloudless sky a swift flitted across his vision with a flash of wings.

England was so damn beautiful. So much a part of his bones and blood. The bird was joined by another, the two swifts darting around each other in a giddy, swooping dance. On the far side of the lawn, Fitzy paraded under a nectarine tree, its ripening amber fruit complementing his turquoise blue feathers. From this distance, tree and bird made a tapestry woven from rich-colored silks.

At the archery range, the ladies stood in clusters, their summer plumage threatening to outdazzle Fitzy's. As he approached, he realized with an odd thump of his heart that his eyes had gone directly to Willa, just as his brother's had gone directly to Diana when they first walked into the drawing room and interrupted the ladies' tea.

Now, those ladies were sipping champagne and looking on as the duke sent one arrow after another sailing toward the target and hitting the center, more often than not. Alaric headed directly to his lady's side.

Willa caught sight of Alaric prowling across the lawn and felt a thrill of pure joy—but the surge of exultation she felt when he came straight to her, as if the duke, duchess, brothers, guests, didn't exist?

It rolled through her like an earthquake.

"Good afternoon, Miss Ffynche," Alaric said, throwing her an ironic glance that said just how much he disliked addressing her in such formal language.

"Lord Alaric," she said with a smile that she knew wasn't a Willa smile. It was an Evie smile. It was the smile she had as a young girl.

"I suggest a contest." Alaric picked up a bow and tested the string. "Whoever wins will be granted a favor by the other." His eyes had a hot, lazy message of their own.

All the same, he was overconfident with respect to his archery skills. From what she'd seen on previous days, they were evenly matched. He shouldn't assume that he would win this favor, even though it felt as if the air had turned to sherry, a honeyed potent wine, making her fingers tremble.

"What favor do you have in mind?" she asked, picking up her favorite bow. It was light and springy, painted green with daisies. Lavinia had given it to her solely due to its embellishments, but the fact was that, if she had to, Willa could bring down a deer with it. Not that she would ever shoot anything more lively than a target.

Not even those women whose eyes followed Alaric with longing. Who tittered behind their fans and ogled the muscles in his arse.

Prudence was the worst of the lot, by far. Even now she was edging around the marquee, her eyes on Alaric. Willa glanced at her, and the girl flinched.

Alaric looked over his shoulder at Prudence. "A walk," he suggested. "Prudence has taken to poking bits of paper into my pockets. I think she knows we sent messages by your locket."

"What do her notes say?"

"They quote Bible verses. I dislike being reminded that I am in need of salvation. Miss Ffynche, please accompany me on a walk. Escape awaits."

"Perhaps, if you win the bout." Willa felt as if she were hugging a wonderful secret to her heart. She had made up her mind to become Lady Alaric Wilde, and the man in question didn't know.

His eyes crinkled as he smiled at her. Heat rushed up her spine.

He knew.

In the distance, the duchess waddled over to her husband and said something Willa couldn't make out. As they watched, His Grace wrapped his arms around her from behind and she leaned into his weight while drawing back her bow.

"Romantic, aren't they?" Alaric asked in a low voice. "I fully intend to be hugging you when I'm fifty. I'd hug you now if you'd allow me."

When it was their turn, Alaric sent his five arrows into the target, one after the other, as casually as if he weren't looking. Four hit the center.

Willa took her time, standing perfectly straight, drawing back her arm. Ignoring Alaric's groan when her stance made her bosom rise in the air.

Four had struck the bull's-eye when Alaric said, "Willa."

She glanced at him. "Yes?"

"Please don't make me return to that tent."

"We needn't," she answered. She was waiting to be

certain that the boy tasked with removing arrows was well out of the way before she put her final arrow to the string.

"If you hit the center of the target," he said, running his fingers up her arm from the elbow to the wrist, "we have to stage another match before I can ask for my favor. Ten more arrows."

Willa shivered as his caress singed her skin. Desire shot through her with a sharp stab, as if she'd been struck by one of his arrows. His touch reverberated through her, making her throat tight.

"I want to ask you to accompany me for a walk," Alaric coaxed, his voice husky and low. "I'd like to show you my favorite boyhood hiding place. What's more, Prudence keeps staring at me behind your back."

She put her bow down so as to not yield to the temptation to wave it in Prudence's direction. "What if our absence is noted?"

"It won't be," he said. "I believe something is happening that will take everyone's attention."

She glanced over at the marquee. All the ladies were clustered around the duchess and even Prudence had been swept into the group. "Goodness! Is Her Grace about to bear her child?" she asked, alarmed. "*Here?*"

"My father will carry her upstairs, if need be," Alaric said. "The last babe was nearly born in a carriage."

Childbirth was not an ordeal Willa was eager to experience. Or witness.

She handed her bow to a groom. "If Lady Knowe should inquire, I have taken a stroll with Lord Alaric."

Once out of sight of the archery field, Alaric dropped Willa's elbow and pulled her snugly against his side. "Horatius, North, Parth, and I spent our days roaming around these fields, when we weren't in the bog," he said, guiding her toward a small apple orchard that clung to the slope of a gentle hill leading away from the castle.

"That sounds like so much fun," Willa said, a bit wistfully.

Alaric kissed her cheek. His Willa would never be lonely again; he would see to it. They entered the shade of the first apple trees and a narrow leafy lane opened before them. On either side, neat rows of carefully spaced trees stretched away.

"They are alphabetized," Alaric explained. "Four Costard trees, followed by four Cox, and so on, ending with St. Edmund's Pippins. The first apples will ripen in September."

The other side of the orchard opened onto a lane bounded by a tall hedgerow. Swallows were swooping around the hedge, diving as if planning to land, and changing their minds at the last moment.

"This way," Alaric said, drawing Willa to the left. They followed the hedge around the curve until a pristine ornamental lake lay before them. His favorite willow tree slanted more steeply over the bank than when he had seen it last. Its branches used to dangle above the surface, but now they trailed in the water with the lethargy of a drunk after his fifth whiskey of the morning.

After they reached the lake, he guided her under the willow's curtain of arrowed leaves and pointed to a platform far above them. "I spent a great deal of time up there. When you're on top of this willow, you have a bird's-eye view of the duchy. It feels as if you're look-ing at a different country, which was irresistible for a boy always dreaming of traveling to foreign lands."

"I've never climbed a tree," Willa remarked. "Girls are not allowed to."

"Ours will be." He watched with pleasure as rosy spots appeared in her cheeks.

"Surely this isn't a natural lake," she said, ignoring his provocation.

It was round as a mirror, as was the circular island in its precise center. It looked like the pad of a water lily that had overgrown and turned to stone.

"It's like a nursery rhyme," she added. "In the middle of a round lake was a round island. And in the middle of the round island was a round . . . What is that, exactly? A folly?"

"It's a classical rotunda built by the duke for my mother, his first duchess," Alaric said. He was following a length of rope tied to the willow's trunk; brushing aside the rushes at the water's edge, he found the punt still attached to the other end.

Better yet, the punt was dry and reasonably clean. Probably his younger siblings had colonized the island. "Would you care for an excursion in my pleasure boat, my lady?"

A minute later Willa was perched in the bow, her voluminous skirts bunched around her. She looked so fresh, happy, and sensual that Alaric had to wrestle with himself. No, he could not topple her into the bottom of a punt and have his way with her.

"Take care; your gown is billowing over the gunwale," he observed, for the sake of saying something, while avoiding the uncomfortable emotions crowding his chest.

She laughed. "I'll have you know this is a remarkably fashionable garment, which means the rear"—she threw him a naughty glance—"is enhanced by a contrivance called a rump."

He gave a bark of laughter.

"This particular rump," she continued, her eyes sparkling, "came from Paris and is made of cork. I'm truly surprised that there is enough room in this little boat for myself and my rump."

"For your two rumps," he ventured. "May I say that I think your own is in no need of enhancement?"

Her smiling mouth was a strawberry-stained pink that called to him as surely as the plumage of a peacock dazzled its mate. Her hair shone in the sunlight.

"This lake looks as if it ought to be inhabited by swans," she said, changing the subject.

"There used to be a very disagreeable pair when we were growing up. Horatius had a scar on one foot given to him by the cob."

Willa cocked an eyebrow.

"Horatius was not one to avoid danger," Alaric went on. "He was a true Englishman, in the best meaning of the word." A few more strokes and he drew the punt up to the foot of the marble steps on the island, where he moored it to a ring sunk into the stone.

The rotunda, only a few years older than he, had scarcely altered, save for encroachments of lichen and moss. Like the silver hair he didn't have yet, he thought, imagining it in another thirty years.

He held out his hand and helped Willa from the

punt. Her dress—with its Parisian rump—looked exquisitely ladylike, and yet the expression in her eyes was wanton.

Marriage to her promised to be fascinating. A merger of sorts, likely with a period of adjustment. All he had to do was persuade her.

Though he had the feeling she had made up her mind. Willa would not have joined him in the punt had she not decided to take his hand and his name.

"Did His Grace allow the rotunda to fall into disuse after the death of your mother?" she asked, as they climbed the low steps.

"Yes, although not owing to grief. The second duchess spent all her time in London, and Ophelia is uninterested in nature."

"Someone has been using it," Willa remarked when they were under the dome. Against one of the spindly, elegant columns was a pile of canvas pillows, a few candle stubs, and a large tin box with a hinged lid.

Alaric crouched down and lifted the lid. "Clever boy," he murmured. The box contained a folded blanket, on top of which lay a couple of bottles, a small knife, a lump of what might once have been cheese wrapped in canvas, and—secreted beneath the blanket—a book in Italian notorious for its bawdy illustrations.

He picked up one of the bottles and inspected it. "Ginger beer. May I offer you one?"

"Please," Willa said. She was standing between two columns, looking back toward the castle, beyond the orchard to the east. "I can't believe you grew up in a fairy tale."

Alaric walked over to stand beside her. To his eyes, Lindow Castle bore no resemblance to those in fairy tales. It was low and wide, with a stolid look about it, as if it were challenging all onlookers to a siege. It had battlements and turrets, but little other resemblance to the whimsical stacks of golden stone he'd seen in France.

"From this distance, one can hardly call it a castle," he said. "My great-grandfather added bits and pieces, and my grandfather built a new tower. We used to spend rainy days exploring little passageways and secret corridors—there are actually three priest holes."

Willa nodded. Dusky eyelashes exactly matched her hair, so she must have darkened them from brown to black. Knowing that cosmetic secret felt like proof of their intimacy. No other man knew, just as no man knew of the creamy skin of her rounded breast and the satin texture of her thighs.

In fact, he had to swallow hard and look away from

her because a primitive roar was rising in his soul, and he couldn't listen to it.

He had to let Willa accept him in her own time. He cut the string from around the bottle's neck, and with a grunt, managed to draw out the cork. "Ginger beer has a bite," he warned, offering it to her. "You can't find a drink like this anywhere else in the world."

Willa reached out a hand and he put the bottle into it, wondering how he'd got so lucky as to find a lady willing to take a drink from a bottle without fussing.

He took one more look at Lindow Castle, sitting on the hill like a fat brown hen drowsing on her nest, and turned back to the box. He plucked out the blanket and threw it over the pillows. Held up the book.

"May I show you my engravings?" It wasn't hard to produce a leer.

Willa strolled over, swinging the bottle from two fingers. "I recognize that book," she observed, smiling at his surprised look.

"Aunt Knowe is right. Young ladies are not what they used to be."

"Lavinia and I spent a year in mourning for her father," Willa said. "There were libidinous Grays among her ancestors, and we made a study of all the naughty books we could find in the family library."

"As one does," Alaric said, deeply amused.

"Don't tell me you wouldn't have done the same! One of your siblings is enjoying similar literary pursuits."

"Leonidas, I would guess," Alaric said. "Though from the look of the cheese he left, he hasn't been here since he left for Eton."

Willa's decision had taken root in her chest and it was only a matter of telling him. She'd had fourteen proposals. That was a respectable number to tell her children about. She'd weighed more than enough evidence before making her choice.

But she didn't want to blurt out, "I'll be your wife," or something equally simple.

In this moment, more than any, she had to be Evie, not Willa. Brave in emotions as much as, if not more than, in words. With that thought, she unpinned her hat and dropped it to the side. Next, she slipped off her shoes and bent over, reaching up under her skirts to untie her garter.

"What are you doing?" Alaric asked in a strangled voice.

She looked up and smiled. "I've decided to accept your proposal." She allowed her smile to turn into something truly naughty. The suggestive smile she'd occasionally seen on other women's faces. It seemed to curve on her lips quite naturally. "I think I might take to being a trollop."

Her first garter fell away. Her stocking was made of gossamer-weight silk; it fell to her ankle and she toed it off.

Alaric appeared to have been struck dumb.

She looked up, saw just a flash of blue eyes before she bent her head again and untied her second garter.

"How am I to have a rational life if I walk around in a permanent state of arousal?" he demanded, almost as if he were talking to himself. "I look at you, any part of you, from the nape of your neck to your ankle, and I'm ready for service. Your service, I mean."

"I have grasped that," Willa said, voice wry. Her remaining stocking slipped down her leg.

"You shouldn't do that." His voice made the blood pound through her body even faster. She was having trouble keeping a semblance of calmness, which was unusual for her. Very unusual.

She tossed her second stocking on top of the first.

"Have you removed your stockings because they are uncomfortable?"

Maybe she hadn't yet managed a properly alluring smile? There had been many occasions, Willa reminded herself, when her first efforts had been unsuccessful—from her first sampler to her first kiss.

"I am removing my clothing." She twisted to reach the tie at the back of her neck. "I have accepted your proposal of marriage. That being the case, it would be very pleasant to continue what we began last night."

That was pure Willa, she recognized too late.

Sure enough, Alaric let out a bark of laughter. "*Pleasant?*"

"Very." Willa nodded. "We are truly betrothed now. So . . ." She had managed to untie the knot that held the lace apron on her gown.

He wasn't watching as she disrobed; he was studying her face instead. "Are you certain, Evie?"

"That I will marry you? Yes." It was easy to untie the strings of her cork rump and let it drop to the ground.

"What about women like Prudence?"

"The number of mad people is small in proportion to the number of sane people, I would think. Once you become a boring squire, merely a duke's younger son with a few travel narratives in your past, I doubt anyone will pay you much attention."

That was a fib.

Alaric was a man to whom people would always pay notice, but she had concluded that she wanted him more than she wanted privacy. She began unbuttoning her bodice. Under it she wore a corset that did very nice things to her breasts, and below that, her chemise.

"You won't embarrass me, will you?" she asked. Her fingers were trembling again, as they had the night before, from a combination of desire and anticipation. "I will be distressed if you refuse me. I might think you are rejecting my figure."

"That's rubbish."

Willa took her bodice off and dropped it to the side, followed by her corset. Then she lay back on the pillows and smiled up at him.

Alaric stared down, incredulity written on his face. "Aren't you supposed to be timid about bedding me? You're a virgin."

Willa let ice slide into her voice. "Do you imagine otherwise?"

"No." He shook his head with a grimace. "I just can't quite grasp the miracle that is Willa Everett."

She was about to say something sarcastic when he abruptly lowered his large, warm body onto hers. She wriggled against the hardened rod straining against her belly, and a groan sounded from deep in his chest.

In the books whose illustrations she and Lavinia had examined, the male tool had appeared faintly ridiculous, like the horn of a rhinoceros. Alaric's, to her delight, felt warm and alive.

He bent his head to kiss her, and Willa relaxed into his embrace and let herself be. *Be* in the moment, although she was lying on a pile of pillows in an imitation

Greek temple. *Be* with Alaric, even though she had never contemplated marrying Lord Wilde.

Be a person who was trembling and panting and unable to think. There were no rules for a moment like this—or if there were, Willa didn't know them. All she could do was feel.

They kissed for long minutes, Alaric's hands clasping her head, his mouth ravaging hers over and over. Before long she was arching against him, inarticulate pleas coming from her throat. Her legs felt restless, aflame, aching with a burn she'd never felt before.

"Alaric," she gasped.

He didn't answer, but looked into her eyes once more. Whatever he saw there must have satisfied him, because he kissed each eye and murmured something about a wife.

Then he kissed his way down her cheek, peppering her with kisses that felt like brands. Just as he reached her throat, one of his hands curled around her breast.

Willa tipped her head back. In the midst of shattering heat and bliss, one thought floated up: this was so freeing. There was nothing more *free* than to allow someone to make you blissful.

Allow?

It should be an exchange. Her hands had been groggily flying over Alaric's back in small caresses. Now she ran a hand straight down the front of his breeches.

He made a hoarse sound, deep in his throat.

"Should I not do that?" Willa gasped. Her fingers curled in embarrassment. Perhaps she wasn't allowed to touch like that. Perhaps that was only for the trollops pictured in those Italian books.

She snatched her hand back.

"If I beg you, will you touch me like that again?"

His aching question made her lips curl up in a breathless smile. "It's acceptable?"

"No rules," Alaric stated. "No rules between us, Evie." He ripped open the front of his breeches as he flicked his tongue against hers. "I'm going to lick your body from head to foot."

Her hand slid down his front again and she curled her fingers around him. He was large and hot. When she tightened her fingers, the breath caught in his throat.

"There is no propriety between us," he rasped, pushing farther into her hand. "You may do whatever you like to me. Whatever you dream of doing. My body is yours."

Heat was prickling through her from her breasts to her legs. She drew in a shaky breath. "I'm not sure what to do with you."

"Do you have any knowledge of the marital act?" he asked.

"Yes, but I'm not sure if there's something I'm supposed to do at this moment," she confessed, the words ragged.

Willa's mouth was so plush and lovely that Alaric leaned down and kissed her again, even as his cock was pulsing in her hand.

A few minutes or an hour later, he pulled back and forced himself to ask, "Are you certain? You don't want to wait until you become Lady Alaric Wilde to bed me?"

She shook her head, eyes bright. "Has it occurred to you that my name will be Willa Wilde?"

He swooped down and kissed her silent, swallowing her giggles. "Evie Wilde, this is your last chance," he said, meaning it. "I will marry you, even though you deserve better than me, even though I am besieged by readers and madwomen."

"I will marry you," she said, as fiercely as he, "even though you are the beloved son of a duke and I'm an orphan, even though you are a famous author and I still haven't read your books, even though you gave me a skunk when I wanted a kitten."

Alaric felt his heart skip a beat. "You will be my bride, in truth?"

His girl nodded, her eyes on his.

A desperate sound tore from his throat as he succumbed to a wave of blinding need, ripping open the neck of her chemise. A moment later his mouth closed around a pink nipple and he suckled her hard.

"More," she gasped.

"May I remove your skirts?" He'd never heard his own voice so guttural and deep.

Coming up on his knees, he tugged off his shirt and came back to her, taking her other nipple between his lips. She squirmed and arched. "Do that again!"

He slid a hand up her smooth leg, all the way up, and she fell silent.

She was sleek and wet. He flipped up her skirts; she was exquisite, deep rose fading to pale pink. "You're too beautiful for me," he said thickly.

He bent his head and licked her flowery, private place without warning. Direct, because Willa was like that. No need for fussing.

Sure enough, her fingers clamped around his head to hold him there.

He kissed her until she cried out, her body convulsing around his fingers, her eyes flying open in surprise. Then he moved, bracing himself over her. Her trusting smile felt like a caress. "This may hurt," he whispered.

His aching cock slid through wet, hot silk. Being Willa, she looked curious, not frightened. Her fingers tightened on his shoulders as he reached down and guided himself inside. No more than the head of his cock slid inside. She was so tight that a rasping sound escaped his throat. Her hips rose to meet him and he gained another inch. "Is there more?" she gasped.

"Quite a bit," he admitted, bringing himself into her with aching slowness, until he was so deep that he felt as if they were melting one into the other.

Her eyes widened, as if she shared his feeling that the unlocking of her body was a still moment in a turning world. A moment that changed her body and his. Brushing a kiss on her lips, he began to withdraw slowly. Her fingernails pricked his shoulders and she cried, "No!"

He kissed her until she relaxed and he slid into her again, but it felt so good that his vision blurred.

"Alaric, no," she said urgently, and he realized that his hips were drawing back, preparing to thrust back in, but she was arching up, keeping him inside her.

He would have laughed but he had to save his breath. "Just wait," he breathed into her ear. He pumped forward, stopped, moved back slowly, stroked forward, willing her to enjoy it, to learn the dance that would bring joy.

He was just reaching the point at which he was uneasily aware that he might lose control, when she whispered, "Alaric, is it possible to go faster?"

His heart hammered in his chest, stealing his breath. He braced on his forearms, hovering over her body, and began flexing his hips over and over, watching carefully for signs of pain, but seeing none.

In fact, her cheeks were turning cherry red and her eyes dreamy, unfocused, her hands stroking his body and leaving ribbons of bright fire in their wake.

Finally, he let himself go into that place of white-hot heat and emotion, where there was nothing but pleasure, and he took Willa with him.

Or she took him with her.

Because when her hips began rising to meet him, sobs breaking from her chest, fingernails leaving little imprints in his skin, it drove him out of his mind. And when she sobbed and flung herself into his hungry kiss, he lost his head entirely.

Words poured from his mouth, astonishing him even in the grip of the most acute pleasure he'd ever known. The echo of them hung in the air, fueling a ravaging joy that swept him away.

Swept them both away.

Alaric roused himself a good while later. Willa's head was comfortably nestled on his shoulder, their legs entwined. "You know the title of that ridiculous play?" he asked.

"*Wilde in Love*?" she asked, her voice a bit scratchy.

"You're my love," he whispered. He eased her onto her back and looked down at his beautiful bride-to-be. "You're at my heart, Evie; you are my heart. I love you and I'm in love with you."

She stared up at him, lips parted, startled.

"You needn't reciprocate," he said, feeling a deep contentment. "The sentence is not like a curtsy that must be answered with a bow. The emotion was a shock to me. To my system."

A slow smile crept over her face and glowed in her eyes. "So the next play should be called *The Taming of Lord Wilde*?"

Alaric pressed a kiss on one of her slender arched eyebrows, already imagining naughty children with enchanting giggles, just like Willa's.

"I am tamed," he said gravely.

That called for a kiss.

Or ten.

Chapter Twenty-nine

That evening

On her way to dinner, Willa stopped at the top of the staircase and paused to regain her composure. She felt as though what happened in the folly had left visible traces, as if everyone would take one look at her and know she was a different woman.

A fallen woman.

She hadn't realized how tightly she had clung to the role of a perfect lady until it vanished. Of course, she was now a betrothed woman, which was a new role as well. The role of wife was coming soon.

Alaric had said, with ferocious emphasis, that he wanted the first banns read in the morning so she couldn't change her mind. If he had his way, she would be married within the month.

When a hand touched her shoulder, she was so startled that she let out a little squeak. "Good evening," she said, drawing in an unsteady breath and trying for a nonchalant tone.

As if she hadn't parted from this man a mere two hours before.

As if she hadn't pushed him out the door of her bedchamber just when he was threatening to toss her onto the bed again.

"Evie," her fiancé said, his voice a low rumble. He bent to kiss her, and never mind they might be seen by anyone, including footmen in the entry below.

Even as that thought went through Willa's mind, Alaric drew her closer, kissing her with such a deep tenderness that her knees weakened and her arms went around his neck.

When at last Alaric drew away, Willa stood, dazed, gazing at her fiancé. She, Wilhelmina Everett Ffynche, was going to marry Lord Alaric Wilde—but not for any of the reasons she'd imagined. Not because he gave her Sweetpea, or because he was so fascinating.

She was going to marry him because she had fallen in love with him.

A polite cough broke into her thoughts. Willa looked

to her left and the Duke of Lindow was standing at her elbow. She jumped back, mortified. "I'm so sorry!" she blurted out, and dropped into a low curtsy. A feverish blush spread all the way from her chest to her forehead. "Please excuse us."

"Good evening, Father," Alaric said, without a touch of regret in his voice. "How is Her Grace?"

"A false alarm," the duke said. "The doctor thinks it best that my wife stay in bed at the moment, which she is not enjoying. How are you, Miss Ffynche?" He didn't look amused but Willa knew, somehow, that he was.

"I am very well," she managed. She felt like a doomed roly-poly, desperate to curl into a ball of pure humiliation.

His Grace regarded his son. "One might consider a more secluded spot for salutations of this nature."

"I'll keep it in mind," Alaric responded cheerfully.

The duke bowed and descended the stairs.

Willa waited until His Grace had vanished into the drawing room before she scowled at her fiancé. "This won't do, Alaric. Stop laughing!"

She braced her hand against his shoulder to fend off another kiss. "No more of that," she ordered.

Alaric just laughed again. Her future husband didn't give a damn what people thought about him, and he never would. "Please don't kiss me in public," Willa ordered, as she twitched her hips away from his hand.

"But I feel like kissing you every time I look at you," he said, his voice like plush velvet.

"Moreover, please don't speak to me of inappropriate things in the company of others. Or in that tone of voice," she added.

"Yours is the only opinion that matters to me."

A smile trembled on Willa's mouth; how often does a woman hear that? All the same, she gave him a mock scowl. "You, Lord Alaric, are going to be Lord Wilde for the evening."

He grimaced. "I don't want to have to please anyone. I'm not writing any more books."

"Lord Wilde is polite and charming to everyone. Quite untruthful, perhaps, but endlessly genial."

"Lord Alaric wants to strip off your clothing and take you against the wall."

Despite herself, a giggle escaped Willa's chest.

Strong arms circled her. "I love that sound," he murmured in her ear. "It's pure joy. The silly side of you. The side only I get to see."

Willa swallowed hard. "Yes, well," she whispered back, "now we must be *proper*."

Alaric sighed. "This is important to you."

"Very." She nodded vigorously, because his eyes were searching hers, and he didn't seem convinced. "Very important."

"May I visit your room later, and bring you roly-polies, and make you giggle?"

She hesitated. "No more intimacies until we marry."

He made tragic eyes at her, but she was right and he knew it. "If you insist." He held out his elbow. "Come along, *Willa*. Did you notice what I called you? Willa." He looked disgruntled.

"By rights, you should call me Miss Ffynche."

Alaric grinned. "That's a step too far. I caught the most desirable young lady in all of London, and I'm damn well going to flaunt my right to use your first name. You can be Miss Ffynche to all the rest of them. I suspect that my aunt will throw one of the grandest balls this castle has ever seen, merely so that I can show off the fruits of my courtship."

"She will?"

"You haven't noticed that my family loves you as much as I do?"

Willa took a deep breath, trying to stop herself from kissing him. "You dislike balls," she observed.

"I want the world to know you are mine. I would shout it from a mountaintop, if I could."

Willa slipped her hand through his elbow. "Will you always be this sweet?"

He considered that. "No."

His smile was pure sin.

Chapter Thirty

The following afternoon

I'm going to take Sweetpea for a walk before tea," Willa told her maid. "No wig, and no powder either. I'll wear the large straw hat, the one with roses and white plumes."

Her favorite walking costume was cherry striped, with ruffles at the neck and around the hips. It had a white apron and was cut daringly short, the better to walk.

And to show off her ankles. Perhaps Alaric would see her from his secret bedchamber in the tower and join her.

"I'll wear the shoes with buckles," she said. "I know

the ruby boots are better suited, but they hurt my feet."

Once dressed, she fitted Sweetpea into her harness, put her into the basket, and made her way downstairs and out into the rose garden. The day was warm, and the roses were blooming in such tawny-yellow and golden profusion that it looked as if a pride of lions were all sleeping on top of each other.

She had been in the garden only a few minutes when she heard a patter of feet. She was stooped over, tickling Sweetpea, but she straightened to find Prudence Larkin running toward her.

Her first inclination was to turn and quickly walk away.

There was something about Prudence she disliked, beyond the simple fact that the woman was in love with her fiancé. For one thing, Willa couldn't dismiss the idea that Prudence had written *Wilde in Love* with the intention of disgracing Alaric, even if it had produced the opposite effect.

At the same time, she was convinced that Prudence was watching for an opportunity to get Alaric alone and attempt to compromise him.

And lastly, Prudence's habit of murmuring blessings was extraordinarily irritating. Only vicars and other clergymen were qualified to bless people, as far as Willa knew. Prudence's father may have been a missionary, but ordination wasn't hereditary.

Shaking all that off, she summoned a polite smile as Prudence trotted toward her, her face pinched and anxious.

"Miss Ffynche, Miss Ffynche!" she cried as soon as she was close enough. She came to a stop before Willa, panting and wringing her hands.

"Good afternoon, Miss Larkin. Is something the matter?"

"It's Miss Belgrave," Prudence gulped. "Miss Diana!"

Willa waited.

"Verily, she has made up her mind to eschew the bonds of matrimony and has returned from whence she came!"

"Ah," Willa said. This news was not particularly surprising, given that Lavinia had said that Diana was gathering herself to make this very decision.

"She left no note, and she didn't even take her maid," Prudence gasped.

"What?"

"Miss Belgrave instructed me to ask you to break the news to Alaric."

Willa's brows drew together at this informality.

"I mean, to Lord Alaric!" Prudence said defensively, adding, "He should be the one to tell Lord Roland."

Diana had left *without a word to her fiancé*? Willa's mind spun for a moment, thinking of the longing, pain, and desire with which Alaric's brother regarded his fiancée.

Diana should have found the courage and grace to inform North herself.

Willa didn't entirely blame her for leaving. A woman ought to love her spouse, no matter how advantageous the match. Still, there were so many better ways to handle a delicate situation like this than running away.

Prudence was still wringing her hands.

"Miss Belgrave told *you*?" Willa asked, unable to contain her incredulity.

"I saw her go." She hesitated. "I followed her and asked her where she was going. I knew she was fibbing to the butler because she had a hatbox. Why would she take a hatbox to the village?"

That made sense. Prudence was always watching from the corners and she was just the sort to spring out and demand an explanation.

"Very well," Willa said with a sigh. "I'd better find Alaric." She scooped up Sweetpea and returned her to the basket.

"I know where he is," Prudence said, taking her arm and tugging.

Willa held back. "How would you know that?"

"I watched from the window as Alaric went down that path." She gestured away from the castle. "I shouldn't watch him, but it is a hard habit to break. I am trying." Her cheeks were pink, her voice pained. "I have decided to return to London."

"We'll all be leaving soon," Willa said, trying for diplomacy as they began to walk.

"I shall leave tomorrow." Prudence's chin led the way. "I tell thee the truth: Alaric has disappointed me. I wrote a play for him; I dreamed of him; I loved him. And how did he repay me?"

"Betrothing himself to me had nothing to do with you," Willa said, untruthfully. "He didn't even know you were alive, remember?"

Prudence threw her a bitter look. "We will catch up with him soon."

Willa stopped. They had reached the stone wall at the eastern end of the garden. The neat gravel walk had branched off and led them to a heavy wooden door, half-obscured by rosebushes, that Willa had never before noticed.

Prudence dropped Willa's arm and pushed open the door, which moved easily, given its heft. On the other side, the gravel was replaced by wooden planks that led straight into Lindow Moss, the peat bog that they had been warned in no uncertain terms not to enter.

The bog where Lord Horatius had lost his life.

Prudence curled her arm through Willa's again. "Shall we?"

"I'm turning back." Willa jerked her arm away from Prudence's. Sweetpea jolted from side to side and sat up with a little hiss, curling her claws on the side of the basket.

"No, you are not," Prudence stated.

"Don't be daft," Willa said, exasperated. "Could you try to be more rational?"

"Did you think I don't know?" Prudence asked in a low, throbbing voice. "Did you think I wouldn't find out about you?"

"Insulting me will not put you in Lord Alaric's good graces."

"Everyone knows how you wooed him!"

"I have no idea what you're talking about," Willa said. The afternoon sun was making Prudence's eyes sparkle like cut glass.

"Sneaking him into your bedchamber," she hissed. "Did you think I wouldn't know it? Or that I won't write a play about it? Wait until *Wilde in the Country* makes its way onto the stage. Everyone in London will clamor to see it!"

Oh, for goodness' sake.

"If you write that play, you will ruin Alaric," Willa

said, making her voice very, very reasonable. "You love him."

"I believed I did," Prudence said. "Perhaps I should give him another chance." She cocked her head. "No, I think not." She slid her hand out of the side slit in her gray dress. "I would like you to walk down the path now."

She was holding a small pistol that looked as if it had been made for her hand. Unbelievably, it seemed that Prudence had been carrying a weapon in her pocket, which she was now pointing directly at Willa's head.

"May I just say that Wilhelmina is one of the ugliest names I've ever heard?" Prudence said, breaking the silence as Willa stared dumbfounded at her. "I hate to offend you, but I have a writer's soul and a reverence for words."

"I'm going to return to the house now," Willa stated, stepping back again.

"Perhaps you assume that I will miss," Prudence said, her white teeth gleaming. "Allow me to disabuse you of that error. I am an extremely good shot, even at a distance—and this is not much of a distance. We practiced regularly in Africa, because sometimes the only thing that can stop a crocodile is a bullet through the eye. Did you know that?"

Willa shook her head.

Prudence gestured with the pistol. "My belt holds additional gunpowder and bullets, in case you're wondering. Go on. Get in front of me. You're going to walk through this door and down the path."

"Why?"

Prudence's brow furrowed. "You have to ask? Because you've stolen Alaric's soul. Men are weak and prone to sins of the flesh. He won't be able to make a reasonable decision until the doxy is removed from his sight."

Willa's mind was whirling. Where were the duke's gardeners, or a groom, or even another guest? With great reluctance, she started down the plank path, because something in Prudence's face suggested she wouldn't hesitate to shoot.

They continued in silence while Willa racked her brain for a way she might save herself. She walked as slowly as she thought she could risk without provoking her captor.

"Do you know that Puritans consider plays to be the work of the devil?" Prudence said abruptly. "My father was convinced of it." Her voice took on a sing-song cadence. "'Such spectacles are filthy infections, such as turn minds from chaste cogitations, dishonoring the vessels of holiness, leading to a state of everlasting damnation.'"

"He sounds like a blunt man," Willa replied. The wooden planks under her feet were placed on relatively firm hillocks. Darker green patches indicated water holes, if she remembered correctly.

"A good description for my father," Prudence agreed. "He abhors unsavory morsels of unseemly sentences."

"Most alliterative," Willa said, trying to stay calm. Might she be able to lunge backward and knock Prudence off the plank, in hopes the woman fell into a bog hole? Was she capable of allowing another human to drown?

No.

What if she didn't have time to rush back to the castle and fetch men to pull Prudence out? What if Prudence thrashed and sank quickly? Look what had happened to Horatius.

What if she could somehow knock the *pistol* into the swamp?

"May I put Sweetpea down?" she asked, slowing to a stop. If they went much farther she would lose sight of the castle.

"My father scorns filthy, lewd, and ungodly speeches," Prudence hissed. "But the words of truth . . . the words I told him were rooted in my heart, those he also condemned as lewd."

It seemed the missionary hadn't believed his daughter's story about Alaric's adoration for her.

"Keep walking," Prudence barked.

Willa continued, more slowly. "Do you intend to shoot me? It is obvious Alaric is nowhere ahead of us on this path. Do you mean to commit murder?"

"Absolutely not!" Prudence snapped. "You are a harlot, yea, an openly shameful woman who belongs in a brothel, but it is not for me to take your life."

"In that case, where are we going, and why?"

"You will go into the bog," Prudence replied, her voice once more clear and amiable. "I cannot abide to exist near such a filthy thing as you are. Alaric has eaten of your words and tasted of your body. He is *poisoned*."

"If you allow me to return to the castle," Willa said, "I will return to London without delay, leaving Alaric behind. You needn't have my death on your conscience."

"I won't," Prudence said, obviously surprised. "If I had to shoot you, it would be different. But I shall leave your fate in the hands of God. My heart is like a lion's; I will not shirk from the Lord's cause."

When Prudence fell into the rhythms of that particular kind of speech, her eyes took on an unhinged look.

"Don't you think the Lord might take his vengeance on me on the road to London?" Willa asked. "I could keep walking on this path and not return to Lindow Castle at all."

Prudence glanced over her shoulder. The castle was little more than a speck on the western horizon, and the afternoon was drawing in. "Time for you to test your fate," she said. "Get off the plank."

She waved the pistol at Willa. "Put that animal down first."

"What are you going to do to her?"

"Nothing," Prudence said impatiently. "It is an innocent, and as such, must be protected by the godly."

This was madness in its purest, starkest form. But unquestionably, Sweetpea was better out of the bog. Willa put the basket down slowly, keeping an eye on the pistol.

"Step off the footpath," Prudence said, almost sounding bored.

Sweetpea sat up so Willa stroked her head with one finger, willing her to stay put.

"You're not going to weep and beg me for mercy?" Prudence asked as Willa straightened.

"Would it make any difference?" Willa couldn't jump at Prudence without being shot; the woman's finger was curled around the trigger.

She would have to cross the bog without falling into a water sink. As soon as she was out of Prudence's sight, she would sit still and wait to be rescued.

"No difference at all. You are in the hands of God," Prudence said. "His will be done. We are placed as pilgrims in this flesh, and must keep it pure lest the ungodly contaminate us."

Down on the ground, Sweetpea had put her paws on the edge of the basket. "No," Willa said to her. "Stay there. Miss Larkin will take you home."

With a wrinkle of her nose, Prudence reached down with her free hand and took up the basket. "Putrid animal," she complained. Sweetpea lost her balance and tumbled on her side. "I'd encourage you to pray, but I have seen from your manner that you are entirely profane. If you feel the wish to prepare yourself for the spiritual life, you may kneel and pray. If you believe the Spirit will move you."

Willa was pretty certain it wouldn't, so she said, "I think you'll have to shoot me, Prudence. I'm afraid to step into the bog."

"That would endanger my soul," Prudence explained. "Off you go or I'll blow this creature's head off." She pointed the pistol at Sweetpea.

"You said she was an innocent!" Willa protested.

"It is an animal. *You*, on the other hand, live in a

Temple of the Lord, which you have defiled and polluted. Why are you taking off your hat?"

"I can't enter the bog in a large hat designed for a garden party," Willa stated, hoping that Prudence would accept it as a fashion edict.

"That is a work of darkness," Prudence said broodingly.

The afternoon was fading and their shadows were stretching across the surface of the bog. If Willa delayed any longer, she wouldn't be able to discern dark moss from lighter grass. What's more, she had a shrewd feeling that Prudence would find it easier to shoot her as time went on.

Prism had told them that the bog was dotted with peat cutters' huts, and if she wasn't mistaken, there was a low roof in the distance.

"*Go!*"

Willa stepped from the footpath, testing a hassock of grass with her toe. A crack of gunfire broke the silence and she screamed. With a hiss, the hot bullet sank into wet grass to her right.

"I'm reloading," Prudence said, her voice utterly calm. "I advise you to run. If you are godly, you will survive the bog. God will show your feet the way. If you are scurrilous and infectious, you will sink."

Willa looked ahead, committing to a meandering

trail of sturdy-looking hassocks that went as far as she could see. Before Prudence could finish reloading, she threw her hat onto an openly wet area, praying it would float, picked up her skirts, and began to run.

Her entire being focused on reaching one hassock after another. The peat was spongy under her feet. More than once a hassock shifted and rolled under her weight, but she had already left it for the next one.

No more shots were fired; Prudence shouted something but Willa was too focused to catch what she said.

She stopped only when she lost a shoe, grabbed by the bog when she put her foot wrong. She turned and watched as it sank with a sucking noise, and then took a shattered breath, fighting down a sob.

Meanwhile, the light had turned golden and would remain so for an hour, perhaps longer. Her frantic dash had taken her to a place where she could no longer see the plank path, or the castle on the horizon.

In this light, the jade-green patches were fading to a mossy brown, like the kind of rocks you see in a Highlands stream. But this was no stream. A whole sea of peat gently rolled to the horizon.

Chapter Thirty-one

Alaric spent an hour or so with the ledger containing the buttery accounts, but he kept thinking of Willa's question about Horatius. It was such a simple one: what kind of person was Horatius? It made him realize that younger Wildes would have little or no memory of their eldest brother, which was inconceivable.

He finally put the ledger to the side and began to write a story drawn from his childhood, about a time when the Duke of Lindow took their family to a hunting lodge high in the Pennines hills one December.

Horatius dug a snow house for Alaric, Parth, and Roland, with two exits and three separate rooms. He'd dropped his dignity and played with them, chasing them on hands and knees through warm, snowy tunnels. Howling at them like the great warrior he was named after.

It was, hands down, the best Christmas of Alaric's life.

He was just finishing when the door was thrown open and North appeared.

"She's left me," he roared.

"What?" Alaric looked up as his brother slammed the door shut behind him.

"Diana's run away. She's left me."

"Bloody hell," Alaric said, dropping his pencil. "That's rotten luck." Of course it wasn't a question of luck, but he didn't think his brother was ready to hear that he was better off without that particular woman, or that he'd find someone better.

North ripped off his wig and threw it at a chair; it bounced and fell to the floor. To Alaric's surprise, his brother's head was shaved. He took off his coat and threw that to the side as well. "She's left me," he repeated, obviously stunned.

Alaric leaned back in his chair. "Just now?"

North strode forward and slammed his fist on the desk. "She didn't even write me a bloody note. Nothing."

Alaric felt a surge of anger toward Diana Belgrave. To go away without an explanation was rude and unfeeling. Cruel, even. Any fool could see how devoted North was.

"Do you know who told me that my sniveling, cowardly fiancée had fled to London?" North demanded.

"Prism?"

"Prudence Larkin!" he bellowed. "That unmitigated, rubbishing Puritan woman was entrusted with a simple message: 'Miss Belgrave has changed her mind about the wedding.'"

"I wasn't aware they were more than acquaintances."

"They aren't," North snarled. "As I understand it, if Prudence hadn't seen Diana sneaking away and demanded an explanation, my fiancée would have left the house without bothering to tell me that she was jilting me. She lied to Prism, who thought she was paying a visit to the village."

He dropped onto the settee and rubbed his hands over his scalp, his jaw clenched in a rigid line.

"I'm sorry," Alaric said.

"No, you're not. You never liked Diana and now you're proven right."

"I didn't dislike her. I just thought she wasn't as deeply attached as you are."

"As deeply? She's not attached at all. She prefers to ruin herself rather than marry me."

"Is Diana ruined?" Alaric had never paid much attention to the rules of polite society. And, at his brother's nod, "Simply because she left you?"

"She's jilted the heir to a dukedom," North said, his voice quieting. "She won't be invited to parties next Season, if ever." He looked up, hands falling into his lap. "Do you want to know the damnable thing?"

Alaric nodded.

"I don't think she'll care. I think she is so eager to rid herself of me that she'd rather marry a chimney sweep. I tried—I tried everything I could think of."

His wig lay on the floor next to his feet. North gave it such a violent kick that it actually lifted in the air before plopping down on the empty hearth.

"That's your Parisian wig," Alaric said. "If this was December, it would be a cinder." He went over and picked it up, patting it into shape the way one might pat a small fluffy dog.

"Do you really think I give a damn?" his brother demanded, the words grinding from somewhere deep in his chest.

"No," Alaric said, placing the wig on the mantelpiece. He sat down beside North, wrapping an arm around his shoulders. "I'm sorry Diana couldn't see the man you are." He hesitated. "Do you think she had already given her affections elsewhere?"

"No. I asked her as much a couple of days ago. Flatly

asked her in the drawing room, when I was trying to imagine our married life."

"She may have lied," Alaric said, trying to decide whether it was worse to have one's fiancée in love with someone else, or simply be in the grip of such disgust that she'd ruin her prospects of a good marriage to get away.

"There were times when our eyes would meet and I could have sworn she was beginning to be fond of me. That I could win her, given time. I told myself she was frightened by all the fuss around the Wildes."

"Because of my books?" Alaric asked, his heart sinking.

"It's not just you," North said wearily. "It's all of us. The whole family. Every damn thing we do is watched and imitated, appears in the gossip columns the next day if we're in London. Those prints . . ."

"I am sorry about them."

"There are prints sold of me, as well as of the duke and duchess. The house. Leonidas, being kicked out of Eton, matched to another of *you* in the same situation. Betsy."

"Betsy! She's only sixteen."

"She's beautiful," North said. "Father managed to have an etching of Horatius struggling in the swamp destroyed, but only after it sold several thousand copies."

That was so distasteful that Alaric bit back a curse.

North returned to the subject at hand. "The evening I asked Diana to marry me, she kissed me," he said, sounding like a man in a dream. "I thought I would never be so happy again. But when I saw her the next day, she wouldn't meet my eyes. I kissed her earlier today, and now she's gone."

He came to his feet. "I have to go after her."

"Do you think you can make a difference?" Alaric asked.

"She'll be ruined. I can't permit her to be ruined. I'll let it be known that I broke the betrothal."

"Are you leaving for London now?" And, at North's nod, "Would you like me to accompany you?"

North shook his head. He was expressionless, his eyes like dark glass with violet smudges under them. "I must make certain that she's safe."

"It wasn't a mistake to have loved her," Alaric said, walking him to the door.

"Better to have loved and lost?" North said, biting off his words. "Bull. I feel as if I was fool enough to walk in the high grass, and now that I've been bitten by a snake, I can hardly complain."

He strode away. Returning to the ledgers, Alaric realized that his brother had left his Parisian wig behind on the mantelpiece, a little worse for wear.

North had been gone for a half hour at most, when the door to the library opened again, and his father entered.

"It seems Miss Belgrave may not have left by herself," the duke said, without introduction.

Alaric put down his pencil and came to his feet. "I assumed her maid had left with her."

"Her maid has been given a soporific and put to bed. The poor woman is convinced that Diana's mother will blame her. No, I am told that Miss Ffynche departed with Miss Belgrave, though I can scarcely believe that both of my sons would lose their fiancées in a single day."

Images reeled through Alaric's mind: the way Willa smiled at him. The way her head fell backward when he . . .

No. Willa did not leave him.

"It could be that Miss Belgrave begged for Willa's assistance in her flight, but in that case, Willa would have explained it to me first."

"Yours was not a true betrothal," his father said, his eyes intent on Alaric.

"Not immediately," Alaric said. "But as you saw last night, it is entirely real now."

His father's eyes lightened. "I did assume as much." Then he frowned. "Prudence Larkin just informed me that Willa had decided to break her betrothal."

"She is lying." Dread surged through him. "Where is Willa?"

"She is not in her bedchamber, nor can Prism find her anywhere in the house or gardens." The duke opened the heavy oak door and Alaric lunged for the staircase.

When Alaric pounded on Prudence's bedchamber door, a voice called, "I am not prepared for visitors."

He pushed the door open. Prudence was seated with her feet in a large pan of water. As he entered, followed by the duke, she shrieked and drew her gown over her bare ankles. Its hem fell into the water.

"Alaric!" she squealed. And then, "Your Grace!" She jumped up without stepping from the basin. "Please forgive me for not being in proper attire to greet you."

Alaric looked down at her feet. The hem of her dress was not only wet, but caked in mud. "Why are you soaking your feet?" he asked—and at the same moment he knew the answer to his own question. He could *smell* the answer. "What have you done with Sweetpea?"

Prudence's expression sweetened. "You mean Miss Ffynche's darling little pet? I have no idea where it is."

"Stop lying," Alaric barked. "I am not imagining that stench. More pertinent, *where is Willa*?"

"Miss Ffynche left with Miss Belgrave," she chirped, blithely ignoring a roar that would have had many young women in frightened tears. "As for the disagreeable odor, I encountered an animal akin to Miss Ffynche's pet in the garden. Her darling would never be so mischievous as to foul my shoes."

"Sweetpea is a North American species," Alaric stated. "You did not encounter another of her kind in the garden."

"Lord Roland left on a fast horse following Miss Belgrave," the duke said, fixing Prudence with a ducal glare. "The veracity of your statements will shortly become clear."

Alaric turned to his father. "Send for the sheriff."

"Why?" Prudence squawked.

"To arrest you on suspicion of causing Miss Ffynche bodily harm."

The duke nodded and left.

"Why would you say such a thing?" Prudence cried. "She left, she left with Miss Belgrave." Stubborn hostility shone from her eyes. "She doesn't love you, Alaric. She doesn't deserve you. Not the way I do." She ended on a pleased note, as if her argument was sufficient to make him stop questioning Willa's disappearance.

Alaric took another step toward her, clenching his fists to ensure he didn't reach out and shake her. "You don't know what it means to love, Prudence."

"I suppose you do?" she retorted, growing a little shrill. "I know—we *all* know—that you are bedding that trollop. Is that love? No! Lust will consign you to the everlasting fires of hell!"

Despite himself, Alaric's hands seized her bony shoulders. He restrained himself from shaking her, just looked into her pale eyes and said, "Prudence, listen to me."

"I could listen to you every moment of my life," she said. But her expression was wary. She was caught in the lion's trap and she knew it. Under all that treacly nonsense was a shrewdly evil, calculating brain. Perhaps not a sane brain, but a shrewd one.

"I am going to marry Willa. Only Willa. I will never marry you, under any circumstances. If you have caused harm to my future wife, I will see that justice is served; you will live out the rest of your life in the darkest, dankest prison in all the kingdom. Now tell me where she is."

"I didn't kill her!" Prudence cried, trying to wrench free of his grasp.

He let go and she stepped backward, tipping over the basin. Water ran across the floor and Sweetpea's distinctive odor filled the room.

"That varmint befouled me." Her voice was a hiss, like steam escaping a teakettle.

"*Where is Willa?*" Alaric demanded. His heart was beating a sickening cadence.

"I'm sure I don't know," Prudence said, rearranging her skirts to cover her bare feet.

"Where did you see her last?"

"Outside, in the rose garden. I would never do away with her; such a thing would be morally wrong. I left her in the hands of God."

"You have just admitted that Willa didn't leave with Diana," Alaric pointed out.

Prudence hunched up a shoulder until it nearly brushed her ear and gave him a coy, sideways glance. "I thought perhaps you would see more clearly if she wasn't at your side every moment, tempting you to sin."

"If you left Willa in the rose garden, she would have returned to the castle by now."

"Must you go after her?" Then, after a glance at his face, "Perhaps she's twisted her ankle."

"Did you injure her?"

"Certainly not," Prudence said, her voice taking on a peevish tone. "She was in the rose garden with that animal of hers. We had . . . *words* and look what happened." Her eyes flashed with rage. "That dreadful little creature lifted its tail and—and urinated on me! On my feet!"

"Sweetpea must have felt threatened."

"I should have broken its neck," Prudence said with venom. "Miss Ffynche chased after that animal when it ran away."

Alaric looked at her, a hard look with menace behind it.

"I kicked it," Prudence said sulkily. "After which, I left Miss Ffynche in the rose garden, searching for her filthy animal."

Alaric had no reason to believe a single word she said, but he might as well search the rose garden. "Do not leave this room," he ordered.

"How could I?" Prudence demanded, dropping back into her chair and slipping her feet into the water. "I reek, thanks to that horrid animal!"

In the hallway, Alaric stopped a footman and instructed him to stand outside Prudence's door and not allow her to stir from the room. Then he ran downstairs and out of the castle to the rose garden.

It was deserted. The house-party guests were in their bedchambers, engaged in lengthy preparations for the evening meal.

Significantly, the garden smelled just as it should, though the scent of roses seemed sickening to him now. If Sweetpea had sprayed Prudence here, the smell would linger.

Prudence had lied.

As he moved between the beds, trying to decide where to look next, he suddenly noticed that the door leading out to Lindow Moss was ajar.

Throughout the chaotic years of his childhood and youth, almost no rules had been in force for him and his siblings. One rule, however, was inviolable: the door leading to the Moss was to remain securely closed at all times for the safety of the duke's children.

That hadn't stopped them from exploring the bog, but they always, always closed the door behind them. Now, as he stared at the half-open door, he felt a deep uneasiness.

Surely Willa wouldn't have followed Sweetpea down the path into the bog.

If she had stayed on the path, she was almost certainly safe. They would find her. If she *had* ventured into Lindow Moss, she was in peril, and there was no time to waste. It only took a second to make up his mind: He pushed the door fully open and surveyed the undulating peat sea.

Before it claimed Horatius, the Moss had simply existed, a part of his world. Now it seemed animate . . . malevolent.

Planks rocked slightly under his feet as he walked, his eyes searching in every direction for any sign of Willa. If Prudence had pushed her from the path into the bog after Sweetpea's defensive volley, the planks would smell, but the only odor was the stink of peat.

Willa would never leave the path on her own. His heart thudded a dark rhythm in his chest as the wooden path zigzagged, following sturdy ground.

Then he caught it. It was just a whiff, traveling on a faint breeze. He stopped and turned in a circle, trying to identify the direction of the odor. The castle was almost out of sight, a spot on the horizon with the sun sinking above it.

He'd lost the odor entirely, so he strode on, willing another breeze to come. Some moments later he caught another whiff and then the smell grew ever more pungent until he spotted a small black-and-white animal on the edge of the path.

Alaric's heart bounded. He crouched down and Sweetpea ran straight to him and launched herself into his hands. She stank to high heaven, but she was alive and evidently unhurt. Her paws were muddy, so she must have ventured off the plank but been smart enough to get herself back on and wait for help.

She had been lucky not to have been discovered by a hawk. Thinking of that, Alaric tucked her into his pocket.

Willa was lost in Lindow Moss. He was certain now. The truth of it clawed at his chest. Could Prudence have struck her on the head? Dragged her body into the bog? He refused to lose another person to this infernal place.

They had never found Horatius's body; the bog hole where his horse was mired fed a swift running river under the Moss. Sometimes bodies reemerged, but most didn't, trapped below the surface and never seen again.

He turned again, even more slowly, and peered across the bog.

Fifty yards from where he stood, a straw hat was floating in the water.

For one sickening moment, he pictured Willa still wearing the hat, her face—*all of her*—beneath the surface of the Moss.

Agony wrenched his gut before logic overruled his imagination: Willa was not under the hat. She had fled into the bog, doubtless in the face of some threat of Prudence's.

Alaric stepped off the plank.

She had left the hat as a sign for him, clever girl. Now that he was actually in the bog, his pulse steadied. Willa may have been fleeing from Prudence, but she was cool-headed. She would never run blindly.

She had dropped her hat to give him a starting point, and she trusted him to understand what she would do next. There was no question but that she would run toward the peat cutter's hut visible in the distance.

Bending over, he spied the imprint of a small heel. Breath exploded out of his lungs. Thank God, her shoes had heels; it would make it easier to track her.

He kept going, examining every tuft of moss or grass carefully. At some point Willa stopped running and began moving more deliberately, which made it harder to follow her, as her feet struck the bog with less force. Paradoxically, her caution put her in greater danger: bog walkers should always keep one foot in the air.

Several times he found she'd had to retrace her steps, looking for solid ground. He followed the faint traces of her footprints. At one point, he came upon a scrap of white lace snagged on a gorse twig. When he found another, and then a third, he knew she'd deliberately planted the scraps to guide him.

The lace trail was heartening, but ice still ran through his veins. It would be so easy for Willa to make a fatal mistake.

She started along a bright ribbon of sedge grass. Following it, he followed her. The deep part of his soul knew that he would follow her anywhere. For all the days of his life, the blades of grass that bent under her foot would bend under his as well.

She kept going, turning and twisting on her way to

the hut. He was having more and more trouble follow-ing her path; the light was fading and he kept losing her trail.

All the same, hope was pounding through him now. The low walls of the peat cutter's hut were coming closer and closer.

Five minutes later he reached the moss-covered door. He thrust it open without knocking.

The hut was deserted.

Chapter Thirty-two

Alaric's heart sank as he looked around the small dark room. There was a pallet to the side, so he knelt and shaped the rough blankets into a nest. He plucked Sweetpea from his pocket and put her in it.

She looked up at him, eyes bright.

"I'll be back," he promised. "I'll be back for you, Sweetpea."

She made a churring sound and curled up, her tail flopping over her nose. Alaric shut the door behind him, stepping into the darkening landscape.

Somehow he'd missed her. He'd made a mistake. He refused to imagine that he missed her because she had fallen into the bog, sunk without a trace.

Not Willa. Not his Willa. She was no Horatius, impaired by alcohol and trying to save his horse like a great, crusading ass.

All the same, panic raged through his veins, accompanied by fury at the filthy bog that had taken Horatius and put Willa in danger.

As he searched the horizon, looking for any sign of her, two lapwings flew over the peat in a mating dance, circling and falling back again, whirling up into the dark blue sky.

When they were boys, he and his brothers had been forbidden to enter Lindow Moss—so naturally, he, Horatius, Parth, and North treated it like their personal playground. He knew this land. Yet he hadn't gone near Lindow Moss since Horatius's death.

As his eyes followed the swooping flight of the lapwings, he realized that Horatius wouldn't approve. As the eldest son and future Duke of Lindow, Horatius had claimed the bog as his own.

He would have scorned Alaric for pretending it didn't exist. For shunning the place. No one loved tales of their ancestor, the first Lindow to conquer the bog, more than Horatius.

Abruptly, the words of a Meskwaki wise man came back to Alaric: "*We love the land that is ours. We are part of the land. If we fear it, it will swallow us.*"

He had spent eight months living with native peoples in the Americas, hunting with them, dancing with them, eating with them. He had learned from them that blades of grass have a language of their own.

But at that moment Alaric grasped that the more important lesson was that this was *his* land. He was one of the Wildes of Lindow Moss. This land was his family's, and had been for centuries. His land would talk to him. But not if he deemed it a violent entity aiming to murder the woman he loved.

Taking another deep breath, he let the perfume of peat and wildflowers sink into his skin. His land. His bog. His moss.

Calm flowed into his veins and he moved slowly back into the bog, retracing his steps. Almost immediately he saw where he had gone astray. He had turned north, heading directly for the peat cutter's hut at the same moment Willa had turned south.

After a few minutes he found another bit of lace stuck on a long thorn, waving slightly in the evening breeze.

Pushing terror out of his head, he concentrated everything he had on the language of Lindow Moss. An evening breeze stirred like a shy spirit, bringing with it the faint scent of chamomile. He froze. Smells of bracken, bramble, and smoky peat dominated, but underneath, like a whisper of song: chamomile soap.

Willa.

Mere minutes later, he found her, just as purple light was settling into the hollows of the bog. His future wife was lying on her stomach on the very edge of what appeared to be a large bog hole covered with a mat of moss. Her head was cradled on her arms and she appeared to be asleep.

He came to a soundless stop. If Willa turned on her side, she might easily roll onto that moss beside her. Even as slender as she was, it would not support her weight. And beneath the moss . . . Some bog holes were straight drops of twenty feet, full of water the color of the strongest pekoe tea.

If he called her name, she might wake abruptly and plunge into the hole.

His heart skipped a beat, before he pushed the thought away and lowered himself to a sitting position. She was here, and she was alive. He could see her breath moving strands of her hair.

Gradually, the sounds of Lindow Moss replaced the thundering of blood in his ears. Curlews were calling back and forth their evening songs, their cries thin spirals of sound.

When he had his body completely under control, he edged toward her, stopping only when the ground before him turned to a springy mat of thin moss covering liquid mud. With utmost care, he shifted onto his stomach. Willa must have been lying on a little island of firmer ground. It was a miracle that she hadn't fallen in.

His head was so close to the peat now that he could hear water flowing under the surface. The moss before him was black, and he knew before his palm brushed its rocking surface that it couldn't take his weight. He backed up, approached her from another angle.

Failed.

Tried again. Finally he came close enough that he thought it safe to wake her. If he had to, he could lunge for her hand. They might both fall into the hole, but at least they would die together.

"Evie," he said quietly. His voice drifted under the sounds of Lindow Moss putting itself to sleep. The curlews were drowsy now, calling irregularly. The burble of running water was louder.

She opened her eyes immediately; she had not been asleep, apparently, but she showed no sign of panic. "Oh, Alaric—I didn't hear you," she said, smiling without moving any other muscle.

Wilhelmina Everett Ffynche was an adventurer, whether she thought of herself as an aristocratic lady or not.

"Darling, please remain exactly where you are," he said.

"I must," she answered, ruefully. "If I shift my weight, everything moves under me, as if I lay on a thin mattress rocking on the waves. I seem safe enough at the moment."

Curses exploded in his head. She was not lying on a firm island. She was, in fact, lying directly above the bog hole.

"I knew you would come," she added.

He smiled back at her, thinking hard. He was a foot away. Inch by painstaking inch, he spread his arms forward, keeping them above the surface of the moss. "I'm going to move toward you, Evie. If I go down, do not move, do you hear me? My father's men will find you."

She managed to express the absurdity of that without twitching more than her eyebrows. "Why don't you go find help," she suggested. "I'll wait here."

He didn't want to frighten her. He really didn't want to frighten her.

"We haven't time for that," he said, because it was all too true. "It's growing dark."

"We could simply wait for morning," she said. But she sounded uncertain.

"You're lying on something we call a quaking bog," he said. "The mud that holds the moss together can warm with body heat and loosen."

Fear went through her eyes, but she didn't let it triumph. "I suppose we'd better do something, in that case."

"Many ladies would be in hysterics at this moment, Evie," he said. "I can't think of anyone I've ever met whom I'd want as a partner other than you."

"Why would I panic when I knew you would come for me?"

"And I have. Now, I'm going to keep my torso on firm ground, so that I can pull you toward me. Can you inch your arms carefully toward me?"

Willa nodded. Even that minute movement made the surface billow beneath her. Slowly, slowly, she inched her left arm out from under her head and straightened it.

"That's it, darling," Alaric murmured.

Willa gave him a lopsided smile. He was lying flat, his fingers outstretched toward hers. But behind his eyes . . .

"I am not Horatius," she reminded him. She'd been lying on this undulating mattress of moss for a good hour, and she could feel where it was thick, and where a mere tangle of weeds separated her from running water.

"I know you're not," he said. His tone was encouraging, but his eyes were stark.

She shifted her weight slightly in order to reach her right arm toward him. One hip dipped low and she paused, waiting until her quaking bed quieted again.

"You have unerring instincts for the bog," Alaric said, his voice drifting toward her. "You could have been born on Lindow Moss."

"Does the house you own lie alongside the bog as well?" She reached her arms forward, but a gap still divided their hands.

"We can sell it," he said, terse. "Do you know how to swim, Evie?"

"Oh, yes," she said. "Lavinia and I have swum in the sea at Brighton."

"Glide one arm forward toward me, pretending that you are lying on the surface of the water, like this."

She imitated him, reaching forward with the right side of her body. It caused a violent rocking on her blanket.

"Easy," Alaric said, so quietly it was hardly more than a breath. "Easy . . . Now little by little, staying level, swing your hip to the left."

"I didn't gain any ground," Willa told him, a moment later, having attempted it.

"You will," he said. His eyes held her, fiercely, as if he could will her over that last half-foot of bog.

"I believe my rump is caught," she said.

"What?"

"My *cork* rump." She managed a smile. "I suspect that the strings that hold it around my waist are caught on some twigs."

"That cork rump," he said, stunned. "It's keeping you afloat, isn't it?"

"Perhaps? When I tripped, my arms and legs went through the moss, but I popped back up. Yet I can't seem to move forward. Or backward."

Alaric made a slow, sinuous movement and reached for her.

"Is your weight moving onto the moss?" Willa asked with a pulse of sick fear. "You don't have a rump to hold you up!"

Another movement, so delicate that it scarcely sent a ripple across the surface. Alaric had perfect control over every muscle, she realized. As he moved, his weight didn't tip to either side.

"I'm all right," he reassured, his voice low. "I have a good grip of a hassock with my knees. Not ideal, but sufficient."

One more movement, so slow that she scarcely saw it, and his hands closed firmly around her outstretched fingers. Willa's smile trembled. "Hello, darling. I'm— I'm so glad you came for me."

"I will always come for you," Alaric stated, matter-of-factly. "Now, I mean to skate you along the surface toward me. Can you bend your knees so that your feet are raised above the surface?"

"I'm afraid I would be made—oh!" she exclaimed. "I believe I understand."

"It will remove the drag of your feet, and your cork rump will prevent you from sinking. I shall give you a good tug to free the strings. On my nod."

Willa kept her eyes on Alaric's. "If I fall into the water," she asked, "will you please stay safely where you are?"

"You didn't answer when I asked you the same question."

"My answer is no." The truth of it came from her heart. Alaric was hers and she was his, and if one of them was lost, the other would go as well. "Perhaps it was best that my parents died together," she added, a sudden thought.

"*We* are not going to die," Alaric said firmly. His hands tightened on hers. "*Now*, Evie."

Instantly she bent her knees, pulling her legs up at the same moment that he pulled her sharply toward him. The rump's strings broke free and she skimmed the rolling surface of the bog like a hoop across a lawn. He flung himself backward and they rolled together onto relatively solid ground.

Alaric's arms closed tightly around her and he buried his face in her hair. Willa was trembling all over, shock making her feel more frightened than she had been a minute earlier.

After a while, she took his face in her hands. "You saved my life, Alaric."

His expression in the darkening twilight was agonized. "One of my readers tried to kill you, Evie. Tried to *kill* you."

Willa shook her head. "Prudence wasn't a reader. She was a madwoman, and like a flash of lightning, nothing could be done about her. You're not responsible for her actions."

Alaric grimaced, but then he carefully stood up. "You're wet and cold," he said, bringing her to her feet. "We have to make our way to the peat cutter's hut before it gets any darker."

"I'm wet, but not cold," Willa said, following his lead as he showed her how to hop from hassock to hassock. "Thank goodness, it's warm today."

When they reached the hut, Alaric helped her inside, leaving the door open so the sun's last rays shone through.

"Someone is waiting to see you," he said.

"Sweetpea!" Willa cried, sinking to her knees. "You're all muddy." She put the little skunk against her cheek but quickly started blinking and held her at arm's length.

"She reeks," she cried. She turned to Alaric. "She's never smelled like this before!"

"She sprayed Prudence," Alaric said, crouching down. "That is how I knew Prudence was lying to me, and how I discovered where you left the path. If not for Sweetpea, you might well have had a night in the bog by yourself. How did Prudence get you off the path, by the way?"

"She has a pistol," Willa said, shuddering.

"Good lord. I am desperately sorry." His arms wrapped around her. "I left a footman guarding her door, and she'll be in the sheriff's hands tomorrow, I promise."

Sweetpea was trying to get down, so Willa put her on the floor, and the little skunk trundled off with her tail in the air. "What do you mean, Sweetpea 'sprayed' her?"

"This odor is her weapon." They watched as the baby nosed her way out the door and peed before trotting back inside. "I'm glad she didn't use my pocket for that."

"Sweetpea has very good manners," Willa said, laying her head against his shoulder.

Dropping a kiss on her hair, Alaric gently nudged

her to the side and investigated the hut. It was the work of a moment to light a peat fire; its smoke banished Sweetpea's lingering fragrance. He even found a couple of tallow rushes to keep the dark at bay, and three earthenware bottles of clear, cold water likely scooped from the same underground river they had almost fallen into.

"My father's men will find us," he said, closing the door so the peat smoke would rise to the hole in the ceiling rather than billow around the room. "This hut belongs to an old peat cutter named Barty, who lives with his granddaughter in the village. As soon as people smell peat burning in an empty hut, they'll know where to look for us."

Willa had seated herself on the pile of rough blankets on the pallet, her back against the wall, and was drinking from one of the bottles. The front of her gown was covered with mud, which made his heart skip a beat. She could have sunk into the mire so easily.

But she hadn't.

His eyes moved slowly up her body, cataloguing her missing shoe, wet sleeves, round chin, smiling lips . . . happy eyes. He froze for a moment, relief washing over him as if he'd ducked under a waterfall on a blistering African day.

Willa was safe. He hadn't really taken it in before now.

"I knew you'd come, and you did," she said. She waved the bottle at him. "Come drink some water. I don't think I've ever been so tired in my life."

Alaric had never been so joyful in his life. He took one stride and fell on his knees, pulling her to him, unable to speak. His arms wound around her so tightly that she squeaked a laughing protest.

"I'm all right," she said, kissing his jaw and then his lips. "We're both safe."

His throat was closed to words, so he just held her, rocking back and forth. She leaned against his chest until he managed to croak, "I was terrified that I'd lost you."

She shook her head, and soft hair caressed his cheek. Holding Willa sent another stab of terror through his heart. "You knew I was coming," he said, forcing the words past that damned tightness in his throat.

"Of course I did."

That was the woman he loved: she who took whatever happened to her, whatever life gave her, and made the best of it.

"Do you ever cry?" he asked, lowering his mouth and brushing hers.

"Extremely rarely."

"Why not?"

"When my parents died, I realized that if I were to begin crying, I might never stop. So I decided not to begin." She ran a hand along his cheek. "Today I knew you would come for me, which made me feel as safe as I used to feel before my parents died, when nothing frightened me."

"I might have missed you," he said, his voice tight. "We never found Horatius's body."

Her brows drew together. "And yet you're certain he's dead?"

"He died trying to save his horse."

"A heroic death," Willa whispered, putting a kiss on his chin.

"No," Alaric said tightly. "It wasn't."

Willa tried to move back, but he tightened his grip and wouldn't let her slide off his lap. "I want to see your eyes," she complained.

He bent his head and gave her a lopsided smile. "I'm looking at you."

Alaric followed the logical workings of her mind by watching her eyes, and he knew her question before she even asked it.

"He'd been drinking, and some fool bet him that he couldn't take his horse safely across Lindow Moss," he said, getting the sorry story out. "Horatius knew every path in the bog. If any man could have come through the bog on horseback unscathed, it would have been he."

"So he died as a result of an idiotic bet, just like my parents," she said.

"It has made me wary of obvious danger," Alaric said. "Hence, no cannibals."

"I'm glad," she whispered.

She pressed her lips onto his, and heat flared down Alaric's body. He bent his head to give her a proper kiss. Her lips opened and he dipped deep into the sweetness of her mouth, telling her without words that she was his.

Telling her of fear, relief, and joy, so tightly bound together that he felt as if the knot in his chest would never untwine. He had the sudden conviction that if he could see his own heart, he would see an image of Willa in the middle of it: composed, brilliant, loving, organized Willa.

Or Evie, to give that image the name by which only he knew her. Evie would always surprise him. Frustrate him, probably. Take care of him, because she took care of everyone in her life.

Love him.

Save him.

Chapter Thirty-three

Willa was conscious of a bone-deep weariness such as she'd never felt before, along with dizzying elation. "Do you know that you have never properly asked me to marry you?" she asked Alaric.

He scowled at her. "Damn it, Evie, you aren't allowed to change your mind. Not about this."

It seemed that was his proposal. None of her fourteen suitors had *demanded* her hand. Their requests had been courtly, flattering.

Alaric's was profane.

It made her laugh.

"Believe me, I had no intention of marriage when I returned to England." The sentence burst from him with an enraged frustration that made Willa laugh again.

"This isn't a humorous matter," he said, running a hand through his hair. If he'd had a hat, it was lost in the bog. "Now I can't imagine my life without you."

"You're framing your proposal with the dispiriting news that you suffer a deficit of imagination?" Willa asked, her smile growing wider.

He dragged his hand through his hair again. "No. I *can* imagine the world without you in it—my mind showed me that possibility over and over in the last few hours—but it's not a world I would want to live in." His eyes were dark with pain. "Damn it, Willa, no one who's lost a loved one too soon suffers from that particular lack of imagination."

"I know," she said softly. "It's often in the back of my mind."

"Since Horatius's death, my imagination readily shows me a world with holes in place of people I love," he said. "My stepmother might die in childbirth; Betsy might succumb to scarlet fever; North might drink himself into a stupor."

"Unlikely, but I understand."

"When I think about your death, it's not just a hole in the fabric of my world, Willa. It's the whole damn thing. It's . . ."

He seemed to run out of words, just when Willa became most interested. He snatched her up and kissed her so fiercely that she melted into his arms, and stopped thinking.

The voice in the back of her head, the one that never stopped observing and commenting—the unruffled, curious, detached voice?

It gave up.

Stopped.

Went silent.

The only thing that mattered was the strong circle of Alaric's arms. He didn't hold her as if she were a fragile crystal statue: he crushed her, his mouth ravaging hers. His tongue demanded she respond—and she did.

When he nipped her bottom lip, she licked his and then gave it a little bite. And another one, because no man should have such a plump bottom lip. While she was at it, she kissed him along the line of his jaw and then nibbled his earlobe.

He was kissing her neck, but when she bit his earlobe, she felt a pulse go through his body as if it had gone through her own.

"Evie," he said, his voice strangled.

"Hmmm," she purred. She'd managed to free his muddy shirt from his breeches. The muscles in his back flexed as her fingers slid over them, which made her shiver and push closer.

"You must answer my question."

"What question?" Willa slid her hands around to the corded muscle over his belly.

"Will you marry me?" an insistent voice asked in her ear.

She pressed her hands against his stomach and looked up, meeting his eyes. "I will marry you." A surge of emotion caught her unawares. "And I'll protect you, Alaric. No one like Prudence will get near you again."

One of his eyebrows shot up.

She slipped a hand behind his neck. "You need me," she said smugly. "All those madwomen, lusting after your thighs."

Willa had the most enchanting giggle Alaric had heard in all his born days. It sounded as if joy took shape and burst into the world in liquid syllables. He kissed her, pushing her gently back on the blankets. He kissed a damp ankle, an ankle that smelled of peat and chamomile soap.

He coaxed her into opening her restless legs so he could kiss her heated flesh. She responded with a husky moan, followed by a honeyed breathless series of commands made incoherent by waves of white-hot pleasure.

He pushed her skirts around her waist and tore open the placket on his breeches.

"Yes," Willa choked, pulling him down on top of her, his masculine weight and strength the perfect complement to her softness, "yes, now, Alaric, *now.*"

He understood "now."

He understood the way his hips drew back. The way his cock fed into a tight, wet place that welcomed him. The way Willa writhed beneath him, pleas falling from her mouth.

He didn't recognize the deep emotion that spread through him at the sight of her face, glistening with sweat, crying out, arching up to press a final kiss on his lips before flopping backward, limp, sweaty, blissful.

But he was beginning to understand it.

He may not have experienced the emotion before, but he knew it would be his for life.

Chapter Thirty-four

Two hours later, Alaric heard a shout echoing over the bog. Willa had fallen asleep, so he roused his muddy, soon-to-be wife and helped her put most of her garments back on, though not the cork rump. Sweetpea was returned to his pocket.

As the shouts grew nearer, he kissed Willa awake again. She was perfectly agreeable until she understood what he was saying. "I don't want to cross the bog again," she said, shaking her head.

"Even if I carry you?"

Her heavy-lidded eyes closed. "Tomorrow."

He pushed open the door to find an indistinct group, three or four men, moving toward the hut, their outlines lit by flickering torches.

They progressed slowly, a few feet at a time, as the

man in front threw down a plank and tested its solidity before the others joined him. When it was clear that the footing was firm, the man at the rear passed the last plank to the front, and the process was repeated.

Alaric realized with some amusement that his deliverers seemed to be playing one of his favorite childhood games, leapfrog, albeit a deadly serious version.

He leaned back against the sod wall and waited as his father and a couple of grooms with coils of rope over their shoulders were distinguishable. Barty was at the front of the group.

"Hullo, Barty," he said, grinning at the old peat cutter. "My fiancée and I were grateful for the shelter of your hut tonight."

Barty's face glowed in the torchlight. "I'd give all the candles I've ever had to know your lady was saved from the bog," he said, smiling in toothless celebration.

The duke stepped off the plank. "Willa is safe?"

"She's asleep. We're both unhurt."

With a stifled noise, his father drew Alaric into a rough embrace. For a moment the two of them stood together, arms around each other's shoulders, relief and love a silent bond between them.

"In other news," the duke said, drawing back, "you have a brand-new sister, Artemisia. I promised we would return as soon as I could, so your stepmother needn't continue to worry."

"I'm very glad to hear that," Alaric said. "And I'm doubly grateful that you made the trip into the Moss under those circumstances." He ducked back into the hut and walked over to his sleeping fiancée.

"Time to go home," he said, bending down to take Willa into his arms.

"What are you doing?" she murmured, her cheek falling against his chest as he came to his feet.

Alaric took a deep breath of his sweet-smelling lady. Even under the odor of mud and moss and dank water, he could still make out Willa's own fragrance. "I'm taking you to the castle." She was asleep again, long lashes motionless on alabaster cheeks.

It took them nearly an hour to get home, even with Barty's knowledge of every tuft of sturdy ground between his hut and the castle wall. Alaric tramped on, his most precious possession in his arms, listening to the sleepy peeps of golden plovers settling into their nests.

He would teach his children to know the bog as well as he did. It was their inheritance, this deceptively beautiful, dangerous land that stretched on every side.

The castle wall loomed larger as they approached. Light blazed in every window, evidence of the fact that the duke's family had been unable to sleep. Finally their makeshift path joined up with the line of planks that crossed the bog, which meant Alaric could walk more quickly, knowing he was on solid ground.

A groom ran ahead, torch bouncing, to tell the household all was well.

Finally, Alaric walked through the door of the castle. Willa opened her eyes, and he set her on her feet.

The entry was crowded with people. Betsy ran to them with a cry of happiness, and the rest of his siblings followed, crowding close with shrieks of welcome.

"Good evening, everyone," Alaric said, grinning at all of them. "We are here, safe and sound, with much thanks for your good wishes and prayers."

"Thank the good lord you are found," Lady Knowe cried, folding Willa into her embrace. "We must have champagne, Prism!"

Now that they were in the brightly lit entry, Alaric realized that his father wore no wig. His hair was cut short but streaked silver in places. His face was unexpectedly lined, his eyes dark. "Was it close?" the duke asked, handing over his coat to a footman.

"Closer than I would like," Alaric admitted.

"Hell and damnation," His Grace said gruffly. "I've lost one son to the bog, and if we'd lost the two of you . . . I always told myself that you were as safe in

Africa as you would be here." He rubbed a hand over his face.

"I was never in danger," Alaric reassured him. "All the hours in childhood when we broke your edicts and chased each other around the Moss proved useful. For her part, Willa was wearing a fashionable piece of cork on her bottom that kept her afloat."

Sparky was the first to burst out laughing.

"She was saved by her rump," Alaric said, grinning.

Once the party retired to the drawing room, Willa didn't pull away from him, or otherwise try to restore propriety. She leaned against him, snug in the circle of his arms. His shoulders ached—every part of him ached—but for the best of reasons.

After glasses of champagne were handed to everyone, including Barty and the grooms, Willa turned to the butler and raised her glass. "I owe you much thanks, Prism. I am safe and well thanks in no small part to your instructions about the dangers of the bog."

The castle butler was overcome, and merely bowed as everyone from Lady Knowe to the duke applauded him.

"To my newest sister, Artemisia," Alaric proclaimed, and everyone chimed in.

After that, they celebrated Willa for her bravery, Alaric for his courage, Barty for his hut.

"Finally, to Sweetpea, for her apt use of a personal weapon," Alaric said, bringing the little animal from his pocket. "This remarkably intrepid creature saved Miss Ffynche's life today."

Sweetpea's unique odor spread instantly through the room, and Lady Knowe made a choking sound.

"I would be grateful if someone could give this animal a bath, Prism," Alaric said. "Perhaps two."

"Warm water, with chamomile soap only, please," Willa said. "Afterwards, she may come to my room; Hannibal must be beside himself with worry."

Prism nodded to a footman, who bore Sweetpea away, his nose wrinkling.

"It's time for bed," Lady Knowe said. "I, for one, feel that *eau de Sweetpea* has brought this impromptu celebration to a close."

"I'd like supper, if you please," Alaric said to Prism. "Where is Prudence?" he asked, turning to his father.

"She remains upstairs, under guard," the duke replied.

"She has a pistol!" Willa cried with alarm.

"I relieved her of it when she threatened to shoot the sheriff upon his arrival tomorrow," His Grace said laconically. "She's in her bedchamber with instructions to pack up her things. I don't know what an attempted murderess is allowed to take to jail these days."

The Duke of Lindow wore all the frills and furbe-lows that the rank both demanded and conferred. But he was a Wilde at heart. His eyes were icy.

"If she hadn't threatened your life, Miss Ffynche, I would have let her free. But now she must be con-fined."

Alaric expected Willa to request mercy, but she just nodded. "It has occurred to me that our children would be at risk."

Children. Children with Willa. It gave him a pecu-liar feeling that he had no difficulty identifying as joy.

"Thank you," Alaric said. His father wasn't the sort of Englishman who lavished affection or praise. But ever since he was a child, he'd known that his father was always there, a man to be counted on.

"Hopefully, the news of this night's adventures won't spread," the duke said, his voice returning to its usual dry cadence. "You are famous enough as it is. A bloodthirsty missionary's daughter would make you legendary."

"What about Diana?" Willa asked. "Prudence told me that she'd left the castle."

"North followed her to London," the duke said. "He will make certain that she returns safely to her mother's care."

Prism bowed. "Baths are being prepared, Miss

Ffynche, Lord Alaric. I will deliver a light repast to your chambers."

"I shall escort Miss Ffynche to her chamber," Alaric said. In truth, he had no intention of leaving her, but he might as well preserve appearances. He took Willa's arm and they made their way slowly upstairs, trailing bits of peat. "It's been a long day," she said unnecessarily, stopping at her door.

He put an arm against the door, over her head, and smiled down at her with voluptuous pleasure. His wife-to-be was disheveled and dirty. He thought she'd never been more beautiful.

"I'm joining you," he informed her. "I mean to make love to you on a bed for the first time, though we may have to sleep first."

For a moment, he thought she was going to refuse. They were back in the castle, after all. Someone might find out. She might be ruined.

"Oh, and I'm marrying you as soon as I can get a special license," he added. "No waiting for banns."

"No one is making love to me before I've had a bath," Willa announced. "Perhaps you can pay me a visit later."

Alaric brought his lady's small, muddy hand to his lips. "An excellent idea," he said, as smoothly as if they were discussing cups of tea. "Except I cannot let you out of my sight. I—"

He dropped her hand.

Impossibly, Prudence—*Prudence*, who was supposed to be under guard in her bedchamber—was making her way down the corridor toward them. Even more impossibly, a pistol was gripped in her right hand.

Alaric's eyes met hers as he gathered himself to lunge.

"Don't move," she snapped. "This pistol is cocked and aimed at your concubine. The duke took one of my pistols from me, but they come in pairs—or at least, mine did." Her eyes burned with a nameless macabre light, but her hand was steady. At this range, she couldn't miss.

At his side, Willa stood frozen, scarcely breathing.

"I wrote that play for you, Alaric, from pure love," Prudence said, in throbbing accents. "That was before I knew you were a misguided sinner, one who will writhe in the pitchy smoke of darkest hell, unless you repent."

"Prudence," Alaric began.

"I love you too much to leave your soul in the care of a trollop," she remarked, as casually as if she were discussing laundry—and Alaric's instincts told him it was a declaration of intent.

At once, he threw himself in front of Willa while pushing her to the floor. The pistol cracked with a deafening report and a flash of light, and the corridor filled with the acrid, sulfurous smell of gunpowder.

For some moments, chaos reigned. Doors slammed open, and Willa heard cries and pounding feet. Alaric lay, face down, on top of her. To her horror, she realized that the warmth she felt was blood. *His* blood.

"Alaric!" she cried, trying to extricate herself without injuring him further.

His face was colorless. "Sorry, darling," he whispered.

Like a guardian angel's, Lady Knowe's face appeared above hers. "Good, there's an exit wound," she said. In one smooth movement, she lifted Alaric and laid him gently on his back.

Willa came to her knees. Her hand instinctively went to the wound in Alaric's shoulder to try to stop the flow of blood gushing from it. She discovered that she was praying, praying harder than she ever had in her life, pleading for Alaric's life with every sobbing breath.

Lady Knowe kindly but firmly pushed her away. As a footman leaned close, holding a lantern, Alaric's aunt ripped open his shirt and examined the wound. She put her weight behind wads of cloth applied above and below.

The duke was standing to the side, holding Prudence's arms clamped to her sides. She was staring at Alaric, crying something.

It wasn't until she repeated it three times that Willa understood. "He saved *her*. He sacrificed himself for *her*."

"We need a litter," the duke commanded. His voice was as quietly authoritative as ever.

"It's just a shoulder wound," Lady Knowe said calmly. "No vital parts."

At this point, Prudence became hysterical, sobbing and shrieking.

"Prism, take a footman and search her luggage to make sure she wasn't carrying the contents of an armory along with her," His Grace instructed. "And find out how in the bloody hell she escaped the room in the first place!"

Prism hauled Prudence away down the corridor, surrounded by three footmen.

That was a good thing, because Willa—who had never had an impulse to physical violence that she remembered—was close to lunging at her and ripping hair from her scalp. Instead, she watched closely as Alaric's aunt lifted the pad covering the bullet's entrance wound. Blood still oozed, but the flow had subsided.

Lady Knowe made a satisfied sound and pressed the pad down again. "Alaric's always been lucky."

"'*Lucky*'?" Willa cried, trying to reconcile the notion with what had just happened.

"The bullet's not inside, and he won't lose use of the arm, unless I miss my guess."

Footmen arrived with a litter, and Willa scrambled to her feet. She looked down at herself helplessly. The mud of the bog was now mixed with blood, so much blood.

As footmen lifted Alaric onto the litter, he opened his eyes. "Someone get a special license," he muttered.

"No need—I have one," his father said calmly. "It was acquired for North, but it will do."

Alaric's eyelids were heavy but he made an obvious effort. "It will be in his name," he said in a harsh whisper.

His Grace shook his head, his lips twisted in a rueful line. "In fact, it isn't. You can thank Horatius for that—North wasn't sure whether he had to marry under Horatius's courtesy title, which he has refused to take, so the archbishop left the license blank."

"Up," Lady Knowe commanded the footmen, ignoring the conversation.

"If I'm delirious, I suppose we could wait a few days," Alaric said, his eyes closing.

"I don't allow my patients to get fevers," Lady Knowe announced. She strode after the footmen, shouting orders to do with boiling water and comfrey-root poultices.

Alaric didn't open his eyes again for well over twenty-four hours. Willa had bathed, washed her hair three times, and eaten something. She was sitting by his bed, having chased off any number of retainers and family members, including Lady Knowe, Alaric's valet, his brother Spartacus, and the duke.

Alaric's father put up the most resistance, and Willa knew he'd be back in a matter of a few hours, no matter what she said. But at least there was some peace in the chamber now.

If *she'd* been torn open by a hot lead ball, she'd want quiet in which to heal.

When Alaric opened his eyes, she started and put a hand on his forehead. "Hello, darling," she whispered.

"Did Aunt Knowe take care of me?" he murmured.

Willa nodded. "She sewed you up herself with all sorts of fussing." She dropped a kiss on his forehead.

He smiled faintly. "My aunt's had practice, with all the hunting and archery done on the estate."

Willa hadn't given much thought to the dangers of hunting. "Our sons will never hunt," she told him. It was terrifying to see Alaric lying so still, his face ashen, his shoulder bound up in muslin.

"Let's conceive the sons before we make rules

for them." Alaric was looking at her from beneath heavy-lidded eyes, his mouth curled in a smile.

"How do you feel?" she asked, hand on his forehead.

"Aches," he said with a grunt, twitching his shoulder. "If I hold off the fever, I'll be up and about soon."

"Up?" Willa cried. "You most certainly will not."

"We're getting married," Alaric stated. He raised his shoulder slightly, winced, and let it drop. "If we have to say our vows here in this room, Evie, I'm marrying you."

Willa smiled down at him. "I daren't refuse, because your brother Leonidas set off for Manchester on horseback last night in order to get Lady Gray's signature on that special license. He should be home in a few hours, and it would be most inconsiderate not to use the license at the earliest opportunity—*if* you are not feverish, of course."

"I won't be."

"You saved my life again," Willa whispered, bending down to kiss his brow.

"No need to get the wind up," he murmured. "Course I did. You're mine, Evie."

A tear slid down her cheek and splashed onto his hand. "I love you so much. I was terrified that I'd lost the chance to say it to you."

"Those words needn't be spoken," Alaric said. "I am loved, and I love."

She smiled at him through tears.

"Even that daft, murderous woman understood that I will always care for those I love. Where is she, by the way?"

"Your father sent her away to Wales under heavy guard. If she was found guilty of attempted murder— and obviously, she would be—she'd likely be given a year's hard labor. None of us wanted that, so he sent her to an institution that your aunt knew of. If she recovers her sanity, she'll be escorted to Africa with no possibility of return. But she might well live out her life there, under lock and key."

Alaric nodded.

"When Lavinia was infatuated with your books, I didn't believe you were a hero," Willa said, a sob catching her voice. "You *are* a hero. I was wrong, so wrong."

"I wasn't a hero."

"Yes, you—"

"Not until I had to be," Alaric said, cutting her off. "Not until I met you. Stop crying, Evie, because you boasted that you never shed a tear, remember?" His eyes closed and he abruptly fell asleep, his hand still held tight by hers.

Willa remained by his bedside as the sun came up, feeling his forehead every few minutes and making bargains with God. No unnatural heat crept under her palm. Alaric turned his head toward her at some point and smiled drowsily.

She crawled in next to him and fell asleep.

Twenty-four hours later, Lord Alaric wore a fresh linen shirt and a waistcoat at his wedding, but no coat; between the bandages and the sling he wore, a coat was out of the question. Willa wore one of her favorite gowns, as simple and plain as his shirt.

He didn't bound to the altar in Lindow Castle's private chapel, but he did walk there steadily. He didn't pick up the bride and carry her over the threshold to his bedchamber in the east tower, but he did kiss her.

Repeatedly.

When they were finally in bed, he lay flat on his back and grinned up at his wife. "I am *terra incognita,*" he said.

"An undiscovered country?"

"Exactly. Yours. All for you."

Chapter Thirty-five

Two days later

I am exceedingly annoyed that so much happened
while I was in Manchester, buying bonnets," Lavinia
complained, not for the first time. "Diana ran away, and
you nearly sank into the bog, and now you have stolen
the man whom I loved for at least three years!"

"But you stopped adoring him," Willa pointed out.
She was trying on Lavinia's new hats. There were eight,
each more delightful than the last. "Did I tell you that
my straw hat with the roses was lost in the bog?"

"A worthy sacrifice," Lavinia said, "in light of what
followed."

"I love this darling veil," Willa said. She held up a

summer hat with a swooping brim, a number of white and lavender plumes, and a veil in the back that floated almost to the waist.

"You must have it! It's my gift, in honor of your wedding. I do so wish I had been there."

Willa leaned over and kissed Lavinia's cheek. "You couldn't have ridden through the night, the way Leonidas did. As it is, he fell asleep in a pew and missed the ceremony." She adjusted the bonnet so the brim hung rakishly over one eye. "Thank you for this lovely gift!"

"You've changed," Lavinia said, narrowing her eyes.

"How so?" Willa readjusted the bonnet so the plumes swept around the side of her face. Which made her sneeze.

"It must be something to do with bedding a man," Lavinia said thoughtfully. "Or perhaps it's a matter of becoming Lady Alaric Wilde. You're more yourself. The way you are when we're alone."

"Oh," Willa said. She threw her a quick smile. "Our rules were only designed for the hunting season, after all."

"Your hunting season is over, since you're married to one of the most handsome men in the country. *And* one of the richest. Mother heard that Parth quadrupled Alaric's and North's inheritances."

"You'll have to stop calling him 'simple-minded,'" Willa said with amusement.

Lavinia shrugged. "Now Mother has come to the conclusion that I should catch North before Diana changes her mind. She can't decide whether to remain here or go to London. I think she'll remain here, because the chances are pretty good that Mrs. Belgrave will have some harsh words for Diana's chaperone."

"As far as I know, neither Diana nor North has sent any messages," Willa said.

"I just wish Diana had confided in me," Lavinia said, twisting a ribbon around her finger. "She's my cousin, after all. I would have helped her. I feel as if I failed her, somehow."

"Diana is the sort of woman who keeps her own counsel," Willa pointed out.

"It's sent my mother into a frenzy, trying to persuade me to entice North to marry me. But—*remember?*—we decided not to accept anyone's hand until the end of our second Season."

"That was before I met Alaric," Willa said, feeling that was an entirely logical response.

"Whereas I still haven't met a man I could bear to live with for more than a week," Lavinia said.

"You've never really considered North, inasmuch

as Diana disqualified him," Willa pointed out. "But I quite like him."

"Diana bumbled it, didn't she? Why couldn't she simply behave like a civilized person? Running away is so dramatic."

"Not only dramatic, but uncomfortable, since she rode the stagecoach," Willa agreed. "I heard that North shouted at poor Prism for not sending Diana to London in one of the estate's carriages. But Prism had no idea why she wanted to go to the village, so he lent her the pony cart, as she requested. Just imagine Diana crowded into a stagecoach!"

"I don't believe she owns a gown that doesn't double her width. All the same, I shall leave North to his melancholy. I have no interest in her castoffs."

"May I wear this hat to the archery range?"

"Certainly." Lavinia snatched up another new hat and put it on. It was smaller and adorned with a great many purple striped ribbons that formed bows and loops that made her look like a stylish ship, albeit with swelling sails. "Did I tell you that Parth Sterling has returned? He was barely inside the door before he insulted me."

"He's come for the wedding ball tonight," Willa said apologetically.

"Don't you dare tell him about all these bonnets!"

"Why on earth would I?" Willa asked, astonished.

"He said that I am a mercenary, grasping woman," Lavinia said. "That I do nothing but visit shops, and am fit for nothing else."

"He's wrong," Willa said, dropping the bonnet and giving Lavinia a hug. "He's terribly wrong and I shall tell him so myself."

Lavinia scowled. "Perhaps I'll slip up with my bow and arrow. I'm a terrible shot, you know."

As it happened, Willa never found out whether Lavinia came close to shooting Parth on the archery field, because no sooner had she made her appearance downstairs in her fetching new bonnet, than Alaric declared himself to be suffering terribly from his sore shoulder.

Which necessitated that they both return to the east tower and go to bed.

Willa did not, on the whole, believe exuberance to be an emotion that adults should indulge in often or at length. It seemed to her a childish emotion, one suited to parties and puppet shows.

Yet she knew perfectly well that the emotion brewing in her chest was just that: exuberance. She couldn't stop smiling, for one thing. If she kept this up, she would resemble Lavinia.

But who wouldn't smile?

She had spent the afternoon intoxicated by Alaric's kisses, not to mention by the musculature of his chest, his long fingers, his eyelashes, his . . . other parts.

The duchess had summoned most of the Cheshire gentry to the castle for a ball that night to celebrate the wedding. Willa had returned to her old bedchamber to dress, while her husband lounged, book in hand, to one side.

Sweetpea had offered him a polite sniff, and then returned to her busy work; to wit, emptying Willa's knotting bag of walnuts and stowing them under the bed, from whence the maid would fish them out and return them to the bag in the morning.

Alaric wasn't sitting alone: stretched across his knees, purring, was a lanky orange cat. Hannibal's fur was starting to shine, and his ribs weren't quite as visible.

"You are the most exquisite lady in this castle, Evie," he said, looking up from his book. "That apricot thing you have on, with all the satin flounces, makes you look like a princess."

Willa glanced down at her favorite ball gown. It was a soft rose, not apricot; cotton organdy, not satin; a gown, not a "thing."

"I am particularly partial to the bodice," Alaric added.

Her corset hoisted her bosom into the air, and the

bodice cleverly stayed just above her nipples, partly because it was skintight. Below her waist, lace and silk rioted in every direction.

Hannibal leapt to the floor when Alaric stood up. He came so close to her that he would crush her gown, but Willa didn't want him to move away, not when he smelled so good that her heart skipped a beat.

She was fairly certain that she betrayed her feelings every time she looked at her husband. Every time she snapped open her fan in order to whisper to him behind its shelter. Every time she put her hand on his arm and glanced about, daring any of his admirers to approach.

It had taken a few days, but Willa had the house party under control. Guests were treating him like an ordinary man, which was a welcome change.

Tonight would be another challenge, but the last such for some time: tomorrow she, Alaric, Hannibal, and Sweetpea would depart for their own house, less than an hour's drive from the castle.

In the last few hours, she had heard coach after coach pulling up in the courtyard, and the sounds rising from the ballroom had grown from a distant sibilant murmur to the clamor of a flock of starlings.

It would probably take a good part of the night to tutor the ladies of Cheshire that Lord Alaric was not the author, Lord Wilde, and that furthermore, he was not to be touched, questioned, or addressed inappropriately.

"We must go downstairs," Willa said, before Alaric's caresses grew too distracting. "We mustn't be late," she gasped, twisting away from a kiss that made her shudder with anticipation. "We mustn't miss your father's . . ."

The word escaped her because Alaric's clever tongue was stroking her lower lip and all she wanted was to yield to him. "Your father's gift," she said with relief, grabbing the right word and holding on to it. "Your father's gift to us, to celebrate our wedding."

Alaric made a discontented sound, but he let her go. "Why in the hell did my father think he had to make such a fuss?"

"You are the first of his children to wed," Willa pointed out. She stepped before the glass and began coaxing her hair back into the elaborate arrangement that allowed her to eschew a wig for the evening. "Do you know what his gift is?"

Alaric didn't reply.

She glanced over her shoulder. "You do!"

"*You* will enjoy it."

"But you won't?" She met his eyes in the glass.

"You're part of the family now, and you're about to be introduced to my father's sense of humor."

Her smile turned to a puzzled frown. "Has His Grace summoned a jester to perform?"

"I only wish that were the case. The second duchess hated his sense of humor so much that we speculated in the nursery it was the reason she fled the country, lover in tow."

"Funny stories?" Willa was unable to imagine the duke laughing at a merry tale.

"No. A pervasive interest in oddities, paired with a strong belief that Wildes should not be allowed to bask in their own consequence."

Willa had that same interest in oddities; it made her feel warm toward her new father-in-law.

"Yes, you are very like him," Alaric said, reading her mind. "Except for the way you look, which is luscious. We'd better go down before I decide I need to have your hips writhing beneath me."

"Alaric!" Willa colored and almost ran out of the room, followed by his chuckle.

When they reached the doors leading to the ballroom, she squared her shoulders. In a way, she had been born for this.

If there was anyone in England who could liberate Alaric of the burden of Lord Wilde and give him the private life that every Englishman deserved, it was she. She had every intention of returning her husband to his rightful place in society as a member of the aristocracy, rather than a deranged scribbling girl's idea of a hero.

She poised the fingers of her hand on his forearm, as if they were about to dance a minuet.

Alaric looked at her. "I wouldn't wish anyone else to accompany me into battle."

"You are cultivating the ability to guess what I am thinking," Willa laughed.

"As do all the best husbands." He seemed completely unperturbed by the fact of their marriage, whereas Willa was in a state of disbelief that a mere fortnight before she had arrived from London. She had felt nothing but amused skepticism about the object of Lavinia's adoration, the famous Lord Wilde. How quickly her circumstances changed!

Now she was *married* to that notorious explorer. Sleeping with him at night. And she would be for years. Decades. For the rest of her life.

It was such an alien concept as to require a flowering imagination like Lavinia's. One capable of picturing the inconceivable.

At Alaric's nod, Prism threw open the ballroom doors.

Instead of musicians and dancing guests, the great space was filled with row after row of chairs. Those in the front were gilt, set far enough apart to accommodate ladies' skirts. They were reserved for the family; a number of young Wildes were already seated, faces shining with excitement. At the sight of Alaric and Willa, there was some yelping, quickly curtailed by two nursemaids.

Behind them, chairs carried in from the drawing rooms were filled with house-party guests and the neighboring gentry who had arrived that evening for the ball. At the back of the room, ladies' maids, valets, and grooms sat shoulder-to-shoulder, with a few leaning against the back wall.

"My father," Alaric said, *sotto voce*, "wants to share the joke as widely as possible."

Willa gasped and came to a sudden halt. "It's the *play*, isn't it!"

"The final performance, as I understand it," Alaric said. "My father had the production closed and brought the actors to the castle before they disband. The last gasp of a murderous playwright." His wry smile made Willa want to kiss him.

Though, obviously, propriety forbade it.

As they made their way to the front row, the audience became even more animated. Willa caught fragments of conversation floating from the assembled guests, who ogled them with the attention usually reserved for royalty, not mere neighbors.

"That's he," a robust lady announced to her elderly companion, who was blinking watery eyes as if she couldn't make out Alaric's form. "He looks a proper—"

Whatever she went on to say was drowned by a squeal from a young lady a few rows forward. "I cannot believe the luck of being able to see *Wilde in Love*! Petra's father had to pay four times the price for—"

"Thighs," a third lady gasped.

Yes, *thighs*, Willa thought affectionately. Her husband's were magnificent, and magnificently shown off tonight, as Alaric was wearing one of North's costumes. He had ransacked his brother's wardrobe for formal attire.

He had complained that North's breeches were entirely too tight, but the truth was that his legs flattered the tailor who had made breeches to that measure.

"I believe I am about to faint," Lady Boston moaned as Alaric passed her chair. Willa gave her a look, just to make it clear that Lord Wilde would not be gathering swooning women from the floor and reviving them against his manly breast.

"You terrify me," Alaric said into her ear.

When they reached the front row, Leonidas jumped to his feet. He and Betsy were dressed for the ball, whereas the younger children were going to be dispatched back to the nursery.

"With the arrival of the lovelorn hero, the play can begin," Leonidas announced, doubling over with laughter at his own joke.

Alaric gave his brother a mock box on the shoulder as he escorted Willa to a chair and then seated himself as close to her as he could, given the luxuriant mounds of silk and creamy lace that pooled on either side of her chair.

Before them, a wide stage had been erected a few inches above the ballroom floor; canvas sheets painted with a jungle scene were suspended behind it and along the sides. An extremely hairy painted lion peeked from between two trees, and a painted crocodile lounged, open-mouthed, at the bottom right.

Green velvet curtains had been hung behind the canvases, shielding anything happening behind the scenes. A certain amount of excited activity could be detected on the other side of the curtains, a low burr of actors' voices.

"How on earth did His Grace arrange for the performance to travel to Cheshire?" Willa asked.

Her husband shrugged. "He told me he was having the production closed down as a wedding present. I suppose he paid them enough to make the trip worthwhile."

It was true that in the days after Alaric's wounding,

she had paid no attention to anything beyond his care. Still, a whole theater troupe had arrived without her notice.

"Good evening," she heard a man say. She looked up.

It was North, but not the same North. For one thing, he wasn't wearing an extravagant Parisian wig, but the sort a doctor, or a man indifferent to fashion, might wear. His plain black coat emphasized the shadows under his eyes, but his bow was as elegant as any courtier's.

"I didn't realize you had returned from London. Please do sit beside me," she invited. "Prism just informed us that His Grace may not be able to attend the performance."

"Ophelia is all right, is she not?" North asked, taking the chair she indicated.

"Tetchy as hell," Alaric said, leaning forward to speak around Willa. "Doesn't like the doctor's prescribing lying in, and is keeping Father dancing at her beck and call."

"As it should be," Willa pointed out. She strongly believed that Nature's rule that only females carried children was unreasonable.

"Should it be that way all the time, or merely during delicate times?" North had a frightfully charming smile.

"In a just world, women would birth female babies and men would birth males," Willa said firmly. "Some male babies are far too large to be carried with comfort."

North looked past her at his brother, his mouth a lopsided smile.

"Yes, I am lucky," Alaric said, grinning.

North's face closed like a trap.

"Bloody hell," Alaric said. "I didn't mean it that way. Did you find Diana?"

"No, and her mother informed me that she is no longer my concern."

From behind the green velvet curtain came the sound of a few violins being tuned. Alaric leaned forward and gripped his brother's knee.

A beaming Lady Knowe arrived and took the seat on the other side of North. "I've seen this play twice already, and I am agog to see it a third time!"

"You do remember that it was authored by a woman who was as mad as a March hare?" Alaric asked.

"And responsible for no little actual drama?" Willa chimed in, curling her hand around Alaric's arm. She still woke up at night, shaking with fear.

Lady Knowe shrugged. "Whoever claimed that Shakespeare was sane? Do you know that he left his wife nothing but his 'second-best bed'?"

"That sounds like a commentary on his marriage, not his sanity," Willa pointed out.

A moment later, the ballroom fell silent when a boy emerged from the curtain and paraded across the stage holding a large pasteboard placard which read,

WILDE IN LOVE
OR,
THE TRAGIC STORY OF
THE BEASTS OF THE WILD
AND THE
MISSIONARY'S DAUGHTER

Willa wanted to laugh at the absurdity of it, but she patted Alaric's knee instead. A helpmeet, she reminded herself, should offer succor in times of distress.

The boy reached the far end of the stage, turned his placard, and marched back the way he'd come. The sign now read,

THE FINAL PERFORMANCE

This brought on another wave of chatter from the audience, only hushed by the sound of violins rising in a crescendo.

A gentleman emerged from behind the curtains and stepped up onto the low stage.

"Oh God, don't tell me he's supposed to be me," Alaric groaned.

"He is not so terrible," Willa whispered.

The actor didn't resemble her husband in the least. He had a narrow patrician face, a carefully powdered lavender wig, and a figure that seemed to have been created specifically for the current slim-waisted fashions.

"I am wearing a *corset*," Alaric hissed, outraged, in Willa's ear.

"Hush!" she whispered back. But she couldn't help laughing.

The gentleman—who was indeed "Lord Wilde"—launched into a long speech about his passion for the wilderness, while Alaric sat back and glared, arms folded over his chest.

It seemed that the presence of the actual Lord Wilde made the actor nervous, because he fairly rattled out a soliloquy that explained his voyage to "*wildest* Africa."

He concluded with a flourish, proclaiming that one hadn't truly experienced life until one had lived among wild animals. At that point, Alaric's expression grew ferocious, and one could definitely have described the poor man's exit as a flight.

North leaned over. "I'd forgotten what a jolly good play this is. I daresay Fitzball could give you some hints about dress, Alaric."

"Fitzball?"

"The actor," North clarified, his expression positively gleeful. "Quite a star already. His soulful performance of Lord Wilde did much to increase your fame."

Alaric's response to this was a rude gesture, so Willa gave him a gentle kick, reminding him there were children present. Then, since they were family now, she kicked North as well. "Behave yourselves!"

"Ouch," North rumbled.

At this point, the missionary's daughter burst onto the stage, and Act One was off. As the play proceeded, Willa discovered that her assessment of the play was different from North's. For one thing, there was far too much reliance on throbbing sentences. For another, the missionary's family was given to blessing each other right and left, which grew tiresome.

She did enjoy the scene in which the missionary's daughter fell into the deep river (adequately represented by rippling blue cloth). Her mother shrieked and moaned, casting blessings on the head of her drowning daughter.

Lord Wilde beat his chest, raging up and down the riverbank while lamenting that his terror of the water prevented him from saving "the sweetest maiden who ever walked the savannah."

The reaction of the audience to this dramatic crisis was divided unevenly between those in the front rows—the Wildes—who were howling with laughter, and the rest, who were howling in terror and suspense.

Happily, it was revealed that the young lady knew how to swim, because she wiggled across the blue cloth and made it to the riverbank, ending Act Two.

"I can't believe this nonsense," Alaric said, in the interval before Act Three commenced.

"It isn't very good," Willa agreed, "although I thought the mother played her part with a great deal of spirit."

"'Dead! Dead! Never to call me Mother again,'" North said, deadpan.

Further along the row, past Lady Knowe, Lavinia and Parth had somehow ended up seated beside each other. Willa just caught Lavinia's retort, "Just because you have no understanding of art—"

Act Three opened before Lavinia could complete her sentence.

The heroine's near death had caused Lord Wilde to see at last that she was the dearest treasure of his heart. Their stolen "moment of delight," represented by feverish kisses, was greeted with approval by the audience, especially the youngest Wildes, whose encouraging hoots could be heard over civilized applause.

The locket made its appearance, and was dropped by the heroine into her bodice; a nice touch, Willa thought.

After that, high emotions came thick and furious. The missionary and his wife uncovered Lord Wilde's perfidious seduction, leading to much gnashing of teeth and wailing about God's providence: "Branded with infamy! Shunned! Degraded! O, my daughter, my daughter, what will become of you!"

Before anyone could answer that riveting question, the cannibals made their attack, though it was conducted behind the scenes. To the front of the stage, Lord Wilde ate a leisurely breakfast, unaware that his lady love had not only been cast off by her parents, but had been captured by bloodthirsty cannibals, and was about to become *their* breakfast.

A few rending screams shook the curtains, followed by the pushing of an enormous papier-mâché cooking pot onto the stage, "fire" wadded underneath. A woman's hand was draped over its rim, the locket poignantly tangled in its fingers.

Even the children held their breaths now, waiting for Lord Wilde to finish his ham and eggs, turn around, and discover the tragedy.

He leapt to his feet with a fine roar of fury. There was nothing he could do other than fight off the cannibals and rescue his beloved's body in order to return it to her family. But he kept the locket, falling to his knees and crying out, "*Never shall I love another woman!*"

A satisfied sigh echoed around the ballroom.

Until Alaric broke the mood by bursting into laughter.

Fitzball threw Alaric a withering glare and swept from the stage.

"I will credit Prudence for getting *one* thing right," Alaric said, rising to his feet.

Willa looked up at him inquiringly.

"I will never love another woman," he announced. He pulled her up, wrapped his arms around her, and kissed her. The audience roared with appreciation.

Willa returned his kiss, because there are rare occasions on which propriety should be ignored, and this was one of them. "Love you," she murmured, her voice almost silent against his lips. "And you?"

"Don't you dare," he murmured back.

She choked back laughter because, after all, it was unnecessary to point out that he was, indeed, *Wilde in Love.*

The whole castle knew it.

Chapter Thirty-six

Three months later
A country cottage in Lancashire

North knocked on the door of a small, dreary cottage with a sense of profound disbelief. His exquisitely fashionable fiancée was living in a tiny house with two rooms at the most?

With a fraying thatched roof, and a fence so rickety that his horse might bring it down by a twitch on his reins? Curtains at the windows that looked as if they'd been sewn from flour sacks? Blindingly white flour sacks, but still . . .

Impossible.

Her favorite wig wouldn't even fit through the door.

There had to be something wrong with the directions he'd been given. And yet, once he had bribed Mrs. Belgrave's butler with a handful of guineas, this was the address he'd been given. No matter how often he asked, Mrs. Belgrave flatly refused to share the location of the daughter she had disinherited.

All for the crime of jilting a future duke.

It was North's fault, the whole of it. If only he'd been perceptive enough to see that Diana didn't love him—in fact, loathed him—he would never have proposed. She would still be in a London ballroom, perhaps dancing with a man whom she could love.

And he?

He wouldn't have spent over a year in yellow heels and towering wigs, trying to match her elegance. Showing off his finery as if he were Fitzy, the family's peacock.

He knocked again, more loudly.

"I'm coming!"

Her voice gave him a sudden sense of vertigo. The sickening part of it all was that Diana may have preferred exile to marriage—but he didn't seem to be able to stop loving her.

That hopeless love had driven him to this visit. His courtship had ruined her life, and he had to make amends before leaving for war.

He would take her out of this pitiful cottage, for

one thing, and make sure that she was never destitute again. He would have to phrase it in such a way that Diana was able to accept his help—with the understanding that there were no strings attached. That he would never bother her again.

The door swung open, and there she was.

When North first saw Diana Belgrave laughing on the side of the ballroom, he thought she was the most beautiful creature he'd ever seen.

But now?

She was wearing an unfashionable bonnet that framed her face. Her eyes were outlined not by black kohl, but by long eyelashes. Her lips were a natural rose.

She was exquisite.

He lost the ability to speak and just stared at her.

Finely drawn brows drew together. "Lord Roland, what are you doing here?" Her eyes swept down his body, and froze. "What are you wearing?"

He glanced down. After months of military training, he no longer noticed his dark crimson coat with its standing collar, plain breeches, and sturdy, beautifully made boots. Or if he did, it was only to thank God that he didn't have to squeeze his shoulders into tight, embroidered coats meant to bedazzle Diana.

"I've bought a commission," he said flatly. "I'm leaving for the war in America."

To his surprise, her eyes filled with horror. "No!" She reached out and caught his sleeve. "You mustn't, North! Is it too late?"

Stupidly, his heart thudded in his chest at her touch. Gently he disengaged his sleeve. "I command a regiment that leaves directly. I came to say goodbye but, more than that, I want to apologize."

Her face had lost all color. She looked as shocked as if she'd really cared for him.

"I spoke to your mother several times over the last week," he said, trying to ease into a discussion of her circumstances.

She shook her head. "A waste of words."

That was true: her bloody-minded mother had actually detailed the money she'd made by reselling Diana's gowns. "I may not be able to convince Mrs. Belgrave to accept you as her daughter," North said, "but the least I can do is ensure that you don't suffer due to my courtship. Why did—"

But he made himself cut off that question. It didn't matter why she had accepted his proposal, or why she jilted him, for that matter.

If possible, she had turned even whiter. "She didn't tell you, did she?"

"Tell me what?"

Sunlight loved her, he thought numbly. It lit the perfect cream of her cheek, the shadow cast by her fringe of eyelashes. Deluded fool though he was, he found himself memorizing every detail so that he could take it with him into war.

Diana didn't want him or love him, but her disdain hadn't killed his idiotic passion for her.

She opened her mouth, then shook her head. "It doesn't matter, Lord Roland."

"You called me North a moment ago."

Just then, he heard a thump from behind her, in the shadowed cottage. As if someone had dropped an object.

Diana's eyes widened, and she shifted to block the cottage interior from his sight.

The truth of it seared down North's body. She had a lover. She had told him that she hadn't—and he had believed her—but obviously she lied.

Likely she fled to the country with someone whom her mother would never accept. A footman, or a grocer, like her grandfather. Mrs. Belgrave had cast off her daughter for that sin; it had nothing to do with him.

She didn't need his help. She had chosen another man, and all those lies she had told were . . . lies. Just lies. No different than the words she spoke when she promised to marry him.

A sensation of pure emptiness filled him, a chilly

wave of nausea in its wake. "I beg your pardon," he said, stepping backward. "I didn't mean to disturb you."

Another thump came from inside: something wooden tumbled off a table and rolled across the floor.

"I must be on my way."

She swallowed so hard that he saw the lump in her throat. "I never wished to hurt you," she said haltingly.

North bowed his head. What was he supposed to say? Thank you for small blessings? She watched silently as he swung up on his horse. He was about to say goodbye when another thump came from behind her, this one followed by a wail. The voice was high and young, full of tears.

A baby.

Diana had a baby.

Epilogue

Eleven years later
An unnamed and uncharted island in the
West Indies

Two young boys ran across the white sand and
threw themselves into turquoise water as joyously
as otters.

Miss Katerina Wilde looked up from her book and
squinted. She had inherited her mother's imperfect
eyesight, and the distinction between the cool, shady
palm and the glaring sun made it impossible to see, especially with her spectacles on. "Don't go too far out!"
she shouted at Benjamin and Shaw.

Their nursemaid, who was infatuated with one of the footmen, was nowhere to be seen.

A footman was a strange creature to find on a West Indian island. But their mother insisted on a proper evening meal, which meant the Wildes traveled with footmen, linen, silver, and china. A cook and a butler.

Katie's brothers had spent the last four months turning brown as nuts, cavorting in the warm water of the Caribbean. Katie preferred to lie around under a tree wearing a pair of breeches so she could dash into the water to cool off. Their mother spent her days studying sea turtles, making delicate watercolors of their eggs.

Their father worked on his next book, of course.

Every night the whole family donned proper clothing and cut their goat stew with silver utensils.

Their mother wouldn't have it any other way.

Katie let her book slide to the ground as she lay back, hands behind her head. Her beloved cat, Sweetpea, was curled up next to her, purring loudly. Sweetpea was the daughter of her father's favorite cat, and named after her mother's favorite pet—but she loved Katie better than anyone else in the world.

Looking up into the waving palm fronds, Katie decided that she was probably the luckiest ten-year-old girl anywhere in the world.

Just this morning, her father had said she was old enough to edit any scene he'd written in which she appeared. Even delete it, if she wished.

Not that she would. She loved Lord Wilde's stories of their family's adventures as much as the rest of England did. Well, England, and France, and even America, now. Father was trying to talk their mother into traveling to New York City next.

Katie gave the palm fronds far above her a happy grin. She meant to marry a man as big and handsome as her father. They would travel the world, returning to England every once in a while.

She didn't want to study animals, the way her mother did. No, she'd rather be a writer like her father. If she took off her spectacles, she could just see a hazy green lump on the horizon that was another island. This part of the ocean was full of them . . . island after island, all waiting to be visited. Waiting to be described by Miss Katie Wilde.

This particular island was pretty, but it didn't have any residents other than sea turtles, wild goats, and birds. If she had her druthers, they'd be living on an island with people, so she could learn another language.

Unfortunately, when her father settled into writing, he liked to find somewhere private.

You couldn't get more private than an island with no name and no inhabitants.

With a sigh, she put her glasses back on and picked up her book. It was one of her favorites, written by an ancient fellow named Pliny. Pliny's uncle had sailed right into a volcanic explosion, trying to save its victims.

Katie would have done exactly the same, except she wouldn't have died in the attempt. She could tell that Pliny agreed with her; his uncle should have been more careful. She fell asleep dreaming of captaining her own ship, steering it (carefully) toward great deeds and even greater adventures.

A while later, a coconut fell beside her with such a thump that it sprayed her face with sand. Katie sat bolt upright, mouth open in shock, which meant that sand from yet another "falling" coconut made her cough and spit.

Sweetpea fled, and Katie was forced to jump to her feet and chase Ben and Shaw round the island, shrieking so loudly that it woke up their parents.

They were sleeping in the shaded platform house whose timbers traveled from place to place in the hold of the *Lindow*, the huge ship designed and built to the highest specifications and with no expense spared. A ship that Lord Wilde had described in his last book as a corner of England that floated from place to place.

At the moment, the king and queen of that small corner of England were lying in a bed covered with snowy-white linen sheets. Hearing shrieks, Alaric raised his head just long enough to discern that the sounds indicated happy rage. "Let's do that again," he said, the suggestion rumbling from his chest.

Willa was sprawled on top of him, breathless, her body glistening with sweat, her hair spread across his chest like tangled silk.

"Too tired," she mumbled.

That made him laugh. Willa was never tired. A new journey, a new island, a new adventure—all of it energized her just as much as it did him.

Alaric could never have imagined a life like this. He had been more than willing to live in England, if that was what Willa wanted. He would have been happy there. He would have helped with his father's estate, and Lord Wilde would have ceased to write books.

But he was so damned lucky. His arms tightened around Willa. He was in love with his fascinating, gorgeous wife, with his nimble-minded, curious children . . . with his life.

Wilde in Love, indeed.

A Note About Bogs, Egyptian Ducks, and Melodramatic Plays

When I began the Wilde series, I decided to place it in a castle far from London. My discovery of Lindow Moss was one of the most delightful parts of my research. Although Lindow Castle doesn't exist, the Moss is a real bog found in Cheshire—a stretch of peaty wetlands, sometimes known as a quagmire, that was originally 1,500 acres wide. In a bog, peat, made from compressed mosses and grasses, forms a floating crust, an undulating blanket, that looks solid, but isn't. A traveler might fall through into rushing water below, or be mired in spongy muck and unable to climb out.

No matter how arcane a bog may seem to urban readers, in the Georgian period, Egyptian hieroglyphs were even more mysterious. The supposition that the hieroglyph of a duck meant "son" is true to the period. As was later understood (and Willa suggests), the hieroglyph actually stands for the sound of the main consonants of the Egyptian word for "duck"; yet without context, that hieroglyph can also mean "son," a word formed by those consonants.

Perhaps you noticed that North is always pocketing the red ball when he plays billiards. Billiards dates back to the 1500s, when it evolved out of a lawn game akin to croquet. By the Georgian period, it was wildly popular. The game itself was still in transition; at this point, two players each have a white ball. They hope to cannon off the opponent's ball and the red ball in one shot.

I turned from history to literature when it came to fashioning my mad missionary's daughter, Prudence. As a Shakespeare professor, I've spent years teaching portrayals of Puritans and deranged lovers; here I am particularly indebted to Ben Jonson's *Bartholomew Faire* and Shakespeare's *A Midsummer Night's Dream*. The actor Fitzball appears as a thank-you to the playwright Edward Fitzball, who provided versions of the mother's lines in *Wilde in Love*.

I owe another literary debt to Robert McCloskey's *Homer Price*. Sweetpea is a nod to Homer's pet skunk Aroma, who travels in a basket and is instrumental in solving a robbery. Obviously, Sweetpea echoes her literary ancestor by thwarting a criminal. Exploring skunks in the past—alas, grow-your-own-tippet sales of American sables were not fictional—and the present was fascinating. Skunks are intelligent, friendly animals, best left in the wild, but making wonderful pets if need be.

I know some of you want to kill me because of the ending of Chapter Thirty-six; as a reader, I agree with you. But as a writer, I have to warn you: every one of the Wilde books ends with a cliff-hanger. They are the sort of family whose lives hurdle onward at a pace we mere mortals can only gasp at.

I hope you have as much fun reading about them as I have writing about them.

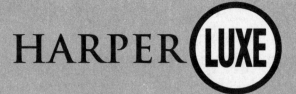